THE PORPOISE

THE PORPOISE

MARK HADDON

Chatto & Windus
LONDON

1 3 5 7 9 10 8 6 4 2

Chatto & Windus, an imprint of Vintage,
20 Vauxhall Bridge Road,
London SW1V 2SA

Chatto & Windus is part of the Penguin Random House group of companies
whose addresses can be found at global.penguinrandomhouse.com.

Penguin
Random House
UK

First published by Chatto & Windus in 2019

penguin.co.uk/vintage

A CIP catalogue record for this book is available from the British Library

HB ISBN 9781784742829
TPB ISBN 9781784742836

Typeset in 11.5/18 pt Adobe Garamond Pro
by Integra Software Services Pvt. Ltd, Pondicherry

Printed and bound in Great Britain by Clays Ltd, Elcograf S.p.A.

Penguin Random House is committed to a sustainable future
for our business, our readers and our planet. This book is
made from Forest Stewardship Council® certified paper.

MIX
Paper from
responsible sources
FSC® C018179

For Suzanne Dean and Simon Stephens

I didn't know the cost
Of entering a song – was to lose
        your way back

Ocean Vuong, 'Threshold'

His doghter, which was piereles
Of beaute, duelte aboute him stille.
Bot whanne a man hath welthe at wille,
The fleissh is frele and falleth ofte,
And that this maide tendre and softe,
Which in hire fadres chambres duelte,
Withinne a time wiste and felte:
For likinge and concupiscence
Withoute insihte of conscience
The fader so with lustes blente,
That he caste al his hole entente
His oghne doghter forto spille.

John Gower, *Confessio Amantis*

The porpoise, how he bounced and tumbled.

William Shakespeare, *Pericles*

CONTENTS

THE PORPOISE

THE FLIGHT

Maja is thirty-seven weeks pregnant. She would not be allowed on a commercial flight but they have been staying with friends who own a vineyard in Bellevue Champillon and one of the other guests, Viktor, has a Piper PA-28 Warrior which he intends to fly back to Popham the following morning. His Land Rover is waiting at the airfield and it will be the simplest thing in the world to drop her at the Winchester house en route to the south coast. Her husband, Philippe, does not like placing Maja in the care of another man, let alone one he has met only two days previously, but the jigsaw falls so serendipitously into place that refusal is almost impossible. He will drive to Paris, leave the car at the apartment, take the Eurostar to London and be back in Winchester a day later.

Besides, Maja enjoys small planes. Travel has become too easy. You fall asleep in Istanbul and wake up in Beijing. She likes to watch the miles tick by – river deltas, irrigation circles, clouds spooling into existence downwind of peaks. She retains a vivid memory of flying over Oslofjord as a girl, island after island, summerhouses, quays, boats, the sun's reflection skimming the water, some revelation which lay just beyond words about the relation between scale and escape and the surface of the earth. In addition, the morning sickness which persisted unnaturally late into her pregnancy has finally faded; she is experiencing the fabled glow and eager to indulge the freedom that comes with it before she devotes her life to a very small and very demanding human being.

Philippe's anxiety is justified. Viktor has a Private Pilot's Licence but no Instrument Rating. This wouldn't matter were he travelling with only his nine-year-old son, Rudy. They would head off early and if the weather or other circumstances were to change he could either postpone the flight till the following day or divert to one of his alternates if they were already airborne. But Maja wakes late and takes a long breakfast and packs slowly and has mislaid a coral necklace which, she insists, can be couriered to the UK if and when it is found, but which becomes the object of a painstaking and fruitless search of what is a very large house. Lunch has come and gone by the time she is ready to leave. Were Maja less attractive Viktor would feel no compunction about inconveniencing her but, having been underwhelmed by her performances on screen, he is surprised to find himself in the company of a woman who makes him fifteen again – thick blonde hair, blue, blue eyes, cartoon-pretty, engagingly shambolic, just this side of plump. There is a scar on her cheek, courtesy of a rook which flew in through her bedroom window when she was ten years old. Viktor's infatuation is enjoyable but mildly alarming for a man who is used to having a courtroom, indeed any room, in the palm of his hand.

The necklace will be found six months later by the gardener, Bruno, tarnished and grubby in a stand of poplars at the very edge of the property where the Beaufours rarely venture, let alone their guests. The only explanation they will be able to find is that some animal, drawn to the bright colour, has dragged it from the poolside, across the grass and into the trees before realising the pointlessness of the effort. They consider sending it to Winchester but cannot find the appropriate words for the accompanying letter, so it is laid quietly at the back of a drawer where it remains for many years.

Viktor rings the airfield to check the weather one final time before they leave the house. The report is not reassuring but he accepts it as a given that they are going to fly. Far from irritating him, he finds to his surprise that the delay has made Maja more endearing. He will not allow himself to appear anxious or ill-prepared in her eyes, so he dons those metaphorical robes which bestow a radiant confidence in the rightness of his own pronouncements, and the clear sky suggests that the weather is as susceptible as any jury to the force of his personality.

They walk out onto the tarmac and Rudy climbs into the plane straight away. Maja watches while Viktor performs the external checks, her visible enjoyment of the process reigniting some of the excitement he once felt himself before every flight. He climbs into the cabin through the single door, sits himself in the pilot's seat then helps her in. He leans across her lap to pull the door shut, shows her how the seat belt works and gives her a headset. They refuel then park up into the wind. He puts the brakes on, checks the fuel is drawing from the emptier tank, switches to the fuller and runs through the power checks. Magnetos, carburettor, trim, full and free movement, hatch and harness. They taxi to the runway and wait for a Hawker 600 to take off, bank right and dissolve into the blue.

They have not left the ground but Rudy is already asleep in the back seat, lullabied by the rumble and bounce. He is ill at ease in the company of most other children but he is utterly self-sufficient, so this holiday has been, for him, a little heaven during which he has had unrestricted access to a pool, a well-stocked refrigerator with double doors and a set of thirty-two Caran d'Ache coloured pencils with which to continue writing and drawing his cartoon epic *The Knights of Kandor*.

His fondest memory is that of swimming in the rain, having the vacated pool area entirely to himself, the pebbled fizz of the surface and the blue silence under. He goes to a boarding school where he is bullied by the other boys in a way that is too unspecific and too nebulous to complain about but which eats away at him, and there are only three more days of holiday left, so he has made the most of his limited time in Bellevue, going to bed late and rising early. Consequently he is exhausted. But he will not be returning to school. In two hours he will be dead.

'Prunay tower. Golf Alpha Sierra at the hold and ready for departure.'

'Golf Alpha Sierra. Clear to take-off, runway zero one. Wind zero two zero degrees. Five knots.'

Viktor has become lax recently but because Maja is sitting next to him he goes through the emergency protocols, reciting the mantra in his head as they accelerate along the runway. 'If I have an engine failure on the ground, I close the throttle and come to a halt. If I get an engine failure when I'm just airborne but have sufficient room I close the throttle and land back on the runway. If I can't land on the runway I pick the safest area within thirty degrees left and right of the centre line and land in it.'

Thirty miles per hour, forty, fifty ... They take off and Viktor turns on track as they climb. He'll head north-west to Le Touquet then north along the coast to Cap Gris-Nez before crossing the Channel to the Dover beacon. They level out at six thousand feet and Maja starts talking about riding a horse called Bombardier on the South Downs – the Clarendon Way, Ashley Down, Beacon Hill ... It's superficial chatter but she seems satisfied with a few well-placed noises of agreement and he likes the sound of her voice. Finally she stops fighting the roar of the engine and gives herself over to looking down at the landscape so that he is free to turn every now and then and imagine what she looks like naked.

Five thousand feet below it's a jumbled parquet of fields, half ploughed, half green, patches of forest over Saint-Gobain and Noyon, the fat snake of the Somme looping down towards Amiens. The sky is cloudier now, the blue fading, the air a little bumpier. He radios Lille Information for a heads-up. A few clouds at a thousand feet, broken cloud at fifteen hundred, overcast at five. Not perfect but they're heading towards Le Touquet anyway so there are no significant decisions to be made and Maja is talking again, about her husband's shortcomings this time, in a way which is sad and funny and surprisingly kind, so that Viktor feels drawn into a circle of confidence from which he has been excluded all week, a sensation so intensely pleasurable when combined with their physical closeness that he pays too little attention to the slowly deteriorating weather. Over Abbeville the cloud thickens unexpectedly. He loses visual contact with the ground and finds that his forward visibility has been reduced to the point where he can no longer distinguish the horizon. He knows precisely what he should do at this point – carefully execute a one-hundred-and-eighty-degree turn and get out of what is a potentially disastrous situation as swiftly as he can. If Maja were noticeably concerned then this is precisely what he would do, but far from understanding the danger they are now in, she seems entranced.

'You can imagine it's Turkey down there. Or Finland. Very Antoine de Saint-Exupéry.'

It is the most foolish thing he has ever done. Their safety – her safety, Rudy's safety – is more important than any other consideration, but there is some caveman part of his brain which is profoundly averse to being seen as less than competent, by anyone, let alone by a woman, and least of all by a woman he finds this attractive. The very act of turning over these thoughts in his mind has postponed the evasive action he should have taken by five, then ten, then fifteen seconds and convinced him that since he's on track he will hold his course and, fingers crossed, soon emerge from the other side of the cloud.

There is an American study everyone quotes during PPL training which says that the average life expectancy of a pilot who flies into cloud with no instrument training is ninety seconds. It had always seemed to him like a tactical exaggeration. *Keep out. Here be monsters.* Or a measure perhaps of the number of idiot farmers in rural Kansas who used crop-dusters like quad bikes. It is the speed with which he must read and react to the instruments which shocks him, and the difficulty of ignoring the messages coming from his inner ear.

Maja gazes out of the window, unperturbed.

It is less than three minutes since they entered the cloud. He is shockingly tired and starting to feel dizzy, his brain so desperate for some fixed point to contradict all these deceptive signals of lift and twist and fall and yaw that he is starting to hallucinate dark shapes ahead. The aircraft pitches and banks. He over-corrects. He needs to lose height. Maybe he can get out from under the cloud cover. A glimpse of the ground is all he needs. He loosens the throttle a little and gently pushes the yoke forwards. Two thousand feet, a thousand feet, eight hundred.

Were he not concentrating so hard on keeping the plane level and straight he might realise the elementary mistake he is making. The altimeter is set to sea level. He is not over the sea. He is over the land. Four minutes. Five. The cloud is not clearing. There is a very real possibility that they are going to crash. He is unconcerned about his own death, but he cannot bear the thought that he will kill his own son, he cannot bear the thought that he will kill a beautiful woman and her unborn child.

In his dream Rudy is playing with his imaginary friend, Babu. They are back at Bellevue. It is night-time and they have taken triangles of La Vache Qui Rit from the fridge and made themselves big tumblers of grenadine and turned on the pool lights so that the water is a turquoise slab of liquid light swaying in the dark.

Maja looks across and sees tears rolling down Viktor's face. He says, in an oddly formal voice, 'I really am so very, very sorry about this.' She is sick with fear for perhaps ten seconds then the fog in front of the plane darkens for the merest moment before they strike the side of a grain silo. They are travelling at seventy miles per hour. The silo is empty so they rip through the corrugated iron. The Perspex windscreen splits and pops out of its frame, the snapped edge taking Viktor's head clean off. They hit the far wall of the silo, rip through that in turn then plough, nose first, into the hard earth. The wheels collapse, the plane pitches forward and the engine block is punched backwards, crushing Maja's legs.

By chance a German doctor, Raphael Bhatt, is driving slowly along a small country road between Gapennes and Yvrench when he sees a green starboard wing light descending to the left of the car. The fog is so thick that he has no idea whether the plane is a Cessna or an Airbus. He hits the brakes for fear that the plane is going to veer across the road, but the light shoots ahead, lower than tree height now, and vanishes. He does not know the area well but he is fairly sure that there are no airfields nearby. He thinks he hears an explosion of some kind but it is possible that he has imagined it. He slows to a crawl and waits for the glow of flames, but there is only the road dissolving into the whiteness ahead. He wonders whether he really saw it, the way one does after extraordinary events which leave no mark on one's surroundings.

He picks up speed. After a few hundred metres he takes a left-hand turning onto a dirt track which leads to a dilapidated farmhouse. A rusted tractor. A stack of old tyres. He suspects that he has come to the wrong place, that the plane landed somewhere else or gained altitude and is now five miles away. Nevertheless he gets out of the car. The only thing he can hear is the fog-muffled grunting of many pigs, the smell of whose shit is almost overpowering. The door of the farmhouse opens, a triangle of light cuts across the muddy yard and a portly woman trots towards him – bun, floral apron, slippers – shouting, '*Venez! Venez!*' as if she were relieved to find that he has finally arrived. She beckons him round the side of the farmhouse whose entire gable wall consists of black plastic sheeting held in place by a grid of wooden battens. An intruder floodlight comes on as they jog beneath it. The woman's husband stands facing them, immobile, pointing a beam of torchlight to his left like a bored usherette at the cinema. They turn the corner of a barn.

It is, by some margin, the most extraordinary thing Raphael has seen in his life. The nose of the plane is buried in the earth, the wings have snapped and slumped forward and the tail is bent over like the tail of a scorpion. Directly behind the plane is a large metal building through which it seems to have flown, though it is difficult to make out details in this Gothic light. He runs over. Through the shattered glass he can see a small, blonde woman wearing a cream rollneck jumper. Beyond that it is impossible to work out what she looks like because her face is crazed with lacerations. She is heavily pregnant. He forgets what country he is in. He says, '*Keine Panik, ich bin Arzt.*' He grabs the handle of the door and twists it. He puts his foot against the body of the plane and heaves. The door opens at the third attempt with a grinding squeal as it scrapes across the buckled wing. He can see now that the woman's legs are clamped between the seat and the instrument panel. She sounds as if she is very, very drunk and is trying to get across some important message but cannot form the words. She needs to be cut out. She needs pain relief. He needs to examine her lower legs to discover how badly she might be bleeding. None of these things are possible. And only then does he see that she is not the pilot. The pilot is sitting beyond her in the far seat. His head is missing. This detail will be kept out of the press but the gossip at l'Arbre de Mai in town will be that old man Moreau found the head in the middle of a nearby field the following day.

The ripped metal of the plane squeals and shifts. Raphael jumps backwards and waits for the structure to find a new equilibrium. Broken glass has sliced a deep channel in the flesh of his arm of which he is completely unaware. He is unaware of many things. Only afterwards, in the flashbacks which will haunt him for the best part of two years, will he worry about the possibility of the plane catching fire. He grabs the farmer's torch and returns to the woman and it is only when he points the beam into the dark interior of the cabin that he sees a boy lying behind her in the rear footwell. He smashes the small triangular window at the back with the butt of the torch so that he can reach inside. He squeezes the boy's shoulder but gets no response. He presses two fingers to the boy's neck. Nothing. He twists the boy's head and pulls his upper eyelids back, left then right. No dilation. Traumatic head injury, probably. Behind him the farmer's wife is praying quietly to herself. '*Pardonne-nous nos offenses, comme nous aussi nous pardonnons à ceux qui nous ont offensés.*'

The injured woman is holding her swollen belly. Is it possible that she is in labour? 'Hang on,' he says. 'Help will be here very soon.' The woman's head is rolling from side to side. He cannot even tell what language she is speaking, but with the aid of the torch he can make out the exposed bone of a broken femur. He takes off his tie and makes a rudimentary tourniquet. She seems unaware of what he's doing. Her wordless drunken moan is growing steadily quieter. The roll of her head is a metronome winding down. 'Be strong. We will get through this together, the two of us.'

He pulls the tourniquet as tight as he can then secures it with a double reef knot. There is nothing more he can do now except wait. He feels her belly. The baby is moving. The following minutes are the most upsetting part of what will be the most upsetting night of his life, waiting for the emergency services to arrive, offering reassurance which feels increasingly meaningless, desperately willing the woman and the child to remain alive. 'You can do it. Help is on its way.'

After a period of time which could be ten minutes or an hour the woman's head sags forwards and she stops moving. She has gone, he is certain of it. He knows now what he has to do. If nothing else he may be able to keep the baby alive.

He unclips the woman's seat belt and steps over her so that he is straddling her belly. There is blood everywhere. The pilot's hand is frozen mid-air, finger pointing upwards, as if he were interrupted in the middle of a speech.

Raphael grips the woman's nose and tilts her head back. He puts his lips to her mouth and blows hard to inflate her lungs. Her chest rises. He pauses and does it again. If he can get enough oxygen into her lungs and keep her heart pumping then he may be able to get enough oxygen to the baby. He leans backwards, places the heels of his doubled hands against her sternum and presses hard. One ... two ... three ... four ... five ... Back to the mouth. Grip, tilt, blow. There is an eerie stillness in the midst of all this. The twisted metal, the fog, the sound of the pigs, the rhythm of his hands. Occasionally the plane creaks. Or perhaps it is the broken metal of the building which stands over them. He pictures himself on an iron ship in the middle of a dark ocean. He and the unborn child could be the only living beings in the world.

He doesn't wear a watch on holiday so he counts, because the paramedics will need to know. Fifty cycles of CPR. Twenty-five minutes or thereabouts. He hears sirens and gunned engines and men's voices and he is suddenly in the middle of a science-fiction film, all thunder and arc-light, helmets and jumpsuits. There is a large vehicle of a kind he has never seen before which might be a fire tender from a military airfield. A pair of gloved hands grip his shoulders and guide him out of the cockpit. He walks away then turns to take it all in – the silhouetted figures, the buckled crucifix of the plane, 'CA-956' in yellow on racing green, pulsing blue lights, the sparkler-fizz of oxy-acetylene torches. It is like a vast Renaissance canvas depicting some new myth. Then he thinks, for the first time, that this is probably a family. The mother is dead, the father is dead, the son is dead. And if the child survives ...? Something happens which has never happened in seventeen years of practising medicine. A flurry of violet hail blows across his field of vision and he sees the mud of the farmyard swing gracefully up to meet his unprotected face. He returns to his body to find himself sitting on a plastic barrel holding a small chipped mug of brandy and the farmer's wife offering him an opened packet of chocolate LU Pépitos. Somewhere a baby is crying.

THE CHILD

Philippe looks across the Avenue du Président Kennedy to the Île aux Cygnes. From this height the Eiffel Tower is visible in its entirety so that it looks like one of the models sold by hawkers below the real thing. A mint-green Line 6 metro train crosses the Pont de Bir-Hakeim. They must have come for another reason. If he can think of that other reason before they reach the apartment then they will not say that Maja is dead. It is like avoiding the lines between paving stones. But he cannot think of any other reason. If there were any other reason they would be talking to his lawyer, to his accountant or to Hervé. The Seine is a ribbon of pitted khaki sliding west. The glass door opens and Hervé leads them out onto the balcony. The man is an *officier de la Police Judiciaire*. Black uniform, two chevrons. He has unnaturally pale skin and a mole like a squashed sultana on his cheek. There is a portly woman standing just behind him in a dowdy beige jumper and a purple windcheater.

People do not enter Philippe's private space unasked. It is the job of Hervé and other members of staff to prevent situations like this occurring. The officer introduces his colleague. She is from the *bureau d'aide aux victimes*. This is not possible. Philippe's mother died instantly of a heart attack while skiing in Lech Zürs. His father spent his last month in a villa in Kefalonia where he could be lifted in and out of the sea by nurses. Philippe is not so naive as to believe that money can alter the brute facts of life but he has always assumed that it can postpone and ameliorate.

The officer apologises for being the bearer of bad news. He flips open a little notebook to check the facts. 'The plane struck a farm building.' The woman is openly admiring the view. Or is she merely avoiding Philippe's glance? How could she be of assistance to anyone? Hervé asks about the other passengers. The policeman explains that both the pilot and the young boy are dead. Philippe is glad. He would not be able to bear the knowledge that Viktor had killed Maja and that he or his son had survived. The woman turns back towards him and tilts her head to one side in order to seem sympathetic. She is a fatter, older, less attractive version of a TV presenter whose name Philippe cannot remember. His own thoughts seem to belong to someone else, running like ticker tape under the scene in front of him.

'She was trapped in the wreckage.'

Ten storeys below, a barge is being hauled upstream, water pleating around the tug's snub bow. Why are they telling him these details?

'The good news, however ...' The policeman pauses and takes a breath. 'I'm sorry. That was badly phrased.' He takes another breath. 'Your daughter is alive.'

Philippe holds the brushed steel rail and looks down at the moat of thorny shrubs that separates the building from the pavement. He had forgotten completely that Maja was pregnant. How is that possible? Steam drifts from a sunken grille. Did she give birth before she died, or did they hack at her like meat to save the child? If he were to lean a little further out then gravity will simply take over. It would be the easiest thing in the world. It would be like falling into bed.

Hervé drives. He is Philippe's factotum and bodyguard, one of the few people who will remain close to his employer as everyone else is discarded over the next few years. Philippe does not want to spend three hours in the presence of someone he does not know and he is in no state to drive himself. He watches the cruel countryside reel past. *Shock* is the wrong word. He is outside his body, airborne, cartwheeling, blank. They had decided on a name but he will not say it, even in the privacy of his own mind, for fear of making her real. He does not want a daughter, but neither does he want her to die. He wants to turn back time and trade her for Maja. What if the child was starved of oxygen? What if she is brain-damaged? What if she is crippled?

Hervé pulls out and overtakes a Dentressangle eighteen-wheeler, a loose tongue of dirty orange canvas flapping so rapidly along its flank that it sings. Hervé is six foot four and seventeen stone and carries no fat. He wears, always, a white shirt under a charcoal suit with no tie. His shaved head shines like a polished apple. He wears Wood Sage & Sea Salt cologne by Jo Malone. He has no interest in other people except insofar as it impinges upon his own plans, needs and well-being. He listens, mostly, to seventies and eighties disco, of which he has an encyclopedic knowledge – Rose Royce, A Taste of Honey, the Love Unlimited Orchestra. He is polite and attentive to those to whom Philippe needs him to be polite and attentive. There is a set to his face, however, when he is displeased which is sufficiently unsettling for him to have needed to resort to physical violence on only two occasions. Nikki, Philippe's secretary, is fairly sure that he would kill someone if asked and feel no compunction.

The Commissariat in Boulogne occupies one corner of a down-at-heel crossroads opposite a tattoo parlour. Inside, a man in a hi-vis, lemon-yellow tabard and a pirate's hat is complaining drunkenly about his landlord. A rank cheesy stink rolls off him. He is ushered from the building by a portly policeman who has donned a pair of disposable blue gloves for the purpose.

Philippe hasn't stood in a queue or waited in a public place since Cambridge.

They are taken to the morgue where Philippe identifies Maja's body. She looks as if she has been flailed. He has always scorned the idea of a soul but the body feels … empty. He will have the same thought about the Alfama apartment, about the Dubuffets, about the sweetbreads and sea lettuce at Mirazur, about Tribune Bay, as if Maja were the lamp that previously lit the world.

At the hospital his daughter is asleep in a box of transparent plastic. There are two hand-holes on the side which makes Philippe think of gloved scientists manipulating plutonium rods from behind leaded glass. A cannula disappears under a Swiss cross of Micropore tape on the back of each tiny hand, giving her the air of a resting puppet. Hervé takes a photograph for the passport. A nurse places her gently in Philippe's arms. He has never held a baby. She has his skin colouring – suede, coffee. Wisps of damp black hair on her head. She opens her eyes. They are astonishingly dark. She is the most beautiful thing he has ever seen. The nurse gives him a bottle of formula milk and he feeds her. Angelica. He will call her Angelica. He will never remember the name he and Maja chose.

Hervé books them into a modest hotel in Château Cléry while Angelica is observed overnight. Philippe has never stayed in a three-star establishment before. Hervé hires nurses and initiates the passport application process. He calls Maja's father in Gothenburg and tells them the terrible news. He says that Philippe is too upset to talk at the moment. He tells Mr Söderberg that he and his wife now have a granddaughter and he hopes that this is some small compensation for the loss of their daughter. Mr Söderberg sounds woozy. Is it possible that he is drunk? Hervé calls the Beaufours.

The following morning Hervé meets the private nurse. Côte d'Ivoire, he guesses. Her name is Océane. She is tall and strikingly good-looking. Philippe will not want the company of someone so extravagantly blessed. Hervé gives her two hundred euros in cash and tells the agency to send someone plain. He buys baby clothes, baby food, a car seat at an Intermarché, jobs well below his pay grade but he wants to keep the circle tight.

Medical checks are running late so Philippe and Hervé sit in a hospital waiting room. Philippe keeps forgetting that Maja is dead, then remembering, the same sick lurch every time. An obese crone pads past in slippers and polyester gown, pushing a wheeled stand from which a bag of pale yellow fluid dangles and sways. A tattooed woman has her head bandaged in a way that Philippe has only ever seen in cartoons.

They return to the ward but the *chef de clinique* is still busy. Philippe is shocked at how much waiting there is in the world of ordinary people and at how difficult it is to do. There are five other incubated babies on the ward. Four are premature – small, wrinkled creatures who could be sleeping in a hollowed oak in a fairy tale. They lie on cashmere blankets and wear tiny, hand-knitted woolly hats. One is Indian, he guesses, or somewhere thereabouts. Long, silky black hair on its shoulders and arms.

An *interne* appears after twenty-five minutes and says that there is some remaining bureaucracy to be gone through. What he does not say, because the situation is difficult enough already, is that this concerns the need for confirmation of paternity. Hervé gives the man a card and says simply that Philippe's lawyer will be in touch. Then they take

Angelica and leave, displaying a presumption so free of doubt that it leaves no opening for disagreement.

Philippe insists that they drive to the crash site. Hervé thinks it unwise but rations his absolute prohibitions to maintain their force. He sits in the car with the baby. Philippe walks down the muddy lane to the farmhouse. He will notice later how dirty his shoes are and think of this as a penance. The farm building of the police report is a tall, cylindrical silo of black corrugated iron. It has been hacked through the middle and now slumps sideways like the bashed-in hat of a nineteenth-century pantomime villain. There are gouges in the earth where the plane was presumably dragged prior to being lifted onto a flatbed truck and driven away. He pictures it in a hangar somewhere, men in rolled-up sleeves taking photographs and jotting down readings taken from smashed dials. *She wouldn't have known a thing.* Is that true? There are dark stains on the earth, some fluid which last night's rain has not washed away. Oil? Fuel? Blood?

An old woman is yelling at him. She belongs to another world. Overhead, the sky is uniformly blue, only two parallel contrails smudging and sliding. A railway for angels. There is nothing here for him.

In the car Hervé receives a phone call from Paris. There are journalists at the apartment. He must find somewhere else for Philippe and Angelica to stay until the passport comes through.

They meet the new nurse at the hotel. She looks as if she works on the checkout at Carrefour – forties, heavyset, the ghost of a tattoo on her right forearm. Agathe Guérin. Philippe feels both relieved and jealous of the ease and warmth with which she handles his daughter, the fluent, unaffected nonsense she talks. *Un, deux, trois, allons dans les bois. Quatre, cinq, six, cueillir des cerises …*

Philippe says he wants to see the ocean. Memories of childhood, perhaps, or simply the comfort of having a whim indulged. They leave Angelica with Agathe, and Hervé drives them to Fort-Mahon-Plage where they stand on the promenade in bright sunshine and a cold wind. Hardy families hunker under umbrellas hammered into the sand. Far off, the gaudy blades of five land yachts – pink, white, orange, orange, white – scoot over the flats. What if he left it all behind – the money, the houses, the investments, the artwork, the travel? What if he took a job and he and Angelica lived in an unremarkable house in an unre-markable town? A boy stands on the beach staring at him. It is Rudy. If Rudy is alive, then it is possible that Maja is alive. He turns to get Hervé's attention but when he turns back to the beach the boy has gone. He is suddenly frightened that Rudy has re-materialised in the hotel and is planning to do some terrible harm to Angelica.

'We need to get back.'

❧

They move into a large villa near Cavaillon. Hervé hires a cook, a housekeeper and three more local nurses to work eight-hour shifts. Much as he loves Angelica, Philippe's own parents were neither very attentive nor very affectionate and he has a limited appetite for baby talk. He does not know how to be a father. He spends much of his time engaged in the raw act of grieving. He thinks about Maja perpe-tually – scenes from their shared life, scenes from TV dramas, nightmare images of her death, nightmare images of Angelica's birth. Sometimes he hears her voice and turns to see an empty doorway or a bird at the poolside. He had a gallstone four years ago in New York, a pain so all-consuming it rendered him briefly blind. This time there is no morphine. He must get down on all fours and ride it out. Hervé says that he can source medication but Philippe fears that it is only the pain that stands between himself and a great void into which he might tumble irretrievably.

There are obituaries in the *New York Times, Le Monde, Süddeutsche Zeitung*. She has two pages in *Aftonbladet*. He reads them over and over. He saw her first in *The Forest*, a television series at which he would have scoffed had it starred anyone else. He watched both seasons in a fortnight, telling himself it was a childish infatuation till he googled her and watched an interview in which she quoted Christopher Smart at length, in English as fluent as his own. *For I will consider my Cat Jeoffry. For he is the servant of the Living God, duly and daily serving him. For at the first glance of the glory of God in the East he worships in his way …* He flew to Stockholm to see her in *John Gabriel Borkman* at the Kungliga Dramatiska Teatern and waited at the stage door with flowers like it was 1954.

He has arranged his life so that there is nothing he needs to do. Housekeepers look after all five properties. Nikki oversees the housekeepers, pays bills and runs maintenance. The accountancy firm retained by the family, Maines, subcontract an investment manager, Quadrant, to run a portfolio on a medium-risk basis that steadily outpaces inflation. He was in the tea business for seven years till rising Indian labour costs required him to tell lies and hurt people, actions which his partner Lem called *deal-making* and *streamlining* and which came to Lem as easily as breathing so that he slipped into that big leather chair on Portugal Street as if Philippe had merely been keeping it warm for him. And now? How does one conjure those engaging, complex, necessary tasks which give one's days shape and meaning from within a life of such ease?

He watches an episode of *The Forest* on DVD every night. It has dated terribly, but it is a magic box which still contains Maja and she is alive and she is young and she is beautiful. Hervé reorders all the books Philippe left in the teetering pagoda by his bed in Winchester, but Philippe can read nothing denser than Fred Vargas and Arnaldur Indriðason, good vanquishing evil in three hundred and fifty easy pages. There are bicycles in the shed. He goes for long rides. Sometimes he has to stop at the side of the road and weep. He floats in the pool and is badly sunburnt. He longs for some more serious ailment.

He returns none of the calls, emails or letters from friends and acquaintances offering their condolences. It is not that he dislikes the idea of seeming weak, or calling upon the kindness of equals; it is simply a transaction he has never learnt. Perhaps it would be truer to say that they are not friends in the way that others might understand the word. He has never lived in one place. He moved school every two years – Sir James Henderson, the Institut Auf Dem Rosenberg, Aiglon, Phillips Exeter ... When relationships, political climates or tax regimes became uncomfortable he moved on, as his father had done, as his grandfather had done. In his adult life he has chosen to spend time with people of similar tastes whose company he enjoys. Why would one do anything else? When those people have difficulties – a serious illness, drug addiction, a teenage child in trouble with the law – he has given them the space he would have wanted in a similar situation. He realises now that he loved Maja because she was the only person he needed. It seems obvious in retrospect, as do many of the hard lessons he is learning.

❧

The French air-accident investigation closes, offering no challenge to what seemed, only hours after the crash, to be the obvious explanation. The coroner passes a verdict of death by misadventure, the police case is closed and Maja's body is released.

Hervé arranges a funeral in Gothenburg. It is a shambles. No press are invited but the information leaks and there is an unseemly scuffle involving a photographer and Maja's brother. When Maja's mother is presented with Angelica she collapses, the way people do in films when given shocking news. Maja's father, Hervé now sees, is in the early stages of Alzheimer's which accounts for his seeming drunkenness during that first phone call and his failure to pass on the vital message. The old man spends a great deal of time at the reception asking for Teddy Lindholm, a name his wife does not recognise. He goes missing at one point and is discovered round the back of the building, kneeling beside a dead thrush and weeping. Maja's agent delivers a dreary eulogy which sounds like her Wikipedia page, to an audience which contains two Oscars, three Oliviers and a Knight of the Realm. There is unremitting rain throughout.

Philippe is pleased. Maja's death itself was a shambles and a shambolic funeral feels right. Besides, he has never greatly liked her family. Brewers and soldiers. Her cousin is an MP for the so-called Sweden Democrats. *Bevara Sverige Svenskt* and everyone else can fuck off. Her father was the only one he had liked. That rebellious twinkle. Court-martialled for putting two cats and a lit Catherine wheel inside a tank containing a senior officer. His Alzheimer's, thankfully, preoccupies Maja's mother enough to stop her trying to pin Philippe down about arrangements for seeing Angelica before they slip out to the idling limousine.

❧

Antioch was designed by Amyas Connell in 1937 for Philippe's grandfather and named after the ancient city on the eastern end of the Turkish Mediterranean coast. Occupying fifty-five acres of land it sits in a saddle between two wooded hills above the village of Braishfield, eight miles west of Winchester. The office and the staff accommodation are shielded by trees at the boundary of the property so that even from the roof garden of the main house no other buildings are visible. The shield of the hills creates a sweet spot where the average temperature is always a couple of degrees higher than the surrounding countryside and cheeringly un-English palms grow happily around the long sloping lawn. On sunny days it is possible to think that one is in the Loire, if not quite Provence.

Connell was a disciple of Le Corbusier though the master's hard lines have been softened a little here. There is a good deal of concrete and many straight lines and semicircles, but everything is painted white and there are big windows so that the effect is more Riviera than Cité Radieuse. The house is Grade II listed and every few months a bold architectural twitcher will wander up the drive which remains without electronic gates because Philippe thinks the fashion vulgar. He returns to the house five weeks after the funeral when Nikki assures Hervé that even the most persistent journalists are long gone. He will remain there with Angelica for eighteen months.

Before Maja was killed Philippe read widely, travelled frequently and collected art, each activity a manifestation of the same hunger for the world, as if the planet itself were a great feast to be greedily eaten. The Milky Way seen from the doorway of a yurt in Elsen Tasarkhai, the Modigliani portrait of Soutine, Leigh Fermor's Danube ... the dividing lines between the world experienced and the world described so porous that sometimes he could not remember whether he had seen a place, a painting or a building through his own eyes or through someone else's words. He reads easily in four languages and can carry on rudimentary conversations in seven, though he always found those languages and their respective literatures more fascinating than its living speakers, using ramshackle modernisations of Latin and Greek, for instance, which confused and amused interlocutors in Italy and Greece. But now? Those paintings, those temples, those archipelagos, those tiny planes dragging their red ribbons across so many pages of the atlas, seem like the kind of cheap trick a conjurer might get away with at a children's party to disguise the fact that there was in truth no magic in the world.

He cannot travel without Angelica. Even in London he is beset by nightmares of her being lowered into a bath of boiling water by an idiot nurse, or rolling off a table and cracking her head on the kitchen floor. Two days in Bonn are a torment. Nor can he travel with a nurse in tow, his wife's absence mocked constantly by a dowdy stand-in, tarnishing the golden memory of one country after another. So he hunkers down and lets the world's callous carnival carry on beyond the trees.

Every so often the senders of the unanswered calls, emails and letters turn up without an invitation, because they happen to be passing, because they genuinely care or because they are intrigued. Philippe assumes that they have all come to see Angelica. She is a thing of such wonder to him that she must surely be a thing of wonder to everyone, so she is brought out by one of the nurses while Philippe and his visitors are served tea and cake and try to keep the conversation afloat. One day Hanneke, Viktor's widow and Rudy's mother, knocks at the door. She has tried to contact Philippe repeatedly and polite rebuffs from Hervé and Nikki have not reduced the frequency of her attempts. Paola, the current housekeeper, gives her the same story she gives the journalists who turn up every so often: Philippe is living in Turkey. He watches from an upstairs window as she walks towards the white Range Rover parked askew on the gravel. He expects her to sit behind the wheel and gather herself before putting the car into gear and departing. To his surprise she opens the passenger door and takes out a small red fire extinguisher. She walks over to his Mercedes and swings it into the centre of the windscreen which slumps into a target of frosting. He doesn't understand. Surely it is he who has the right to be angry. She leaves the fire extinguisher protruding from the rectangle of shattered glass and drives away and Hervé's instinct not to press charges is correct because it is the last time she attempts to make contact.

Maja's mother telephones on several occasions, wanting to arrange a visit so that she can see her granddaughter again. Hervé pencils in some vague dates which are never firmed up. She is, he guesses, increasingly preoccupied with her husband's deteriorating condition. For whatever reason, she finally stops ringing.

Maja's death has become, for a small number of people, an obsession, fostered and sustained by the Internet which, to Philippe, seems like nothing more than a great machine for connecting the deranged and angry people of the world. So, five mornings a week Angelica goes to a local nursery under an assumed name. After she leaves the house, Philippe swims one hundred and fifty anaesthetic lengths. He cannot imagine talking to anyone about his sadness. He does not want the burden shared or halved. He could no more give away this hurt than he could give away Maja's clothes, her piano, her awards. He plays the music she once loved (*Simon Boccanegra, Tristan und Isolde, Káťa Kabanová* ...) on the speakers built into the walls of the house and pretends that she is in a nearby room. He sees Rudy sometimes, standing at the end of a corridor, or in the gloaming under the palms. It does not surprise him. It seems natural that biology and physics have been fundamentally altered by the same impact that shattered his heart.

He goes for long walks on the Downs where Maja used to ride. The Clarendon Way, Ashley Down, Beacon Hill. Inhuman nature calms him with its long, slow rhythms and its million different greens, the wind in the long grass, buzzards overhead. He doesn't see Rudy out here. The boy is an indoor phenomenon, a product of those vibrations human beings leave ringing in bricks and glass and steel.

Angelica toddles, then walks. She speaks late and her first word is 'water' and Philippe is unaware of how peculiar this is. She hears her father talk about the paintings on the walls of the house and describes her first pictures – a forest of Twombly-esque loops – as 'abstrack'. She likes all fruit except oranges and hates all vegetables except spinach. So she calls orange a vegetable and spinach a fruit because she likes categories not to overlap. For several years she will call the uncomfortable overlapping of categories 'making things brown' because it is what happens when coloured paints are allowed to mix. She gives her twenty-two soft toys names which begin with successive letters of the alphabet, from a rabbit called André to an orang-utan called Very Very. She likes *Barbapapa* and *Madeleine* and *Dear Zoo* and *Peepo!* She likes *Le Renard et l'Enfant* and *The Incredibles* and *Le Petit Poucet*. Her baby-fat falls away. She is tall for her age and skinny with it, that same dark skin which surprised him in the hospital in Boulogne set off now by glossy, mahogany hair. Philippe could gaze at her for ever, but to other adults her looks can be disturbing, the darkness of those extraordinary eyes, so dark you feel as if you are looking *into* someone not *at* them. Philippe explains to Angelica that her mother acted in films and on television, that she was loved by people who had never met her, that she flew away and didn't come back. These things fuse in Angelica's mind so that she will always think of Maja as a faerie figure borrowed by the physical world before she was called back home.

Philippe owns houses in Sri Lanka, Berlin and Skiathos. They are rented out, less to save money than to keep the staff on their toes. The villa outside Antakya remains empty. He cannot bear the idea of anyone else inhabiting what has always been thought of as the ancestral home. The family has owned the estate for as long as written records exist, so it is said. According to their own private myth they have been there since Antakya was Antioch, since Antioch itself was founded, surviving all the subsequent revolts, sieges, conquests and earthquakes. In the very centre of the house is a low-lit room where archaeological relics from the city's early days are kept behind glass – bowls, amphorae, seven Roman dice, two vanishingly rare Domitian Tetradrachms from the city's mint, a substantial piece of mosaic flooring which should technically be in the Hatay Museum. Is the story true? Perhaps it matters only that this is a family which has always prided itself as part of a global aristocracy, doggedly secular but with Muslim, Christian and Jewish roots, citizens of the world not in aspiration but in simple fact.

❧

Angelica's birthdays are simultaneously anniversaries of Maja's death. Philippe ignores both. On her third birthday, however, Paola the housekeeper starts a tradition of taking her to Legoland in Windsor, and Philippe is too preoccupied with his own memories to be haunted by images of his daughter falling from a roller coaster or being abducted by a stranger.

The fourth Christmas after Maja's death Philippe tries to make up for his self-absorption by throwing a party for Angelica and a few friends from the nursery. The temperature drops unexpectedly the night before and by the time guests arrive there is snow on the palms and on the grass, fat flakes against a dark, pearly sky. If the noise of their shrieking is any measure the children are clearly enjoying themselves, sweeping from room to room in a raucous shoal. Only one girl stands apart, walking the room the way a cat does, following some kind of path invisible to everyone else. She climbs up and sits on the wide white mantelpiece at one point, like a presiding sprite, until her mother lifts her down for jelly, and Philippe can't suppress the suspicion that she has some connection to Rudy, an emissary, a lieutenant. Hervé is not at ease among children. He hovers at the periphery only because the event carries so much potential for disaster. Two fathers start talking to Philippe without introducing themselves and he realises, belatedly, that he met them at local events years ago, when Maja was still alive. A number of the parents have clearly tagged along only to see the house and the grounds and spend the entire time looking over the children's heads and out of the windows as if they are thinking of buying the place. One has to be extracted from a bedroom. The children eat Würstchen im Schlafrock and mini-pizzas with pineapple and ham. They drink magic punch containing gummy bears in ice cubes. They play Snake's Tail and Pass-the-Parcel and Chinese Jump Rope. Nikki has hired Safari Sam who brings a boa constrictor, an iguana, a tarantula, a fat, black millipede and twelve cockroaches which the children are encouraged to place on their faces in order to horrify their parents. One of the fathers has to sit in his car for the best part of an hour until he is certain that the animals have gone.

The whole event has the heightened colours of a folk tale, as if it is taking place inside one of those houses that spring up on the solstice, at which the weary traveller knocks and is asked inside to find a blazing fire, fine food and sweet wine. Angelica is happy and Philippe cannot imagine anything better than being here, now, with these people, his sadness gone, his wanderlust stilled, the snow, the palms, the music. But as always happens in the folk tale there comes a point where abundance tips into surfeit and the faintest of shadows falls. He is resentful of all these people who seem capable of making his daughter happy in a way that he cannot. He is frightened that they will spirit her away, not today and perhaps not literally, but that they will spirit her away nevertheless.

He asks Paola to bring the party to a sharp close at the prescribed time, but it is one of the few occasions when she stands her ground. This is Angelica's day and she is enjoying herself. Hervé extracts Philippe on the fictional pretext of an important phone call, and ushers him into the upstairs study whose windows look onto the unpeopled white woods at the rear of the house and from where the noise of the party is faint enough to be covered by the Juilliard's rendering of Bartok's third string quartet. Before Hervé leaves he glances out of the window and sees, on the strip of snow-covered lawn that separates the gravel path from the beginning of the trees, a roebuck, motionless, fox-orange. He waits for it to spook and bolt, its white rump flashing as it vanishes into the foliage, but it remains completely still. The two men watch it for a minute, two minutes, three. Philippe wonders if the animal is sick. It reads like a symbol of something, though what the meaning is he has no idea. Perhaps it is this insolubility that will keep the image bright in Philippe's mind for such a long time afterwards. Hervé wonders if the deer believes that it will remain unseen as long as it doesn't move. If this is true then they are scaring it. Hervé turns away and heads back to the party and when he glances from the staircase window the animal has gone.

❧

When does Philippe's touching move from innocence into something more sinister? Is he conscious of having crossed a line at all? Or was the way he held her and played with her compromised from the beginning? If Philippe gives it any name, he calls it love. He cares for her unconditionally in a way that no one else will ever be able to care for her. They need one another, more even than he and Maja needed one another. She is made from his body, from Maja's body. How could there be a boundary of any kind between them? The only woman he ever truly loved was torn violently from him and, in return, he was given this gift. Sometimes, he palliates the recurring nightmare of the crashed plane by thinking not that Angelica looks like Maja but that in some obscure way Angelica *is* her mother, that in those terrible final seconds some vital spark jumped between the dying and the living body in order that it might remain in the world. Nor, as she gets older, will he be able to bear the thought of sharing Maja with another man. The pictures, the sounds, the sensations this possibility brings to mind make him nauseous. And it is a dangerous world out there, especially for a young woman as innocent as his daughter. Who else could protect her in the way that he can protect her? He will refrain from full intercourse until she is fourteen. He thinks of this as a kindness.

Does he know, in some corner of his mind, that what he is doing is wrong? Or, if you have never been forbidden absolutely, if you have never been harshly criticised by someone whose opinion genuinely matters to you, if you have never had to face the consequences of your own mistakes, does the quiet, critical, contrary voice at the back of the mind grow gradually quieter until it is no longer audible?

34

Angelica does not resist his advances. Sometimes he must cajole, but he never needs to threaten. That, surely, is sufficient confirmation of his integrity. That, surely, is the measure of any relationship.

The staff both know and do not know that something is not right. Hervé does not care greatly. He has little sympathy for Angelica. Hervé, though Philippe would be shocked to know it, has little sympathy for either of them. In truth Maja's death pleased him, giving him a problem sufficiently complex to tax him at long last. When he is off duty, in the company of his partner and his friends, he does vicious and accurate impressions of the family and their circle. His lack of concern is precisely why he is good at his job. His objectivity is never clouded by emotion of any kind. Nikki cares but she took the financial bait laid by Andrew Maine and was shown evidence of her clumsy embezzlements at a meeting of which Philippe knows nothing, a meeting where Andrew made a theatrical show of sliding a sealed brown envelope of incriminating documents into a safe. It is something he has done quietly on behalf of many wealthy clients, a trick learnt from his father – simple, deniable and, so far, infallible. Her loyalty, he hopes, is now guaranteed.

The cooks, the housekeepers, the cleaners, the gardeners … some can't quite put a finger on the problem, some are more convinced, but what can anyone do with such information beyond sharing it with friends and family who pass it on in turn to friends so that it merges with the vapour of fantasy which always surrounds the rich, powerful and reclusive.

Nevertheless, Philippe treats Angelica during the day with an affected coolness and never touches her until the staff have retreated from the main house. He makes sure that she always returns to her own bed. He tells her that it must remain their secret, that other people might

35

not understand. He tells her that those people would be jealous if they knew and would try to separate the two of them, that this life of ease and luxury would then come to a terrible, crashing close. He invokes the ghost of Maja and imagines her casting a posthumous blessing on their union.

There are close calls. When she is six years old a teacher finds her rubbing a doll between its legs, saying, 'Do you know how much I love you?' He does something he rarely does and attends a meeting on his own behalf. He is offended by the suggestion of impropriety. You stroke dogs because you love them, you stroke cats because you love them, you stroke people because you love them. How is a girl as young as Angelica meant to know that certain areas of the body are out of bounds? They are reading their own prurient narratives into events of no consequence. Nevertheless he withdraws Angelica and they move to a rented penthouse apartment in Vancouver.

The class is on a trip to the zoo in Aldergrove when Angelica sees a gazelle with an erection and says, 'It's like Papa.' The head of her new school is more insistent and less willing to bend to Philippe's argument that Angelica is simply pointing out that men have penises. They leave Canada. Back in Winchester he removes Angelica from formal education altogether and arranges for tutors to teach her at home. She is eight years old. He tells her that she is so far in advance of other children academically that she needs personal attention and work tailored to her own special talents. She has spent so much of her life around adults that this is largely true, and already other children are aware of something different about her, something which makes them instinctively keep their distance. Consequently she is untroubled by the prospect of a solitary life, and the flattering suggestion that this is happening because of her intellectual superiority only sugars a pill she was already happy to swallow.

Philippe never imagines that he will be found out, that he will be charged with wrongdoing. Such things are inconceivable. And that anxious thrum which runs constantly like the vibration of a ship's engine in the walls and floors? Those moments when you are woken in the small hours by the conviction that a stranger is walking up the stairs ... are they not universal feelings? Are they not simply the price of being human?

◆

She takes it as normal at first, what her father does to her. How would she know any different? She accepts, too, his insistence that she keep it secret and not discuss it with anyone. This is not a threat. It is simply the way things are. Some of the things he makes her do are disgusting and some of them are painful, but so many things to do with the human body are disgusting and painful and must simply be borne. Only as she gets older is there a growing sense of something wrong.

Her father does not allow her to watch TV and there is no Internet access in the main house. Indeed, she has been taught to think of the Internet as dangerous. It matters little. She has grown up knowing that problems will always be solved and questions answered by kind and efficient staff. She has no mobile phone and no friends she might call. She reads newspapers and magazines from an early age, but those occasional horror stories she cannot help but notice about sick men who prey on children bear no relation to her own experience. They are stepfathers, teachers, neighbours, strangers. Her father doesn't hit her. He doesn't lock her up. He loves her. He tells her so repeatedly.

She tells no one about her unease. Her father is a good man. People respect him. She has never heard him criticised. He is the biggest thing in her life. It is not possible that he is in the wrong. So it must be she who is at fault, and the fact that she doesn't know in what way she is at fault only makes the growing unease harder to bear. Who in any case would she tell? She is close to some of the staff, the housekeepers in particular – Paola, then Naomi who cycled to China, then Mariam the mountain climber from Tbilisi, then Dottie who can juggle and wears heavy-metal T-shirts under her uniform – but they are employees and seldom stay long, sensing, like so many of her father's employees, something deeply out of kilter.

She knows, too, that her father's threat is real. If someone outside the family learns of their secret then this charmed life might indeed come to an end – whatever food she wants cooked whenever she wants, clean clothes every day, new clothes every few months, endless hot baths, a wooded garden where this world and the other world merge so effortlessly one into the other, the fact that they can open the atlas at random and, by the following evening, be looking at the marble caves of General Carrera Lake, or cruising through the Qutang Gorge on the Yangtze. Above all she would miss the library at Antioch.

If she and her father were separated, if she were placed in the care of strangers and forced to live elsewhere, then how would she survive?

Fourteen, fifteen. She never fights, never complains. She allows these things to happen, and the gap between acceptance and encouragement is a very narrow one. The longer it goes on the more she feels like an accomplice. Sixteen years without a complaint. Is that not tantamount to saying that you enjoyed it, that you wanted it?

So she reads. For company, for solace, for escape. She reads beyond her years. She has fewer languages but she shares the omnivorous hunger her father once felt for the written word. At the same time she has retained a child's ability to sit still for long periods and lose herself entirely in a fictional world. Not children's books, not contemporary novels. She does not want to be mocked with visions of other lives she might be leading. Nor does she read poetry. Poetry scares her, with its glimpses of the abyss between the slats of the swaying bridge. Her favourite stories are the old ones, those that set deep truths ringing like bells, that take the raw materials of sex and cruelty, of fate and chance, and render them safe by trapping them in beautiful words. And every night, when her father comes to her room, she recites silently to herself the magic words which bring one of these other worlds into being and wanders there, far from the body he is using for his pleasure.

She watches Arjuna string the great steel bow and fire an arrow through the eye of the mechanical fish to win the hand of Draupadi. She travels for a day with Gilgamesh along the subterranean Road of the Sun under Mount Mashu to the Garden of the Gods. She smiles at Rumpelstilzchen spinning himself into angry pieces. She is frightened by the knight who rides into the court of Genghis Khan on a magical bronze horse, bearing a mind-reading mirror, a ring that translates the language of birds and a sword whose deadly wounds can be healed only by a touch of the same sword.

She has no one with whom she can share these stories. She is both teller and listener. She forgets, sometimes, where the page ends and her mind begins. She recounts these tales to herself in idle moments, inevitably changing them a little every time and comes to believe, in some occult way, that these are stories of her own invention, that she is bringing these lives into being, as if she is one of the Fates, those supernatural women who make and cut the thread of life. She is the abducted Helen sitting high in the Trojan citadel weaving her *great purple web of double fold*, the tapestry which describes *the many battles of the horse-taming Trojans and the brazen-coated Achaeans*, so that it is hard to tell whether she is simply describing the scenes far below her chamber window or whether she is creating them. Who in any case can say what is real? The Trojan War, Helen's tapestry or this other quiet room in which we are recreating those scenes in our own minds?

There are darker tales about women who weave stories. Arachne the shepherd's daughter, for example, who boasts that her extraordinary handiwork is not a gift from the gods but something she has taught herself. She challenges the outraged Minerva to a contest and two looms are strung so that they may compete against one another. Minerva begins, weaving a picture of the twelve Olympians seated in their majesty watching Minerva herself strike the ground with the tip of her spear so that the olive tree is born. In the corners of the picture she depicts mortals who have been transformed as punishment for defying the gods – Haemus and Rhodope who became mountain ranges, the Queen of the Pygmies who became a crane, Trojan Antigone who became a stork, Cynaras whose daughters were turned to stone.

Arachne responds with a weaving which shows Jupiter taking the form of a bull to rape Europa, the form of an eagle to rape Asterië, of a swan to rape Leda, of a satyr to rape Antiope, of a shower of gold to rape Danaë, of a speckled serpent to rape Ceres ...

Seeing that the work is better than her own, Minerva tears it to shreds and beats Arachne with her boxwood shuttle. Too proud to endure this humiliation, Arachne hangs herself, but Minerva refuses to let her die and transforms her into a spider, forever dangling from a rope, for ever weaving, punished by metamorphosis exactly like the characters depicted in her own tapestry.

The house is cleaned scrupulously and Angelica is no more likely to stumble across a cobweb than she is to stumble across a dead mouse, but she finds them in the garden sometimes, strung between branches, picked out early in the morning by the tiniest drops of dew which hang from the individual filaments, and she wonders every time whether they were made by a woman who was punished for telling the truth.

❧

Old friends have largely given up trying to stay in touch. There are fleeting encounters in hotels and restaurants, but Philippe takes her to hotels and restaurants less and less frequently once she becomes a teenager. Her gawkiness has gone, she has become a young woman and it is painfully obvious to him that when she walks into a room, men turn to look at her and have trouble looking away. Sometimes they tell him how attractive she is. Sometimes they say this to Angelica herself. They do not spell it out but they are saying, *I want to have sex with your daughter.* Angelica cannot understand this. Dangerously naive, she is flattered by their attention. She acts as if she were living in a fairy tale, as if she were a princess and these were her admirers. Sometimes she responds in a way which could be described as flirting, if she knew what flirting meant. He finds it unbearable, though what he finds most unbearable is a possibility he hardly dare articulate, that she is looking for a white knight, someone to hoist her onto his saddle and bear her away.

So they holiday in isolated locations, they stay in cities where he knows no one, they stay at home. Stories circulate, nevertheless, about the aloof but radiant daughter of the famous mother, the stories made more compelling by their sinister footnotes. Angelica rarely speaks, it is said. Some suggest that she is unable to speak. Is it possible, in spite of her beauty, that she has a learning difficulty, or a brain injury as a result of her traumatic birth? Others, who have heard her speak, say that she is shockingly naive, an unnerving mix of sophistication and childishness. Might she be mentally unwell? It would not be wholly surprising given her motherless, hermetic upbringing. Some wonder if there is a nastier story, though it is rarely spelled out any more clearly than in remarks that it's not quite right for a father to keep a daughter so close. To be explicit would be to say that one knows but does nothing. Far easier to dismiss it as baseless innuendo and bored gossip.

❧

Bobby Koulouris is an art dealer, in twentieth-century prints mostly – Käthe Kollwitz, Otto Dix, George Grosz, Louise Bourgeois ... He sells work to Philippe and, occasionally, buys work from him. He is as near to a genuine friend as Philippe has and these transactions are as much conversation as commerce. He has a reprobate son, Darius, of whom he despairs and about whom he has complained on many occasions, a vain, idle boy who was thrown out of two schools, turned up his nose at university, flirted sporadically with paid employment and now leads a life of dissipation among minor European aristocracy and trust-fund beneficiaries of equal vanity and idleness. Predictably, he has no interest in art, and rejoices in his ignorance. But when his father dies unexpectedly of pneumonia in Laos, Darius takes it upon himself to go through the contents of his father's apartments in Athens and Berlin where work rests on its journey from seller to buyer, intending to squirrel away a few valuable pieces with no paper trail. In doing so he stumbles on an exchange of emails between his father and Philippe in which his father says that he is hopeful of getting his hands on a complete signed set of Hockney's Brothers Grimm fairy-tale etchings which Darius has been looking at only moments before and has, uncharacteristically, recognised.

Remembering the stories about the elusive and beautiful Angelica and thinking that he can both solve a mystery and have himself a small adventure, he rings Philippe on the private number known only to a very small number of people. Philippe ignores the first three calls but Darius is persistent and when he finally picks up, Philippe's annoyance is undercut immediately by the news of Bobby's death. Darius moves swiftly to capitalise on his advantage and says that he will *by very happy accident* be passing through Hampshire in the next few days and will drop a set of prints off, politely drawing the call to a close before Philippe can demur.

Philippe no longer feels the same hunger for the pictures – he no longer feels the same hunger for any pictures – but there will be some satisfaction in the purchase, given that he already possesses complete sets of the Cavafy and the *Rake's Progress*. It seems, too, like a small, belated recompense to a friend whose final communications he left unanswered.

Three afternoons later Darius comes to a halt in a white BMW 3 Series with an ostentatious little skid on the gravel outside Antioch, sporting an elderly, sun-bleached, denim shirt and a hundred and seventy-five thousand euros' worth of art slung over his shoulder in a portfolio, for all the world as if he were carrying a few watercolours of New Forest ponies he'd knocked off that morning.

Hervé walks out onto the drive to give the interloper the once-over and to allow the interloper to give *him* the once-over and take on board the knowledge that Hervé will be somewhere in the building for the duration. Judging the young man harmless he leads him inside.

Philippe has not done the appropriate calculation and when Darius turns up, Philippe discovers that he is a decade younger than expected. His swagger is a surprise, too, just self-mocking enough to charm

43

everyone apart from the person who was the centre of attention before Darius walked into that particular room. He shakes Philippe's hand with a grip halfway between exuberant and overpowering and Philippe feels that he is being bested in a contest whose rules are not wholly clear. He considers saying that he has to leave post-haste to deal with some unforeseen business complication but he imagines this supremely confident young man fixing him with a wry stare and simply refusing to believe him. As they walk through the house, however, Darius makes enthusiastic and knowledgeable remarks about the work of Amyas Connell ('He was born in New Zealand, if my memory serves me correctly') whom he googled over a pub lunch en route, so that by the time they are being served with a pot of first flush Darjeeling and slices of rhubarb-and-pistachio cake, Philippe is rowing back on his presumptions. He asks the obligatory questions about Bobby's death and Darius lingers a little on the ghoulish details.

Angelica hears the soft rip of gravel when Darius arrives and goes to the window to look, visitors being a rare entertainment. The young man who gets out of the sports car and removes a portfolio from the boot is more entertaining than she could have hoped for. He is clearly not someone employed by her father – a lawyer, a banker. He is utterly uncowed by the house and garden and looks, for all the world, as if he might own the place. Is it possible that he is a friend of the family?

His looks are unimportant. He is young and wealthy, he comes from the Great Elsewhere and there is a dash about him which suggests that in his company anything might happen. But on top of these things he happens to be almost comically handsome – slim hips, a wave of thick hair the colour of black coffee, a feline ease in his own body. She has read about Lydia Bennet's elopement with George Wickham, about Marie Melmotte falling for the rakish idiot

Sir Felix Carbury but she knows little of the world and it is often hard to recognise stories when you find yourself inside them, so that by the time she has found Darius and her father sitting in the slatted sunshine of the roof terrace she is already in thrall to an imagined future in which he takes her away from all this, and the knowledge that the fantasy is ridiculous does nothing to sour its addictive sweetness.

Philippe's hackles rise as soon as she appears. If he had known a little more about Darius in advance he would have explicitly excluded her from the meeting. He says, without thinking, 'You shouldn't be here,' taking her subservience for granted. This, he will realise later, is the mistake that changes everything, goading her in front of Bobby's son.

There is a moment of stillness. A woodpecker rat-a-tats somewhere in the garden. Darius says, to Angelica, calmly but brooking no contradiction, 'Sit down with us. I've heard a great deal about you,' and Angelica thinks, for once, to hell with her father. She pours herself a cup of tea and takes a slice of cake and it is hard to tell whether her hands are shaking from excitement or fear, because she looks at Darius and knows that they are in league together against her father.

'Where do you go to school?' asks Darius, though he is pretty sure from what he has heard that she hasn't been allowed near a school in a long time. 'Or university?' There is something sexual and yet utterly unsexual about her that puzzles him. She doesn't look sixteen. She looks twenty. Or twelve. And the rumours about her looks are true. Those extraordinary eyes.

'I don't go to school.'

'So you're stuck here with your old man.' He looks at Philippe and gives him a warm, knowing smile which both men know is a provocation.

'Darius's father died a couple of months ago,' Philippe says to Angelica, trying to regain control of the situation. 'Robert Koulouris? I'm sure you remember him. Darius has thoughtfully delivered some artwork which Robert was tracking down for me.'

Darius is not looking at her father. Darius is looking at Angelica. She is drunk with attention. There is something in his expression that she has never seen before at this close a range, something anarchic, something joyous. He likes her a lot, she can see it and feel it. She has no idea how these things work. What if they jumped into the car, span on the gravel, roared down the drive and never came back?

Darius says, 'You should come for a drive.' Can he read her thoughts so clearly? 'It is the most glorious day. We could be at the seaside in an hour.' He has no idea how long it would take to get to the seaside, nor what constitutes the seaside in these parts. Donkey rides and deckchairs? An oil refinery?

Angelica takes a little breath to control her voice before saying, calmly, 'I would very much like that.' She can tell him on the way. Not the truth – she will never be able to tell him the truth – but some close cousin of the truth. Just enough to let him know how grateful she is and to guarantee that he does not bring her back.

But Darius's sexual interest is already waning. He can see that she is needy and fragile. An hour in her company might be diverting, but three would be purgatory. Angelica's feelings, however, are neither here nor there at this point. It is her father's reaction that is driving this little drama. Darius might know nothing about Kokoschka or Balthus but in his own way he's as good a salesman as his father and unwilling to walk away from any encounter without believing himself the winner.

Philippe says, 'I'm afraid that won't be possible.'

Angelica says, 'Why not?' Her giddy imagination is running away with itself. She is picturing herself and Darius in front of a log fire in Norway or the Highlands of Scotland, one of those cold, damp locations her father hates. Outside the window a great blade of silver water lies between foggy mountains. Darius's arm is around her shoulder.

Philippe is not used to being angry, let alone having to control that anger in front of people beyond the household. He wants to call Hervé, but to do so would be an admission of defeat all too visible to this strutting little cockerel. 'Now you must leave us.'

Angelica feels close to weeping. The gift is being taken away before she can open it. 'Papa ...'

'Be quiet.' He stands up.

Darius performs a little pantomime of shifting his sitting position, leaning back in the chair to make himself even more comfortable. Philippe calms himself. The boy will take his time but he will go. There is nothing for him here.

'Papa, why are you doing this?' Angelica has so few weapons at her disposal.

'Your father is jealous.' Only when Darius says the word, the precise word – not *protective* but *jealous* – does he realise how accurate it is. Sexual jealousy. It is like reaching into a dark box and touching something cold and clammy and alive.

'Mr Koulouris ...' It sounds wrong. 'Darius ...' Philippe moves a little closer so that he is only a centimetre from the toes of Darius's polished, conker-brown Chelsea boots. Has Philippe misjudged this? Might it end in a physical fight?

Darius looks at Angelica. She is on the edge of tears. This is not the kind of adventure he wanted. Something is very wrong in this house and if he stays any longer he will become entangled. He gets to his feet.

'Philippe.' He turns from father to daughter. 'Angelica … It has been a pleasure.' He holds her eye to make it clear that this sentence is addressed to her alone. 'I am very sorry I cannot stay any longer.' He turns back to her father. 'I will leave the prints with you. Let me know if you change your mind. I'll send you an invoice later.' It is an excellent final gesture – cavalier, trusting, unruffled, unanswerable. But he needs to leave before Angelica spoils it by breaking down. 'I can find my own way out.'

He drives to the seaside. No oil refinery, no donkeys, no deckchairs. Lepe Country Park – some cars, a row of Scots pines, a grey sky and a welcome cold wind to clear his head. There is a boxy, baby-blue café with big rectangular windows onto the beach. He buys himself a mug of what his English friends call *builder's tea* plus an egg-mayonnaise sandwich. He needs a levelling dose of a normality he would usually despise. He will not let his worst imaginings come into focus. It is a thing that happens in boarding schools and broken homes. It does not happen in his social circle.

He books a room at the Viceroy in Winchester. Provincial tea-room rococo, though the clientele leave something to be desired. There is a difference between dressing casually and dressing badly and the world has become blind to the distinction. There are two men in the bar wearing Arsenal shirts in some ghastly synthetic material. His bedroom looks onto a lawn where three putti urinate into a circular marble trough, buffeting an empty Carlsberg can back and forth. He showers, changes and goes downstairs. The menu is trying a little too hard (he has wood pigeon with asparagus, peach and seaweed) but proficiently done. After supper he sits on a bench at the far end of the lawn smoking Sobranie Black Russians. He had imagined emailing friends, sticking a few photos of the fabled house – maybe even the fabled siren herself – on his private

Instagram account, then, given the almost certain absence of local nightlife, getting a decent sleep before his early flight back to Athens. He wishes now that he had driven straight to Heathrow and was airborne so that the matter was definitively out of his hands. But a teenage girl is suffering and he finds that for once he can't walk away. That desperate look she gave him as he turned and left. He had acted dishonourably and far from being a victory his departure had in fact been a shameful admission of defeat.

He throws back a double espresso to counteract the Malbec and only when he is in the car does he begin to wonder precisely what he is going to do when he arrives at the other end. He has not answered the question by the time he parks on the public road by the end of the drive. Everything is submarine, the colours going out one by one as the world sinks into the dark. He will ask to talk to Angelica alone. And if Philippe will not allow that ...? The gravel on the drive is ridiculously loud under his boots, so he slips into the trees. A large cobweb wraps itself around his face. He flinches and brushes it away. When his heart has slowed he continues up the slope, a steady zigzag between the soft pine trunks, relying almost entirely on touch to navigate. There are long slashes of mauve sky up ahead. He steps onto the lawn. Four lemon rectangles burn like open stove doors in the silhouette of the house. Palm leaves are black swords overhead. He can smell gorse, creosote and septic tank. He keeps to the edge of the grass, ready to slip back into the trees if his movement triggers a bank of floodlights. He ascends the twelve concrete steps. The only noises are the hush of his breath and the faint scrape of grit under his feet.

He jumps again. Angelica is sitting on the patio with her back against the wall in the wedge of shadow between two big lit windows. Her head is in her hands. She is not taking the night air; she has been thrown out, or she is hiding from her father. 'Hey!' he whispers. No reaction. He says it again, more loudly this time. She looks up, gasps and scrabbles crab-wise away from him. He steps into the light. 'Angelica. It's me.' He holds his open hands wide. 'I really didn't mean to scare you.' She settles. He takes a few steps towards her and crouches, as if she is a cat he doesn't want to startle. 'I came to say sorry for earlier.' He pauses. Saying sorry is not what he came to do. He must think clearly. He may have very little time. 'I wanted to make sure that you were all right.' He sits himself against the same wall, a metre or so away from her, companionable he hopes, but not intrusive. He can see now that she is very much not all right because there is a sticky wound on the side of her head. She has tucked her hair behind her ear to keep it away from the drying blood. 'He hit you.' There is only the faintest human glow from over the hills. They could be a hundred miles from anywhere.

'I fell over.'

'He hit you.' He says it more gently this time, meaning, *You can tell me.*

But it is the truth. Philippe never hits her. He is not stupid. He came to her room an hour or so after Darius had gone. He called her a whore, a bloody idiot. She said nothing. She never says anything. Her tactic is always to make herself small and quiet and wait for the storms to blow themselves out. Her father apologised. He said he was angry and shouldn't be taking it out on her. He said that it was his own fault for letting *that jumped-up coxcomb* into the house. He said, 'We're safe now,' and put his hands around the back of her neck and tried to kiss her.

When her father had forced Darius to leave the house earlier in the day he had thrown away something precious. He had made it clear that he would do everything in his power to prevent her having the thing she wanted more than anything in the world. Emotions had churned inside her which she could neither name nor vent. It had been like having a high fever. She had scratched at her arms with her fingernails and there was some comfort in the pain and the puffy wheals she raised and the blood which began to flow when she had finally broken through the skin.

So, later, when her father tried to kiss her she squirmed away, something she had never done before. He gripped her upper arm and hissed, 'You have no idea what is at stake here,' the anger he had graciously put aside now roaring back unchecked. She twisted free a second time, stumbled and banged her head on the wooden column at the corner of the bed-frame, blacking out briefly and coming round with her face pressed against a bloody carpet.

Now Darius has returned and far from being pleased she is frightened and confused. These shocks and reversals are the stuff of other people's lives. What is he doing here? Her father is inside the house doubtless trying to clean her blood from the carpet right now, ineptly, with a bowl of soapy water and tea-towels in the hope that the staff won't realise what it is.

'Angelica ...?'

She touches the wound on the side of her head. 'This doesn't matter.' She must seize the moment. It has been sixteen years coming and if she loses her chance now it may never come again. 'You're going to help me.' It is part desperate plea, part simple demand. She does not recognise her own voice.

'Yes. I'm going to help you.' What in God's name has he got himself into? He must think this through, and think it through fast. He will take her to a hospital. There must surely be one in Southampton. A friend-of-a-friend, Francine, is a criminal barrister in London. He can get her number easily enough. She will help, or she will know who can help. 'Come on. We can do this.' He holds out his hand.

To her surprise, Angelica starts to cry. 'I thought you'd abandoned me.'

Darius feels a sudden, stabbing doubt. Is she unwell in her mind? Is the wound something she did to herself, perhaps? Is it possible that she is hidden from the world because she cannot cope with the world?

But she gathers herself, takes hold of his hand and gets to her feet and says with complete clarity, 'I know that this will be difficult and dangerous for you, but I really don't think I can stay here any longer.' She cannot be passive. This is the moment upon which her entire life pivots. They will do this together, she and Darius. They can make it happen. 'We have to move quickly because if my father isn't looking for me now then he will be looking for me very soon.'

Darius cannot see her face. It is too darkly silhouetted against the light of the window, but he hears her sudden intake of breath and knows that something is wrong before he hears the soft click of a latch behind him followed by the snaky hiss of a sliding door. It must be her father. Who else could it be? He turns slowly, to demonstrate that he is unfazed. It is a mistake. Philippe has already swung something high above his head and Darius has time only to lift his right arm to protect himself. The object above Philippe's head is the cast-iron poker that stands beside the wood fire in the living room. He brings it down as hard as he can and they all hear Darius's upper arm snap under the impact, halfway between the elbow and the shoulder, the dog-leg of the broken bone clearly visible inside his shirt. There is no pain yet but he can no longer move the arm. Philippe hoists the poker for a second blow. Angelica cries out, 'No!' and time slows, the way it slows during all terrible events – the car upside down in mid-air, the child falling from the balcony to the street. She sees Darius step backwards but cannot warn him in time and must watch as his foot misses the edge of the concrete patio; he loses his balance and, unable to put his arms out to save himself, he tumbles and rolls down the grassy slope to the flat of the dark lawn. Her father pauses briefly then runs down the slope after him, carrying the poker.

Darius is tougher than his foppish good looks suggest. Three teenage boys who tried to separate him from his wallet and phone in the Marais the previous year beat a bruised and bloody retreat, but right now he is on his back and one limb short and he has never encountered someone this determined to hurt another human being. He can hear Angelica screaming. She sounds as if she is a very long way away. Philippe stands over Darius, gathering himself for a decisive second blow because this preening little shit is trying to destroy two lives for no other reason than the fact that he cannot have Angelica for himself. He is the reason Philippe cannot let her go out into the world, the kind of man who thinks he can take anything he wants. Philippe's anger is exhilarating.

Angelica yells, 'Papa, stop! Please stop!'

Darius kicks hard at Philippe's ankle and the older man topples sideways. Darius lifts himself with his good arm and scrabbles to his feet. The pain is starting to arrive and he must carry his broken arm as if it were a basket of eggs. He pauses. He is dizzy. If he runs now he will fall over. He must not look at his arm. Philippe is getting to his feet. Dizzy or not Darius has no choice. Zigzagging but upright, he runs towards the palms and pines. He reaches the edge of the lawn and realises that returning the way he came earlier in the evening is foolish. He does not know the garden as Philippe doubtless does. It is too late now. He enters the dark between the trees and after only a few paces, runs smack into a trunk and is hurled sideways onto the ground. And now the pain decisively arrives. It is hot metal poured into the broken bone. His eyes are full of fizzing light, like an old TV between stations. He is briefly absent from the world then returns to hear the soft crumple of feet on pine needles. He can see nothing. He knows only that Philippe is very near. Seconds pass. The poker does not descend. Has Angelica's father seen sense or is he pausing to take careful aim? Darius has no easy way of standing up without rolling onto his front and making himself even more vulnerable. He tries to speak but when he fills his lungs he feels the broken bone-ends grate against one another inside his upper arm and the sensation consumes him utterly.

'You arrogant little shit,' says Philippe. 'You are so proud of yourself. You understand nothing. About me. About my daughter.' He takes a big breath and Darius knows that he is raising the poker high over his head as if it were an axe and he were preparing to split a log.

❧

She is briefly in hell. She is going to see her father murder Darius by smashing his head open in front of her and she cannot prevent this from happening. Darius's arm is broken horribly. There is no way he can win any kind of fight. Then her father falls and Darius gets to his feet and it seems to Angelica that he stands a chance of getting away. But her father is on his feet, too, and Darius vanishes into the trees at the bottom of the garden and her father vanishes into the trees at the bottom of the garden. Then there is silence. The world is perfectly still. Were it not for her thumping heart she could have simply stepped outside to take in the night air. Darius? Her father? Did any of that happen? She feels embarrassed, as if she were recounting the events to a fourth person and they were smiling indulgently at her overheated imagination. Such things are not possible, not in a place like this, not to people like them.

She looks up. The clouds have cleared to reveal a moon only a couple of nights away from fullness. The craters, are they extinct volcanoes or dents left by meteorites? She knew once but she can no longer remember. If only her heart would stop beating so fast. A fox barks in the distance. Darius had come to take her away. She cannot connect this fact to anything.

Then she hears the noise, a damp *thunk* from the trees at the bottom of the garden. There is a second *thunk*, then a third. They could be the sounds of a poker striking the trunk of a tree. They could be the sounds of a poker being stoved into a human head. She doubles over and throws up onto the patio. It is the strangest thing. She doesn't feel sick. She doesn't feel anything. She doesn't think. Her body is reacting to something which her mind is refusing to accept.

After a long time the dark at the end of the lawn thickens to the figure of a man walking slowly towards the house. Might it be Darius?

It is her father. If Angelica were a different woman she might run, but running is a skill she was never allowed to learn. Running means having somewhere to run to. She cannot picture herself elsewhere and alone. Beyond those dark hills right now it might as well be Nunavut. It might as well be the Skeleton Coast. Rusted hulks and sun-leathered corpses. It might as well be Pentapolis or Ephesus.

A terrible sadness presses upon her, as if she were lying beneath a mattress and stones were being laid on top of the mattress. She is so profoundly tired. She uses a sleeve to wipe a final strand of sick from her mouth.

Her father walks up the concrete steps holding the poker. His white shirt is ripped and soiled. He is going to kill her, she is convinced of this. She hopes only that he does it quickly. 'Go to your room.' She will look back and think of this as the greater cruelty, letting her life carry on precisely as it was before. She does not move. 'Go,' he says, more sternly this time. She turns and steps through the glass door. Her father follows her into the house. She heads into the hallway. As she climbs the stairs she hears her father say, into his phone, 'Hervé? I need you to do something for me ... Yes. Now.'

She opens her bedroom window and leans on the sill. The light of the full moon throws a black silhouette of the house over the rear lawn, and in the centre of the silhouette lies a skewed trapezium of room-light, and in that skewed parallelogram lies the silhouette of a girl. It is impossible to tell which of them is more real, the flesh or the shadow. Bats slip through the dark, too fast for the eye to follow, their nights ablaze with squeaks and echoes. The world of sound which sits inside the world of light. Nothing happens for a long time. In the distance she hears tyres on the gravel. Doors slam. Silence. Doors slam again. Tyres on gravel.

Darius is dead, or he escaped and ran away. She does not know which is more terrible. The police will not help even if they are asked. Like doctors, like lawyers, the police are functionaries. She has seen it happen before. The law bends before wealth. It is the way the world works. She tries to cry but she feels scraped out, raw and empty.

It is the first night in a very long time that her father does not come to her room. She should feel relieved. Instead she feels scared and abandoned. She is disgusted with herself for feeling this. She cannot sleep. The wound on the side of her head has scabbed over but the pain still pulses in time with her heartbeat. She turns off all the lights and squats in the space between the cupboard and the wall, hugging her knees and rocking gently back and forth to calm herself. The house clicks and creaks. The fox barks again. Shreds of moonlit cloud change shape as they track across the uncurtained window. Every so often the wingtip navigation light of a plane passes in the opposite direction and she has the same thought she used to have as a small child, that it is her mother, made into a star by God.

Dawn comes. The staff arrive at eight. She feels drained and wretched but safe enough now to go downstairs for breakfast. She tells Dottie that she fell in the bathroom and banged the side of her head the evening before. Dottie nods. Anyone else would know that Dottie is sceptical about this story, but Angelica has never learnt to hear the conversation which runs beneath a conversation. She eats scrambled eggs on sourdough toast and drinks a black coffee. She says that she has a headache. Dottie gives her two paracetamol. Her father enters the room and Dottie slips away, saying she has chores elsewhere. He tells Angelica that he is very sorry but he does not say precisely what he is sorry for.

He comes to her room in the evening. He undresses her. He says he loves her. She leaves her body behind. It is only an animal which houses the mind after all. She enters that foggy border country between dream and story. She is seated high in the citadel, far above the armies at war on the plain below. She is weaving another world. And right here, in the very corner of the tapestry, is Darius, clamping his injured arm to his side as he jogs down the drive to the main road where he is very nearly hit by a clanking farm pickup which squeals to a skewed halt in front of him. Sheep bleat. Hooves scrabble on metal.

❦

A twig snaps nearby. The two men freeze. Darius is on the ground. Philippe stands with the poker raised above his head. The dark between the trunks is absolute. Another twig snaps. Someone – or something – very large is standing very close to them. There is a smell of burnt hair and cellar damp. There is deep, regular breathing like that of an iron lung. The thing is too big to be human, though surely even the biggest stag would have bolted by now. Darius does not care what it is. The only thing that matters is Philippe's distracted attention. He grabs hold of a low branch with his uninjured left arm. There is a wall of flame he can pass through if he pushes himself hard and moves fast. He grunts like a weightlifter and hoists himself. The pain is spectacular. He is on his feet. He clamps his broken arm to his side and steps between the trees. He is on the gravel. He jogs towards the main road.

He will not be able to drive. He is five miles out of Winchester and it is nearly midnight. He will have to knock on someone's door or hide in a field. As if in answer to his desperate need, however, the hedge on the far side of the road begins to glow. He picks up speed in case he is too late, reaches the gates, runs into the road and is very nearly hit by a clanking farm pickup which squeals to a skewed halt in front of him. He hears sheep bleating and the scrabble of hooves on metal. The driver leans out of the window – cigarette, baseball cap, some kind of sore at the corner of his mouth. 'Get in, then.' He sounds like a tired father retrieving his teenage son from a party. Darius cannot persuade his left arm to give up its role of splinting the right in order to open the passenger door, so the driver gets out, shaking his head wearily. There are little furred faces behind the barred air vent at the back of the vehicle. 'There you go, mate.' The driver takes a last drag on his cigarette and pings it into the rural dark. Darius swings his legs one by one into the footwell. The farmer slams Darius's door and walks back round the mud-spattered bonnet. Through the driver's window Darius sees a shape moving rapidly towards them down the drive. Whether it is Philippe or the unseen creature intent on doing to him what it has very possibly just done to Phillippe he doesn't know. The farmer climbs in, slams his own door and restarts the asthmatic engine. Something bloody and terrible looms briefly on the far side of the man's baseball-hatted head, the ill-tempered gears mesh and they pull jerkily away, the sheep scrabbling and bleating behind them.

The driver glances across at him and laughs wryly. 'Looks like you've had a bit of an evening.'

Darius wonders if the man has been drinking. 'Thank you. Thank you for stopping.' He leans back against the burst leatherette headrest, detaches himself from the world and is aware of very little beyond the flaming circle of his hurt until he is stretchered into a curtained bay in A & E at Southampton General. Hoops scoot noisily along a metal rail and a plump nurse leans over him. Her hair is purple and she has shaved three little stripes into her left eyebrow. Darius looks around. The only traces of his Good Samaritan are a faint smell of dung and some agricultural stains on the chinos draped over the orange plastic chair together with his shirt which seems to have been cut off. Two hundred pounds from Louis Vuitton.

The nurse says, 'What happened to you, then?'

He says, 'Someone tried to kill me.'

She says, 'That's not nice, is it.'

He wonders if it is a regional thing. She administers four squirts of nasal diamorphine and a doctor appears. The man is a mad professor – bald pate, curly hair, round glasses, a Polish accent or somewhere thereabouts. He examines the break in Darius's arm, nodding appreciatively so that Darius feels obscurely proud of having sustained a proper injury. He should get in touch with the police but the diamorphine is kicking in and time has turned to toffee. Another nurse appears with a trolley. They are going to plaster his arm prior to surgery. He is given a mask and told to breathe in as hard and as frequently as he can while they align the bone, so he sucks and blows and sucks and blows and a great white balloon lifts him into the air so that he is looking down on the whole world as if it were the largest and most detailed model train-set in history. Far below a tiny Darius is lying in a tiny hospital bed. The tiny mad professor hauls on the wrist of the tiny Darius the way a stevedore might heave on a rope to bring a tug alongside a jetty while the second nurse wets strips of plaster in a kidney-shaped metal bowl of water and wraps them around the tiny Darius's upper arm. It reminds Darius of making papier mâché at school. 'Nearly there.'

Then the mask is removed and the air goes out of the balloon and Darius descends rapidly and the two Dariuses are recombined and he feels really very sick indeed. He vomits into a bowl of cheap grey cardboard a nurse is holding under his chin. Wood pigeon, asparagus, peach and seaweed. He loses track of time. At some point he is given a pre-med then taken into surgery where the mad professor is arguing with another doctor about whether Real Madrid or Bayern Munich are going to win the UEFA Champions League. The other doctor slides a cannula into the crook of the elbow of Darius's unbroken arm and suggests he count from ten to one which Darius had assumed happened only in films. He reaches seven and instantly he's coming round, terrified that the anaesthetic hasn't worked and that they are about to cut him open; but the ceiling is different and the room is different and his arm is now sealed inside a tube of petrified slate-grey carpet. There is a third doctor but he's wearing black and smells of wood sage and sea salt. A faint alarm sounds in the back of Darius's brain. He fights his way through layers of milky sleep. He can't remember how you tell your body to sit up. Shaved head, white shirt, grey suit. The PA-cum-bodyguard who met him on the drive. Sweet Christ. Suddenly he is awake. The man has unscrewed the top from the suspended bag of saline and is topping it up from a small brown bottle.

Darius swings his plastered arm. It is no more than a rudimentary flipper but it is heavy and it is hard. The stand topples and the cannula is yanked out, the long tube flicking towards the ceiling like a fishing line being cast, an arc of bloody fluid airborne in its wake. The shaven-headed man is unfazed. Darius swings his arm again but the man steps back the way you would step back to avoid your shoes getting soaked by the next wave on the beach. 'I'll see you later.' He turns and leaves the room.

The pain in Darius's arm is very unpleasant indeed. He remembers that there is a poker-shattered bone inside the plaster. He waits for the pain to ebb a little. The room spins the wrong way, not round-about but ferris wheel. He grips the steel rail until it slows down and comes to a halt. His other arm is bleeding where the cannula was ripped out. There is an empty bed to his right and two against the opposite wall. There are many medical machines of incomprehensible function. There is a low, scientific hum. The bladder of saline continues to empty itself onto the tiles. He stands up, wobbles, sits down, waits, stands up again and takes a few careful steps across the wet floor. Using his only functioning hand he removes a small red fire extinguisher from its wall-holster. It is the only object in the room that comes close to being a weapon. He listens for a few moments at the room's only door then opens it onto an empty corridor. Voices far off, the buzz of a striplight. There is a window onto some dead plants in a drab little courtyard. It is daytime. Many hours must have passed while he was unconscious. There are five ghastly abstracts on the wall – slashes of orange on blue backgrounds, slashes of blue on orange backgrounds. He turns two corners and finds himself on the hospital's main thoroughfare. Oncology and Paediatrics. Threadbare dressing gowns and white coats. Three elderly ladies with identically bandaged ankles cackle together like witches. No shaven-headed man. He stands the fire extinguisher against a wall and wipes the blood from his leaking arm. His car keys and his wallet are in the pocket of his chinos. God alone knows where the chinos are. Now is not the moment for worrying about such matters. Now is the moment for getting away from this building as fast as possible. He will get a taxi to the Viceroy. He will borrow the fare from the hotel reception. He will do all this wearing nothing but a backless cream hospital gown. He remembers the man with the shaved head, the utter blankness of his expression, the little brown bottle. He has no choice. He strides confidently through the main doors of the hospital onto the forecourt.

Harbour Cars. A triple-masted schooner in silhouette behind the name on the passenger door. It costs thirty pounds on top of the meter to override the driver's qualms about giving a lift to a manifestly crazy person, but the Viceroy rises in Darius's estimation when they lend him the cash without so much as a raised eyebrow. He is walking across the hotel lobby, however, when he glances into the lounge and sees, in the bay window, the shaven-headed man selecting a scone from a mini-ziggurat of silver traylets being proffered by a waiter. The man looks up. That same blank stare. No surprise whatsoever. Five, six seconds. The man looks back to the table and charges his knife with butter. Darius runs up the stairs, locks the door of his room and sits on the bed. He has a passport but no wallet. His car is ten miles away, the keys are ten miles in the opposite direction. Two men want to kill him. One is very rich, the other is possessed of borderline supernatural powers. A jackdaw sits on a branch which bobs and sways outside the window. Black body, little grey hood, half nun, half pilot. It twists its head, its tiny eye glints and Darius finds it hard to shake the suspicion that the bird is trying to deliver a message of some kind. He rubs his face. He will call his father's lawyer. He needs to be on home turf. The two of them will put aside their deep historical differences because there are more important things at stake. Stephanos will book him a flight. Security, too. Several large, trained men will stay with him until he boards the plane. It is something he did for Darius's father on occasions. Even Philippe and his henchman can't bring down an Airbus. Once he is in Athens he will be safe.

He stands and walks to the table where the hotel phone squats like a black toad. He is about to lift the receiver when he glances down at the urinating putti and sees the most extraordinary thing.

❧

He hoists the sash and whistles ineptly. Helena breaks off from conversation with her two nautical colleagues, looks up, tilts her head sideways in the manner of a dog analysing a faint but interesting sound and is doubtless about to make some dry quip about her friend's unclothed state and broken arm when Darius puts a finger to his lips and beckons her silently upstairs, raising nine fingers for the room number. Helena does an *aye-aye-captain* mini-salute in return and flips her cigarette into the fountain.

She is wearing a Sonic Youth T-shirt – *I stole my sister's boyfriend, it was all whirlwind heat and flash ...* – and khaki utility-trousers with square black knee patches and more zips than necessary. She has nut-brown skin and blonde hair so salt-stiffened and wind-tangled that she appears always to be squinting into bright sunlight and a strong headwind. She does not acknowledge the serendipity of their vanishingly unlikely meeting. She would approach an alien invasion or a flat tyre in the same way. She is picking up a refitted wooden schooner for a wealthy client whose name, for once, she genuinely cannot share. 'The *Porpoise*. 1972. Three masts. No fibreglass. Twenty-four metres. Five cabins. New engine. Not fast, but she is bloody lovely.'

It is some measure of the unexpectedness of Darius's story that Helena keeps one eyebrow raised for a good five seconds before saying, 'I think we can solve this problem.'

Helena helps the injured Darius into his warmest clothes – ripping yet another Louis Vuitton shirt to accommodate his plastered arm – and ten minutes later the two of them are walking swiftly downstairs while Hervé's attention is diverted by Helena's colleague, Anton. Hervé, however, is unconvinced by the large Russian man who claims to recognise him. 'Frankfurt, perhaps. Did we meet in Frankfurt? Were you in Frankfurt in April?' The man is blocking Hervé's view of the hotel lobby and Hervé very much wants to keep an eye on the hotel lobby. There is a rapidly escalating altercation which involves, in its final stages, a pot of scalding tea, upturned furniture and a pastry fork which has, thankfully, been dulled by a century of parkin and Chelsea buns. It ends with Anton running from the hotel entrance, hand clapped over a bloody neck wound, with Hervé in pursuit.

Anton yells, 'Go!' and throws himself through the open back door of the rented Toyota Yaris. Marlena, who completes the party, whoops excitedly, Helena puts the car into gear and the shaven-headed man thumps the roof so hard that the dent is visible from the inside. They pull away and take several corners almost but not quite on two wheels before joining the M3 and heading south to Poole Harbour.

THE PORPOISE

What Darius knows about ocean-going yachts was picked up during a week's tour of the Baltic with Helena and a small group of mutual friends and amounts to little more than a memory of seasick hangovers and the dimensions of a toilet too small to enable one to sit down and shut the door simultaneously. But even he can see that the *Porpoise* is beautiful – polished oak, polished brass, everything singing with little bursts of sunlight. There is a ship's wheel with protruding handles at which you could stand and be Barbarossa or Vasco da Gama, there are cream canvas sails which belly and ripple and slap, there are portholes and winches, there are proper ropes of twisted sisal.

They cast off and motor out of the marina into the body of Poole Harbour. There is a steady wind astern so they hoist a single sail to help propel them towards the ocean proper. The deck tilts as the sail fills, only a couple of degrees but it reminds Darius of how ill-suited his physiology is to this form of transport. Right now, however, he would choose to be hoisted in the talons of a giant eagle as long as it was heading in the right direction and there were no more comfortable option.

To their left, above the beach, sits a row of preposterous mansions – a wedding cake, a baby-blue New England townhouse, a planetary outpost from *Star Wars*. 'Football managers, DJs and TV presenters,' says Marlena.

Darius can see now that Marlena has a slight limp, though it seems not to hamper her gymnastic clambering. 'An altercation in Sicily,' apparently, though she gives no more details. Anton's neck is still bleeding but Helena insists that salt spray and a cool wind will prevent it becoming infected. Sun dances on the water and gulls are their outriders. A Condor catamaran thunders slowly towards the harbour mouth waiting to pick up speed in open water en route to Jersey. It is the size of a recumbent tower block. Tiny people wave from the rail.

The *Porpoise* yaws and twists as they climb into the wake of the ferry. Darius starts to relax and as he does so he is able to admit how frightened he has been over the last twelve hours. Someone was trying to kill him. *Someone was trying to kill me.* He says the phrase out loud and finds himself laughing then sobbing a little. He thinks about Angelica. He decides not to think about Angelica. He cannot help her if he is dead. Right now he is going to concentrate on not becoming dead. He sits against the cabin housing and takes the weight off his throbbing arm.

The tide is rising and as they reach the bottleneck where the chain-link ferry connects Sandbanks to Studland the squeezed and speeded water thickens and twists under the hull. Boats entering the harbour scoot past them on the flood – plump white yachts with downed sails and high, bevelled sterns, a fishing boat stacked with lobster pots, two whiny jet-skis, a yellow pleasure cruiser – *Maid of the Islands* – chugging straight out of 1974. Their own speed relative to the land slows to a stroll. A blue double-decker bus drives onto the waiting ferry at the Studland end of its tiny shuttle route. Darius is pretty sure there are naked men on the beach, though that seems unlikely for England.

Five minutes and they are out at sea. The engine is turned off and the injured Anton holds the wheel while Helena and Marlena raise the other three sails. The swell is higher and has a longer wavelength out here. This water is a different kind of substance. The sky is enormous.

He should have called his parents. He imagines his father's voice at the end of the line. *Μπα, ο άσωτος υιός μου τηλεφώνησε.* He remembers that his father is dead. That he forgot this fact troubles him as much as the fact itself. He looks at the jigging, scalloped surface of the sea, seeking solace. He doesn't yet know the details of his father's will. The old man liked to keep his offspring on the back foot. Too late for buttering up now. There looms the very real possibility of Darius having to earn a living. There are kitesurfers far off. He wonders if they get tangled mid-air. He really should have tried a little harder in school.

His eye is caught by something in the water. He will look back and tell himself that he was in a disturbed state of mind, that it was a trick of the light, but he will never wholly convince himself. It is not a dolphin, nor is it flotsam. It is the body of a woman a metre or so under the surface of the water. Dark brown hair, light brown skin. She does not slip past like something merely floating in the water. For a good ten, fifteen seconds she is moving parallel to the boat. His first thought is that she has become tangled in one of their ropes, but there are no ropes trailing overboard. The way her image is jumbled and warped by the surface of the waves makes it hard to tell, but he cannot entirely suppress the idea that she is swimming.

❧

The air becomes sweeter as they sail south. The towns on the coast seem smaller and more widely spaced – no pylons, no chimneys, only the occasional horse-tail of woodsmoke. The stars are powdered glass on velvet. There are more fish in the water – mackerel, tarpon, black-tipped sharks, swordfish, marlin, yellowfin tuna – though Darius knows the names only because Marlena points them out. One afternoon a churning shoal of herring revolves under the boat for half an hour so that it feels as if they are riding a great silver drum. Battalions of gulls dive repeatedly into the glittering mass and haul out with the silver winnings in their beaks. Just before the herring disperse there is a brief, panicked scattering and a humpback whale broaches the shoal, fish and water pouring from the monumental black bucket of its grooved lower jaw. One night they glide through a sheet of luminous plankton, the like of which the others have never seen. Darius takes it all for granted, part and parcel of ocean-sailing, some compensation for the nausea and the pain in his arm. Helena, Marlena and Anton, however, know that something is very wrong. There is no weird uptick in the weather, no alteration in sea currents which can feasibly explain this fecundity. Marlena counts thirty-six species of seabird – petrels, albatross, frigatebirds, boobies, shearwaters, razorbills …

The radio fails. Except that they can find nothing wrong with the radio. Then the GPS signal vanishes. The wavebands are as clear as the glassy water below the hull which no longer contains plastic flotsam or iridescent slicks of oil. They pass fishing vessels with oars and hand-stitched sails more like those out of the coastal villages of Guinea-Bissau or The Gambia.

Helena, Marlena and Anton are not easily perturbed, but this frightens them. They are navigating old-school, using charts and compass, and there are whole towns missing along the coast. They discuss going ashore but feel safer out here. When Anton says, 'The zombie apocalypse is finally upon us,' it is neither funny nor less rational than any other explanation they can summon.

Darius's arm begins to swell. His hand is white and he can no longer move his fingers without considerable pain. Anton cuts the plaster away with his Gerber Scout. It takes a long time and leaves several bloody gashes where the knife breaches the last millimetres of plaster with unexpected ease.

Helena, Marlena and Anton tell Darius nothing about the disturbing nature of the changes in the world around them. He has been through enough already and the situation is so peculiar that, even as a group, they are wary of admitting their concerns for fear of seeming crazy.

Two nights later, however, they fall asleep to the slap of waves on the hull and the shriek of shearwaters while riding at anchor in an isolated cove just above the Spanish border. In the small hours Darius is woken by noises which he does not recognise and cannot easily explain – creaks, thumps, scrapes. He climbs out of bed. The movement of the boat is different, a wider, slower roll. He can smell tar and wet wood. He thinks about waking the others but this seems like a good opportunity to restore a little of his badly undermined manhood. He mounts the steps, girds his loins, slides the hatch back and climbs onto the deck.

There is a man standing in front of him, wearing a soiled leather jerkin over a bare torso. He has a tattoo of a griffin with talons raised down one muscular arm, and a compass inked onto the centre of his chest. The man's black hair is plaited down his back and he is so filthy that it is impossible to tell the colour of his skin. His eyes are narrow, Mongolian perhaps. His smell is the smell of someone who sleeps in the street and soils himself and does not change his clothes. Mixed with dog-breath and incense. There is an elderly, wooden-handled knife tucked into the rope that holds his trousers up. He looks like a man for whom killing other people is easy, if not habitual. He smiles at Darius. He has a small number of yellow teeth randomly arranged inside his mouth. Darius assumes it is an ironic smile, an indication that any resistance would be hilariously ineffective. 'All is good. Back to sleep.' The accent is indecipherable, part Dublin, part Bangkok, part Lord alone knows where. Darius is having trouble breathing. The man is surely not alone. Two more like him and they will find themselves thrown overboard at best. People have been held for years on becalmed tankers off Mogadishu. It might be best to jump the rail now and swim, but he has one functioning arm and no memory of how far they are from the shore. He looks at the long rip of absolute black between the stars and the starlit chop of the waves, and this is when he sees what has happened while he was asleep.

'Shitting Christ.' The exclamation is so in tune with his own feelings that he thinks they are his own words, but Anton climbs up onto the deck beside him, looking not at the stranger but up into the air. 'Holy shitting Christ.'

Darius looks up. The sails are different. The sails are huge, and square, and there are way too many of them. The deck shifts unexpectedly. Not *moves* as such but ... *expands*. Darius stumbles. Anton falls. Helena's head rises through the opened hatch. She looks different in a way that Darius can't quite pinpoint. 'And who the fuck are you?' She is addressing their tattooed potential murderer.

The man laughs as if this is an old joke the two of them have shared many times. 'All is good. All is very good.' He reaches down and helps Anton to his feet.

The boat is bigger. There is no polish and nothing sings with light. There are barrels, there are actual cannons – black iron shafts, wooden bases, solid wooden wheels. There is a second man whom Darius has also never seen before. He has a dense ginger beard and a wooden leg which looks as if it was sawed from a chair. Two clinkered gigs are roped to the deck. Darius is taken aback by the ease with which the term *clinkered gig* comes to mind.

The most disturbing thing of all, however, happens inside his head. He has an overwhelming need to be on dry ground in a world where you can go to sleep and wake up to find everything exactly as it was when you closed your eyes. Since this is not possible he rides that long chute back through the years until he is sitting in the little circular cupola at the very top of the eastern tower. His pet monkey crouches over a bowl of pistachios, selecting nuts in turn, splitting the shells exactly as Darius has taught him, eating the kernels and throwing the shells over the balustrade, the tiny bell on his red collar tinkling as he does so. The monkey's name is Kremnobates. It is winter and a light drizzle is falling on the ring of terracotta roofs by which he is surrounded. Beyond them a grey sea shades imperceptibly into a grey sky. There is a leather-bound book open on his lap, more parchment than paper. The words at the very top of the page read:

> *Talia iactanti stridens Aquilone procella*
> *velum adversa ferit, fluctusque ad sidera tollit.*

They flip effortlessly into English:

> *As he throws out these words, a screaming north wind*
> *hits the sail full-on and lifts the waves to the stars.*

Except that Darius has never learnt Latin, never owned a pet monkey, never lived in a building with a tower. And yet these images are utterly convincing – the pistachios, the little bell. Worse, they are part of a larger world he knows in equal detail. Below the hatch upon which he is kneeling a spiral staircase leads down to the long gallery with its terrifying tapestry of Phaethon failing to control the chariot of the sun. On the floor below that, his sister is being taught to play the cittern, her ill-tempered tutor chopping the air with his bony hands as if he were slicing a sausage. *One and two and . . .* His father swings between rage and sadness. Courtiers bow and flatter and cave. Slaves scurry from the royal presence like cockroaches from the light. Everywhere and nowhere, his mother's ghost, more present than anyone.

Darius tries to put these images out of his mind and reach into the real past and summon the place he always felt safest and happiest, the villa in Kozani to which the Koulouris family retreated every summer, the cool of the stone-flagged hallway, the stuffed owl and the smell of cigarettes in his father's study, the Rouault clown on the wall of the dining room. But the house is being swallowed by a fine, grey mist. He tries to remember his mother's face and nothing will come . . .

He is back on the ship. It is night-time, he is lying on the deck and he is shaking uncontrollably. His mind has always been robust. He would have avoided a few scrapes if he'd been a little more anxious in advance of certain activities and a little more regretful afterwards. He has never quite believed in mental illness and has therefore caused grave offence on a number of occasions. Now he understands what it means to lose your mind. He is being carried away by a dark flood. There is nothing to which he can cling for safety and very little Darius left to do the clinging.

The tattooed man puts the metal spout of a water pouch to Darius's lips, lifts it and squeezes. The liquid tastes of latrines and bay leaves and contains grit which he can feel between his teeth. The man with the ginger beard bats the pouch away and replaces it with a bottle. Darius takes a swig. He has never tasted petrol but it cannot be greatly different from this. He takes two large swigs and tightens his grip on the bottle lest it is taken away.

His mind has no centre any more. There is only a flurry of sensations and feelings. Nothing binds them together. He is a flock of birds, he is a field of grass, he is the aftermath of an explosion, the splinters flying away from one another. Arms lift him. He has no strength left. He is carried below decks, wrapped in a fleece, laid in a hammock and swayed into the relieving dark by the rot-gut and the roll of the hull.

❧

He wakes in the Great Cabin. Images of the stuffed owl and the Rouault clown linger briefly, as resonant and troubling as the dispersing wisps of any nightmare. His head is heavy. He must have been drinking. He gets to his feet. Sunlight pours through the long window which runs the width of the stern. There is a wardrobe and a chest of drawers and a low-backed beechwood chair with wide legs. There are hourglasses of three different sizes. There is an astrolabe, a quadrant and a cross-staff. There are declination tables, astronomical maps and a shelf of charts held in fat rolls by ageing blue ribbons. Spread out on the table, its curly corners pinned down by four cast-iron balance-weights, is a vellum map of the Mediterranean.

His name is Pericles, Prince of Tyre, and this is where he is at home, in motion, incommunicado, hundreds of leagues from those chill and melancholy halls once warmed and lit by his mother's generosity and goodwill. Two years since her untimely death. His father's worst self unconstrained now, petty, angry, the runt of his own father's litter, a small man with too much power. One third of the court desperate to carry out his every whim, one third hiding, a final third seizing the opportunity to use the chaos to their own advantage, much as men leash ill-tempered dogs and encourage them to hurt others, his sisters protected only by the fact that they are women and therefore have little value and demand little attention.

Another ten days and he will be back inside that godforsaken palace. One cannot remain at sea for ever and he owes a duty to the people over whom he will one day rule if not to the man from whose dead hands he will eventually take the crown. Is he a coward to hope that a violent confrontation between the two of them will justify a swift return to this peripatetic life of travel and trade? Assuming the city has not been eaten up by the canker of his father's anger, or fallen to some neighbouring king who has taken advantage of eyes turned inwards. And if it has, so be it.

He clears his head by splashing his face with cold water from the fat-bottomed tin jug by the privy, then takes his pea coat from a hook and steps out of the door. The helmsman is checking the compass, gimballed in its teak box. He stands upright and executes a cursory but respectful nod. 'My Lord.'

Pericles nods back then rises into the light and the fresh wind of the upper gun deck.

Above him sails ripple and sway – top-gallant, topsails, courses … Men spider through the rigging. He knows every inch of this ship from the stern lantern to the wooden mermaid with long tangerine hair, painted lips and full but slightly chipped wooden breasts. Three hundred and seventeen tonnes laden, nineteen carriage guns, a hold packed with bisket, Holland cheese, neats' tongues, mutton, lemons, good wine … and secreted under these, the Barbary gold which they have earned trading Venetian glass.

Rubbing his arm, which hurts abominably for some unknown reason, he climbs to the quarterdeck and stands beside Helicanus who asks if he has any objection to them resuming their journey. He has none so they weigh anchor and tack into deeper water to gain the benefit of the propitious current then turn south towards Lisbon and the mouth of the Tagus.

His captain, Helicanus, has nut-brown skin and salt-stiffened blonde hair. Unnaturally young and still beardless, he nevertheless radiates a confidence which outstrips his youth. His two junior officers have done sterling service in some very tight spots on both this and previous voyages – Marlenus whose nimbleness belies the limp he sustained falling from a horse in Sicily, and the burly Antonio whose more recent wound has healed well in the salt air, though it will leave a scar on his neck which will either keep him out of respectable houses or make him the centre of attention depending on the sensibilities of the womenfolk in that particular city. The other hands have been taken on in Tyre or picked up en route. One man was lost overboard in a storm on the Dogger Bank, a second vanished among the fleshpots of Copenhagen and a third died of a fever. It's a decent average for a trip of this length.

They round the cape at Sagres and turn towards Cádiz. Other ships pass them with increasing frequency as the ocean traffic of the eastern Atlantic thickens near the Strait of Gibraltar. When they enter the Mediterranean Pericles expects to feel more at home – small tides, fewer storms, more accurate maps, languages he understands – but something is wrong, a pebble in the mind's shoe. There is a task which has to be done, of that he is certain, but the name and nature of the task eludes him. He lies awake at night, unable to sleep. They pass the Balearic Islands, they pass Sardinia, they pick up fresh water in Syracuse. There is a meteor shower at night, brief scratches of bright white light high in the north-west which send the more credulous sailors below decks for fear of contagion.

He sleeps and dreams that he is in a wood and badly injured. A man stands over him holding a weapon of some kind. Burning hair and cellar damp, a sound like the air going in and out of a great pair of bellows.

They pass between Cythera and Cydonia, they pass Rhodes. They are rounding the southern coast of Cyprus when he sees, swimming in the water, parallel to the boat, some twenty yards out, a pure white albino dolphin. Or a porpoise maybe, the ship's eponymous twin. He considers telling Helicanus, or indeed Marlenus whose knowledge of marine creatures is seemingly inexhaustible, but he is nervous that the crew will take it upon themselves to harpoon the creature. He watches it keep pace with the ship for perhaps a quarter of an hour. It neither broaches the waves nor rises close enough to the surface for him to get a clearer view. Then Helicanus calls, he turns briefly, and when he looks at the water again the creature has gone.

Just out of Tyre they see a small royal cutter riding at anchor. Pericles' heart sinks. It is, presumably, waiting to give an expansive welcome to the fleet of some minor potentate expected in the next few days. The palace will then be swept up in a great dance of empty pomp for the coming week. It is precisely the kind of vapid activity which drove him to sea in the first place.

He is wrong. They are not waiting for a foreign embassy. On the contrary they have got wind of his own arrival and want to make contact before he docks. As the two ships close upon one another the cutter sends out a small gig, eight men rowing an elderly dignitary. Helicanus slows the *Porpoise* so that the gig can tie up alongside. Is it possible that his father has died? He can think of no other news which must be delivered before he enters the harbour. Is he now king? A terrible weight settles upon him. His whole life has been moving relentlessly towards this point but he has doggedly refused to look in its direction, like a man being swept towards a cataract who sees only the birds overhead and the fish jumping and the trees lining the riverbank.

He stands at the rail watching the cutter tie up. He recognises the old man. Alkaios, is it? He is clearly unused to being on the water and even less comfortable climbing up the side of a ship and must therefore be assisted by several undignified hands supporting his pantalooned backside. He stands on the deck for perhaps a whole minute getting his breath back. 'My Lord … Oh dear … Give me a few moments … My Lord, forgive me … Welcome, of course, though I must skip the usual diplomatic niceties to deliver … some alarming news.'

Pericles is wrong for a second time. His father is not dead. It is his own life which is in danger.

'Three days ago a frigate of Antioch docked unexpectedly. The captain, a man of prodigious height who wore black and sported a shaven head, went by the name of Kallios. He begged an audience with your father and claimed to have met you on your travels. He had arrived here at your invitation and was rather surprised to find that you had not yet returned. His knowledge of you and of your vessel was detailed enough to convince your father that you and he were indeed friends. The stranger apologised and said that he would resume your acquaintance when he was next passing Tyre, but your father, greatly cheered to hear that you were on your way home, insisted that he remain as a guest until they might be reunited with friend and son respectively.'

'And why have you intercepted my ship to tell me this?' Pericles has no memory of the name, but it is eminently likely that he has, after strong drink, offered such an invitation.

'My Lord, of course, again my apologies, I'm approaching the burden of my message …'

The following day the king's spymaster asked for a private meeting. Once he and the king were alone he opened a leather bag and unrolled a little brown bottle from a swathe of green velvet. 'Buried in one of the travelling trunks of our guest.' He held up his hand to soften the king's outrage. 'A moment will, I think, justify the breach of etiquette.' He whistled loudly and one of the king's hunting dogs trotted through the door. Fearing what was to come, the king sat forward and patted the snout of the beloved animal. In truth he loved his dogs more than any human residents of the palace, but if the spymaster was correct then he had a more pressing problem to deal with than a dead dog. 'Let us hope, Strider, that our friend here is mistaken.'

The spymaster took a small slab of horsemeat from the bag and donned a pair of hawking gloves. He twisted the tiny cork from the bottle and gingerly poured six drops of fluid onto the flesh. He recorked the vial and dropped the meat onto the flagstones. The dog tore enthusiastically into the steak and was convulsing before the gloves and the wrapped vial were returned to the bag, neck, back and tail gripped in a savage rictus, limbs trembling, eyes rolled back into their sockets. It died soon after, bleeding from every opening in its body. The sight and its implication were so distressing to the king that the yells and crashes coming from elsewhere in the building seemed like the world quite naturally expressing the same horror he himself felt. But the spymaster was already at the door, saying, 'Throw the bolt and do not allow anyone in unless they call out the dog's name.'

Kallios must have left a pebble on the lid of the trunk or memorised the arrangement of books inside. He and his lieutenants fought their way to the harbour with such supernatural vigour that many of those who witnessed the running battle talked of them as devils. Seven men of Tyre died. Only one man from the ship of Antioch lost his life and his last act before he tumbled into the harbour was to grab his destroyer and haul him backwards so that they drowned together. The following day when the bodies were winched out of the water, the demon's hand was still locked around his victim's wrist and had to be broken away, finger by finger.

The elderly counsellor – Ampelios, that is his name, he remembers now – asks quietly if Pericles knows of any reason why someone might wish him ill. 'I ask on behalf of your father.' He clearly does not like to pry, least of all into the affairs of a young prince who disappeared over the horizon, possibly to sow wild oats away from judging eyes.

Pericles wonders if this is some ruse his father has cooked up to keep him away for reasons which are not immediately obvious. But surely neither his father nor this old man has the imagination to concoct so vivid a story. Judging by the looks on the faces of Helicanus and Marlenus they give the courtier's account similar credence. But it is something more peculiar and more personal which convinces Pericles. He has no idea who wants him dead, but in his bones he has been expecting this moment for some time. And far from being frightened or mystified he feels unexpectedly cheered.

Helicanus looks at him, puzzled by this visible alteration of mood. 'My Lord ...?'

Pericles barely hears him. The news feels like the answer to a question he did not realise that he had asked. The unease he has been feeling for the past week looks, in retrospect, like the heart's anxious pacing before the beginning of a journey, the tug of the kite string, the bending of the bow.

'It was night when they left the harbour,' says Ampelios. 'They carried no lights. We lost them almost immediately, for which I am truly sorry. The only weapon I can give you is a detailed description of the vessel and the crew.' The counsellor hands him a small scroll which has clearly suffered much folding and wetting and drying out. 'We think it best if you prolong your journey and avoid, for the immediate future, all places where you are known. I saw this Kallios with my own eyes and I do not think such precautions are excessive.'

Pericles turns to Helicanus. 'Then we must place ourselves in the hands of God, close our eyes and thrust a pin into the map of the world.'

❧

Angelica stops speaking. It happens a couple of days after Darius's visit. Mid-afternoon her father finds her in one of the armchairs by the fire-place. There is Elizabethan court music playing quietly in the back-ground. Lutes and viols. He suggests that they take a trip – San Francisco, Lisbon, Sydney, an old favourite, somewhere new ... anywhere she wants.

Angelica does not want to stay in a hotel in a foreign city with her father. The presence of the staff at home forces him to keep his distance during the day at least. But how can she refuse without angering him?

'What do you think?'

She stares down the garden. Clouds like swansdown pulled from a torn pillow by a bored child. They would be beautiful if they did not float above those trees and this house.

'Angelica?'

She has always deferred to her father, always done what he tells her to do, but as this silence extends the balance begins to shift. It is such a new feeling that she does not recognise it at first.

'Angelica, tell me what's wrong.'

She looks directly at her father. He is on the far side of a thick sheet of glass, like a tiger in a zoo, an ape, a snake. He cannot touch her.

He gathers himself. 'I'm sorry. I acted selfishly. You are the most precious thing in my life. I would rather lose everything than lose you. It's hard for anyone to be rational when their most valuable possession is threatened.'

She stands and walks to the window. A woman is singing. *Dona nobis pacem*. Outside, a robin lands on the rim of the white concrete bird bath, dips its beak into the water then flies away.

'I understand if you're angry.'

She walks away without saying a word. It is exhilarating.

'Angelica?'

She goes to her room. She puts on walking socks and her cream Shetland hoody with the wooden toggles and goes outside to the stripy hammock from which the house is invisible and the only building to be seen is the squat tower of St Mary's Michelmersh. Sheltered from the wind by a thick stand of box and rowan, it is just warm enough to lie here for an hour and let herself be rocked gently out of the world. She read here throughout the summer and the place is still woven into the remembered plots of *Les Trois Mousquetaires*, *Dr Zhivago*, *The Street of Crocodiles* ... But there is only one story she wants to tell now.

... the Porpoise *is beautiful – polished oak, polished brass, everything singing with little bursts of sunlight. There is a ship's wheel with*

protruding handles at which you could stand and be Barbarossa or
Vasco da Gama, there are waxed cream canvas sails which belly and
ripple and slap ...

Philippe comes to her room that night. She is reading in bed. He sits beside her and brushes the hair from her face. She is wearing a man's dress shirt many sizes too large in a colour that is neither quite pink nor quite orange. She acts as if he does not exist. He finds the shape of her breasts under the linen arousing but when he begins to unbutton the shirt and she does not react he feels, for the first time, as if he is being watched by a third person, and in that person's eyes he appears foolish, pathetic, perverse. He takes his hands away. He reminds himself how poorly things turned out the last time he allowed his anger to get the better of him. He says, 'You obviously need time.' He gets up and leaves.

... a skeletal boy is standing in the shallows off the little pebbled beach
using a sharpened stick to catch the tiny fish that have sustained him
since his parents died, but he is weak and his hands are shaking and
the sun is hot and what he wants most of all is to lie down in a dark
room and sleep. He glances up. There is a boat about a league out ...

❧

It arrives with rats stowed away in a shipment of grain from Sidon. Black Death. *Yersinia pestis*, clogging the guts of infected fleas so that when they bite into the flesh of a host the bacterium is washed back into the wound with the host's own regurgitated blood.

Three of the sailors are already sick before they reach Tarsus, swellings the size of apples in their groins and armpits. Talents are handed over and the sacks of grain are swung onto the hot quay, the captain lingering long enough not to arouse suspicion then casting off, heading west to Myra to pick up another cargo.

The first two men to become ill work on the docks. The next victims are the ones who care for them – wives, mothers, daughters. The rats are everywhere by now, in roofs, cupboards, sewage tanks, licking the dust from the dirty corners of empty grain stores. Where there are rats there are fleas, and where there are fleas there is plague. A red X is painted on the door of every plague-ridden house. Uninfected family members found out of doors are fined. Infected family members found out of doors are executed. The houses of dead families are burnt. Those who visit the sick – quacks, priests, do-gooders, the greedy and foolhardy who earn money by burying the dead – carry red wands so that they can be avoided in the street. Only those too weak to leave their homes are spared contact with the disease but they are already taking leave of the world by another, slower route.

❧

And if the merchants of Tarsus had known of the invisible cargo being delivered along with the grain, would they have turned the ship away? The city is starving. There has been no rain for four months. Cisterns and irrigation channels have run dry and even the deepest wells produce little more than cups of foul, gluey liquid. Crops have failed. Markets are empty which should be stacked with apples and nectarines, spelt flour, sesame seeds, chickpeas, butter … There is fish but it goes to fishermen's families, their wealthy customers and those bold enough to rob either at knifepoint. Most of the donkey trains from the Anatolian plateau which run the gauntlet of the Cilician Gates are ambushed, the traders' throats cut, their wares, made precious by scarcity, sold to the highest bidders in Tyana or Issus, or traded for gold through black-market intermediaries to the royal family who hunker in the citadel burning incense to cover the smells of unflushed sewers and rotting flesh which rise from the rush roofs between the ramparts and the sea.

The poor live on acorns and bitter vetch. The dogs were eaten long ago. There is no meat left with which to make a sacrifice to the gods. Rumours are spreading that young men are dying in fights, their bodies vanishing before they can be buried.

The citizens' growing resentment is blunted only by their fading strength. A battle with palace guards ends with little more than surface wounds, neither side having the energy to do much damage. The guards, in any case, are starving too and unwilling to give their lives to protect masters who wash quails' eggs and flatbreads down with sweet wine from Khirokitia and fresh water in calfskin bladders.

The sea swaying and sparkling beyond the harbour is empty of sails. Everyone from Rhodes to Jerusalem now knows that this cursed corner of the Cilician Strait is to be avoided. The only visitors are the increasingly bold gulls who no longer scatter when people try to stop them feasting on the dead or the near-dead lying in the streets.

King Cleon feels no pity for the citizens. They are like leaves or cattle, no generation greatly different from the next. The architecture, the history, his family, the city's standing in the wider world, these are the things that matter, and, for the first time in his life, they are in danger. He and his queen, Dionyza, are young but childless. Cleon is terrified not simply that he will die but that he will do so without leaving an heir, though if the gods do not change their disposition there will be nothing for such an heir to inherit. He walks through the linked courtyards of the walled garden with their filigree stonework and coloured tiles of dizzying symmetry, their mosaics depicting sea-battles, gods, a rhinoceros hunt. The fountains and the watercourses are dry, the lemons and persimmons dead. Only the cacti in the fourth courtyard survive, sitting in their clouds of angry needles. Cleon pictures the palace in twenty years' time, arches fallen, temples ruined, the citadel a starling roost, tawny foxes padding nimbly over the tumbled stones. To be angry with the gods is to risk falling even further out of favour so he becomes angry instead with advisers, courtiers and servants, about the quality of the food, about the cleanliness of bed linen, about the failure of his underlings to maintain good cheer.

Dionyza is the cactus. She quietly despises her husband and is aware of the low esteem in which he is held by those over whom he wields power. Every so often she orders acts of theatrical cruelty to ensure that their grip does not loosen – the cook whose thumbs are cleavered off when he is found to be smuggling food to his family, the kitchen girl whose tongue is cut out when she is overheard discussing the possibility that their superiors might be overthrown.

Finally, after three months, the plague peaks and falls away. Three quarters of the population are dead. If there were food and clean water most of the survivors would gradually recover, but there is no food and there has been no rain for seven months now. The people are cadaverous and lethargic. The roads north through the Cilician Gates are empty, the bandits hunting richer traffic elsewhere. The flow of food to the palace is drying up, and neither petulant rage nor random cruelty can magic sustenance from the empty air. An embassy is sent to Kition but does not return. Cleon dares not send another. There is talk of leaving by road but the thought of travelling, let alone dying, like an itinerant merchant is inconceivable.

Cleon's chief adviser, the Lord Chancellor, dies. He is rail-thin, as they all are, but there seems to be nothing else obviously wrong with him. They find him one morning kneeling in the corner of a chamber, as if looking for a dropped coin. His body is already rigid.

A bearded vulture sits on the parapet outside the royal quarters, watching, waiting. The guards trap it and kill it. Cleon and Dionyza are offered the paltry meat. She eats but he declines.

The sky darkens one afternoon. The citizens gather on the quay, along the harbour wall, on the rocks. They hear thunder and watch a rainstorm slide across the ocean far out, a fat column of grey where the sky drains onto the sea. There is a cool breeze for just over an hour. Then the sun comes out, the same hot, cruel blue overhead.

Ten days later a skeletal boy is standing in the shallows off the little pebbled beach using a sharpened stick to catch the tiny fish that have sustained him since his parents died, but he is weak and his hands are shaking and the sun is hot and what he wants most of all is to lie down in a dark room and sleep. He glances up. There is a boat about a league out. It was not there when he last looked. It is sailing towards the city and it is sailing fast.

Before it has halved the distance everyone knows of its approach and most are watching. Cleon and Dionyza stand on a balcony in the citadel. Even at that height they sense it, the moment when collective relief turns to collective fear, triggered by those with the sharpest eyes. The ship carries no colours and therefore professes allegiance to no monarch. These are clearly pirates and the confidence and speed with which they are heading straight for the harbour suggests that news of the city's parlous state has spread. The plague is over and they are now easy pickings.

❧

The gods point the *Porpoise* in the direction of Tarsus, though it is a spun-silver talent rather than a blindfold and a pin through which his intentions are made manifest. Helicanus suspects that the city's position in a fold of the map is of greater significance but he is not going to argue with a method of divination that has so improved his master's ill mood.

In the night's long watches Pericles wonders whom his pursuer, Kallios, might be. Whom might he have injured grievously enough to justify so violent a reaction? He is exuberant. To the sober he is very possibly brash. But that has always been the prerogative of youth and the complaint of age. Seekers of adventure are attracted by a possibility that anything might happen in his company, and they are correct. He has killed a number of people, albeit ones of little account. But even the family of the portly count who rashly challenged him in Xeres surely did not have the wealth to finance a retaliatory sea-voyage. There were girls, of course, there were always girls. It is entirely possible that he has fathered children, of which he prefers not to think, for God alone knows what has become of them. But he has always tried to pick his way gingerly through the flower garden, taking care not to pluck the daughters of fathers, and the wives of husbands, who might be capable of turning their anger into action. Has he, perhaps, been grossly misled as to the social status of one of his conquests?

He looks at the jumbled moon scattered on the choppy water. He listens to the wind and the canvas talking. It is an intriguing puzzle but in truth it does not matter greatly. The things that matter are those that lie ahead – rocks, hurricanes, pirates. Behind there is only a wake which rapidly becomes indistinguishable from the rest of the limitless sea.

They move swiftly across the Mediterranean, avoiding all other ships in order to throw Kallios off their trail. They do not pause to pick up news from other mariners and therefore hear nothing about the fate that has befallen the city at the end of their journey. They are consequently taken aback as they approach Tarsus, first by the absence of sails and masts in the harbour, then by the vast, ragged crowd which has gathered to witness their arrival, then by the presence of the king and queen – if that is the identity of the splendidly arrayed young couple on the quay backed by a chorus of dour nobles.

Helicanus stands at Pericles' shoulder and quietly voices the general fear. 'Plague?'

Pericles has, in the way of many rich young men, a conviction that the world should bend to his will. Moreover, he has, for the first time in his life, an inexplicable sense of purpose, a conviction that there is something as yet unnamed that he must do. Will this be the moment when he proves himself?

They drop anchor in the deeper water of the bay and lower a gig. With Helicanus in temporary command of the *Porpoise*, Pericles is rowed ashore by four men, accompanied by Marlenus and Antonio and a complement of small arms should the welcome prove a ruse. They tie up loosely, leaving two men on the gig to facilitate a swift retreat if necessary, then ascend the stone steps, the smell of putrefaction thickening as they rise to the cobbled dock. Pericles wonders if he is being foolhardy. They are not even possessed of a ship's surgeon. He puts the thought to the back of his mind. There is no turning back now. Of all things, he is least desirous of being counted a coward.

The three men stand side by side, taking in the gathered crowd. The royal couple wear silk and lawn and scarlet and look not greatly different from the royal couples one might find in any city state along this coast. The queen's face is hypnotic – dark, flawless skin, jet-black hair which drinks the light which falls upon it, eyes that do not look away. Behind them the nobles are gaunt and dirty. Further back their subjects look like the risen dead, every head a skull covered by too little skin. They have the legs of birds, their hands are claws, their faces are patched and stained with lesions. A woman crumples onto the hot ground as they watch. None of her neighbours move to raise her. Somewhere a child cries. Hungry gulls patrol the perimeter.

The prince strides boldly forwards and announces himself. 'My name is Pericles, Prince of Tyre.' The king drops to one knee. The queen does not. Years later he will recall the scene and read the warnings to which he was originally blind, being preoccupied with the unfolding drama of his own heroism.

The king says, 'I was once ruler of a great city. We ate veal and peacock. We drank Gascony claret and Malmsey from Crete. Branches snapped under the weight of our olives. The rivers were dammed by their own fish. I am now the king of nothing and nowhere.'

The queen stares directly at Pericles and does not turn away. 'His name is Cleon.'

'You did not hear of the plague?' asks her husband.

'We did not.'

'Though even that has abandoned us in search of better prey. Now only hunger and thirst pick at our bones.'

Pericles laughs at the opportunity for munificence which has tumbled so plumply into his lap. Raising his benevolent hands he calls out, 'We mean you no harm.' There is a pause. Then relief passes through the malodorous crowd like a breeze through wheat.

'My name,' says the queen, 'is Dionyza.'

'Stand,' says Pericles to her husband. The reversal of etiquette is thrilling. The king gets to his feet with the effort required of a man twice his age. The queen stares into the sky. Her face is unreadable. 'We have a ship fully stocked with both water and food. We will put it all at your disposal.' There is no reaction. Pericles repeats himself.

'Why would you do that?' asks Dionyza, coolly.

He must think for a second to answer the question accurately. He feels that he is an instrument of some force he does not comprehend but knows no way of putting this into words without seeming both grandiose and deluded. 'If I sailed away without having helped I would not be able to forgive myself.' The nobles murmur. Is Cleon weeping? 'Come.' He puts a hand behind the king's shoulder and ushers him towards the steps that lead back down to the gig. The queen follows them. A small group of courtiers follows the queen. Pericles escorts them out to the *Porpoise* where they are dined with all the ha'penny pomp the ship can muster.

Marlenus and Antonio remain on the quay with two armed men while barrels of food and water are delivered by the returning gig. When it ties up a musket must be fired to hold back a surging crowd who push a mother and her child into the harbour. The children are given a cup of water, the old and sick are given two, the women three, the men four. Bisket and bread are handed out in similar proportions.

Marlenus and Antonio have seen nothing like it. Some tear at their food like animals, some close their eyes and savour every mouthful, some stare at it as if they have forgotten what to do with it, some cry, some laugh. An old woman dies with a crust in her hands, killed perhaps by the shock of her own salvation. Lemons and hunks of Holland cheese are distributed. Gulls grown bold steal food from the hands of the weak and must be driven away with sticks and yells.

On board the *Porpoise*, Cleon and Dionyza are given watered Rhenish, salt beef and apricots. The silver fork shakes in Cleon's hands. He retches and brings the food back up. Everyone pretends that this has not happened. Cold water is poured into his silver tankard and plain bisket is laid on his silver plate. Dionyza tells Pericles the story of the last six months. She does not mention the citizens once.

Late in the afternoon an eiderdown of big-bellied, dove-grey clouds slides over the sky and the city is bathed in the pearly light that precedes a storm. Tarsians who had sought shade to sleep off full stomachs are drawn back outside by the general clamour. They stare at the sky like devotees awaiting the descent of a god. A deep quiet seizes the city. The only sound is the fizzle of waves sinking between pebbles, and rising, and sinking.

The first fat drops vanish on impact, sucked up by the hot, dry earth and the hot, dry stone. Their successors splash and spread. Forgotten colours re-enter the world, deeper greens, deeper browns. Roof tiles play music. The surface of the sea is white and stippled and dancing. The air is cold for the first time in a year. Gutters fill, troughs fill. People stand with arms outstretched and heads tilted backwards so that the rain falls onto their faces. Long-imprisoned smells are set free – thyme and wood-sap, tar, seaweed. The merciless sunlight which yesterday picked out every line softens and the distance vanishes in a foggy blur behind the bars of the rain.

Cleon and Dionyza watch from the long window in the great cabin, drops drumming the planks above their heads, the whole chamber scented by wet oak. Pericles stands on the quarterdeck while boys arrange empty barrels in a row to save this unexpected and prodigal gift. He turns it over in his mind, this story in which he finds himself. The cork-stoppered vial of poison, the serendipity of arriving in this belea-guered city with a laden ship, the timing of this saving deluge. There seems to be a significance to these events but it lies just beyond the reach of his mind.

Thunder rumbles in the shrouded hills.

The downpour continues overnight and halfway through the following morning. When they can do so without the indignity of being drenched, Cleon and Dionyza are rowed back to the quay then returned to the palace in the company of four carts of supplies from the *Porpoise*. Cleon insists that Pericles and his three senior officers remain as guests for a week at the very least. Pericles' heart sinks at the prospect of becoming trapped by the pointless ceremonial round, but to refuse would be unchivalrous and impolitic. So he and Helicanus and Marlenus and Antonio are installed in four adjacent rooms looking over the hippo-drome to the sea. Pericles cleans himself with perfumed soap from Gaul and jugs of hot water and sleeps between cotton sheets and eats his own food served in fine, hand-painted bowls and must feign a gratitude he does not feel. His status as saviour relieves him at least of the obli-gation to toady and scrape, but watching others toady and scrape is thin entertainment.

The company is some compensation. Cleon could be a bookish older brother, denied the opportunity to explore the wider world by his father's early death and eager for travellers' tales. Pericles tells him of cannibals and volcanoes, of the Northern Lights and shrunken heads and spirits observed in obsidian mirrors, of St Elmo's fire and ships broken on the backs of breaching leviathans, and if he embellishes somewhat, he does so no more than authors of the travelogues in Latin, Arabic, Hebrew and Greek which furnish Cleon's library. The king likes both listening to and playing music. He sings and accompanies himself on the cittern and if Pericles finds this effeminate at first, there is sometimes a snag in his heart when he listens.

Ah poor bird,
Why art thou
Singing in the shadows
At this late Hour?

Ah, poor bird
Take thy flight
High above the shadows
Of this sad night.

Dionyza has unbuckled the armour she wore to survive the onslaught of the previous year. There is a softness he had not expected. She refuses to smile when he smiles at her, but he turns occasionally to find her staring at him. She always takes a few moments to turn away. He finds this infuriating and beguiling in equal measure. Dionyza's husband is oblivious. At other times she stands just a little closer to him than is proper, just inside an invisible orbit of which he has never been aware before. She never catches his eye when she is doing this. She is talking to him in a language no one else can understand. If she touched him it could not be more intimate. He cannot move away without seeming discourteous. He does not wish to move away.

News of the city's recovery travels quickly and it is a matter of days before merchants begin to arrive once more bearing figs and dried fish and sacks of barley. The court eat godwits and plovers, they eat ox and antelope, they eat marzipan and candied figs and a model of the very palace in which they sit made out of dyed sugar. In the harbour the hull of the *Porpoise* is caulked and tarred, the boat swabbed inside and out. Ropes are mended. In the city burnt houses are pulled down like dead trees and new houses start to grow in the gaps they leave behind. Sacrifices are made and the dead are given the due ceremony they failed to receive during hasty burials.

Pericles longs for action. Glory and gratitude, he realises, are more pleasurable in the earning than the receipt. But the alternative is a graceless departure. He dreams of Kallios. He wishes now that they had not shaken off their pursuer quite so easily, but had laid a trail of bread-crumbs in order that the pursuit might continue a little longer. He pictures the otherworldy fighters described by his father's counsellor and his sword-hand itches.

He does not understand yet that adventure is the easiest of all challenges, when the monster has a face and a name and you can place a boot on its chest and pull out that long wet blade and know that it will not rise again. He does not understand yet that there are things that keep one awake at night which are more terrifying than pirates or reefs, and cannot be avoided by the dousing of lights at dusk and the possession of a good map. He does not understand yet that sometimes the monster is other people, sometimes the monster squats unseen inside one's own heart, and sometimes the monster is the brute fact of time itself.

His mind drifts, not to the scrapes and skirmishes of the last two years, nor to the extraordinary sights he has witnessed on his travels (in truth he has never knowingly met cannibals though he did see the Northern Lights unnaturally far south in Bergen at the New Year). He revisits, instead, scenes from his childhood. He is hiding in the cupola at the top of the eastern tower, he is hiding in the little temple at the end of the orchard, he is hiding behind the sacks and jars in the storeroom at the back of the kitchen where the cook Mustafa brings him lokum and salep, telling nurses and tutors that, no, he hasn't seen the young master anywhere. He is troubled by the seductiveness of these pictures, he is troubled by the fact that he is hiding in these scenes, troubled that he might have been a coward, that he is still at heart a coward. What difference is there between a child who hides and a man who runs away?

He wishes he could talk to Helicanus in the way they do at sea where they are engaged in a shared task and rank matters little, but here in the court Helicanus is a social inferior and in spite of Pericles' encouragement Helicanus can act the role of friend no more convincingly than he can dance a gavotte. Indeed, if Pericles learns anything during these interminable days it is that he has no true friends, that he has never had any true friends. How has he spent so long blind to this obvious truth?

It is not a friend, however, who rescues him, it is an enemy. Rumour pays out as swiftly as any ball of wool, and the markets of Aleppo sell things more valuable than ambergris or Chinese silk. Sixteen days. That is all it takes. They come at night, having followed the figs and fish and barley through the Cilician Gates. The peace generated by having little worth stealing has made the sentries careless and sleepy. With a rope and grappling hook the strangers scale the walls unseen then move quietly through the sleeping city to the cries of nightjars and scops owls. Shadows are holes punched into the world. A jackal ripping at some dead thing stops at the far end of an alley and watches them pass, tiny candles of moonlight in its eyes. A nightwatchman is lowered gently into his own blood. Another dies the same way. They slip past the gymnasium and the temple of Athena, past the silent brothels and the empty butchers' shops, past the goldsmiths and the vintners. Dying flames dance lazily in a single brazier beside the common pump. The earth beneath their feet turns to flags and cobbles as they zigzag slowly uphill to the city's moneyed heart.

Pericles wakes to the wrong kind of silence, an alarm ringing in his blood. It is the middle of the night. He climbs out of bed. Stockings, tunic, boots. They have come, he is certain. No moon, absolute dark. He has a dagger but his sword is respectfully sheathed on the *Porpoise*. He can hear them now, distant shouts, faint echoes of metal striking metal. He needs some instrument to keep an attacker at bay. Footsteps on the stairs. There is a trunk, there is a water jug, there is a coverlet on the bed. These three objects are his armoury.

The door opens. A man steps into the wedge of light thrown by the sconces in the hallway. He is unnaturally tall and wears a beard like carved black wood. His shoulders are the shoulders of a bull. He wears a bronze cuirass, a black tunic and greaves. There is a backsword in his right hand and a chain in his left fist.

Pericles cannot win a straight fight against this man armed only with a dagger so he must use some other advantage. It comes to him in a moment. He knows the shape of the room whereas his opponent does not. He grabs the coverlet. It's not a gladiator's weighted net but it must suffice. He swings it, tangling the man's sword just long enough for him to dodge sideways and push the door shut. All light vanishes. He jumps the trunk and stands on the far side. The man revolves slowly. Pericles can smell leather and sword-oil and sweat like boiled onions and make out the faintest silhouette with his dark-adjusted eyes. Can his attacker see the trunk between them? Is he waiting for his own eyes to adjust? 'Come at me,' says Pericles, though only the gods know what language the man speaks. Pericles hears a deep jingle as his attacker raises the chain above his head and begins to swing it. The noise is like the wingbeats of a great bird. The man steps forwards. He has not seen the trunk. He stumbles and pitches over with the crash and clatter of a full dining table being upended. He does not cry out either in surprise or pain. Pericles throws himself onto the man's exposed back but the dagger refuses to enter the skin. Chain mail. The man twists and kicks so that Pericles has to ride him like a baited bull. He grabs the lower edge of the vest, hauls it up and shoves the dagger into the exposed flesh. Still the man makes no noise. Is he mute? Pericles cranks the handle of the buried dagger back and forth to damage as many internal organs as possible. The man grabs Pericles' hair in one hand and sinks his teeth into Pericles' shoulder and only later when he cleans the wound will Pericles look at the size and shape of the scar left by the teeth and wonder if he was wounded by something not human. But now the man bucks hard and Pericles is thrown clear, the blood so thick on the stone floor that he skids and slips as he gets to his feet. The only noise coming from the man is the squeak of leather and the grating of bronze body-plate against stone. It grows quieter, then there is no more noise. Pericles throws open the door, wider this time, and the same sconce-light falls on a sight he will not forget for a long time. His attacker is lying not face down in a pool of blood, but face up, back arched, bent like a bow, only head and feet on the floor. His lips are pulled back from long, yellow teeth in the grimace of a snarling dog and his eyes are wide open as if it was not the dagger that killed him but the sight of some hovering black angel.

Pericles steps outside and sees something else he will have trouble forgetting. Marlenus squats over Antonio. He knows immediately that Antonio is dead. They do not have time to grieve, nor do they have time to speak. Helicanus appears at his side and hands him a borrowed sword, its handle slick with blood. They know what they have to do.

They must assume that they are the quarry and save themselves by getting to the ship, hoping that it is neither holed nor burning.

There is a second, smaller staircase down to the courtyard at the rear of the palace complex. They turn as one and run down the corridor. Through the arched openings to their left Pericles can see the bodies of two palace guards spreadeagled under the mulberry trees in the peristyle. Pericles has already forgotten about Antonius. He has entered his element. He is a falcon unhooded and off the glove. He is pure body. When he sees the man he killed running up the staircase towards them it does not seem like devilry, only another situation to be dealt with. But it is not the man he killed because there are two more men coming up the staircase behind him and they all possess the same black beard, the same shoulders, identical monsters from the same litter. Marlenus shouts, 'Out of the way,' because he and Helicanus have lifted a heavy wooden bench and are running towards the mouth of the staircase. Pericles steps to one side as Helicanus and Marlenus hoist the bench down the staircase where it strikes the legs of the bearded men, sending them tumbling backwards as silently and uncomplainingly as Pericles' attacker in the bedchamber.

Pericles, Helicanus and Marlenus run down the staircase, vault the bench now broken-backed and wedged between the walls, then slash hard at the backs of the knees of the fallen men to cut their tendons before running into the courtyard. The smell of dust and fox urine, the little music of fountains. A wolf howls miles off. The rear wall is high but they clamber over it, feet in cupped hands, Pericles and Marlenus leaning down to haul Helicanus up behind them. More bearded pursuers materialise between the trees, black tunics, swords, greaves, chains. But the three men are flying down cobbled alleys now, the way one flies when running through a silent city at night, speeded by the rake of the streets as the city tilts towards the ocean. But their pursuers have climbed the wall, too, or perhaps these are different men who appear at the junction ahead so that Pericles, Helicanus and Marlenus must skid to a halt, run back uphill and turn and turn again to avoid a similar meeting at the next junction. The sky widens as they cross the market square and briefly they see the black headland and the wave-glitter and the hulk of the *Porpoise* sitting on a road of moonshine. Then they are swallowed by alleys once more until five more steep streets spill them onto the waterside. They turn left to the quay at whose far end the gig will hopefully be tied up so that they can jump in, cut the painter and push off. But as they run out onto the stone arm that curves around the harbour they see four more men waiting at the far end. One of them is Kallios. Pericles knows it instantly. Bald head, no beard, a little shorter, a little less muscular but no less forbidding for that. Pericles shouts, 'Swim.' Most sailors refuse to learn so as not to prolong a grisly death when swept overboard, but Pericles spent his childhood in and out of rivers and the sea. The bearded men will doubtless be wearing armour which they will have to unbuckle if they are to enter the water. He picks up speed, Helicanus on one side, Marlenus on the other. He feels more alive than he has done for a long time. He could whoop for joy had he breath to spare.

They run towards the four men then veer right at the last moment, reaching the very end of the quay before dropping their weapons and springing from the stone lip, arms stretched out to meet the freezing smash of the water, then down into darkness, eyes closed, swimming hard under the surface for as long as possible before the need for air forces them upwards, breaking the surface, arms churning. Pericles turns just in time to see a flash on the polished point of a thrown spear which vanishes into the water only a hand's breadth from his shoulder. A second falls short. He counts the silhouettes on the quay. Still four. None of them have given chase as yet. He turns and swims again. The *Porpoise* is a good deal further out than she appeared, the water colder than he expected and he cannot swim as well as he had thought. He has never needed to cross a stretch of water this wide, and fear and determination can only compensate so much for a lack of training. Already he is slowing. It dawns on him that he may not be able to make it. Did Kallios know this? Is he letting nature complete the task on his behalf? They are only halfway. Helicanus, too, is struggling, his thrashing arms losing energy like a spun top before it falls. Pericles cannot see Marlenus. He turns onto his back. He needs to rest. He can float if he keeps his arms moving. But the cold is entering his bones. He cannot move his arms. He is starting to sink.

Helicanus says, 'Look!'

Pericles turns his head. He sees the hoisted foresail of the *Porpoise* first and then the topsail rising. His first thought is that the crew have decided to leave without them. Then he sees the swaying lantern and pinpoints the source of the yells across the water. The second gig is rowing towards them. He turns onto his back again. Orion stands overhead, cold and vast and uninterested. All he has to do is to keep his head out of the water. One simple task. The rhythmic chop of the oars becomes the swing of a rope tied to an oak tree, then the rocking of a cradle. Then darkness takes him.

❧

Southwark Cathedral, the present day. It is early morning, the stillness before the first visitor, only the angled sunlight and the night's dust lifted by the air the warden has disturbed by his first circuit of the building. On the northern side of the nave a life-size stone Shakespeare reclines in a niche, head on hand, like a dreaming teenager in a spring meadow, an effect enhanced by the real petals worshippers have placed at his feet, the sprigs of herb they have placed in his hand and the wreath of roses they have placed around his head. He is everywhere the colour of dirty alabaster except for his elbow, the hand which holds the flowers and his raised knee, which have been rubbed to a creamy paleness by a thousand caresses. Facing him across the nave is the tomb of John Gower, already long dead when Shakespeare was born. A brightly painted wooden effigy of the senior poet lies inside an open-fronted wooden marquee in the Perpendicular Gothic style – panels in red and gold and racing green, three high, pointed arches. His hands are pressed together in prayer and his head rests on a very uncomfortable pillow consisting of his three major works – *Vox Clamantis, Speculum Meditantis* and *Confessio Amantis – The Lover's Confession.*

No one touches Gower. No one rubs his elbows bare. He is merely chipped by the occasional small accident and faded by centuries of sunlight and smoke. There would have been a time, however, when Shakespeare himself would have stood right here. The Globe was a stroll away. This was his parish church for a period and twenty shillings were paid to St Saviour's – as it then was – for the burial of his brother Edmund *with a forenoone knell of the great bell.*

Perhaps Shakespeare reached out and placed his hand on the forehead of his celebrated predecessor, perhaps his eye ran down the spine of those three volumes and perhaps *Confessio Amantis* opened in his mind's eye as he recalled the old story of Appolinus of Tyre at the beginning of Book 8.

... grete Antiochus,
Of whom that Antioche tok
His ferste name, as seith the bok,
Was coupled to a noble queene,
And hadde a dowhter hem betwene:

Great Antiochus,
from whom Antioch took
its first name, as the book says,
Was married to a noble queen,
And between them they had a daughter.

The queen dies and Antiochus, who has great wealth, unchecked power and no conscience, lusts after his own daughter and rapes her. Having done this he can neither risk giving her away in marriage nor risk the suspicion which will be aroused if he refuses to give her away, so he issues a proclamation stating that any young man wanting her hand must either solve a riddle or lose his life. But the riddle is more than a simple puzzle. It is Antiochus' confession hidden in plain sight. Many suitors have failed to solve it and met the promised grisly end before Prince Appolinus arrives, drawn by rumours of the princess's beauty. When he hears the riddle he understands immediately.

It toucheth al the privete
Betwen thin oghne child and thee,

It touches on all the private matters
Between your own child and you.

This is not a scenario for which Antiochus has planned. Clearly, Appolinus must die, otherwise he will broadcast Antiochus' infamy to the world. But

Antiochus cannot take his life immediately or the world will ask some very difficult questions. So he gives the young suitor thirty days in which to reconsider his answer. Appolinus heads to his ship, weighs anchor and sails home to Tyre. Antiochus sends an assassin in his wake. The prince escapes, of course, and his adventures begin. He relieves a famine-struck city, he is shipwrecked, he marries a princess. She gives birth to a daughter during a storm at sea. The mother, presumed dead, is thrown overboard in a sealed casket ... But of Antiochus' abused daughter we hear nothing more, except that she and her father are later killed by lightning in an act of divine vengeance because they share blame for the crime of incest.

Was it standing here that Shakespeare decided to borrow the story and turn Appolinus into Pericles? Or perhaps it wasn't Shakespeare. Because the play was not his work alone. The first nine scenes were almost certainly written by George Wilkins, victualler, pimp, minor criminal, abuser of women and author of one other play, *The Miseries of Enforced Marriage*. Perhaps it was Wilkins who found inspiration standing on this spot with his hand resting on Gower's forehead, his eyes running down those spines. Perhaps it was Wilkins who gave the abused princess no name and two empty lines welcoming Pericles. Perhaps it was Wilkins who called her father's crime 'incest' and insisted that she was equally to blame.

> *Bad child, worse father.*

Perhaps it was Wilkins who has Pericles say of this woman whom he wanted to marry only moments previously and of whose suffering he has just learnt.

> *Fair glass of light, I loved you, and could still,*
> *Were not this glorious casket stored with ill ...*
> *I care not for you.*

The same Wilkins who now lies asleep in the main bedroom of the inn-cum-brothel he runs on the corner of Cow Cross Street and Turnmill Street in Clerkenwell. In five minutes he will be dead, for George is a drinker of much unwatered ale, a lover of bacon and sweetmeats and the descendant of a long chain of men killed by their own weak hearts. Over time, deposits of cholesterol have built up on the walls of all the major arteries throughout George's body and hardened into calcified lumps, many of which are inflamed and ulcerated. Increasingly in the last two years he has been visited with bouts of crippling chest pain. He has suffered a small stroke, as a result of which his left hand is little more than a claw. It hurts when he walks. On several occasions he has blacked out and collapsed. He has great difficulty remembering the names of certain objects – keys, buckets, shoes …

The largest of these calcified lumps has recently ruptured and formed a thick clot of gluey, coagulated blood. The pulsing passage of thinner blood has gradually loosened it from the plaque which secures it to the arterial wall. But now it rips away and is swept by that red tide into the chamber of the aorta where it jams hard in the neck of the right coronary artery. Half the muscles of George's heart are now starved of oxygen.

At this point George is dreaming. Milder men might be visited at night by images of the debauchery they are forbidden in their daily life and for which some dark part of them secretly yearns, but there is no bestial act George has been unable to perform or have performed upon him by women and girls who need his money or his protection from beadles and bailiffs. George dreams instead of the innocence and sobriety he has lost for ever. He sits on a quiet bend of the Wye just upstream of Bredwardine where he was brought up by his maternal aunt before being apprenticed to a London silversmith. He is seven years old, it is Sunday and he and his older brothers have been given two hours for roaming before sundown.

Richard and Robert are emptying and resetting their rabbit traps but George needs this brief solace before the joshing and the sparring recommence.

It is spring and the river is in spate. Midstream, an egret has landed on a rock. It is startlingly white. It turns towards him and George cannot shake the suspicion that the bird is trying to deliver a message of some kind. But there is a great weight on his sternum and suddenly he is back in the bedchamber with two bracelets of fire travelling down his arm as if someone were peeling the skin from shoulder to wrist.

Large parts of George's heart are now damaged irreversibly. Only one side of the organ is beating. There is no movement of blood and no working pressure in two of the four chambers. The wall between the chambers is thin and ballooning and becoming weaker with each surge of pressure on the functioning side until, at last, the flesh tears and there are no longer four chambers, only one wrecked vessel of twitching flesh in which the blood pools and squelches.

The year is 1618. George is a lucky man. There are many ways to die unpleasantly in Jacobean London. His uncle was consumed by a carbuncle which began as a boil on the side of his head and grew so large that his own head seemed like the monster's outgrowth. George's brother spent two years losing a long battle against a belly wound received from a fur-clad savage in the bogs of Antrim. George himself was in the crowd outside St Paul's, eating a cup of mussels and drinking a bottle of ale, when the conspirators Grant, Bates, Wintour and Digby were strung up, cut down, castrated in front of the cheering crowd and forced to watch their disembowelled guts slither onto the splintery planking before they died.

George, on the contrary, feels unexpectedly peaceful. The pain has lessened. He is falling down a great well, looking up at a circle of daylight which grows ever brighter as it shrinks inside a growing black corona.

Then it occurs to him to wonder where this long descent will end. The irrefutable answer is that he is going to hell. He has spent his life ignoring this possibility, rehearsing sometimes, in his cups, radical ideas about God being a fiction born of childish fears, and heaven and hell merely the carrot and stick to cajole those donkeys the true believers. But he has known all along, in his bones, that he is deceiving himself, that in truth he is a lost traveller singing a ribald song to cheer himself as night comes down. He will burn and the flames will neither consume nor reduce him and the pain will be unending and he will envy his monstrous uncle who said his prayers and now sits at the right-hand side of God. George wishes he could have realised this truth a little earlier. The pain in his chest has returned. He is very, very scared.

The light becomes a sixpence. The light becomes a pea. The light becomes a grain of rice. The light becomes a single star. The light vanishes. He hits the bottom of the well. He opens his eyes. To his surprise he is not floating in a pond of fire being forked hard by snarling demons. He is back in his own room, lying on his own bed. A man is silhouetted by the harsh morning light that glares through the hexagonal panes of the casement behind him.

'Good morning, George,' says the silhouette. 'This will doubtless come as something of a surprise.'

❧

Angelica doesn't speak for three days, for a week, for two weeks. The staff accept the situation, as they are paid to accept all situations. There is, in any case, little she needs to tell them, and she in turn always listens graciously to what they need to tell her. They are, perhaps, a little flattered by this minimal attention which is withheld from her father. Seeing how it goads him, some of them quietly cheer her on. Her three tutors adjust rapidly. She is attentive, writes fluently and prepares work in advance which they mark in her presence, giving feedback as they go.

She draws too, something she hasn't done for a long time, recreating the pictures she drew as a child – castles, palaces, little villages – mesmerised as she was back then by the ease with which you can fly over imaginary hills created with just a few strokes of pencil. She remembers the story of Wu Daozi who was imprisoned by one of the Tang emperors and ordered to paint a vast mural for the Imperial Palace – mountains, waterfalls, caves ... When he had finished the work he stepped inside one of his own painted caves and vanished.

Philippe considers giving her a pad and asking her to write a message of some kind but he is nervous about what that message might be. Now that she is not talking he is more scared than ever about what she might say. He stops coming to her room at night. In truth he is aroused by the thought of making love to Angelica while she is utterly unresponsive, but in this fantasy his arousal and his fury become tangled and he pictures himself doing something to which even he must give the name *rape*, and he is both shocked and ashamed that he could imagine stooping to such a thing.

At the end of that first silent fortnight he enters the main living room to find her curled in an armchair reading by the fire. The staff have gone home. He tells her to stop playing this pointless game. He is shouting. He tells her that she is ungrateful, that he has done more for her than she can possibly imagine. He walks to the window and rests his forehead against the cold glass.

'If you are unhappy then you need to tell me why, and we can make things better.'

She turns a page.

'Have I ever denied you anything?' He walks over and squats in front of her. 'Have I?'

She carries on reading. He slaps her hard across the face. The book falls to the floor. She holds her eyes closed for a few seconds, her head pushed to one side by the force of the blow. She lifts her head slowly upright, reaches over the arm of the chair to retrieve her book, refinds her page and continues reading. He can see, already, the mark of his hand reddening on her cheek. He goes to his study and sits and weeps.

The welt is visible on Angelica's cheek when she comes down for breakfast the following morning, so clear that he can make out the shape of individual fingers. Dottie says nothing. Philippe cancels the tutors for a week, saying that Angelica is unwell. When her father is not in the room, Dottie asks Angelica what happened. Angelica reaches across the table and holds Dottie's hand, as if it is the housekeeper who needs comforting. It is the only time they have touched one another. Dottie asks if she should tell someone. Angelica squeezes her hand and lets go. Dottie feels uneasy about remaining in the house but knows that she would feel even more uneasy abandoning Angelica. She will be the last housekeeper. She will stay till the end.

Angelica is at ease in a way that she has never been before. She is surprised to discover how strong it is, this simplest of weapons, one that has been lying unused within her reach all this time. She takes up less space than she once did, but she is not reduced. She has been compacted. She was a branch, now she is a blade. She can cut through anything. She cannot be broken.

After eight weeks she stops eating.

You sink and rise three times before Neptune drags you down, or so they say. They see Pericles vanish and reappear twice, so they have only moments to spare. They put on a final surge of speed then haul him up over the side by his armpits. His eyes are closed, he cannot speak and he is shaking uncontrollably. They lay him face down so that his lungs drain. They haul Helicanus on board. 'Marlenus,' he says, 'Marlenus,' but can add nothing further. Little Mobbs is convinced that he saw three men dive from the quay and the boy has the eyes of an owl. They raise the lamp and scan the dark water but they can see nothing. What they *can* see is a small boat rowing towards them, so they turn about and haul hard because the counsellor's story of the devilish pursuers has taken firm hold among the crew and they need no convincing that these are the same men.

Once the gig is alongside the *Porpoise*, Pericles and Helicanus are winched aboard with much speed and little dignity like sacks of millet. The gig is roped and left to trail astern, there being more important tasks on hand. They turn seawards and fire four rounds of grapeshot from the demi-falcon gun, less in the hope of hitting so small a target than as a statement of intent. Mobbs climbs to the foretop with the glass. His opinion is that the craft following them is nothing more than a borrowed fishing boat, four oars at most and no sail, but the first mate prefers to err on the side of caution and they sail steadily through the remainder of the night until dawn rises on an empty sea.

Helicanus is sufficiently recovered by the following morning to tell the crew of Antonio's death. In turn he is told of the loss of Marlenus and the prince's fragile grip on life. Helicanus is not a sentimental man – sentimental captains do not last long – but the loss of Marlenus is a blow. He knows stories from Marlenus' childhood that no one else knows – how his father fell and struck his head and no longer recognised his children, the cousin who lived as a woman. He will treat the hurt like a broken bone. He will hold it firm with a splint and he will adjust his behaviour so that it no longer has to bear any weight. He has, in any case, more weighty problems to ponder. He must assume that they are still being pursued and that the pursuit will continue even if the prince dies. He drinks sugared ale and sits in the sun on the quarterdeck, sheepskin-wrapped, considering these things, hidden from the men who do not need to see their captain so distressed.

Pericles, shattered and feverish, rides the long border between life and death haunted by images visible through the diaphanous curtain which separates the two worlds. A woman throws a bucket of herring and cold water over a sleeping boy. A dwarf spins straw into gold. A big blue box stands on a beach below pine trees. A young woman who was beautiful once lies emaciated in a bed, smooth, transparent ropes coming out of her body so that she seems like a spider weaving the world around her.

The truth is that it would be easier to step through that curtain than make the long journey back towards the light. Marlenus could not swim. Pericles knew this but in his excitement he had forgotten. He told a man to die in order that he and Helicanus could escape. He retains a single clear image of Marlenus airborne beside him, black against the night's deep blue, not hesitating for a moment. Then the freezing dark of underwater. Was he run through by a spear hurled from the quay so that he died quickly? Or did he panic, paddling desperately like a dog, fighting to keep his head above water, his strength ebbing till he sucked down that fatal draught? Pericles has never felt genuine regret before, always moved too fast, never forged those bonds that can be broken only with lasting damage. He feels it now for the first time, that impotent desire to turn back time, forced to bear the one burden which cannot be put down because it is carried in the heart. There is a window in the cabin. There is sunshine on the far side of those little squares of thick, bubbled glass, but there is ice in his chest, under his skin, in his bones.

Weak pea-and-mutton broth is spooned into his mouth.

He wants to sleep for a long time. He wants to let go of life completely. But those demons. Sword-oil and onion-sweat, identical as chess pieces or scorpions. If he steps through that curtain will they follow him? Time passes. Hours, days, weeks? He is not sure. His pet monkey Kremnobates squats at his side, shucking pistachios, the bell on his collar tinkling as he casts the shells into the water, tiny wooden boats which capsize almost immediately and are swept away.

It is fear that wakes him, as it has woken him on so many occasions, forcing him to rise and dress before he knows the reason. He opens his eyes and sits up. The boat is pitching, the roof lantern swinging wildly. It is dark outside. A great wave smacks the glass of the cabin, shattering two panes. Stationed in the armchair is Hatem, whose knowledge of sheep, goats and cattle has made him ship's doctor in the absence of anyone more qualified. Pericles swings his legs over the side of the bed, tries to stand and staggers sideways.

'Ho there!' Hatem catches him. 'You have to rest.'

'No.' Pericles stands again. 'Help me.'

Is it his own weakness or the movement of the ship making this so difficult? He gets into his breeches and boots. They step outside into the main stairwell. Abraham is at the whipstaff. 'Rocks at half a league. Landward gale and the mizzen down.' He is too preoccupied to be surprised by the prince's sudden recovery.

'Helicanus?'

Abraham nods upwards.

'You are not strong,' Hatem insists. 'You will be safer down here.'

Ignoring this advice will save his life. He grabs the rails on either side of the main staircase and hoists himself upwards step by careful step, slides back the hatch and rises into the howling storm. Foam smashes over the deck, obscuring the scene. Two lanterns still burn somehow. Helicanus is shouting orders to the men who are trying to bring down the sails to save the mainmast. Their job is surely impossible in this weather and even if they succeed they may be too late because Pericles can see the black silhouette of cliffs and a faint star-blue ribbon of waves breaking and booming. The boat lurches to starboard. Twenty-five, thirty degrees. He grips the rail around the great skylight so as not to be swept away. One of the men who has failed to do something similar slides across the wet deck and vanishes into the dark. There is a high squealing creak Pericles doesn't recognise, audible above even the roar of the storm. In his confused state he wonders whether it is some sea creature intent on swallowing the ship. The sound is wood being bent and twisted to breaking point. The creak becomes a long ripping crack, the ship lurches another five degrees and the mainmast finally snaps at the foot. The entire ship judders and Pericles can see the white of the broken wood, a starburst of splinters, rope-tangled, jabbing the air like a great angry finger.

Now that the wind has less purchase the hull should right itself but this does not happen. The keel must be held fast on sand or rocks. Pericles looks up and is convinced, despite the darkness and the distance, that he can see the figure of a man standing on top of the cliffs. The man is in charge of this whole drama, playing with the boat like a toy. Pericles is convinced that the man is Marlenus, but does not understand why Marlenus would do such a thing. A great wave breaks over the higher, port side of the ship and knocks Pericles' legs from under him. His falling weight comes near to tearing his weak fingers from the rail. He regains his footing and works his way round to the far side of the skylight. The boat lurches yet again to starboard. One man is hanging from an arm of the capstan. Three others skate down the slick deck into the tangle of netting along the starboard side. He can hear Mobbs screaming somewhere.

The deck is near vertical now, a wooden cliff above his head to match the rocky cliffs where the whole vessel will soon be smashed to pieces. He is lying on the port flank of the skylight. One of the gigs comes loose and breaks apart as it strikes its twin on the opposite side. He feels a series of juddering booms which must be the port guns rolling and hitting the starboard side of the vessel. The lanterns are out now. He can no longer see Helicanus. He can no longer see anyone. If the ship capsizes completely he will find himself trapped under the hull. If he jumps he will find himself in a churned mess of canvas and knotted line. He remembers why he was in bed. He nearly drowned in the still water of a harbour. Marlenus was unable to swim, and now he is taking his revenge. Below deck the cabins will be filling with water, the trapped men drowning one by one. If these are his final moments in the world then he will never do penance or receive forgiveness.

He must let go and jump, not cower and be taken, make another move in the game, keep fighting. But it is too late to make that decision for the freezing water rises suddenly and rips him from his little perch. He is under the waves now, with no sense of up or down, no sense of where the ship is or where the land is. He does not know in which direction to swim. He must trust the buoyancy of his own body to surface.

He is rising and then he is no longer rising. There is a rough membrane over his head, holding him down. Canvas. He is under a sail. His luck has run out. He hopes that there is another world.

Sun sparkles on an earring. 'Will?' George sits up and shields his eyes from the glare. 'Is this a commission? Or are you shopping for a fuck?' He coughs to loosen the phlegm in his throat and hawks it into the chamber pot. 'It's a little early in the day for such sport, though I'm sure we could wake one of the little baggages and sluice her down.'

'Gather yourself,' says Will, for it is indeed him, 'and think a little harder.'

George thinks a little harder. 'You are dead.' He rubs his face. 'You *were* dead.'

'Two years. I am a little offended that you could forget so easily.'

'I assume the reports we heard were mistaken.' George's mind is all thorns and shadows.

'The reports were true. Typhoid in Stratford after escaping so much contagion here.'

There is something in George's chest which is not pain as such, but the absence that follows pain, like the ringing silence in a street after a pistol has been fired. He had a bad dream, a very bad dream. 'Are you some kind of …?'

'Finding the word for what I am seems a bootless exercise at this point,' says Will. 'This is not a meeting you will be called upon to describe to your friends over supper.'

'Are you still angry about *Pericles*?' A queasy spiritual vertigo is taking hold of George and a solid, simple reason for Will's presence would be very welcome. 'I had debts. The playhouses were closed. The company was not, I am convinced, planning to publish the play itself. I turned it into a novel. It was not theft. As such.'

Will shrugs. 'It was a long time ago and it was a poor book which sold in small numbers. Your subsequent failure to write anything new seems punishment enough. Besides, none of this is of much consequence now.'

George is nervous. 'So your reason for being here is …?'

'Come. I have something to show you.'

George is unwilling to move nearer to a man who claims to be dead.

'I really do quite literally have all the time in the world,' says Will.

George waits for a good minute before getting reluctantly to his feet. His legs ache, his head aches. He takes three stiff steps across the room in the direction of his unwelcome guest. Will looks surprisingly healthy – ruddy cheeks, a smoother forehead. Is it Will or perhaps an actor playing Will? George has angered enough people to justify revenge of many colours, but few of them would rise to anything more sophisticated than violence. The likeness is certainly compelling.

'Turn around.'

'I am nervous of presenting my back to anyone with a grudge.'

Wearily, Will raises the wings of his cloak to demonstrate that he is carrying neither a sword nor a knife. George turns and gasps audibly when he sees a man lying face down on the bed. He is fat and old and, from what George can see of the face crushed against the dirty pillow, very ugly indeed. Worse, the man has soiled his breeches. Was it possible that he and this man were jointly carousing last night and fell asleep on the same bed? His memory is unclear. 'Who in God's name is that?'

'If you really need confirmation,' says Will, 'examine the two moles beside the right ear.'

'No.'

'Take a look.'

George steps a little nearer to the bed. The world is wheeling, the way it might wheel if he were forced to climb a church spire. The man's chest does not move. His skin is the pale blue of the most costly china. Is George Wilkins really that ugly? Is *he* really that ugly? *Was* he really that ugly? The smell is catastrophically bad. If this is hell then hell is less painful but more disturbing than he had expected. He turns to his visitor. 'What happens now?'

Will smiles the faintest of smiles as if he knows precisely what is going to happen now, as if he has written the little drama himself. There are heavy steps on the creaking stairs and the chamber door is pushed open by a blowsy woman of middle age with a tinderbox and a basket of kindling. It is Mrs Brokehill the housekeeper.

She looks at the body, shakes her head and quietly mutters the word, 'Pig,' before turning to the grate. She glances briefly at Wilkins and Shakespeare and nods. 'Gentlemen.' She seems both to see and not see them. It troubles George more than the insult. She opens the little tin, takes out her equipment and summons a flame in her cupped hands. Then she becomes still. Is it the smell, or does her half-woken morning-mind finally put the evidence together? She stands, rotating slowly as she does so, then extinguishes the flame with her own scream.

A serving girl runs into the room. Two bleary-eyed prostitutes wander in after her. 'The master shat himself,' says one of them, wrinkling her nose and waving her hand in front of her face. Mrs Brokehill leans against the windowsill recovering her composure. A customer, naked from the waist down, steps through the doorway, retches and beats an immediate retreat. The second prostitute says, 'Christ's fucking thumbs,' and a lad enters, no more than nine or ten years old.

George feels a surge of sadness for the old man lying on the bed. It is the first genuine feeling he has had for another human being in his adult life, which is doubtless an explanation for many things.

The gathered onlookers seem unsure what to do next, as if they have found themselves in the presence of an obscure dignitary. Mrs Brokehill says, 'I do believe he is dead,' though she is clearly wary.

There are so many things George wants to say – *Be kind to him ... Help me ... I'm sorry ... What is happening ...?* He opens his mouth to speak but what comes out is the cry of a cornered animal. Mrs Brokehill turns briefly in his direction, as if she has heard a beam creak or a bird tapping at the window. A young lad steps forward, taking a bent silver spoon from his jerkin pocket, doubtless purloined from a sleeping customer. Tentatively, he uses it to prod the arm of the recumbent man. The recumbent man does not react. Emboldened, the boy pokes the man's head, then does it again, harder.

'Dead,' says Mrs Brokehill.

'Dead,' they repeat after her, like witches catechising.

The boy turns the spoon round and idly pushes the handle into the man's eye. George squeals because it hurts and because it doesn't hurt. Mrs Brokehill says, 'Stephen, for the love of God ...' but someone else is laughing and a second person is cheering and the entire household seems to have arrived in the room. Will stands and puts his hand on George's shoulder. 'Now is, I think, a good time for us to leave.'

They move through the dense little crowd much as they would move through the crowd at a bear-baiting, people stepping aside but keeping their attention fixed rigidly on the entertainment. George and Will leave the room as one of the women climbs onto the bed, squats over him and urinates voluminously onto his head to general approval.

Downstairs in the parlour George slips his feet into his boots and the two men step into the daylight on Cow Cross Street. 'Follow me,' says Will and begins walking towards Cripplegate.

THE FAMILY

The priest places the tip of the blade against the bull's neck, on a patch of skin that pulses to the heart's rhythm like a struck drum. The opium in that morning's grain has made the animal drowsy and compliant. His horns have then been decorated with gold leaf, which will be discreetly peeled away for re-use before he is butchered and burnt. Three eagles turn in overlapping spirals high up against the unblemished blue as scents of orange and pine drift from the royal gardens. Distant buildings ripple in the heat like flags. The priest offers prayers to Jupiter, to Pallas Athene, to Demeter their civic deity. A cough is stifled among the gathered crowd. The rub of sandals on dust.

The priest thrusts the knife in then pulls it swiftly down to sever both the artery and the windpipe. There is a loud outbreath from the crowd, part awe, part excitement, part relief. The priest steps backwards as the glossy tongue of blood spews out. The first attendant leans in to fill a silver bowl, his free hand holding back his white robe, though not quite far enough to avoid it being splashed at the hem. The animal sinks to its knees. It can no longer bellow. Instead the air from its lungs hisses and bubbles through the wound. Blood splashes and steams and runs along the cracks between the paving slabs. The butcher steps forward, a wiry little man wearing a leather apron and a belt of knives. He opens the belly with a deft swipe. The entrails slip out, the heart still beating, the intestines clenching and releasing. He snips the vessels leading into the heart then slices the gristle that locks the organ in place. He lays it on the wooden platter held by his oldest apprentice, then cuts out the liver and a single kidney. The priest carries the offerings away, while the butcher and his apprentices hack the body apart and load it onto a nearby cart so that it can be wheeled to the royal kitchens. At the altar the offerings are burnt and wine is poured onto them. Old women with brushes and rags and pails of water clean the soiled stone in the public square.

Nearby, in the marketplace a sandy ring is roped off, checked for sharp stones then raked flat. A rowdy crowd is gathering as the royal family take their seats in the block of slanted shadow under an awning of striped linen – Simonides of Pentapolis and his queen Lucina, their three sons and their sons' wives. Their daughter, Chloë, arrives last as always, a symptom of the obstreperousness that means she remains unmarried, having refused the suitors who didn't refuse her when she ventured an opinion. Simonides, however, is indulgent. His sons have cemented the necessary alliances, and his daughter's wilfulness is surely his fault to some extent, having allowed her to read books and ride horses. Most of the suitors were, in any case, ridiculous young men who would have made tiresome sons-in-law.

She sits down next to Demetrius. She looks like no one in her family. She has thick blonde hair and blue, blue eyes which have made her the subject of intrigue and fascination throughout the entire region. The only flaw – if it is a flaw – is the tiny half-moon scar on her cheek, courtesy of a rook that flew in through her bedroom window when she was ten years old.

'You have no respect,' says her brother, who is not indulgent and who wishes he himself had been used to cement a different alliance.

'You are an obsequious spaniel.'

'And you are a spoilt lapdog.'

'I know,' says Chloë, stroking her arm as if it were covered in the very softest fur, because agreement can irk as much as dissent and what are brothers for but goading? He looks skywards and shakes his head as if accepting the commiserations of gods who find the girl equally exasperating.

The Saxon and the Ethiopian are fighting first. Princes both, they stare at one another from either side of the ring, unblinking, intractable. Attendants tighten the fighters' loincloths and rub oil into their limbs and torsos to deny their opponent an easy hold.

'Well, this should be edifying,' says Chloë, and, for once, her brother manages not to rise to the bait.

The Saxon has white skin, tangled blonde hair and a red beard. His freckle-dusted shoulders are broad as a yoke. He is a bear who has wandered out of the forest and into a human village. The Ethiopian's head is shaved and pearled with sweat. The whites of his eyes are almost blue. The muscles in his back move under the skin like the muscles in the flank of a good horse. He is night made flesh. The two men sink their meaty hands into bags of chalk then clap them together, turning the air to smoke.

The praefectus stands in the centre of the ring and shrinks in size as the beckoned combatants approach. They could tear him in half if they chose to. He makes them lean in close so that he can repeat the simple rules in words they neither hear nor understand, for in their hearts and heads nothing exists but the coming fight. The Ethiopian is smaller by a hand and a half, and he carries no spare weight. The crowd is rooting for him, their near-neighbour against this pale ogre from the map's uppermost margin. The Ethiopian bounces lightly from foot to foot, the noise of the crowd responding to his movement as if he were gently strumming an instrument of human lungs. The Saxon shakes his head like a fly-pestered ox and spits a great gobbet of phlegm onto the ground beside the Ethiopian's leg.

The praefectus steps back and everyone expects the men to fall upon one another, but instead they begin to turn, locked together only by a bronze-hard mutual stare, feet spread wide, weight low, searching for that single heartbeat of inattention when their opponent's body is off-balance.

There is a graveyard between the cliffs and the lemon groves which receives at least one more body every year, the weather too hot to ship them home unputrified. Broken necks, bleeding in the brain, open wounds become septic. There will be another two residents by the end of tomorrow. Chloë yawns operatically. Demetrius glares at her. She smiles back sweetly.

The crowd are becoming impatient. 'Grapple …! Come on …!' Simonides moves to the edge of his seat. Lucina maintains the perfect smile of the inwardly appalled diplomat.

Is it the cry of a child, the passage of a bird across the empty sky? The Ethiopian's eyes are briefly elsewhere. The Saxon surges forward. His darker opponent swiftly copies him. There is a wet, juddering slap as sweating black flesh smacks into sweating white flesh. The crowd erupt. Shoulders and necks are now locked into one another, the two men making a great human crab. The grunt of breath, hands slapping and grabbing. The Saxon twists and yanks, trying to flip the smaller man sideways, but the Ethiopian is quicker, his legs always under him, that untippable triangle, swift feet kicking up sand as he dances. 'Bring him down …!' Suddenly – unbelievably – the Ethiopian falls. But while the two bodies are airborne everyone realises that this is not a fall. He has let the Saxon throw him and is twisting lynx-like so that the Saxon's shoulder meets the ground first. The crowd hear the deep bull-thump of it, then feel it in the soles of their feet, then see it ripple upwards through the fighter's flesh. Grounded now, he keeps his arms tight round the torso of the darker man but the Ethiopian has a hand free and the Saxon has no way of defending his face.

Simonides leans a little further forward, decorum forbidding him an audible cheer. Chloë examines her fingernails. Lucina is looking at the fighters but is seeing the fountain at the heart of the spiral privet maze in the higher garden. It is a skill she learnt early and has relied on ever since.

The crowd are eager for cruelty but gouging of the eyes is not permitted, so the Ethiopian pushes the man's face backwards until his nose collapses under the palm of his hand. The blood is thrilling against his white skin. The crowd roar with pleasure. The Saxon yells in pain, his grip loosening momentarily, so that the Ethiopian can break the imprisoning hoop of his opponent's muscular arms and get to his feet. The crowd whoop. It remains only for the Ethiopian to administer the *coup de grâce*. He drops heavily, knees first, onto the Saxon's shoulders, pinning him down. 'One ...!' shout the crowd. 'Two ...! Three ...!' The Ethiopian rolls away and lies on his back, staring up into the searing blue, the joyous yell washing over him. His oiled skin is coated in sand. He is the colour of ground black pepper.

Attendants help the Saxon up and walk him stiffly away, a bloodied bear. It is possible to see already the sunburnt skin which will redden through the evening and blister overnight. The Ethiopian rolls over and climbs to his feet. Approaching Simonides he goes down on one knee. The king commends his prowess, wishes him luck against his opponent in the next round and looks forward to seeing him at the evening's feast. The Ethiopian throws the quickest of glances sideways at the king's daughter and it is enough to confirm that she is both startlingly beautiful and looking doggedly elsewhere.

A Libyan fights a Cretan. An Irishman fights a Spaniard. An important message is garbled in translation and the Scythian fighting Demetrius' older brother, Kimon, breaks Kimon's forearm, unaware that he is the king's son. Only an intervention by Simonides himself prevents an outbreak of more general violence.

Chloë struggles to feel sympathetic. It is precisely the kind of thing which is going to happen sooner or later if you fight muscular Scythians, and she has never much liked her brother. Mostly she is bored. In her cheeriest sing-song voice she tells her father that she wants to leave because she is not feeling well. Demetrius upbraids her. What will people think if they see their father's authority publicly undermined? 'They will think me liberal and fond,' says Simonides, who likes to see Chloë enjoying freedoms he is himself denied. He turns to his daughter. 'Go. Go before the next fight starts.'

But Chloë does not go because her eye falls on a wrestler being oiled for that next fight. Simultaneously the wrestler's eye falls on her. They should look away but neither of them does. He is a young man, twenty years old perhaps, her own age or thereabouts, but poor, judging by the attendants borrowed from the royal household. He is doubtless one of the underdogs her father lets compete to demonstrate his generosity and for the occasional entertainment of seeing foreign potentates badly hurt by men who keep pigs or make barrels for a living. The moment stretches. The fighter looks away only when his borrowed trainer grasps his chin, turns his head, looks into his eyes and says stern words which Chloë cannot hear.

Puzzled by her stalled departure, Demetrius follows her line of sight and, dim as he is, understands immediately. He would mock her were he less appalled at the implications. He is comfortable with the prospect of his sister marrying a man but the idea that she has sexual feelings makes him queasy and the fact that she is having them right now about a destitute foreigner only magnifies that queasiness. He says, snappily, 'Will you either leave or sit down?' She sits down and for once makes no spiky rejoinder. She is only vaguely aware of her brother. The fighter seems too handsome to be poor, though she has seen a good number of kings who look like donkeys. He has a swagger about him, and something self-mocking about the swagger, as if he is engaged in a hugely enjoyable game. She has the strangest sense that she knows him, though that is surely not possible.

The Moroccan against whom he is pitched has a thick black ponytail, no visible neck and angry little eyes. She is scared for the man she is thinking of already as *my wrestler*. Her father turns. 'You stayed.' She simply nods, aware that she might give herself away if she speaks.

The praefectus draws the men together in the centre of the circle. The crowd want the stranger with no retinue to win. The peace treaty with Morocco is pragmatic rather than fraternal and relations are tetchy. The crowd know that they will likely be disappointed. Underdogs rarely win against men with cooks and trainers. Many are buried on the hill, which is considered a high honour, if not by the families who previously depended upon their labour.

The praefectus steps backwards and the Moroccan lunges, but to everyone's surprise the stranger skips deftly sideways so that the Moroccan stumbles into empty air and must use both hands to stop himself landing face first in the sand. The Moroccan turns and stares at the stranger, cursing in gutter Arabic. His eyes are nails hammered into the wall of his face. He lunges and again the stranger dodges nimbly out of his way. It happens a third time and the crowd begin a slow hand clap. The stranger's tactics are starting to look cowardly. They like underdogs but they like violence more, and injury and a death if at all possible. The Moroccan is shaking with rage. He walks towards the stranger. There is open jeering now. More of this and the crowd will take matters into their own hands – not now, not in front of the king perhaps, but later when the stranger tries to slink away. It has happened before, and the victim does not end up in the graveyard between the cliffs and the lemon groves.

Then everything changes because the stranger does something none of them have seen before. Out of nowhere he jumps into the air, pirouettes and kicks the Moroccan in the side of the head. The crowd fall silent. The Moroccan stares at his opponent, staggering a little, his head ringing like a hammered gong, surprised, affronted and in a good deal of pain. Before he can gather himself the stranger pirouettes in the opposite direction. The Moroccan, still groggy from the previous blow, lifts his arms to defend his head, but the stranger swings his foot lower this time and strikes the side of the Moroccan's knee. His legs buckle and he topples sideways onto the ground.

The crowd explode. Chloë leaps from her seat and cheers, which is very much something she should not do. But no one has eyes for the princess. They have eyes only for the stunned and prostrate Moroccan who is clumsily rolling over and getting up onto all fours like a dog. A boy shouts, 'Kick his head off.' Is it possible that such a thrilling thing could happen? They have never seen anyone fight in this manner before.

The stranger seems immune to the recommendations of his new supporters. The Moroccan is having trouble getting to his feet. Still on all fours, he sways woozily. Surely now is the time for a fatal blow. Instead the stranger turns towards Chloë as if asking for her advice. Or does she imagine this? He turns back to the Moroccan, puts a foot on his shoulder and pushes gently. The Moroccan topples sideways, thumps the sand and rolls onto his back, both shoulders pressed unequivocally to the ground for one … two … three seconds. There is a desultory cheer from the crowd which dwindles like the gush of air from an abandoned pair of bellows. Unconcerned, the stranger walks over to Simonides and goes down on one knee. He is supernaturally self-possessed for a man who commands no slaves. Simonides asks for his name. The stranger looks up and pauses just long enough to suggest that he is plucking an alias from thin air. 'My name is Appolinus.'

He does not fight again, his opponents in the next two rounds excusing themselves on the grounds of injuries picked up during their earlier victories. The risk of losing a fight against a social equal is one thing; the certainty of being kicked in the head by a peasant is another. The crowds would have loved the stranger had he been beaten – or indeed killed – in the final round. But his victory by default has severely undermined their sense of solidarity. His coolness likewise. They want burly woodcutters and grunting butchers who play to the crowd on whose behalf they fight symbolically against all the men who live richly off their labours. The stranger has not looked at them once.

They must content themselves instead with the prospect of the following day's racing – hubs clipping the pillar, wheels tangling on the straight, men churned by hooves and bronze rims and shattered spokes. Consequently they have all but drifted away when the stranger approaches Simonides for a second time to receive his prize.

Chloë wishes she knew some way of overturning the adamantine protocol and getting a commoner invited to that evening's feast. But Demetrius is already suspicious and there are limits both to her father's generosity and to her own otherwise formidable diplomatic skills. So she is shocked when her father offers the invitation unprompted. Is it the disparity between his embarrassment at the meagreness of the prize traditionally offered to vulgar fighters and the ease this man radiates? Certainly the stranger seems only politely impressed by the bushels of corn and the painted clay krater. Or is this another loop of that same golden thread that entered the fabric when they caught one another's eyes earlier in the day?

If so then it continues to weave itself through the evening when their eyes are able to meet down the length of a table laden with beef cuts and sweet Andalusian wine and bright shoals of sugar fish turning in glass bowls. Later, when she sees him slip onto the balcony she slips her own leash to follow him outside. He is silhouetted at the balustrade, beyond him the vineyards decorate the hills with black and turquoise stripes. He does not turn when she says his name. Perhaps he has run out of the energy to sustain the sophistication he carried off so convincingly earlier in the day. She says, 'It is very rude to stand with your back to me.'

'I hope you will accept my apologies.' Still he does not turn.

She feels a sudden sympathy. She imagines what it would be like if their situations were reversed and she found herself in some squalid shack surrounded by yelping, dirty children and goats bleating on the far side of the dividing wall. She shivers with disgust. 'I do not recognise your accent. I can only assume that you are a sailor.' He says nothing. 'Or a merchant of some kind.'

He has spent his credit. This is beneath her dignity. She is about to spin and march haughtily away when he turns. He is weeping. It is the last thing she expected. 'I am indeed a sailor. My friends were also sailors.'

It takes her a few moments to absorb the meaning of this. 'I'm so sorry.'

'We were two days out of Tarsus ...'

He tells her everything – his mysterious pursuer, the plague, his restlessness, the death of Antonio, the night swim ...

Inside the hall, the feast continues. No one goes in search of the missing princess. Her unannounced departures are usually occasioned by a foul mood which makes her absence something of a relief. As for the stranger, it is presumed that he has run away or drunk too much and become lost in what is, for him, doubtless a confusingly large building.

On the balcony Pericles explains how he clawed his way to the sail's edge, grabbed a shattered plank and was churned in the freezing foam. At one point he was thrown onto a domed rock and the great wave receded around him. He slid down the gritty flank of the basalt and found sand under his feet. He knew that he had only seconds to reach higher ground before the wave rose to reclaim him, so he ran, following the rising slope of the beach until he found himself in a gap of rock whose sheer, wet sides it was impossible to climb. He braced himself as stoutly as he could between the walls of his narrow prison and listened to the roar of the sea in the impenetrable dark behind him. Then the wave came back with a great hollow explosion as it hit the rock. The water reached his waist. The second wave came up to his chest, the third to his knees. He counted three hundred waves. Five hundred waves. The waves no longer reached him. The storm was easing. Eight hundred. Dawn was on its way.

They found him when they were scavenging for salvage. He was sitting on a grassy berm above the high watermark, drying off in the weak sun when he heard a dog barking and turned to see two women and a boy carrying the low-backed beechwood chair from the great cabin. It seemed like a decent price for a human life. They took him to a cottage overlooking the adjacent cove and fed him hake, mussels and samphire.

It finally occurs to the royal family of Pentapolis that the two empty seats at the table might be connected and a panicked search takes place to find Chloë before she is ravished in an alcove.

'So your father is the King of Tyre,' she says.

'No one beyond your family must know,' replies Pericles. 'As long as the world thinks I am dead then I am safe.'

It is Demetrius who bursts through the double doors onto the balcony first. He is brandishing a sword but it is short and largely ceremonial and when he lunges and says, 'Stand back from my sister,' the stranger does not move and his sister says, 'Oh, do grow up, Demetrius.' At this point he remembers vividly what the stranger did to the Moroccan earlier in the day and decides not to press his point. The queen appears behind him, Chloë introduces Pericles and her mother is in quick succession horrified, mollified, astonished, charmed and then relieved that, for the very first time, her daughter is not insulting a suitor, presuming that he *is* a suitor, which she very much hopes because it would be an excellent match, though she would settle for anyone willing to take her daughter off her hands by this point. Simonides can read Chloë better than anyone and by the time he arrives he can see that the marriage is all but contracted and what he feels mostly is a terrible sadness at the forthcoming loss of the only person in the palace who can tease him and disobey his orders and make him laugh and to whom he can talk with complete freedom.

The truth about the prince's identity is kept within the immediate family. Should it slip out, the gossip would spread like blood in these warm waters and Pericles does not want Kallios to discover that his job is not yet done.

Chloë is besotted. This prince has walked straight out of a storybook which is in equal parts thrilling and sad. If he himself is not a great consumer of literature he is nevertheless articulate and kind and, most importantly, a traveller. She has spent her life trapped in this palace reading about fantastical locations – Giza, Algiers, Olympos, Jerusalem – which have suddenly become real places which they might visit together if … if … The fierceness of her need scares her. Wanting something this much feels like a rope around her neck. So she succumbs and protests and succumbs and protests. She stares into his eyes, catches herself and mocks him mercilessly in compensation. She is desperate to be in his company then equally desperate for solitude.

'I only feel truly at home when I am at sea.'

'I am going to take that as an insult.'

'You misunderstand me.'

'I understand you very well. You would rather be in the middle of the ocean than sitting here.'

'That is untrue.'

'Not that it matters greatly. You will be bored soon enough and desperate to get away.'

'You might be many things but you are not boring.'

'Men accuse women of being fickle, but their minds change with the wind.'

Pericles has never known a woman like her. In truth he has never known a woman, if to know someone is to try and stand in their shoes, to wonder what the world looks like through their eyes, to wonder what *you* look like through their eyes. Certainly he has never met anyone whose company demands such constant hard work, but it is company that consumes him utterly. Only when they are together does he not think about Helicanus, about Marlenus, about Antonio, about the crew, about the destruction of the *Porpoise*. No one has ever held his attention so completely. Does she love him? Does he love her? He has never found a puzzle so difficult to answer, nor one whose answer matters so much.

He will marry her. Everyone else knows it even if they do not. The queen is delighted. She is a snob, but she worries, too, about the fate of an unmarried daughter when they are gone. Chloë will not fare so well in the courts of her brothers. Demetrius himself wavers between declaring that Pericles will finally tame her and declaring that the man must make his swift exit before the jaws of the trap close. And Simonides? What can her father do but let their own games postpone the day when Pericles begs an audience and asks the question officially? He likes the man. Nor has he ever been able to deny his daughter anything she truly wants. It will be the hardest thing he has done. He has never lost a precious object he cannot replace.

Pericles begs an audience. Simonides gives his blessing but makes the couple wait five weeks until the next auspicious date to defer his inevitable bereavement. No messages are sent to Tyre. One intercepted letter, one boarded ship, one loose word could be the prince's undoing. The newlyweds will travel incognito later.

To the women who fed him hake, mussels and samphire Pericles sends, anonymously, a crate of salted ox, some marzipan and twenty bottles of sweet wine together with a sealed leather wallet of silver coins.

Five weeks become four.

Pericles feels restless and confined. There are attractions in Pentapolis which neither Tyre nor Tarsus possessed, of course, but love is exhausting and his confession was truthful – he has never felt entirely at home if the floor is not rolling a little. He yearns for light and space and weather and the great incommunicado of the ocean. So he rides, sometimes, into the hills behind the city, following foresters' tracks which rise through woods which become thicker, greener and damper with the growing altitude. Aspen, oak, poplar, mountain ash. He is no rider but the chaperones are thrown off easily enough. He climbs onto a rock and looks down to the coastal plain and the beckoning blue beyond and feels something in his chest loosen and breathe. Then out of nowhere he feels a terrible loneliness and the conviction that Chloë is in some kind of danger so that he is both worried for her safety and angry at himself for feeling this way, and angry at Chloë for making him feel this way, and angry at her father for not allowing them to come up here together. He returns to the palace feeling more restless and confined than he was when he set out.

Four weeks become three.

Pericles and Chloë have an argument of such intensity and volume that the entire palace hears it. The argument is about his failure to praise in sufficiently high terms a pair of sandals that she is wearing. It is not really about the sandals. It is about the danger of placing the remainder of your life into the hands of another human being. It is about the fear of not being loved enough. They hate one another for an entire afternoon.

Three weeks become two.

Chloë knits a wedding dress of white wool with a good deal of assistance from her attendant women because she is neither patient nor careful.

Pericles tells her the stories with which he entertained Cleon – volcanoes and the Northern Lights. They no longer have the same charge. She is a new world herself and the old one seems smaller in comparison. She knows immediately that the cannibals are an invention.

'An embellishment.'

'A fabrication.'

'A tale told by a very creditable source.'

'Whom you cannot name.'

She fails to understand the hardships he has been through, the hardships anyone must go through to earn the right to tell any such stories. He comes close to telling her about the brothels, about the boy who was eaten by a shark, about the man who entered his chamber in Tarsus and did not live. He wants to hurt her. He wants her to see that he once lived a life in which she would have been powerless. He says, 'I killed my friend. He drowned. But I killed him.' She cries and apologises. He thinks, *He was not my friend. I am a liar.*

It is not that she is unimpressed. She is refusing to be impressed. She is ashamed that she has no story of her own to tell, exasperated that she has had to sit in these quiet rooms while sons and fathers, merchants, diplomats, soldiers and explorers sped to the horizon and returned with the invisible cargo that makes men's lives rich. Pericles will be her story. They will have adventures together. She will override his objections to this as surely as they will ride out storms. Her coolness is not unkindness. She is frightened only of letting him know how much these things matter to her. She is not heartless or unimaginative. She understands that stories demand suffering. How could they not?

But she does not understand, in the same way that someone who has never placed their hand in a flame does not understand that fire burns. Before the year is out, however, she will have a story to tell as terrifying as any of her husband's and she will want, more than anything, for time to run backwards so that she is returned to these rooms where linen curtains sway in the hot breeze and slaves swat flies from the trays of sweetmeats and there is nothing of any significance to do.

Two weeks become one.

Pericles and Chloë have worn themselves into a weary, delirious acceptance of one another's love, and general relief attends a modest marriage of which the larger city knows little and cities further afield know nothing. It would be dangerous to let the curious ponder the identity of this new royal son-in-law, and there is, as yet, no second family to flatter and impress. Even Chloë accepts the plan, consoling herself that the secrecy grants this marriage more importance than the vast sums spent in neighbouring kingdoms on her brothers' lavish nuptials.

The night before the wedding they give one another gifts – a ring of ivory, a ring of gold. Chloë carries a blue childhood dress and a music box to the fig-tree courtyard at the rear of the palace and lays them at the shrine devoted to the household deities, those two badly painted little men who have always danced above a badly painted gecko in the little alcove at the far end. Later, a servant will carry them away and discreetly burn them on the gods' behalf.

The day of the wedding arrives. Chloë dons her dress of white wool. The seven-year-old grandson of her father's chief adviser lights a torch and leads Chloë, her attendants, her parents, her brothers and their wives on a symbolic walk around the palace to the wing where Pericles is staying. Two priests carry gold rhytons of holy water. They stand in the courtyard outside his chamber. Simonides kicks gently at the door while, in the absence of anyone from his own neighbourhood, Chloë gives a copper coin to one of the house slaves who has been spruced up for the occasion.

The door opens and Pericles steps out. At his side is a similar boy carrying a similar torch.

'Aquae et ignis communicatio.'

The rhytons are emptied into the fountain and the torches laid side by side to burn out at the pool's rim. Chloë is lifted up and carried over the threshold of the chamber by her attendants. They put her down. She says, 'Where you are Gaius, I will be Gaia.' He says, 'Where you are Gaia, I will be Gaius.' They join their hands together.

Everyone else retreats to the small temple in the palace grounds where two sows are led out to be slaughtered and offered up to Juno, the goddess of marriage. The second sow sees this being done to the first and is not pleased with the arrangement. She slips her rope and must be chased by one of the priests in a robe not made for pig-chasing in a confined space. Vases are broken, the priest twists an ankle, the pig is cornered. Her end is not pretty. Ironically, the only person who would be entertained is Chloë, who is very specifically not told about the inauspicious event.

In Pericles' chamber, the shutters are closed in accordance with tradition and the wool dress is luminous in the quarter-light. He is not innocent and she is not ignorant but they do not know yet if they can communicate in this language. If they were the children of herdsmen or carpenters they might have discovered themselves already in some wooded clearing, but their actions are too freighted with consequence for such freedoms.

A new coverlet has been made for the bed, embroidered with scenes from the courtship and marriage of Peleus and Thetis – Peleus gazing down at the sea nymph in wonder from the deck of the Argo as it sails to Colchis in search of the Golden Fleece, guests mortal and immortal (Chiron bearing gifts of alpine flowers, Penios carrying whole trees ...), Peleus and Thetis in the quarter-light of their own bedchamber, Thetis giving birth to Achilles.

Chloë has imagined the act of sex many times, sometimes with horror, sometimes with excitement. She has imagined lying naked and ill-tempered under some bumptious neighbouring prince as he plants his seed inside her. She has imagined doing things too scandalous to put into words with a variety of far more attractive princes who have singularly failed to pitch up and ask for her hand. Now it is about to happen in an actual room and there is a daddy-long-legs on the bedpost and a donkey braying in the distance and she is a little bloated by the vast breakfast her mother insisted upon as if she were about to embark upon a forced march. There are two people involved and Pericles is not a character in the mind's puppet-theatre and he has his hands cupped stiffly under her breasts and his manhood is prodding her like a broom handle.

He is nervous. He has never wanted to give a woman pleasure before. More often than not he has paid to do this kind of thing, though he is trying hard not to think of this kind of thing as that kind of thing. More often than not the pleasure lay mostly in going incognito, slipping off his royal name along with his clothes. Now he is himself completely, and more naked than he has ever been.

Her nerves bubble into laughter, at the clumsiness of this man who is so accomplished in so many other ways, and at the sacred hush around this ridiculous thing that bulls do to heifers while the heifers are trying to eat hay.

He is angry. She has made him feel like an idiot. The broom handle declines.

'I'm sorry. Come here.' She takes his hand and leads him to the bed. She lies down, leaving space for him to lie beside her. She lifts the white woollen dress which will not come out of this well. She is naked underneath and becoming wet already because this doesn't have to be different from the inside of her head, does it. She can make him do the things she has already made him do a hundred times in her imagination. She takes his hand and opens herself with her other hand and places his two fingers against that wetness and moves them in a little figure of eight. 'There. Like that.' It's hard to make out his expression in the gloom, but he must surely be a little shocked. She hopes that he is a little shocked. She says, 'Afternoons in the palace are very long, and you can only read so many books.'

He has the rhythm now so she lets go of his hand and closes her eyes and arches her back and reaches over to take hold of him. 'Keep going.'

They stumble into the daylight the following morning, love-sore and squinting at the glare of the world they left behind (the now-stained white dress will go up in smoke just like the music box). There is a feast during the afternoon, modest in size but opulent in content, a small zoo baked, stuffed, roasted, boiled, fried and iced, though Pericles and Chloë would be as happy with oatmeal and a pitcher of good ale. The pendulum of shadow under the scarlet awning which covers the great square table swings with exquisite slowness from west to east. There are musicians and tumblers and dancers. A man with dark brown skin and pale blue eyes blows flames from his mouth and juggles a pole with fire at either end. There are sober blessings and generous speeches and bawdy songs. Another sow dies. Another bull dies.

Chloë and Pericles are outside time. They walk the circuit of the castellated walls, looking out onto the ocean, the vineyards, the cliffs, the graveyard, the lemon groves. They look different to one another, overlaid with the secret of their nakedness. They return to his chamber early in the evening and make love again, taking more time, being gentler, starting to trust that this is a gift they have been given for ever.

They have received another gift, too, for those little swimmers have wriggled their way to a fertile egg and Chloë is carrying her own female Achilles – one cell becoming two, becoming four, becoming eight ... a girl, whose life will be neither as violent nor as storied as that of the great Achaean warrior but who will be dipped entirely in the vessel of magic potion, though this will be proved only by trials that no one should be forced to undergo, least of all a young girl.

They watch *Amphitryon* by Plautus. They watch *Electra* by Sophocles. Pericles goes out hunting boar with Demetrius. Chloë refuses to attend the games in the modest amphitheatre on the grounds that they are too gruesome and Pericles finds that he, too, is now repulsed by the sight of men fighting to the death. They read Horace, and Pericles is surprised to discover that it moves him. *Vides ut alta stet nive candidum Soracte ...* Chloë's belly begins to show. They play latrones. Her parents insist that she is carried around in a litter and she demonstrates that marriage has not reduced her ability to be loudly intractable. She walks with Pericles in the hills. They take a small, armed retinue and he dresses as a body-guard to allay suspicions if they are spotted. In the bedroom they act out their own private drama in which a princess has a love affair with her bodyguard.

One hundred and twenty-eight, two hundred and fifty-six, five hundred and twelve ...

Both of them are restless now, wishing they could be elsewhere, Chloë trapped inside her growing body, both of them trapped in the palace. Days in his wife's company are increasingly similar and no longer have the power to distract Pericles from feelings which wash in and out like the tide, sadness for his comrades, shame at his own actions. He and Chloë have an argument about a subject so trivial that any memory of the content is wiped out immediately by the shock at having an argument of any kind so soon after their wedding. To his surprise he finds himself missing his own parents.

Chloë has been pregnant for ninety-three days when Pericles hears of a small fleet of Tyrian merchants docked in the harbour. He is hungry for news of the place he increasingly finds himself calling *home*, hungry, too, for Tyrian halva and sultanas. Through a palace intermediary he sends a message to the captain of the *Pelican* and arranges a meeting at the caupona under the sign of the twin pulleys.

He dons the drab outfit of a minor official and leaves the palace by one of the kitchen doors. He does not tell Chloë, less because she will think him reckless than because she will want to abscond with him. It is an unnaturally gloomy day for early summer, an end-of-day redness to the sun at noon. Desert sand whipped up by the wind, they say, which will later fall as orange rain. Flocks of starlings swill and sway above the roofs, disturbed by sudden dimming of the light.

The captain is sitting in the far corner of the darkened room in the juddering glow of an oil lamp. He has a dark brown birthmark beneath his left eye as per the description. Pericles sits himself down on the near-side of the trestle table. The man looks at him and nods, the expression neither friendly nor unfriendly. Pericles wonders if he has seated himself in front of the wrong man. The captain stands up and moves aside. A second man slips into his place. It is Kallios.

❧

After three or four days without food Angelica is no longer able to read properly. Her attention wanders, longer sentences require two or three attempts, she loses the thread of plots and arguments. She is most comfortable lying down, and holding a book over her head for any length of time is now hard work. She can draw but she cannot draw well enough to make it a satisfying activity and while she sometimes

146

puts music on, it is rarely more than background noise. If she were any other girl of her age she might watch TV but she has absorbed her father's prejudices on this and many other subjects, and the few snatches she has caught on the little portable set the cook keeps squirrelled away in the cupboard beside the food mixers have done little to alter this judgement.

There is a big screen in the smaller lounge at the back of the house, but it is intended solely for playing the collection of DVDs shelved alphabetically behind the sliding panel on the opposite wall, from *Nosferatu* to *Magnolia*, from *Lagaan* to *Un Prophète*. She finds herself running her hand along the spines one afternoon, eager for distraction, something low-key, undemanding. She doesn't want to be dragged to the edge of her seat or have her heartstrings tugged.

She is on the point of giving up her search when she notices the box on the right-hand side of the bottom shelf. She has slid this panel back many times and never seen it, in the way she has managed not to see many things over the years. It is a relic from another world, the tan cardboard frayed at the corners and punctured by clumsy handling in several places, *Cannings Removals* printed in cheap blue ink below a soaring gull. She knows exactly what's inside.

She lifts it onto the carpet. The four flaps are deftly tucked into one another like the spiral petals of a camera lens. She eases them apart. Under the lid are scrunched-up balls of Swedish newsprint, already a little yellowed with age. She removes several handfuls, turns the box on its side and slides out the black metal body of the old VHS player, plug and leads clattering out behind it. She reaches down into the box and pulls out the four cassettes in their cheap plastic boxes.

She has never watched them. Apart from the odd scene, she has never sat down to watch any of the seven films on the shelves above in which her mother has a role, and no one has suggested she do so. It is assumed that she would find the experience too upsetting. On the contrary, the scenes she has seen have left her feeling only embarrassment at her failure to feel any kind of strong emotion. And why should she seek that emotion out? Why go in search of pain?

If she has any connection to her mother she finds it in places other people would neither predict nor understand – those wingtip lights of planes tracking across the night sky, the skitter of an unseen animal over the roof, bright, complicated sunsets ... remnants of childish fantasies which she has never shared and therefore never needed to rewrite.

She connects the machine to the sockets at the rear of the bottom shelf. To her surprise it works, the word *standby* blinking eagerly in boxy green letters on the little black panel. Even this small amount of effort has made her dizzy and breathless. She lies down for five minutes with her eyes closed before sitting up again, placing the first cassette into the slot and waiting for the noisy mechanism to grab and swallow it. Should she be doing this?

Vertical black lines ripple in a sandstorm of white noise followed by a jittering rectangle of rainbow stripes and some numbers which come and go too quickly to read. Then we're flying behind a raven as it soars over thickly wooded hills in what must be northern Sweden, the green of the trees giving way to bare rock on ridges and summits. Melancholy piano. *Maja Söderberg* in a dated yellow font. The raven descends rapidly and veers away, leaving the camera to plunge through the foliage and emerge into the cathedral-light of the forest interior. *Henrik Ivarsson* in the same font. The camera weaves and dodges between trunks, bursts from the trees into the air above a lake then plunges through the waves into the bubbling green murk below the surface. *SKOGEN* in a bigger font, all caps. The melancholy piano fades, but we are still moving through the dirty translucent water at some speed. The sequence goes on for just a little too long to be comfortable and, then, out of nowhere, something looms from the dark at the screen's base. A sunken boat? A corpse? An animal swimming? We see it for only a fraction of a second then we cut to a woman's hands on a steering wheel in bright sunlight, a single finger tapping the black leather in time to a jaunty pop song on the radio.

Her mother.

The blue Saab speeds along a motorway, then along a single carriageway through farmland, then along a minor road winding its way through an undulating forest landscape. The woman seems drained and anxious. She lights a cigarette. Angelica is surprised to discover that her mother smoked and has to remind herself that her mother is pretending to be someone else.

With no warning the woman hits the brakes hard and the car squeals to a halt, wheels in the gravel between tarmac and ditch. The woman gets out of the car and begins walking back down the road, leaving the driver's door open. She takes a final drag and flicks the cigarette onto the road before turning into the trees. Ferns, low bushes, mossy rocks. There is something in the undergrowth, the size of a big dog, about five metres from the road. How did she manage to see it from the car? She crouches. The creature's fur is matted with blood and there is a fist-sized hole in what looks like the head, a chunk of flesh mashed in or hacked out. The woman is unfazed. She rolls the body over. It has the eyes of a girl but the muzzle of a dog, a little yellow canine poking over the lower lip. The woman places her hand on the forehead of the dog-child and lifts an eyelid. The eyeball is amber, the pupil a vertical black slash like that of a cat.

And now we are watching from further inside the woods. Blurred branches frame the scene. Are we looking through another person's eyes? The woman takes a phone from a pocket. No signal. She walks back to the road.

As far as Angelica is concerned the actress could be anyone, but there is something pleasingly hokey about the story, the way you can almost but not quite predict the next twist. The woman is a police officer of course. With a troubled past, of course, her own daughter having died ten years before in mysterious circumstances. When she returns with the local police to the place where she found the otherworldly creature it has, of course, vanished. The local police think she is mad. She believes they are hiding something. She gets to work sorting out her dead father's estate. Meanwhile, divers working on the old dam discover a mysterious underwater structure which doesn't appear on any of the designs.

There is something about the landscape, too, which calls to Angelica – lake-light between birch trunks, those great boulders sitting improbably among the trees where they were deposited long ago by glaciers, those raven-haunted valleys. A place her father would never choose to visit.

Three episodes in a row ... Dottie puts her head round the door. 'I've been looking for you everywhere.' Predictably, Angelica turns down the offer of a sandwich or a drink, but Dottie's growing anxiety is tempered a little by the sight of the girl doing something which makes her look like an ordinary teenager.

Four episodes, five ... Perhaps it is the weakness brought on by not eating, the way things blur and overlap now that she does not have the mental energy to draw clear lines. Perhaps certain patterns become visible only when you step aside from the heady onrush of the world. She starts to recognise, not her mother, but something more nebulous, a succession of images which repeatedly strike some deep chord so that she feels, increasingly, as if she is watching a coded version of her own life – the dead children who press their faces to the windows of their old homes in the gloaming, the wealthy aristocrat in the big house who plays the piano and carves tiny wooden models of everyone in town, birds delivering messages, the submarine structure into whose tunnels several police divers have vanished and not returned.

Angelica is exhausted. She presses *pause* and sits back against the armchair. So engrossed has she been by the programme that she has not noticed the change in the weather. The sun has gone, rain falls from low grey cloud. Evening is coming on. Angelica feels woozy. The only light in the room comes from the screen where a still image sits juddering. The dog-child lies inside an oxygen tent in the local hospital. There are tubes in both her arms and an oxygen mask over her face. The picture is in poor quality black-and-white. We are looking through a CCTV camera installed high in the corner of the room. The woman stands beside the oxygen tent. At the foot of the picture run the subtitled words, '*Are you my daughter?*'

❧

'My employer is dead,' says Kallios.

'How did you find me?' asks Pericles.

'You can return home.' The man takes a mussel from the bowl in front of him and levers apart the two halves of the purple shell.

'How dare you sit here and declare what I may or may not do.'

'It seemed a courtesy.' Kallios forks out the small meat and puts it in his mouth. 'If I hadn't come it might have taken years for you to summon the courage to set sail.'

'Do not insult me.'

'And you would have spent the rest of your life seeing the flash of a blade in every darkened doorway.'

Pericles pauses to gather himself. He has too many questions. And the man is right. If he were braver and Kallios were an ordinary man he would drag him across the table and beat him. 'Who is your employer?'

'They were riding in a chariot when they were struck by lightning. Out of a clear blue sky. So I was told.'

'They? Who are *they*?'

'But the common people enjoy drama and these stories become rapidly embellished.'

'I asked you for their names.'

'The father and the daughter? Their corpses stank so much that even the priests refused to bury them. Of which I am equally sceptical. Is lightning not fire? And are we not meat? The smell, I imagine, would have been oddly pleasant. If they were locked up in a hot little room and left to starve and rot, on the other hand ...'

'Which father? Which daughter?'

Kallios looks at him and smiles the smile of one who knows that he is in no danger whatsoever. He opens another mussel. 'There were so many daughters, weren't there. So many fathers.' He puts the meat in his mouth and chews. 'I could be one of many charged with restoring a family's honour. Though I would be disappointed if I were not the most persistent.'

'You will not leave here alive.'

'On the contrary.' Kallios reaches into his cloak and retrieves a knife which he places in front of him on the table; the lamplight runs up and down an oiled blade which looks sharper than any Pericles has ever seen. It is serrated with little scallop teeth for a thumb's length at the tip, the shape so precise it seems impossible that it was made by human hands. The ridged grip is formed of a material he does not recognise. Its colour is extraordinary, the kind of vivid orange one might find in the tail of a peacock or a beetle shell, but spread without the smallest blemish over the entire object. The surface has the dull sheen of wax but the material is clearly denser even than lignum vitae judging by the way its owner held it and the noise it made when it was laid on the wooden tabletop. Pericles wants to lean across and pick it up out of simple curiosity.

'How do I know that you are not lying?'

'How does one know that anyone is not lying?' Kallios looks into his eyes. Pericles sees only a blank, animal disinterest. Kallios' shoulders drop a little and his tone changes. He seems human suddenly. 'I could have killed you when you were out hunting with Demetrius.' He gets to his feet. 'I could have killed you when you were walking in the mountains with your new wife.' He re-sheathes the knife. 'She is a beautiful woman. I wish the two of you much happiness.' He steps over the bench, adjusts his cloak and walks to the door.

He has, of course, vanished by the time Pericles runs outside. The old market is a cobweb of alleyways and pursuit is pointless, though Pericles suspects that he would have disappeared with equal ease if the building stood alone on salt flats.

Pericles waits for two days before telling anyone. Accepting the truth of it takes time. A tightness in his muscles of which he has been previously unaware begins slowly to ease. He feels lighter, younger. The world seems suddenly larger and more inviting. He tells Simonides that if the king is willing to lend them a ship then he and Chloë will make for Tyre immediately. Both Simonides and Lucina, however, think it highly inadvisable that any woman should travel anywhere so late in her pregnancy, least of all on a sea-voyage. But neither Pericles nor Chloë is inclined to listen to advice at this point. In any case, says Pericles, he has not seen his parents for more than a year. They do not know if their son is alive or dead. And now that he is to become a parent himself he is beginning to understand the pain his absence will have caused them. He must go home. It is his duty.

Lucina's fears are justified. A long journey undertaken late in pregnancy is not wise, but Pericles does not fully understand this until two weeks later when they are becalmed midway between Pentapolis and Tyre and Chloë goes into early labour.

He is standing at the rail looking at the terrible mirror of the sea. The sails hang slack, no ripple on the surface of the water, no cloud in the sky. He returns to the chamber. On land he would remain outside and receive bulletins from the women in attendance but he cannot bear to be away from a wife who has no one else to comfort her but an old nurse, Lychorida, and the surgeon who accompanied them at Lucina's insistence. Chloë has been suffering contractions all day and what began as an ordinary human event taking place in the wrong location, has become an escalating emergency, for the light is falling and Chloë is exhausted and neither nurse nor surgeon can hide their fears any longer.

He takes his wife's hand. 'Be strong. The child is nearly born. It will soon be in your arms.'

She is only faintly aware of his presence. Her skin is white and greasy, her grip weak. He takes a linen cloth and wipes away the pearls of sweat which bead her forehead. When she opens her eyes she seems unable to focus on anything in the room. He cannot bear to see her in pain. He would have his own arm cut off if she could be returned to herself. She cries out as another spasm begins. It seems to him that she is no longer pushing, rather she is being pushed, some force inside her squeezing and twisting and causing her unbearable agony. He has never seen her weak. The Chloë he knows is difficult, spiky, wilful, opinionated, determined. She is losing this fight and it terrifies him.

The surgeon puts a hand on his shoulder and beckons him outside. Pericles is reluctant to leave Chloë with only Lychorida but there is an unanswerable sternness in the surgeon's face which brooks no refusal. They step into the passageway. 'We do not have time so I will be blunt.' The surgeon pauses to gather his strength. 'I can cut the child out. I do not have the surgical equipment to hand but I am sure we can find adequate tools on board.' Pericles assumes that he must have misheard. 'I can, I think, save the child at the expense of your wife. If, however, we let events continue in their present direction I fear that we risk losing both.'

Pericles puts a hand flat against the man's chest and pushes him hard so that his head bangs against the bulkhead behind him 'The expense of my wife?' For a few moments he is so angry he goes blind. Some part of his harrowed mind is convinced that he can pay for the lives of both his wife and his child with the life of this man. The anger ebbs, his grip loosens. 'My apologies. I didn't ...' The surgeon opens his mouth to speak but Pericles holds up his other hand to silence him. 'You will not take a knife to my wife. You will not speak again of taking a knife to my wife.'

When they return to the room, however, Lychorida says, excitedly, 'The child is coming.' Pericles steps forward and sees a smeared ivory globe in the mess of hair and blood and flesh between his wife's legs. It is shockingly large. He feels sick. The surgeon slips away to the corner of the room, nervous of what the prince might do if he has too intimate a view of his wife. Lychorida's voice is a lullaby. 'The child is coming. Push, my lady, push again.' The head emerges a little further. She places a hand above it and a hand below it and gently rocks it back and forth.

Pericles wants to tell her to be careful, to make sure she does not harm this tiny person, to take care of his wife, but he knows nothing about these things. He is powerless. 'Push, my lady, push again.'

A bloody shoulder slips out. Lychorida takes the weight of the baby's head in one hand, hooks a finger of her free hand into the tiny armpit and pulls. The arm slithers out. The second shoulder slithers out, then the second arm. 'You've done it, my lady, the child is here.' The torso and legs slide out, trailing the umbilical cord on a tide of dark red sludge. He is filled with love, revulsion, terror and amazement. The scene is as beautiful as it is disgusting.

Lychorida says, 'It's a girl.' The child lets out a great gull-squawk followed by a high, extended wail. Pericles is horrified by the amount of blood, in the bed, on the floor. Lychorida wipes the child with a towel, puts it to one side, wraps it in a second towel and lays it against Chloë's breast. Taking a tiny brass sickle from her linen bag she cuts the cord and knots both ends. Chloë is making no effort to hold the child. Lychorida sees now that her mistress is not conscious. She nods towards the empty chair and tells Pericles to sit. She carries the child over and places it in his arms. 'Call her Marina.' It would be an offensive presumption in any other circumstances but this is her demesne and the demand has a force he cannot gainsay. 'Because she was born at sea.'

He looks down at this tiny creature his wife has been carrying for the last eight months. The raw, red skin, the tiny fists, the lick of dark hair. Lychorida returns to the bed. The surgeon is with her. They huddle over his wife. Something is very wrong. He knows it in his guts.

A memory comes back. He fell once, from the Jacob's ladder when they were moored off Karchedon, high spirits undone by poor judgement, his life saved only by a great stack of folded sails forty feet below. Not a heartbeat can have passed between him losing his footing and his back striking the canvas, but he seemed to have more than enough time to look around and observe the world he was about to have taken away from him. There was a ragged little fishing boat heading home under a swarm of gulls. Some kind of sexual act was occurring behind the port gig. It had been a long, hot, dry summer and there was a forest ablaze on the headland.

It is happening again, but there are no folded sails to break his fall this time. That is his wife and this is his daughter. There is an abandoned sandal, a dented tin jug and a blood-soaked towel. This is the precious world which is about to be torn from his hands. He hears the words, 'She is not breathing,' and tries to stand. Lychorida is picking the child up from the floor. He must have dropped her. He does not remember doing this. The child is screaming. His wife is lying motionless on the bed. He can smell sweat and shit and blood. There are men in the cabin whom he does not recognise. The surgeon must bring his wife back to life, but the surgeon is doing nothing. He yells at the surgeon. The men he does not recognise drag him out of the cabin. He tries to resist but he does not have the strength. He is bundled clumsily through a small doorway and forced down onto a bed. He tries to strike the face of one of the men but the air is like water and his fist moves too slowly and the man simply leans back to dodge the blow. Then the surgeon is standing beside him, saying, 'Drink this. It is for your own safety.' A wooden spoon is forced between his teeth and a kind of bitter treacle is poured down his throat. The spoon is removed and the surgeon says, 'He will fight for a few more minutes,' which is precisely what he does; then the individual parts of the world start to separate from one another like the beads on a necklace when the cord is stretched and he is still angry and frightened but his fear and anger are moving further away from one another and then the cord snaps and the beads scatter.

When he comes round he has no idea how much time has passed or, for a long moment, where he is. The memory, when it returns, is like bone breaking. Chloë is dead. The boat is pitching. He can hear, over his head, the howl of wind and the creak of wood under pressure and the crackle of canvas. This is the wind which should have carried them to Tyre. If only it had come a few days earlier. He gets to his feet. He must find his wife's body. But he is still under the influence of whatever was forced down his throat before he fell asleep. Everything revolves and the wall of the cabin hits the side of his face. Two burly men lift him to his feet and the captain appears. The man has a shiny pink scar connecting his ear to the corner of his mouth. 'Bring him outside, but keep a tight hold of him.'

It is daytime, though whether this dim light is morning or evening he cannot tell. The air is full of sea-foam and driving rain. His wife's body is lying in a coffin on the half-deck. It has been wrapped in a shroud. Two sailors are holding a section of sail aloft in an attempt to keep the body and the coffin dry. The lower part of the shroud is bloodstained. It is not a real coffin. It is the box in which rare spices were packed as a gift from Simonides and Lucina to his own parents. A split bag of turmeric makes the planking briefly orange before the driving rain washes it clean. The captain takes hold of his shoulders and leans in close. 'Neptune is angered by the presence of a corpse on board.' Pericles tries to reach Chloë but his legs are not working properly and the two men are strong. A small hessian bag is laid beside her body and the lid is fitted into place. The captain says, 'Superstition or not, I depend upon the loyalty of the crew. And they are mutinous.' Two men drive nails through the lid of the box. A third slaps hot tar all over it to form a watertight seal, the tar hissing and steaming in the cold air. The storm is getting stronger. A loose barrel topples and rolls across the deck. The captain yells at the men to secure it. Prayers are said to Neptune. There is no time for the complications of burnt offerings so a cup of wine is poured into the sea. It is stolen by the wind before it strikes the surface. These men want his wife thrown into the ocean. Pericles could kill every single one of them.

The coffin is lifted onto the rail. Someone yells, 'By the gods, just get it over with,' and the coffin is pitched end over end into the waves. It sinks then it bobs up again. It moves slowly away from the boat. It disappears into a valley between the waves. Another wave hoists it high and flips it over. It disappears, appears, disappears. Pericles thinks, *She will be seasick.* He thinks, *She will be terrified ... What if the coffin is not sealed well enough ...? What if water leaks in and she drowns inside her tiny, tumbling prison?*

He is in the cabin again. The two muscular sailors sit on either side of him. Outside, the storm has abated and the sea is calm. His wife is in his arms. 'Chloë,' he says, 'you came back.'

'This is not Chloë,' says the nurse. 'This is your daughter, Marina.'

❧

They enter the city proper at Cripplegate and walk south down Little Wood Street. It seems to George like any other London day. The Walloons are sitting in a semicircle waiting to be shaved at the sign of the Pheasant. A dirty ragamuffin with a tame squirrel sitting on his shoulder is begging for money. At the corner of Silver Street a woman throws water over a vagrant lying beside her front door. He seems untroubled so she hits him with the bucket and still gets no reaction. It is entirely possible that he is dead.

'Where are we going?' asks George.

'I do not know,' says Will. 'We will doubtless find out when we get there.'

'Christ's teeth,' says George.

'In a general sense I assume that I am escorting you out of this world.'

'Enough,' says George. 'Enough.' He comes to a halt and rubs his face.

A man is walking towards them carrying a small cage containing a pair of songbirds. He has powder-blue stockings and a square-cut ginger beard. George waits until the man is passing then grabs hold of his upper arm. The man's arm feels wrong, too soft, too insubstantial. Nevertheless, the man stops. He seems confused. He looks at George. No, that is not quite right. He looks *through* George. He wears the expression Mrs Brokehill wore when she both saw and didn't see the two of them in the bedchamber. The man smells of lavender and nutmeg, and he is frightened now. The cage clatters to the ground and rolls over several times in the mud. The man is completely unaware of this. The birds chirrup, their little wings drumming on the fine willow bars. The man starts to tremble. George has seen this look on weak men walking to the scaffold. A woman with a brace of rabbits slung over her shoulder stops and stares, wondering whether she should help this troubled man in his ridiculous stockings or walk away as quickly as possible. The man is weeping now, tears running down both cheeks. George lets go and the man sinks to his cornflower-blue knees, the splashed mud spattering George's own nightgown.

George turns to Will and narrows his eyes. 'What *are* you?'

Will shrugs. 'I am as surprised to find myself in this situation as you are.'

Two boys have run off with the caged birds. Some ragged cove is helping the bearded man theatrically to his feet and will doubtless seek payment for the service.

'Follow me.' Will turns and continues towards Cheapside. What he said to George is not the whole truth. He has not the remotest conception of the route they are following, but when he puts one foot in front of the other he knows that he is travelling in the right direction. It is a strange but pleasurable sensation. The fact that he is dead seems of little consequence. George reappears at his shoulder.

They cross Cheapside. There are geese and capons for sale, there are parsnips and melons. There are oranges arranged in a pyramid on a large velvet cushion. A cheesemonger excavates gobbets from inside a stilton. Sparrow the Butcher, one of George's regular clients until he gave Charity the pox, is hacking cuts from a skinless carcase hanging from its own portable gibbet. Blood for black pudding drips from the cut neck into the bucket underneath.

Seeing a trolley of pies George is suddenly hungry, partly for breakfast, partly for the feel of something solid in his hands, in his mouth, in his stomach. The cloak of invisibility would make the theft easy, but he is afraid that the pie will have the softness of the bird-man's arm. Besides, Will has entered Bread Street and George must hurry if he is not to be left behind. He skirts a lady on her palfrey and gives chase.

Next door to the Neptune three men are digging out a privy. They have dirty rags across their faces and breeches buckled round high leather boots to keep the rats out. There is a big barrel of juniper to freshen the emptied pit and a boy who looks as if he is made entirely of turd apart from two white eyes. The smell is eye-wateringly bad. At the side of the street sits a high-sided cart full of excrement bound for some lucky Essex pigs. They pass Snelling the luthier and the burnt-out house where the Tweedy children died in the fire. He wonders, for a second, whether he will meet them now that he, too, is dead. The thought opens an abyss. He backs away.

They pass All Hallows and St Mildred, two churches he has been fined for failing to attend at one time or another. The comforting scents of woodsmoke and horse dung again. They cross Pissing Lane onto Bread Street Hill. He can see water-light now beyond the roofs. There are gulls overhead and the reek of waterweed and rotting wood in the air. They turn right on Thames Street then left down to Broken Wharf opposite St Mary Somerset. The river opens out in front of them, the surprise of space after the tightness of the crowded city. Cold wind, oar-slap and a squadron of swans midstream. Across the river he can see the tops of the Bear Garden and the bull-baiting arena. He has a sudden vision of being over there, eating hazelnuts and a rabbit-meat pastry, some young girl fresh from the shires at his side. An old horse is led into the dusty ring with a monkey on its back, the dogs going at it till they bring the horse down and rip the squealing monkey to pieces. The joyous, gaudy, vulgar human swill of it all. He has not been well enough to go there for many months. He will never go again. A desperate, sick sadness washes through him.

'Our transport waits upon us.' Will is standing at the end of the jetty gesturing to a wherry below. It is not a boat of a kind George has used before, nor one he has ever seen on the Thames. There are no oars and the wood of the hull is stained black inside and out. The upholstery and the canopy are also black. The single waterman stands at the stern, cloaked in black and hooded so voluminously that his face cannot be seen. It is an image from a play, intended to chill the heart onstage but almost comical out here in the bustle of an ordinary morning. George steps into the boat which yaws a little under his feet. Buoyed again by the brief hope that this is all some theatrical illusion he ventures a little humour. 'This is an unexpectedly Virgilian manner in which to be leaving the world.' He sits himself on the far side of the double seat.

'You should be thankful. If we were departing in the Christian manner you would be in a furnace for ever,' says Will, climbing in after him and handing two coins to their pilot. 'That is my assumption at least.' He sits himself on the other side of the seat. 'I should probably know such things given my present condition but I find myself strangely ignorant.'

George wants to continue the badinage but he is distracted by the boat moving away from the jetty with no visible means of propulsion, as if it were attached to the back of some great fish. He turns and sees the waterman standing impassive behind him, untroubled by the growing bob and twist of the hull as they move out into the tangled wakes.

They pass through a thick hedge of sweet smoke; four geese crank themselves into the air over the wherry's bows and they enter the traffic of the great river. No passengers or pilots in other vessels turn to look at the black boat and its impassive, faceless Charon. It seems to George that they are as invisible on the water as he and Will were in the streets. But whatever animating power is in charge of the vessel guides them dextrously, if not comfortably, through the gaps between the packed, unheeding craft.

When they embarked George was convinced that they were crossing the Thames but to his surprise they turn downstream. This scares him more than what might have awaited them on the south bank because he sees now that the ebb is at its height, those two hours when fares rise and small boats navigate the strongest part of the stream swiftly and at some peril. The current has them in its grip. George looks under the seat. Some of the costlier wherries have life-preservers made from pigs' bladders. This boat does not. He grips the gunwales. Four shirtless African men are working the sails of a whaler. Some fool is transporting a cow on something not much more substantial than a punt. To their right, the thatched barrel of Henslowe's Rose and the Globe, both painful sights ever since the Muse abandoned him and the ink ran dry. Looming up ahead the airborne street of the great bridge tiptoes over the river on its nineteen feet, balanced upon it the palatial town houses of mercers and haberdashers with their terraces and balcony gardens. The great wooden toy of Nonsuch House. He wants to be up there, behind those buildings, in that warm, stinking crowd, walking past the White Horse and the Looking Glass and the Dolphin and Comb. He catches a glimpse of heads, legs and unidentifiable chunks of quartered bodies on the spikes which rise from the roof of the southern gateway. 'Will, this is not wise.'

'You are already dead, George. We are both dead. Dying should surely be one of the matters we no longer have to worry about. Besides, our steersman seems more than competent.' Though he can see George's point. A small boat shooting London Bridge is more often than not a few bloated corpses and a scattering of wet planks at Wapping.

'Sweet Christ,' says George.

The surface of the water buckles as they approach the prows of the cutwaters which scissor the Thames into twenty thick ribbons. The boat slips sideways into the lowest part of a trough between the stone starlings. Their already prodigious speed doubles. The sky is briefly blotted out. They enter the echoing roar. A thousand tons of water compressed. The boat exits the bridge, breasts the hill of a standing wave and thumps down onto the flatter water beyond, the currents on either side of them braiding and curling as the liquid ribbons reunite and George is greatly relieved to find the boat upright and himself undrowned.

Botolph's Wharf, Lyon's Key, Somar's Key, Billingsgate ... the bank itself invisible behind a flooded forest of masts and sails and rigging. Caravels and carracks, galleys and galleasses. Longshoremen hoot and holler. Sacks and crates swing from turning cranes. The boom of empty barrels dropped onto flagstones. Wine tuns and Turkish rugs. The Tower rising to their left, black water slopping in the open mouth of Traitor's Gate.

They veer round a barge which sits at anchor awaiting the turn of the tide, twenty-one oak trunks roped to the deck. Bermondsey, Shadwell, the kilns of Limehouse. The ships bigger now, no other wherries certainly, the river too wide, the chop too big. Waves are starting to splash over the prow. George looks down. His boots are sodden. Are they going to capsize? Would it matter? He is gripping the side of the boat and the edge of his seat very hard indeed. He is seasick in his stomach and in his heart. He glances over his shoulder. Their waterman seems entirely unaffected by the movement of the deck beneath his feet, remaining constantly upright like the little wooden soldier George was given by his carpenter uncle when he was a child, which couldn't be knocked over because of the lead weights hidden in its rounded feet.

Redriff and Millwall Dock, the stone stumps of the Roman bridge on either side of the river at Deptford. Times start to slip over one another, the way a reflected image lies upon a scene viewed through glass. The faint ghost of longships riding the tide at Greenwich where the Danes beat Ealpheg to death with ox-bones six hundred years ago. The Isle of Dogs, the dead hounds running for ever in search of their drowned masters. The river is a mile wide now, the featureless marshes of Erith, creeks and inlets. Ribcages of mud-stuck wrecks in assorted stages of decay. A vast sky. George has spent his entire adult life in London. Brief crossings of the river apart, he has lived for thirty years bound by walls of one kind or another. If this vast plain were a meadow it would terrify him. The fact that it is made of water fills him with inexpressible dread.

They pass through a floating island of excrement, solid enough to support the weight of two resting gulls. It is, thankfully, not on fire, unlike the similar island which passed downriver in the summer, causing great entertainment among some and persuading others that the end of the world was upon them.

They pass the chalk pits of Greenhithe. In the submarine dark a hundred feet below them the Black Shelf begins. Onto Fiddler's Reach where, so they say, the spirits of the three drowned musicians make the waves dance in the hope of bringing sailors down to join them in their cold and lonely home. The river curves to the right and they see, distantly, Tilbury on the left bank where Elizabeth blessed the fleet before they went to meet the Spaniards. *We have been persuaded by some that are careful of our safety* ... Then Gravesend where the jurisdiction of the river pilots begins, the port of Cliffe-at-Hoo, the Isle of Sheppey, Canvey Island where the Dutch reside. The river is five miles wide now, not in truth a river any more but the beginning of the ocean, one undivided substance connecting their tiny craft to Greenland, to China, to the map's blank borders. The counties of Kent and Essex are no more than dark lines that separate earth and sky. George wants desperately to go home. He has never felt this way before. But he does not have a home, he has never had a home, not since he was a child. He is close to weeping. But he is distracted by the sudden conviction that something is about to happen. He is not sure yet what that something might be. He looks at Will. He looks at their robed pilot. There are no ships. Is this what has triggered the alarm? Forty square miles of water and not a single sail. They are the only vessel. 'Will?'

Will looks at him with an expression of … what is it, compassion, sorrow? 'Goodbye, George.'

'Will …?'

It is like nothing George has ever seen. Will is sitting beside him made of flesh and blood and fustian and leather. Then George can see the glow of daylight from the other side of him, as if he were made of paper. Then he can see the rowlocks and the horizon through Will's chest. Then Will is made of smoke. Then wind bears the smoke away and Will disperses over the grey water and is gone. George turns round, hoping to see the waterman whose company has previously given him no reassurance whatsoever. The waterman becomes translucent, then transparent, then smoke, then blows away.

George is alone in a tiny boat many miles from land with no obvious means of propulsion and no one to whom he can signal his distress. He is wearing boots and a nightgown. He is very cold. And now he begins to weep properly. He knows that he will not be rescued. He is going to die for a second time and it is going to be lonely and painful and slow.

He closes his eyes and tries to imagine that he is on land, but without the distraction of the visible world the rocking of the hull is even harder to ignore. He opens his eyes. He is shivering. He puts up the black canopy to block the worst of the wind but it also blocks the view of any vessel that might rescue him. He puts the canopy down again. The sky is a uniform dirty white. He has no way of telling the time. There are still no sails. Something is profoundly wrong. Fear sweeps through him like wildfire. The light starts to go down, a general dimming at first, then the spectral gloaming of the day's end. The temperature drops further. He is not sure which will be worse, dying at night or surviving the night to find himself still alive and alone in this watery desert in the morning.

And this is the moment when they start to rise slowly from the water, one by one, around the boat. Lank, wet hair and salt-bleached skin. Sunken cheeks and eyes like chunks of coal, eyes you don't look *at* but *into*. Devils? Ghosts? He cannot breathe. Five, seven, nine of them. Drowned but alive, clad in sodden shrouds that stick to their breasts and bony shoulders. They are talking in a loud whisper, words overlapping so that they emit only a general hiss. Ten, eleven. He turns round. The wet, cadaverous crowd circle the boat completely now. One of them is Ann Plesington, or some demon wearing her body. No pupils in the dungeon black of her eyes, but he knows that she is looking at him. He knows that they are all looking at him. He beat her with a strap and one of the blows hit her face and left her permanently scarred. Bound over to keep the peace in the Clerkenwell magistrates' court.

Rebecka Chetwoode. Dorothy Lumbarde. Magdalen Samways. Hollow-cheeked and fish-fleshed, ankle deep in the water as if they were only five yards from the beach. Twenty? Twenty-five? No longer countable, though he recognises every one of them. Judith Walton. Allison Packham. Susanna Medeley whom he kicked in the belly when she was pregnant. The Old Bailey this time. And only now does he see, beside her, the child who died in her womb, too young to sit up but standing in the water nevertheless, a domed hairless skull above the naked body of a baby bird, tiny versions of those same black eyes staring at him when they should be closed. Joane Chatwyn whom he took by force. Isabelle Fletcher whom he took by force. Frideswide Chase who died when three men used her for their pleasure. Lettice Alfraye whom he sold to Lord Buckleigh. Charity Cooper.

The sky is darker. He is shivering. The water slaps and wobbles, the boat rocks under him but the women remain as fixed as stanchions. Is this a punishment? It was bad enough being led here by his offensively prolific one-time collaborator, but to discover that the sex too weak to have dominion in the physical world are possessed of demonic powers in the other is hard to bear. Dear God, he gave many of these women employment. If it weren't for his business they would have been on the streets at best. The thought is pointless. There is very clearly no one here to whom he can plead his case.

The hissing stops. Their eyes are on him but their mouths are no longer moving. In front of the prow the crowd of women separates, not stepping sideways but sliding smoothly apart. This is the denouement. For years everything has been travelling steadily towards this terrible moment. He wishes now that he were simply adrift in a tiny boat in the Thames Estuary with night coming and a long, painful death ahead of him.

Something – or someone – is swimming below the surface, along the path of clear water between the women, the image jumbled and warped by the waves but becoming clearer as it reaches the surface. A head appears, then shoulders. She is sixteen or so, Barbary skin and mahogany hair. The same sunken cheeks, the same black eyes, but this girl is different. He does not recognise her. She is the kind of girl who would never work for him, the kind of girl punters would refuse for fear of her provenance, who wears damask and lawn and sleeps under clean sheets and washes her soft hands between courses.

The other women begin talking again, that viper hiss, mouths moving faster now, some witchy incantation. The girl is moving slowly towards him. She is beautiful despite the transformation she has undergone. The hissing is louder now. He could reach out and touch her.

Who are you? The words form in his mind but he has neither the breath nor the control over his muscles to say them out loud.

She opens her mouth. Instead of the milk-white teeth he expects, her gums are ringed with thorns like the mouth of a lamprey and it is expanding until he can no longer see the rest of her head, only a well-shaft ringed with knives. She lunges too fast for him to react, fastening herself to the flesh of his face, spikes locked in hard enough for him to be hoisted off his feet and dragged forward, his ankles banging clumsily on the prow as he is hauled down into the cold and the dark.

The hissing stops. One by one the women slip into the water. The rippling circles they leave behind mingle rapidly with the general waves until there is only an empty wherry bobbing and rolling five miles from land as the last light of the day dies over London in the west.

❧

Her first thought is for the baby. She reaches out. She can't reach out. She has become tangled in a sheet and is unable to move. More than tangled. The sheet is wrapped tight around her face. Someone is trying to suffocate her. She shouts but the sheet muffles her voice. The room sounds wrong. And it is completely dark, not a candle, nothing. And the bed is rocking violently. They are at sea. She remembers now. The bed pitches more violently in the opposite direction. They must be sailing through a storm. She tries to sit up. She cannot sit up. There is a hard, flat surface in front of her face. She slides sideways and hits a wall. The bed flips over. She hits another wall. She is not in bed. She is inside a box. She is at sea and she is inside a box. How is that possible?

She does not know how to swim. She cannot even free her arms. She is going to drown.

Her child. She gave birth. She remembers now. After that she remembers nothing. She was exhausted. She must have passed out. The awful truth begins to dawn. The makeshift coffin flips over. She cannot put her hands out to protect herself. Her face is smacked against the lid. She feels her nose break. The pain is a small thing beside her terror. Pericles believes that she is dead. Everyone believes that she is dead. They have sailed on. No one is coming to rescue her. She is a strong woman but she has been cosseted her whole life. She is more frightened than she has ever been, more frightened than she believed possible. Outside she can hear the smash and howl of a wind-whipped ocean.

The coffin is flipped over, more violently this time. The back of her head is hammered against the wooden base. But she has managed to free one of her hands. She begins to work away at the rest of what must be the shroud in which she has been wrapped. She frees her other hand. The coffin flips again. She frees her arms. Only now can she feel how small this box is. She cannot even reach up to unwrap the shroud from her face. The coffin turns over. And turns over again. She cannot protect her head with her hands. She is breathing too fast. She must calm down. She cannot calm down.

There is water inside the coffin. She has no idea how long she has been trapped like this, or how long the box has been leaking. She can open her mouth a little. She tries to bite through the material but it is wound too tightly and she can get no purchase. She tries to sing, to comfort herself, to take some small portion of her mind off what is happening. She knows a hundred songs. She cannot remember the words to a single one. The coffin lurches and a loose object bumps into her right hand. She grabs it with the tips of her fingers. It is a bag and it contains something hard. She hopes against hope that it is a knife. The coffin lurches again and the bag slips out of her grasp. She weeps. The coffin flips. She finds the bag again. Her grip is firmer this time. She can feel through the rough material. Coins. It is filled with coins. She is holding the cost of her own funeral.

The coffin stops turning over. She is lying face down. She has no way of turning onto her back or of turning the coffin over. And the movement of the coffin is different now. It is seesawing slowly from end to end. When the end containing her feet rises up she slides and bangs the top of her head on the top of the coffin. Worse, the water in the coffin runs downwards and her face is briefly submerged. She sucks in a lungful of salt water the first time and coughs it back up. The second time she is coughing too hard to prepare herself. The third time she takes a deep breath while her head is out of the water then holds it while her face is submerged. This happens again and again. It is a relief when the coffin shifts once more with respect to the waves and it is rolled like a log like before.

She starts to count the number of times the coffin revolves. It is the one thing she can force her mind to do. Every time she loses track of the number she starts counting all over again. She never gets past fourteen. She is losing her mind, becoming something animal, stripped down, hollowed out. Is this what the rabbit feels in the fox's jaw? Is this what men feel on the battlefield when a spear is buried in their chest?

Time passes. She is on her back. She stays on her back. The coffin rocks but does not tip over. The sea is becoming calmer. She is lying in shallow water. The constant rolling has loosened the shroud. Her eyes and mouth are uncovered. She can still see nothing but she can breathe more easily. She tries to push the lid but there is no discernible give. They have sealed the coffin tight enough so that it cannot be opened but not tight enough to make it waterproof. If she could get her arms above her head she would be able to push with her hands and feet simultaneously, but what then? What if she made a hole big enough for the water to pour in but not big enough for her to get out? And if she did get out? She has no idea where she is. She has no idea whether it is day or night outside. She has no idea what creatures might be circling the box, sensing that something edible is struggling inside.

She lies still. There is nothing else she can do. She realises for the first time how bitterly cold she is. She can keep her legs together and put one hand in the other. That is all. Her teeth are chattering.

Slowly the water rises. It laps at her ears. It covers her ears. She has no idea how long this takes. If the coffin turns over now she will be face down in seawater and unable to twist her mouth into the shrinking slab of breathable air.

She is no longer in the coffin. She is kneeling by the little shrine in the fig-tree courtyard. The two badly painted little men are riding the gecko like a horse and singing loudly, '*Aquae et ignis! Aquae et ignis!*' She is lying on a bed in a darkened room, Pericles beside her. She is on the battlements watching an eagle the size of a chariot land on the walkway, its talons screeching on the stone. It speaks in the voice of her father. 'What does a month matter when you have delayed so long?'

She is back in the coffin. Water laps at the sides of her face. Her mouth fills. She spits the water out. Water runs up her nose. She lifts her head to breathe in. She lays her head back down and breathes out through the water. She lifts her head again to breathe in. It is astonishing that she is still alive. Perhaps she is not alive. Perhaps she died a long time ago. Perhaps this is what it means to be dead.

❧

Within minutes the wind lessens; within a half-hour they are sitting under a canopy of stars on a calm sea in the gentlest of breezes. The crew believe that this absolves them of any guilt for their threatened mutiny. They are calm at least, so the captain must bite his tongue until they are in port and he has larger, more loyal forces to hand. He has, in any case, a more pressing problem to deal with. He wraps his sodden jacket round the stove chimney in his cabin, then returns, with some trepidation, to the prince's chamber. The man no longer needs restraining by the pair of burly attendant seamen, but he is still crazed with grief, unaware of his surroundings and making little sense. The captain would very much like to know if and when Pericles is going to return to sanity and what opinions he will then hold as to his wife's death, her burial and his own treatment. Decisions which seem unavoidable at sea can be hard to explain to one's superiors on land, and whilst Simonides is a man of fairness and steady temper a granddaughter may prove insufficient compensation for the fact that his dead daughter has been pitched overboard and his son-in-law has lost his mind.

So they head for Tarsus. Allegiances change with the weather in this part of the world but their royal passenger will surely get a friendly reception in the city he saved. And should things go badly wrong and the captain has to make his escape, better to start in a city which is neither Pentapolis nor Tyre.

At this point, however, the prince has never felt less like a man worthy of high esteem. The loss of Antonio and Marlenus weakened some vital foundation which has now been undermined completely. He was a man who could withstand any physical pain, face any danger, take rational decisions in situations where lesser men would crumble. Now he wants to die. He has always considered this cowardice. Why settle for the eternal blankness of the afterlife when you can throw the dice one more

174

time? He understands now. It is a decision taken not in the head or the heart, but in the belly.

He dares not leave the bed. If he leaves the bed he will open the door and climb up on deck and throw himself into the ocean. People try to hold conversations with him – the captain, the two men who sit in his chamber, the surgeon, the nurse. They speak the language of a country he left a long time ago. He does not respond. He remembers sometimes that he has a daughter. He does not want a daughter. A daughter is a poor replacement for what he has lost.

Marina, in contrast, seems happy and healthy, unscarred by the events which have destroyed her immediate family. Lychorida walks the child repeatedly up and down the deck, partly to soothe her, partly because she herself feels constantly seasick and needs air and light. She has never been on a ship before. Only the drama of that fateful night briefly suppressed the nausea. Now she must contend with the constant yaw and roll and a view of nothing but water which seems to extend for ever in all directions. Every so often she pauses to place Marina in a rug-lined crate before leaning over the side to bring up whatever small portion of food she has managed to force down since the last time she did this.

She is a kind woman, and she is moved by Chloë's death, but she does not grieve. The rich and powerful have ample consolation before they are taken from the world. She has, however, against her better judgement, fallen in love with Marina. She feels, foolishly, that the child now belongs to her in some way. This will not end well. In a few days' time the girl will be taken from her and they will never see one another again.

But this is not what happens.

Perhaps it is her constant presence on deck, perhaps it is the fact that she is a woman and therefore invisible to men who talk in her hearing as if she were a gatepost or a sheep, but she is the first to realise that there is an understanding growing among the crew that they have not been absolved by the storm's sudden abatement. One Josephus has convinced them that if they do not take matters into their own hands they will be collectively put to the sword in Tarsus. He has five daggers tattooed below his left ear, one for every man he has killed, Lychorida presumes.

Terrified, she begs an audience with the captain who grants equally small weight to the opinions of women, dismisses her concerns and, as a result, wakes that night just before the end of the middle watch to find his arms pinned, a dirty hand over his mouth and Josephus cutting an artery in his neck with a rusty blade.

Pericles is deeply asleep, clambering through the tangled undergrowth of some dark wood. Then there are yells and thumps overhead and he is awake and the surgeon runs into the cabin and bolts the door behind him. The prince's burly attendants jump from their hammocks. A longing to be dead is one thing, the prospect of being killed is another. This is a dance Pericles knows, and one which requires an absolute focus on the present moment. He gets to his feet and demands of the surgeon, 'Tell me everything,' and if his two guards have thoughts about siding with the mutineers then the prince's transformation persuades them otherwise.

The surgeon is terrified and his story garbled. It is clear, nevertheless, that the majority of the crew have thrown in their lot with Josephus. The captain and the first mate are dead. It seems wisest to presume that no loyal sailors remain alive outside the cabin.

The head of an axe rips through the upper panel of the door. Marina is in the adjacent cabin with her nurse. If the mutineers do not have her now they will have her shortly. Pericles has no weapon and the other men have only the knives they carry to cut themselves free of tangled rigging before it tightens and severs a foot or a hand. They all hear Lychorida scream. Pericles is looking down on the events as if they are a game of chess. This is not the endgame. There are moves available if only he can see them. The axe rips through the door again. Another blow and their attackers will be able to step through the ragged hole. He swings open the stove and uses the tongs to shovel hot coals into the chamber pot. 'Open the door.' The surgeon is unconvinced. Pericles' hands are burning. 'Open the door or I swear by the gods ...' The surgeon withdraws the bolt, the door swings wide and Pericles throws the hot coals into the face of the midshipman who has raised his axe for a decisive blow. The man drops the axe and cries out, hands to his burnt face, jerkin smoking. Over his shoulder Pericles sees the nurse being dragged away by the Irish cook, his baby daughter dangling from the arm of the second mate like a rabbit in a poacher's hand. He picks up the dropped axe and runs after them.

What follows is a story upon which he would previously have dined out, a story he would have shelved beside many similar stories with which to entertain himself or others in the idle hours some men fill with poetry. It means nothing now. He saves his daughter and her nurse. The mutiny is crushed. He kills seven men himself, two with the axe, five with the swords of the two he killed with the axe. The burly sailors commissioned to watch over the prince in his cabin now fight beside him, killing a further six. The cook and the second mate jump overboard like devils going home after a failed raid on the world of light. Josephus and his henchmen are bound heavily, though Josephus will die of his injuries before they dock in Tarsus.

The nurse has a black eye and three broken fingers and there is a gash in the arm of his baby daughter. He should be relieved but he sits on the deck with his back against the gunwale, bloodied and breathless, the thrill ebbing already, trapped again in the airless gap between a past he is unable to change and a future he is frightened to enter. The surgeon cleans and stitches wounds and the bodies of dead mutineers are rolled overboard. The moon is full. Some say it is another world, a great desert in the sky, hills, plains, valleys. He is already there. The barrenness, the impassable distance.

In other circumstances Lychorida would rejoice in his survival, thank him for saving their lives then lay Marina in his arms but the ferocity with which he fought to save them terrifies her almost as much as the actions of their captors. She has learnt not to have opinions about one's superiors lest they become words one cannot unsay, but she believes that the prince's grief has turned him into a monster. Marina might owe him her life but she deserves a better man for a father. It takes three days to reach Tarsus with a crew of four operating a single sail. In that time the prince makes no attempt to see his child. Lychorida is relieved.

They enter the harbour unannounced but flying a royal ensign, causing a frantic stir on the quay where fishermen and merchants are shooed aside and an ad-hoc welcoming ceremony is rapidly concocted – banners, pergolas, dignitaries, a trio of priests. Pericles is only vaguely interested. They could be docking in Orkney or halfway up the Nile. The surgeon is now the most senior crew member on board and it is not his place to chivvy and upbraid a prince. Only when he hears that the royal couple, Cleon and Dionyza, are at the quayside does Pericles deign to board a gig and let himself be rowed ashore.

They climb onto the quay in a blare of inappropriate trumpets, Pericles flanked by the surgeon and Lychorida carrying Marina in her arms. The two surviving sailors walk behind them, both sporting bandages and one limping badly. No one needs to see Pericles' vacant stare to realise that something is terribly wrong. They are the survivors of a massacre stumbling into camp. The trumpets go silent one by one until an exuberant young man blowing joyously with closed eyes has to be cuffed about the head.

'We heard nothing,' says Cleon, who has not seen Pericles since the murderous night-time visitation. 'We feared that you were dead.' He throws brotherly arms around Pericles who returns a feeble imitation of the gesture. The surgeon stutters an apology for speaking out of turn and examines the ground between his feet. 'A great misfortune has befallen the prince ...' He tries to give his account some concluding uplift by describing how Pericles saved their lives during the mutiny but it has the hollow ring of boyish adventure after the description of Chloë's death and burial.

Cleon and Dionyza place simultaneous hands on Pericles' shoulders as if they are a single person consoling him. 'I am profoundly sorry,' says Dionyza, 'and cannot begin to imagine your sadness.'

'Come,' says Cleon. 'This will always be your home.'

A pair of carriages convey the six passengers uphill through the cobbled streets to the palace where the prince is installed in a suite of mocking opulence, in the hope that the feverish delirium of his grief will pass with time. There is a tapestry above the bed showing, unhelpfully, the flaying of Marsyas.

The extraordinary events of the last week have given them all a dazzle which briefly trumps social distinction. So the surgeon and Lychorida and Marina are placed in two nearby suites of modest rooms, and the two sailors who would, in another port, be happy to sleep on any flat, dry, surface now share a guest room overlooking the palace forecourt. They are given clean sheets every day; slaves deliver hot water for morning baths; pistachios, anchovies, oranges and local pastries dusted with powdered sugar sit on trays which are constantly replenished; jugs of wine magically refill. The sailors gorge themselves queasy over several drunken days until they are quietly removed to a tavern.

The prince is invited to dine with Cleon and Dionyza that first evening. Plovers and marzipan, swordfish and pineapple. He apologises for the seeming gracelessness of his failure to send a message after his rapid and bloody departure. He tells them about the downhill sprint through the moonlit town, the icy plunge, the storm, the spectral Marlenus, the samphire, the Moroccan wrestler with angry eyes … This is hard enough. He can say no more without weeping.

Cleon tells him how the men with the beards and chains dissolved into the night leaving only fear and corpses behind, how Marlenus' body was washed up the following day, how both he and Antonio were given funerals befitting heroes and are now interred within the graveyard of the palace itself.

The prince seems to be looking not at them or the room but at someone or something that moves in a world superimposed upon this one.

Dionyza says, 'We too have had an eventful week.' The phrase is wrong, but she cannot think of a better one. 'We have a newborn daughter of our own, she is five days old. Her name is Phoebe.' The coincidence is startling enough, though it is only the nurse Lychorida who will later do the calculation and realise that the two girls were born at the same hour on the same day. For reasons she will not quite understand this fact will seem dangerous and she will share it with no one.

Dionyza hopes the news will cheer their guest, draw him back into the present, make him think of life instead of death, but the subject unsettles him in a way that nothing else has done. They watch him weave his fingers together to stop his hands shaking.

The penitential meal is drawn to an early close and Pericles is released to the solace of his chambers. The following day Cleon delivers Pericles an open invitation to dine with them whenever he wishes, to ride, to walk in the garden, to take a steam bath, to witness the September games which commence in a week's time. Pericles sends a reply saying that he is not fit company for any person. Nor does he visit his daughter. This is not considered negligent. Dionyza leaves her own daughter in the care of nurses for the greater part of each day and Pericles is merely a father. But there are other omissions which are less excusable. He does not write to Simonides and Lucina to explain that their daughter is dead. He does not write to his own parents giving the reason for his continued absence. Cleon must do both of these things on his behalf.

News begins to spread that the Prince of Tyre has lost his mind.

Losing his mind would be a blessing. Pericles' thoughts are painful and refuse to be ignored. Memories mostly – the way Chloë swung herself confidently into the saddle of the dappled stallion her father said she couldn't ride, her thigh against his thigh as they picked at quail while the fire-juggler held everyone spellbound, snatches of her voice so clear and precise he thinks she is in the room. They are more real than this chair, that bed. He longs to be rid of them, but when the details start to fade the forgetting is more painful still and he longs to be hurt again by their previous clarity.

Most nights he has a variation of the same dream in which he jumps overboard after the makeshift coffin. He can't see it. Or he can't swim.

Or he can't reach it. Or he finds it and can't open it. Or it tumbles slowly down into the bottomless dark on a chain of silver bubbles. Sometimes he clings to the box as it descends and at the moment of his drowning he wakes, sweating and trembling, into the taper-light of his unshared bed. He stumbles to the window to clear his head. Faint woodsmoke and a cream-coloured moon.

His body is failing him. He can feel injuries from which he thought he had recovered – an ache in the base of his spine where he fell at Karchedon which forces him to move like an old man when he rises from a chair, a jagged pinching under his right arm where a Frenchman's blade grazed his lung, a low throb at the rear of his skull where he was struck during the mutiny, a blur which comes and goes like fog in his right eye. These things are punishments, of that he is certain.

He does not want to eat. He drinks only because his body demands it. He runs his hand along the spines of books in the library but when he opens a volume his eye will not hold the page. He forgets one line while he is reading the next. Nothing makes sense, nothing remains. He visits the tombs of Antonio and Marlenus. He feels too little, then too much. He stands on the balcony where the hooded crows queue along the marble balustrade to escape the glare of the afternoon and he is untouched by the majesty of the view, roofs like turned clods of orange clay running down to the harbour, the forest of masts, the slashes of white canvas, the sparkle of the ocean, the trio of little islands. He walks in the Egyptian garden with Cleon every other day, so as not to seem ungrateful for his hospitality. He watches his host feed sunflower seeds and macadamia nuts to his three pet parrots, but he does not dine, he does not appear in public. Gradually he turns from a visiting prince into an old dog nearing the end of its days who is gently exercised every so often but mostly left to sleep undisturbed.

⤸

It is just after dawn when they see the box. They are returning to port, exhausted and ill-tempered with yet another meagre catch in the half-empty baskets at the stern – wrasse, bream, a young tiger shark which does not look healthy. They are tempted simply to sail by. The box contains something, certainly, given how low it is riding in the water, but the gods have shunned them so doggedly over the last few months that it will doubtless turn out to be filled with rancid meat or sodden flour or shat-tered earthenware. It promises some small entertainment, however, and none of them can resist the faint hope of treasure which will transform their lives. So they pull alongside, slip a rope under each end and heave.

It is very heavy indeed, doubtless full of seawater, though why someone should go to the trouble of tarring it like this is a puzzle. And if someone went to the trouble of tarring such a box why would they do it in so amateurish a manner?

'I'm breaking my back for a piece of junk someone threw overboard.'

'Do you really want to hear another crew bragging about how they hauled in a crate of opals?'

'Here it comes.'

The box bangs down hard onto the deck and rolls over. There's water inside, certainly, but some heavier mass sloshing back and forth in the water, something big.

'Open it, then.'

Gaius grabs a knife and stabs it into the point where the lid meets the corner under the sticky black covering. The wood splinters. He lifts his foot and stamps on the handle of the knife to drive the point further into the gap, as if he were driving a spade into hard earth. The lid splits away and water gushes onto the deck. And with the water out flops a hand, pale, thin, unmoving. Everyone steps back.

'*Neptuno has ago gratias meo patrono,*' mutters Nonus to himself, '*qui salsis locis incolit piscolentis …*'

'What if it's not human?' says Nikolaos.

'You are a child, Nikolaos,' says Mettius. 'Do all of us a favour and hold your little tongue.'

Gaius drives the knife into the opposite corner of the box. The lid comes away in its entirety and a woman's body is washed onto the deck by the remaining water. She is wrapped in sodden grave clothes, bruised and bloodied with a broken nose. Nikolaos makes a noise like a small, frightened boy. This scenario did not feature in any of their imaginings. Then Mettius stoops and picks up a sodden hessian bag none of them has yet noticed. He hacks it open like a rabbit's belly. Gold coins clatter onto the wet deck. Tetradrachms? They have no idea. They have never seen currency of this value before. Mettius throws his head back and cries like a wolf and everyone feels the mood shift. They are poor men, everyone has a knife in their belt and accidents happen all the time at sea.

'Hoist her overboard,' says Mettius. No one moves or speaks. 'She's no use to anyone now.'

But Korax is holding a sheaf of parchment he has retrieved from the bag Mettius has dropped. 'Nikolaos?'

Nikolaos takes the parchment. There is writing on it, in Greek, which he can read after a fashion. The ink has run badly but the script is still legible. His shipmates are illiterate. If he thinks fast he might be able to invent a message which will get them all back to harbour alive.

'Read it, philosopher,' says Mettius, who is picking up the gold coins one by one.

The message is so extraordinary, however, that any thought of saying something different slips from Nikolaos' mind. '... *and use this money to grant her a burial befitting the daughter of a king.*'

Mettius takes the parchment from his hands, rips it into four pieces and throws them overboard. 'What difference does it make who she is?' He lifts two stacks of gold coins between his forefingers and thumbs. 'This is what matters.' He holds everyone's eye in turn to make sure they understand. He drops the coins into his pockets and grips Nikolaos' chin. 'What did we find in the box?'

'We found a woman's body.'

'So clever but so stupid.' He slaps Nikolaos' face and grips his chin for a second time. 'What did we find in the box, boy?'

'She's moving.' It is Nonus.

Mettius lets go of Nikolaos. Everyone looks down. The woman twitches, then rolls over, coughing bile and seawater onto the deck. Mettius bends down and grabs her arm. 'Let's get her over the side before you bed-wetters start having qualms.'

He has lifted her by the armpits when Nikolaos hits him. The boy is not strong and the playground blow lands awkwardly but it is enough to knock the bigger man off-balance so that he lets go of the woman and stumbles face down onto the washboard. Gaius takes the woman and drags her under the standing shelter. Nikolaos has no plan. He is simply no longer able to control the anger which he has stoppered up over three years of humiliation. He pulls the knife from his belt and stabs Mettius in the back of the thigh. Mettius roars. Korax and Nonus look at one another, then over at Gaius. It is obvious what they must do right now, but they need to know that they are all going to share responsibility.

Mettius cannot stand. 'Help me!'

Nikolaos lifts the knife again but the other men move him aside. He has already done his part. They each put a hand under Mettius' legs and hoist together so that he pivots over the transom into the water. He turns and grips the rudder. Korax raises his own knife so that Mettius has to let go before his fingers are sliced off. 'Row!' shouts Korax. Nikolaos grabs an oar. Nonus grabs an oar. Mettius flails in the water. He cannot swim. Nikolaos and Nonus fit the oars into the rowlocks, sit themselves on the bench and pull hard. Gaius is wrapping a tarpaulin around the sodden woman.

'I have the gold!' yells Mettius. He is holding up one of the coins and laughing, as if he is going to paint hell red at their expense. Korax rehoists the sail. Mettius slips under and resurfaces for one final time. Then he is gone.

His erstwhile colleagues are an hour out of port, enough time to hone the details of the story of how their captain roped a lead weight to his own ankle before stepping overboard. It seems plausible that a man filled with so much anger should finally turn it on himself. Besides, no one is going to ask questions, least of all his widow, though they would like to have given her a gold coin or two to help her feed her children.

Each man donates a piece of dry clothing. The woman is shaking and cannot talk but she is alive. None of them have seen royalty in the flesh before, and none expected to see royalty in so sorry a state. The wife of Pericles of Tyre, so the parchment said, though they can tell no one, lest someone comes asking for the other contents of the bag. She looks as if she has lost a long boxing match against a much stronger opponent. Was it a punishment or a mistake? Did family or enemies do this to her? The men are in a fairy tale. They fished a princess from the sea, for a whole minute they were rich beyond their wildest dreams, they killed a man and then they were poor again. The loss feels like some kind of recompense for taking a life, but those coins will glitter in their dreams for the rest of their lives.

THE SERPENT

There are whole days when Pericles forgets that he has a daughter. Perhaps it is for the best, since every memory of her is followed immediately by a memory of that blood-spattered chamber and a vision of the box being nailed shut and tarred and tipped into the sea.

Cleon is pained that his friend is suffering and disappointed that they cannot talk as they once did. No volcanoes, no leviathans. Dionyza's feelings are more complex, as they always are. She is more intelligent and more capable than her husband but has never been given a task befitting her skills. So she must ape subservience and act upon the world through subterfuge. No one will say this, but she steered the royal house through the roughest of storms. In that part of the mind which works neither by reason nor by argument she believes that Pericles was both the city's saviour and her own reward. Then he was taken from her. Now he has come back, married, widowed, destroyed, in the company of a child born at the same time as her own. The universe is mocking her.

And Marina herself? If she has no father then she has Lychorida. It is taken for granted that the nurse will remain here then continue to Tyre with her charge when the prince is no longer indisposed. She is not asked for her opinion about this. She is rarely asked for her opinion about anything. She is fifty years old. She earned her freedom in Pentapolis. One more year and she would have been sharing a smallholding with her sister and her brother-in-law. She was looking forward to an old age in which she learns how to please herself, how to use time and make friends, sewing her own clothes, growing walnuts and figs, keeping chickens, watching whole sunsets and sleeping past dawn. It will not happen now. Such agreements are never written down and to remind new masters of old obligations is unthinkable. There are compensations. She is not washing soiled linen or tending to an incontinent uncle with a softened mind in some distant outbuilding. She is past the age when her body could be used freely by young men of rank. She is genuinely fond of this tiny child who lost the wrong parent at the moment of her birth, and increasingly Marina is treated as a companion to Phoebe, which places Lychorida within a charmed circle. She is safe, she is warm, she is fed well. How many women of her age and status can say such things?

There is no answer from Pericles' father in Tyre so after a diplomatic interval Cleon writes a second letter, hypothesising that his previous message may have gone astray. A swift reply from a praetor explains that, 'The king was not minded to answer your last, being aggrieved by his son's continuing absence. He was sick, however, and grows sicker. I write therefore, privately and without the king's knowledge. He will, I fear, not last. I therefore urge that the prince returns home at the earliest opportunity.'

Pericles has few feelings about either his father's impending demise or his own subsequent accession, but duty and expectation compel him. The journey has lain ahead for the last three years. He will let it happen. He asks Cleon and Dionyza to look after Marina. She is a complication he does not need, they are better parents than he will ever be and only the gods know how a tiny child will fare in the anarchy that will overtake Tyre if he cannot stay the jackals who will doubtless gather around his father's corpse.

The *Serpent* and its crew are gifted to him. It is the least they can do, thinks Cleon, though he cannot help but see it is a reasonable price for lifting a cloud from his own mind in particular and the palace in general.

Pericles steels himself to say farewell to his daughter. It is a measure of his lack of interest that he needs directions to the chamber overlooking the third court where she spends the greater part of each day. She is lying on a rug of black sheepskin in a tiny chair which rocks back and forth as she wriggles. The polished wooden sides are silhouettes of elephants. The nurse is leaning over her, shaking peas inside a sealed length of bamboo. Pericles is relieved to see that the queen's daughter and her own nurse are also in the room. Their presence will keep the encounter formal.

He holds the nurse's eye. Lychorida. He remembers her name now. He is afraid that if he looks at the child, if he uses her name, then something vital will give way inside his chest. 'I am returning to Tyre. My father is dying. I fear that the inevitable chaos . . .' Why did he come here instead of simply leaving? Did he want absolution from this old woman? 'And I am not good company for anyone. I would not like those near me to be preyed upon by that which preys upon me.' The confession surprises him. Why is he saying this to a slave? It does not matter. He leaves in the morning. 'The ocean will be a kind of quarantine.' He imagines sailing on, past the harbour mouth at Tyre, to Cithera, to Syracuse, between the Pillars of Hercules then turning north and ploughing the Atlantic to where the maps run out and the ice begins.

Lychorida is angry at his coldness, and scared lest he see this. It is the first time he has shared a room with his child in a month. Even now he cannot bear to look at Marina. In truth he is not looking at anything. His eyes are blank. Her anger evaporates. There is no one to be angry at. This is not the man who left Pentapolis. He looks like a dead body – smaller, paler, emptier. He could enter a room and no one would turn their head.

'I take my leave ...'

The departure is not publicised. Cleon does not want to advertise an opportunity to ogle a great man broken. There is no ceremony. There is unseasonal rain. If it were not for the royal couple and their guard the boat could be returning a minor diplomat or shipping a cargo of painted tiles to the coastal cities of Egypt. Gulls squabble and hop. A shirtless strongman quarters a tuna with a cleaver. A trio of Moroccan sailors play jacks under a half-mended sail propped up by oars.

'I have been a tedious and ungrateful guest.'

'We have had far worse,' says Dionyza, but no one is in the mood for humour.

Cleon says that they will treat Marina as if she were their own daughter.

'I'm so sorry.' Pericles says this to the sky.

'There is nothing any of us can say which will make this easy. We can only wish you well.'

Everyone is relieved when Pericles turns and walks out from under the canopy into the fine rain. A stray dog spooks a horse which rears and whinnies at the back of the tiny gathered crowd. He steps onto the gangplank. A slight wobble where it refuses to lie true on the cobbles. Some small comfort in that, leaving the hard and unforgiving earth. The captain greets him. Dark, weathered skin, a single gold tooth and a lopsided smile. Khalid. Hand flat against his chest and the smallest of bows. No sense of the man's character. Pericles has lost the ability to judge other people. He turns at the rail and looks back at the city. The whistle is sounded. Ropes are unwound from capstans on the quay and hurled up to the waiting sailors on deck. The gang-plank is stowed and the pilot skiff roped to the prow, ten rowers ready to heave the ship through the harbour's narrow mouth on this near-windless day. The hull is poled away from the hemp buffers lining the quayside.

Should he wave? It would surely make him look like a child. But to do nothing would seem ungracious. He is about to lift his hand when Cleon and Dionyza turn and start to walk to the waiting carriage, four courtiers walking beside them so that the canopy remains over their heads. The rowers take up the slack and the pilot begins the raucous song that will keep the oars in time.

He is going home.

It will take him fourteen years to realise that this is the most foolish thing he has ever done.

❧

When they have docked, Gaius and Nikolaos unload the baskets while Korax and Nonus take the woman up the hill to the doctor's house. He is not a doctor as such but he owns books, which is qualification enough in this tiny town. They do not mention the gold which they found then lost but ask politely if they may hear news of the woman's condition and old man Kerimon promises that he will leave a message with the harbourmaster in a few days' time. He gets his house slaves to wrap her in clean, dry blankets and sends the two fishermen away with the salt-caked shirt, the waistcoat, the woollen cap, the breeches and the boots in which she was delivered.

In truth she does not need a doctor. Her bruises will heal. Her nose will set of its own accord, if a little off-centre. But something important has broken in her mind and it will never heal completely. She will not sleep for many days and even then she will never sleep deeply, knowing that she will wake at some point during the night to find herself back inside that floating coffin. Every time she enters a small chamber or a dense crowd her heart will race, she will start to sweat profusely and feel sick and find it hard to breathe. She will always leave doors open and if one slams behind her she will weep. She will never enter a cave, a cellar or a tunnel. She will, after many years, agree to travel by sea but it will be painful and she will do it only once. She will only ever feel truly comfortable out of doors, in sunlight, away from the coast. Even then she will be struck by moments of blind panic that overtake her with neither warning nor explanation.

She talks for the first time towards the end of the third day. She thanks Kerimon for his kindness and asks that similar thanks be given to the fishermen. She apologises for the fact that she can tell him nothing of how she came to be here. It is both a lie and not a lie. There was a king's daughter who married a prince and they loved one another beyond measure. It happened a long time ago and far away and there is nothing to connect that woman to the woman sitting here on the terrace under the vines.

She says, 'My name is Emilia.'

She was at sea for a couple of days at most, but it was enough to rip away the shell in which she had lived her entire life. She is ordinary now. Life is fragile and she can no longer take anything for granted. Days are all she has and they can be wasted or cherished, difficult as they sometimes are. To walk on warm dry stones is good, to eat fresh bread is good, to drink clean, cold water is good. If she met that prince now, what would she be able to offer him? What could he offer her? And her child? Thinking about this is the hardest thing of all, a hole in her belly which hurts like the labour that very nearly killed her. She does not even know whether the child survived. If they did then they will grow up cosseted and pampered and have nothing in common with Emilia, not unless they pass through a similar ring of fire which strips away the privilege and the presumption. And who would wish that on anyone, least of all on a child of their own? Better that Chloë is dead to all of them, to her child, to her husband and to herself.

~

It is a chill November afternoon. In the shuttered light of a great chamber the body of an old man lies on a bed, his lower half covered respectfully with a linen sheet. Branches of cypress and pine flank the doors. Thirteen people in dark togas stand around the bed. Two young women stand closest to the corpse, one on either side. The air is so still that smoke rises from two gold frankincense burners in fine, white flutes to head height. Then a physician steps forward and moments later they break into curls and clouds. The physician gently rolls the man's head to one side. Discreetly he pushes a short ivory spike into the back of the neck, taking care that this seeming outrage is not directly visible to anyone present. The dead man does not react and the wound bleeds only a little. The physician retracts the spike, covers the hole with a folded swab and returns the man's head to its original position. He nods to each of the women in turn, then retreats. The older of the two bends to kiss the man on the lips. The gesture is more formal than tender. There is an uncomfortable silence which is finally broken by an obese middle-aged woman who says the dead man's name out loud. A bearded man with lined, conker-coloured skin and a tremor in his hands says the man's name out loud. Two more of the gathering say the man's name out loud. The two women are the last to join in with the general chant. There is little enthusiasm at first, but once individual voices begin to blend with the greater noise it gathers weight and feeling, not heartfelt lamentation perhaps but something released and given voice. The sisters become silent and one by one everyone follows suit. The oldest sister says quietly, '*Conclamatio est.*'

Four burly slaves, freshly laundered, closely shaved and hitherto invisible at the room's corners, lift the man from the bed and place him on the ground just as he was lifted in the arms of a nurse and placed on the ground when he came into this world. A priest kneels. He is elderly and his legs are stiff. He removes the stopper from a small glass bottle and pours a little oil onto the first two fingers of his right hand. He anoints the forehead of the dead man. He wets his fingers again and anoints the man's chest. The smell is sweet and sickly and does not complement the incense. Terebinth and cardamom. He stoppers the bottle and is helped to his feet.

The dead man is then dressed in a fresh toga. This could be clumsy and comic but the slaves have done it so often that it has become a kind of performance. There is a brief pause after they are finished, as if they are waiting for applause. The man is adorned with a wreath, a cunning arrangement of wires slipped under his briefly lifted head so that it remains firmly in place.

The priest kneels again. The dead man will need an obol for payment lest he remain stranded on the shore for ever watching legions of the dead being ferried to their final home. But the man's jaw will not open. The priest leans in to give himself more leverage but to no avail. The corpse is as intransigent as the living man. In different circumstances the priest might twist a knife between the teeth so that the coin could be slipped through as if the head were a money box, but he cannot risk doing this to the king. He must think fast. He parts the toga to reveal the man's chest. There is uneasy movement in the crowd behind him. He places the obol on the man's sternum, the sticky film of oil keeping it in place. He covers the coin with the rearranged toga then, one by one, places the hands over it, hoping that he has performed the actions with sufficient aplomb to suggest that they are an official variation on the standard procedure.

He stands, crosses his own hands in front of him and waits for the room to come to attention then says, '*Rex mortuus est.*'

Just out of Tyre the *Serpent* is intercepted by a cutter flying the royal colours. If the portly civil servant is shocked by the change in Pericles his demeanour registers nothing. The man offers his condolences for the death of his wife. Pericles feels again that sick lurch in his stomach every time Chloë is mentioned, one more confirmation that it really happened. 'I am afraid to say that I have more bad news.' Pericles is too late. His father died only the day before. 'The citizens, however, do not know this yet. They know only that the king is gravely ill. The secret can perhaps be contained overnight, but no longer than that.'

Pericles looks at the city framed by the jaws of the harbour. The architecture of his childhood – the temple to Athena, the long retaining wall of the dam, the cupola of the eastern tower where he hid with Kremnobates. He is now king of this city. Once upon a time he would have taken the elevation in his stride. The presumption that he is superior to everyone in Tyre now seems preposterous. The portly counsellor is wrong. He is years too late. Even before Pericles set sail his father was turning one man against another. It seems unlikely that he has become a healer of wounds in the interim. The gods alone know what is about to be unleashed. Pericles is about to walk onto a battlefield. He needs advisers, he needs staff, loyal troops, knowledge. He is utterly unprepared for the most difficult task of his life. Why did he not plan for this? He must be very careful indeed. If he gets this wrong, people will die and yet again it will be his fault.

'I recommend travelling to the palace incognito. Rumours of your father's serious illness have stoked strong feelings. Your safety is my primary concern. I fear that dignity must wait.'

Pericles is rowed ashore and ushered swiftly into a closed carriage. There is a crowd in the agora. Soldiers ring the temple to Proserpina. A mob have set a shop alight. Fishmongers, bakers, carters. Two bodies lie slumped against a trough like dozing beggars. There is a crackle in the air like the crackle before a thunderstorm. A statue of his grandfather has been toppled and covered in mud or excrement. Chloë's ghost rides beside him the whole way. He will speak to his sisters. Blood is the only thing he can rely on now. They will tell him which men he can trust. Think of the city as a ship. Think of a mutiny brewing.

They move swiftly past a noisy crowd waiting for news outside the palace and enter through a small gate in the rear of the main wall, normally used for goods and slaves and waste. Following the portly counsellor and flanked by two guards Pericles walks through the kitchens. A few heads are dipped as he passes, but what he sees mostly is puzzlement and blankness. Perhaps they see only a nameless dignitary with a military guard, perhaps they recognise the young man but despise him for his long absence, perhaps they are biding their time before deciding their allegiances.

There is a faint oceanic roar echoing in the building which he does not remember and which unsettles him. He understands only when they pass a second-floor window which overlooks the central court whose fourth side opens onto the ornamental lawns between the main buildings and the northern wall. The area has become a camp for a thousand, two thousand, armed men. There are seven rows of tents, there are horses and wagons and water barrels stacked in towers; a field of spears thrust shaft-first into the earth glitters like grass after rain. He can smell dung and leather. Whinnies, yells and the clatter of metal on metal dissolve into one general din. He pauses. The soldiers accompanying him pause. He does not want to appear foolish by asking what is happening.

'It is best if we keep moving,' says the counsellor.

They walk down the Hall of Shields and along the corridor whose swirling blue marble floor he lay on as a child, imagining that he was swimming like a fish through the depths of the ocean. They lead him up the final flight of stairs and enter the council chamber through the big double doors with their curled brass hinges and intricate carvings of knotted snakes and hovering falcons. And in the next long moment he is simultaneously saved and humiliated. His sisters sit beside one another at the head of the table where his father raged and banged his fist. Polished walnut, the zigzag mother-of-pearl inlay running round the edge. No one gets to their feet, no one calls him king, no one performs obsequies of any kind. Is he in danger? He had not expected this.

Ennia stands and walks over. His sisters have become women. Why should this be a surprise? Was time meant to stand still in his absence? 'Brother, welcome.' Her voice is stiff and official. 'We were all very sorry indeed to hear your terrible news and we will later be able to

201

give your story the attention it deserves but for the moment it must be put to one side.'

He wants someone to tell him exactly what is going on, but when he imagines himself making this angry demand he hears it spoken in his father's voice and it throws him off balance. *Take a breath. Proceed with caution. Be gracious.* 'I apologise for the lateness of my arrival.'

'If anything, you have arrived too soon.' This is Corinna. 'You are a complication we could have done without.'

Ennia touches him on the shoulder. 'You must be exhausted from your journey. Perhaps you would feel better if—'

Corinna cuts her off. 'He needs to be here.' She fixes him with a hard stare, all the better to examine his response. 'I presume you are relieved by our father's death.'

Suddenly he wants to defend the old man. He looks around. His armed escort stand by the door.

'We have no time for diplomatic niceties.' Corinna will not look away. 'People are dying.'

'I left to escape our father. I would have thought that spoke for itself.'

'Some of us did not have that luxury.'

He is being outplayed. He was outplayed before he knew the game had begun.

'Take a seat,' says Ennia.

Diodoros stands and offers Pericles his chair. Or is it Pleuron? One of his father's generals. He cannot remember their names, yet he had expected to command them. The seat is near the head of the table but it is not at the head of the table. He gathers himself before sitting. 'Will someone tell me what is happening?'

Corinna pauses, turning some unspoken question over in her mind. 'Lykomedes is gathering troops for a coup.' Pericles does not recognise the name. 'A third of the army will support him, a third are stationed here in the palace, a third will follow the prevailing wind. There are riots. People are using the cover of wholesale unrest to settle old scores. It will get rapidly worse if something is not done. My sister and I will go before the people today to announce our father's death and offer them an alternative to a military dictatorship. It would help a great deal if you kept your head down and did not muddy the water. Rumours have preceded you and the way you look does nothing to contradict them.'

He realises now that the counsellor was waiting in the cutter not to welcome him but to hide him. Fourteen granite-faced men are staring. They are impatient and their sympathies are not for sale. There was a time when he could have walked into this room and taken command of it. There was a time when he could have walked into any room and taken command of it. He has never believed in the Fates. You shape your own life, you see the available futures laid out before you and you choose the most advantageous. He can see now that this is a delusion from which you suffer when the path chosen for you is a profitable one. When the path veers into darker, more difficult terrain you finally understand that what you thought was weakness in others is not weakness at all; it is simply the structure of the world.

Pericles sits down. There is a map in the centre of the table. There are tiny stones on the map, presumably showing the locations of garrisons – at the barracks, the hippodrome, the harbour. There are two boards of bread and olives and halva, all uneaten.

Another of his father's generals whose name he does not recall says to Corinna, 'The promise to lower taxes makes you seem weak. Nor will they believe you. They will assume it is an empty gesture.'

Diodoros says, 'Lykomedes offers nothing but nebulous ideas of glory and patriotism.'

'And the fact that he is a man.'

'Offer them trade and stability. Everyone who matters will understand. Glory and patriotism are indulgences which come second to feeding your children and keeping a roof over your head.'

It is a way of working he would never have considered. He is embarrassed to think that were he in his sisters' shoes he would have simply played a less confident, less competent version of their father. He gets to his feet and says that he will retire. The atmosphere in the room stiffens a little. Two of the guards step forward. Corinna says, 'Let him go.'

The portly counsellor appears at his shoulder. 'Your old suite has been made ready.'

He is escorted from the room. The conversation resumes as soon as he has crossed the threshold.

He stands at the window of his apartment. He was born in a room at the end of this corridor. The nursery is a stone's throw away. Halved limes float in a glass bowl of water on the table. There is sausage, there is incense, there are two carved ivory giraffes. He can still feel the airless panic that drove him away, but he no longer has the energy to fight it. He wants to hide in the storeroom at the back of the kitchen eating lokum and salep. But Mustafa the cook died years ago and his father had Kremnobates strangled when he took a bite out of Ennia's hand. He is fairly certain that the soldiers would not allow him to go to the cupola in the eastern tower. He is so unmanned that he no longer has the energy to feel outrage. A fresco covers the wall opposite the table. The capture of Briseis. The burning of the ships. The suicide of Ajax.

A tiny scorpion scurries along the hot sill. His rooms are at the rear of the palace. He can hear nothing, he can see no gathered troops, no rising smoke, no insurrection, just the overblown town houses of wealthy merchants rising and giving way to hills.

You grow up learning that kingship is natural and eternal, royal lineage a great arch with curves overhead from the forgotten past into the unknown future, giving a city protection and purpose. But it is, in fact, a piece of grand theatre, nothing more than a custom, like money, like honour, and if the majority decide that they will no longer agree to tell the old story then it collapses. At which point there is no turning back. One cannot re-believe when the veil is torn.

There are storks' nests on the taller chimneys, spatters of white shit on the roof tiles around them.

Let it all burn. None of it matters any more. If this city did not exist, if there were only kelch grass and stone pines and spider crabs and black-backed gulls and the perpetual, unwitnessed accounting of the waves, would the world be richer or poorer?

On the far side of the palace his sisters rise with their generals and counsellors and take their claim to the people.

❧

Angelica sleeps for a little longer each day and rarely leaves her bed. Occasionally she sits in the armchair by the fire. She no longer comes to the kitchen or the dining room. Still she does not talk. She no longer reads or draws or watches videos. It needed work at first, pushing further into this strange country. It is easier now. Perhaps it is the knowledge that she has come too far and that the journey back will be more arduous than continuing. Perhaps it is the gravity of the dark interior which pulls at her with increasing strength as the distance shrinks and her own strength fails.

Philippe insists that she will give in to her growing hunger after two days, after four, after a week, but it is obvious even to him that Angelica needs medical help. To ask for such help, however, would risk his daughter being taken to a place where she may say things they will both regret. He will look after her at home, as he has always done. He will devote himself to this task. They will weather the storm as they have weathered others.

He tells her that he will give her anything she wants if only she will stop hurting herself like this, if only she will stop hurting everyone. He asks Dottie to make the foods Angelica liked best as a child – smoked salmon bagels, tiramisu, whitebait, steamed pears in vanilla custard. He takes them to her room and leaves them on the little table by the window. Even the smell of them makes Angelica queasy, the sweetness, the fatness, the physicality. It is the same queasiness she used to feel when they were travelling abroad and she saw gutters filled with sewage or amputees begging at the roadside with their stumps uncovered. Too much of the world.

Philippe asks Dottie to talk to his daughter. Dottie sits beside the bed. Again, Angelica smiles and holds her hand and again it is hard to suppress the feeling that, despite her failing health, Angelica is the stronger of the two.

Dottie confronts Nikki. If they do not tell someone outside the family then they are complicit, legally and morally. The question of why Angelica has stopped speaking and eating hovers unspoken. To ask it now would be to admit that they should have asked it a long time ago. Nikki says that she will do something, if only to end a conversation that makes her profoundly uncomfortable, and perhaps for half an hour or so she really believes that she will indeed do something, but she has worked for Philippe for too long and absorbed a view of the world in which difficult problems are offloaded to someone who has been paid to deal with such things, the difference being that Nikki does not have the money to pay for someone else to solve this problem.

She does not sleep for two nights. Every time she lets herself drift off she is haunted by the images she has kept behind a locked door for many years and it is less the images themselves that horrify her than the fact that she is seeing them and doing nothing. She has her phone in her hands several times, the dial tone whining. Who can she ring? A hospital? The police? Some local GP with whom Angelica has never been registered? She writes a letter of resignation citing a serious illness in her family. She leaves the letter for Hervé and takes a thousand pounds from petty cash, a sum so small it will hopefully go unnoticed in the confusion her departure will create. She drives to Manchester and knocks at the door of a brother who has not seen her for five years. She sells her car and takes a temporary job as a hospital receptionist and hears nothing more about Philippe and Angelica until they appear on the front page of the national newspapers.

In other circumstances Hervé might find a replacement for Nikki and tell Philippe only when he has resolved the problem, but he is not going to be able to replace Nikki and he is not going to be able to solve this problem. It is the beginning of the end and he is intrigued by the way it will play out, as if he were watching the final episode of a TV drama.

Angelica has lost twelve kilos. She had precious little spare fat to begin with. She no longer leaves her bed except to walk slowly to the toilet and back. Her breath is bad. Her joints hurt. It seems to those around her that she is becoming increasingly confused, but inside her head she is increasingly clear that Darius will come back to her once he has learnt the meaning of love and loss.

Hervé calls a private doctor whose details he was given some years ago by a wealthy friend of Philippe's. The fee is shockingly high but when he arrives at the house the doctor treats the situation with sang-froid. His name is Kellaway. He is clean-shaven, a small, forgettable man with spectacles who smells faintly of old-fashioned furniture polish. He examines Angelica while Hervé sits in the corner of the room and Philippe stands at the window looking down at three magpies bouncing between lawn and trees. Three for a girl, is that right?

Angelica acts as if the doctor does not exist. It is impossible to tell whether this is an act or a symptom of her deteriorating condition. The doctor says, with no readable intonation, 'So, it has been decided that the patient cannot be moved to a hospital,' as if that decision has been taken by God himself. He wriggles his left hand into a thin, blue rubber glove.

'Tell me what can be done,' says Philippe, but Kellaway is not an employee, however much he has been paid.

'Let us not jump to conclusions.' He takes Angelica's pulse. He listens to her heart. He taps her chest. He shines a light into her eyes. 'Catabolysis. The body is digesting muscle and tissue in order to protect the heart and the nervous system. She is also badly dehydrated.' He touches the dry cracked skin of her left elbow. 'She has a yeast infection in her throat.' Philippe flinches. Kellaway throws back her bedsheets. 'Skin rashes but no oedema. I will assume some level of non-compliance so it's hard to accurately assess her level of consciousness.' He clicks his fingers in front of Angelica's face then clicks them above her head. 'But she responds to noise and voices.' He pinches her arm as if she were a piece of meat. 'And she responds to painful stimuli so I am not greatly

208

worried for the moment. However, she is on the verge of becoming very sick indeed, heart failure being the primary concern. I am going to send a nurse. We will put her on a drip to rehydrate her. Will she need restraining?' He turns to Philippe who simply shrugs. He is both reassured and scared by the way in which this man has taken charge of the situation.

'If necessary we will then fit a nasogastric tube so that she can be given liquid food.' He removes his glove and drops it alongside the stethoscope inside an accountant's black briefcase.

Philippe watches from the window as Hervé escorts him back to the green Volvo parked discreetly in the far corner of the gravelled rectangle. When the car is gone he turns back to Angelica and feels that bruising wrestle of love and hate. What if she dies? And behind that question, unspoken, its dark twin – what if she lives?

❧

Kerimon is a generous host. He, too, found himself washed up in this coastal town, in his case after his fellow senators died in a coup in Samaria. He has been deprived of the company of social equals for many years and with the exception of this one bloody episode, about which he says nothing, the details of which Emilia later learns from Drusilla, the oldest of the house slaves, he recounts stories constantly, about his childhood and about the town news he hears via the documents he is asked to write and decipher for the illiterate or innumerate. He tells her about the early death of both his parents and the paternal uncle who beat him daily till his maternal aunt stole him away in the middle of the night, how he then grew up in his maternal uncle's household as Allectus moved through a series of civil service postings along the Persian Gulf.

He tells her about the lesser marvels of their own town – the sailor's son with no toes who could see the future, the widow of seven years who remarried a month before her shipwrecked husband finally returned home, the man who bequeathed his small fortune to a horse.

Kerimon is nearing sixty, a saggy man with a hangdog face and a tendency to drop objects and bump into furniture. He has no sexual interest in her. He is, however, besotted with a succession of young men whose attention is never wholly free of mockery. He has a large library – 'a sad fraction of what I once possessed' – and is devoted to the garden laid out along a series of terraces descending to the river which feeds into the harbour. Every so often a grizzled traveller will arrive at the villa bearing a seedling from the world's end and be rewarded with the kind of money other people spend on carnelian or garnet – mountain rhubarb, a bottlebrush tree, evergreen magnolia, fiercely spiked orange cacti … On occasion, instead of supervising his slaves, he gets down on his knees and digs the earth with his own hands.

She thinks, sometimes, about her rescue. There was money in a bag. If the fishermen took it then they will have made better use of it than she could. One of them tried to throw her overboard. His fellows then threw him overboard. He will have drowned, surely. She has difficulty thinking of these acts in terms of right and wrong. What does she know of the stories which lie behind their actions? How much does one ever know of the stories which lead to the present moment? She has stepped out of life. She no longer has an investment. She can see it clearly now. Everyone inhabits a different world.

She needs to be useful, to do something with her hands. So Drusilla is teaching her how to weave. It calms her, the way the body starts to operate without the mind's bidding once you have learnt a skill. She is a good student this time around, she takes more care, she has more patience. She weaves a bedspread patterned with orange and blue diagonal lines. She is starting to learn how one weaves figures, landscapes, stories.

Sometimes Kerimon finds her weeping. He seems embarrassed. He fetches a rug and places it over her as if it is cold from which she is suffering. He sits beside her and says nothing. Sometimes she looks at him and finds that he is weeping, too, though whether he is weeping for her or on his own account she never asks.

Four or five weeks after her arrival one of the young men beats Kerimon about the head before stealing a ruby necklace and two silver cups. Emilia finds him in his chamber, sitting on the floor, a bloody gash running through his thinning hair, his right eye puffy and purpled. She cleans the wound then leads him to a stone bench in the corner of the garden where vines create a wedge of dappled shade. She lays the same unnecessary rug over his lap and sits beside him and reads from the Argonautica.

Ἀρχόμενος σέο, Φοῖβε, παλαιγενέων κλέα φωτῶν μνήσομαι ...

Beginning with you, Phoebus, I will describe the famous deeds of men of old, who, at the behest of King Pelias, drove the well-benched Argo down through the mouth of Pontus and between the Cyanean rocks, in search of the golden fleece ...

Autumn is turning to winter. It has been three months since her rescue and she is growing restless. She needs movement, purpose, responsibility, she needs to engage in some kind of business with other people. But none of the skills she possesses have much value at the end of this particular road where every woman weaves and Kerimon has cornered the market in the interpretation of legal documents and the writing of letters. But where else would she go, and why? She is fond of Kerimon. He welcomed her into his home when she had nothing. And as she once needed him now he needs her. Since the beating he moves like an older man who is nervous of falling. She does not like the idea of him living alone.

One of her pleasures is walking in the hills behind the town, about which these maritime people seem largely incurious. She enjoys the quiet and her own company and likes the idea that she could simply carry on in any direction and nothing could stop her, the absolute freedom of it. She is returning to the villa one afternoon by a winding route she has not taken before when she chances upon a small deserted temple once dedicated to Diana but now derelict. Four columns under the portico and a single room behind the rear wall. The former priestess died years ago, Kerimon tells her later, and these are Neptune's adherents, albeit sceptical ones, too inured to the weather's fickleness to put anything but superficial trust in prayer.

Her walks keep leading her back to the same spot. It is not the most beautiful of locations, a junction of five cart tracks, used enough to churn the mud but not enough to discourage weeds, two wooden byres left to rot, trees and scrub all around, a view of sorts down to the scruffier end of a scruffy town, other unremarkable hills beyond. There is a row of swallows' nests behind the pediment. The temple must have been falling into disrepair even before the last priestess left. The wall paintings are sun-bleached and peeling, moss has made its dogged inroads, the initials of children and courting couples are scored into the plaster and builders have begun purloining the more extractable stones. But she belongs here in a way she cannot articulate. Perhaps it is the very unexceptional nature of the place which resonates.

Kerimon no longer has anyone else to indulge and the project promises to keep Emilia in the villa for the next year at least so he is willing to pay for the work. Two men take on the roles of stonemason, builder, roofer and plasterer. They are not craftsmen but one is hard-working and the drunkard is eventually replaced by the hard-working man's son. The frescoes are restored by a painter of figureheads and shop signs. They are not accomplished pictures but they have a rough vigour and they are certainly eye-catching. Here is Diana hunting with her companions, a large dog at her side. Here is Diana presiding over a childbirth. Here is Diana in a forest, surrounded by a troupe of not wholly believable wild animals, one of which appears to be the offspring of a badger and a horse. Here is Diana bestowing authority upon an unspecific ancient king.

Emilia never becomes the priestess in any official sense. Rather, she realises belatedly that she has been something approaching a priestess in the eyes of the townspeople for a long time, even before she chanced upon the temple. She has possessed since her arrival an aura of the preternatural, the woman fished from the sea, dead then not dead, about whom nothing is known and who knows nothing about herself, the woman who walks alone in the hills and dwells in the villa of the wise man, casting her gaze over them all.

She thinks they are coming to see the results of the restoration or to catch a glimpse of the crazy woman who has taken on this ridiculous job. She does not realise that the conversations these people strike up are anything beyond the ordinary, and it is this perhaps which gives them some of their power. They talk about children who have died of fevers and young men lost at sea. They talk about pregnancies and legacies, about violent husbands and unhappy wives, about wilful children, about wounds to the body and to the heart. She listens. And being listened to by someone held in such high esteem, by someone not quite of this world, makes them feel a little stronger, a little more in harmony with a discordant world, a little more able to solve their own problems without divine intercession. Most go away thinking they have been given wise advice which in truth they have told themselves. Perhaps this is what all prayer is, when the ceremony and the theology are peeled away, a serious stillness in which one talks quietly to one's own best self.

Marriages are consecrated. Funerals are performed. Small sacrifices are made at the little altar at the rear of the portico. Votive tablets are hung on the wall, plaster tiles bearing crudely drawn names and pictures of fishing boats and babies and naked couples and ploughs and farm animals and coins.

Belatedly she finds herself thinking about the goddess whose intermediary she has accidentally become. Chloë gave the gods little consideration. They were a large and restive family ruling a neighbouring kingdom who demanded regular tribute and needed careful diplomatic handling. Even in her floating coffin she called out to none of them for intercession. But now? As Emilia she pictures Diana in the woods behind the temple, bow in hand, dogs at her side. Increasingly, at dusk, she will see flashes of something between the trees, and while she knows that it is probably the scut of a running deer, she feels … unalone, watched over.

She returns to the story of Actaeon which had appalled her as a child – how the grandson of Cadmus is hunting in the valley of Gargaphie when he stumbles upon Diana bathing in a clear, shaded pool in a sacred grove. Her nymphs cry out but are unable to shield the goddess on account of her height. Having no weapon to hand, she throws water at him and cries out, 'Go and tell the story, if you can, of how you saw me naked.' Horns spring from his forehead, his neck lengthens, his ears grow pointed, his hands become hooves, his skin a spotted hide. His dogs can no longer see their master, only a frightened stag. They give chase and drag him to the ground. Forming a ring around the fallen animal so that each dog has a place at the table they fix their snouts deep into the flesh. Terrified and suffering unbearable pain, Actaeon fills the valley with screams which are neither human nor animal. Then he screams no more.

The story is still cruel and unfair, but she knows now that life can be cruel and unfair. There is perhaps some small justice in an innocent man, for once, being the victim of a woman's capricious anger. But the myth hints at something else, the dangers of looking into the heart of the mystery. Questions always lead to more questions which lead to more questions. Do not seek out the sacred grove. Better to keep running with the hunt. She thinks too about those dogs. Were they, like Actaeon, human once? Did Ovid simply not have the time or the ink to tell their stories? She imagines them, sated and bloody-chopped, looking around for their master, finding themselves abandoned, their warm kennels far away and night coming down.

She never utters the name *Pericles*, even in the privacy of her own mind. It edges into her field of vision sometimes. She pushes it gently away. She doesn't know the name of Chloë's child. It is perhaps better that way.

Winter turns to spring. The hills smell of thyme and sage again. There is chamomile and dittany. There are heliotropes and gladioli. She sees kingfishers and, occasionally, a hoopoe. Two boats go down in a freak storm. Nine men are lost. A wife is left blind in one eye after she is punched in the head by her drunken husband. A house is destroyed by lightning. Nine couples are married. Thirteen people die, five of them babies. The body of a teenage boy is found high in the woods a month after his disappearance. A monstrous fish is caught, its weight beyond anyone's guessing. It has to be towed back to harbour where a crowd of men haul it up the beach on log rollers. It has an ill-tempered expression, a mouth a child can climb inside and grey skin so smooth and shiny you can see your own blurred portrait in it. Opinions are divided as to whether it is a blessing or an ill omen, though everyone agrees that the meat is delicious. Only a small amount of it can be eaten, however, before the carcase starts to rot and emit a stench so strong it can be smelled leagues downwind. By this point the fish is more substance than object and must be put back into the sea over several weeks, stinking greasy shovel by stinking greasy shovel.

Spring turns to summer. Kerimon is more frail, more easily fatigued. He takes as much interest in the garden as he ever did but he no longer clips and weeds and plants himself. The illiterate and innumerate come to the villa just as frequently, but after untangling a poorly drafted will or a long bill of lading he will sometimes sleep for an hour on the terrace. The difference in age would make them father and daughter but Emilia pictures them, instead, as two birds sitting on a wall, two horses at a fence, the way animals sit so peaceably in one another's company with neither noise nor fuss nor explanation. She asks him if they should seek the advice of a doctor from another, larger town. He believes that doctors are charlatans and that it is the quality of years which counts, not their number.

Autumn and winter, mild as they are, take their toll. He finds it increasingly hard to breathe and is often racked with a cough that can be soothed only a little by Drusilla's concoctions of honey, gentian and liquorice. He sometimes dozes off while Emilia is reading to him. He can no longer lie down at night but must sleep propped on a bank of pillows.

Emilia deals with much of the paperwork that continues to arrive at the door. It blends seamlessly with her role at the temple. So much sadness flows from broken promises and monies unpaid, so many tragedies leave bureaucratic chaos in their wake.

Both Kerimon and Emilia know, without speaking of it, that he will die in the spring. He is able to comfort her less and less when the memories ambush her during the day, but caring for him lightens her own burden. He can no longer read. His sight is milky and he cannot see much of the garden. His life has become a small thing.

In his final month he talks about the coup in Samaria, how he watched from an attic window as one of the other senators was skinned by a mob, how he himself escaped by burying himself in a pile of dung on the back of a cart pulled by a merchant friend and how he still bears the scar left by an investigatory pitchfork thrust into the dung at the city gates. She tells him in turn about Chloë and Pericles and the child whose name and gender she never knew. She tells him about the wrestling and the marriage and the birth at sea and how she woke to find herself adrift in a sealed crate.

In his last two weeks he becomes increasingly confused. He thinks he is in Talmena. He thinks he is sailing on the Sea of Azov. He sees elephants. Woken by noises in the small hours they find him sleepwalking, moving with an ease and energy he has not possessed for years. They steer him gently back to his chamber. Come morning he is bed-bound once more. He asks repeatedly about an escaped bird called Autonoë and cries, asking his uncle to stop beating him. He has moments of clarity. In some he is frightened. In others he seems utterly at peace with the world. One afternoon he says, 'I seem to be making rather a performance of my departure. You must be exhausted.'

He dies at night in the garden. They find him in the morning curled around an acacia. Drusilla assumes he became disoriented, went outside, could not find his way back in and died of the cold, but Emilia finds a key in the earthenware bowl from which she eats her wine-dipped bread every morning. He must have known that it was his final day. She likes the idea that death did not come to take him away but that he decided to go and meet it.

She finds the locked box which the key opens. It contains papers which transfer ownership of the property and fortune to her. *As if such things matter here in Ultima Thule,* Kerimon has written in the accompanying letter. *You have been my one true friend. Live well.*

His body is burnt in front of the temple. The crowd stretches into the shadows beneath the trees in every direction so that the forest seems to have grown from a field of people. One by one men and women climb the steps of the portico to share stories of his generosity. She sees none of the young men who hung about the villa in the early months of her stay. She waits long into the evening for the crowd to disperse. Dark descends and the last embers are still glowing inside the ashy pyre when a woman comes up to her and says that her mother died a year ago but that she still wakes in the night and sees the old woman standing at the end of the bed. Emilia listens. Life has started up again already.

She gives a generous parting gift to the house slaves who wish to leave. Drusilla and Hamda, one of the younger women, choose to remain.

Spring turns to summer. The heat is vicious. A forest fire comes close enough to the temple to leave the southernmost side of every column smoke-blackened. Many plants die in the garden. Someone breaks into the villa at night and steals a little marble bust of Eurynome and an oil lamp in the shape of a lion. The bust reappears in the garden ten days later, slightly chipped. On the same day she hears news of a young man falling to his death from a roof. It is pointless asking whether the events are connected

Summer turns to autumn. She reads several treatises on plants from the library. She starts to restore the garden. She has never done physical labour like this before. She is surprised to find that she likes the dirt under her fingernails that she can never wholly remove. She walks to the temple every day. She is rarely alone. She prays to Diana. She draws up contracts and tries hard to soften the impact of letters containing bad news.

Autumn turns to winter. The days grow shorter. They close the shutters at sunset and put logs on the fire.

This is her life. It is simple. It is complete.

꩜

The gold sits in a small crucible suspended over a fierce little fire which burns white in a tube of stacked stone. It starts to bubble and spit. It is hot enough. Wearing thick leather gloves Hazhmek places the clay mould between the claws of the blackened iron tongs and holds it over the fire. The mould looks like a large and heavily crusted scallop shell. There is a hole in the top no larger than the end of a child's little finger. Hazhmek sings quietly to himself to time the process. The mould blackens. The song ends. He lifts the mould away, turns it upside down and pours the liquid wax back into the pot which sits on the smaller, cooler fire. The translucent liquid goes pearly as it folds into the parent mixture. He returns the mould to the hotter fire and picks up the crucible of molten gold by one of its two long handles. He lets out a long, slow breath because the gold is precious and spillages are hard to recover. Gently he rotates the handle and a slender tongue of hot metal pours from the narrow spout into the narrower hole. He keeps pouring until a luminous button of hot metal rises in the hole. He rights the crucible and places it back over the fire. He waits for the hot button to scab and darken, then drops the mould into a pot of water sitting behind him.

He removes his gloves, quietly sings another verse to himself then takes the mould from the water. He cracks it against a stone, takes out the cooled metal, brushes away the remaining crumbs of clay, polishes the object on the corner of his jerkin and passes it to Pericles. It is a buckle. There is an emblematic tree in the background. In the foreground a hunter has released an arrow. It is mid-flight in the centre of the buckle. On the opposite side a fleeing boar twists its neck, mouth open, eyes wide. It is a design Pericles has never seen before. The very briefest of moments snatched from time and made into metal.

'Good?'

'Very good indeed. The best yet.' He pats the crouching man's shoulder.

Hazhmek takes the buckle back. He selects a file from the tool kit and starts to rub away the plug of gold which rose in the mould's mouth, so that it becomes the base of the hunter's quiver.

Pericles walks past the wall of wagons to the edge of the encampment. They will all remain here until the growing warmth brings the horseflies and midges and they are forced to drive their flocks further up the valleys. Smoke rises like horse-tails from the chimney hole of the other tents. He can smell mutton boiling. He can hear the whoops and hoots of children, the whinny and jingle of bridled horses, the scrape of men whetting blades. Women sing as they mend felt and leather. He reaches the small tent they have loaned him and for which he is very grateful. It is only the beginning of spring, the nights are still bitter and his journey has been a long and cold one. His camel is resting, bony legs folded under its belly on the moss bed under the little stand of pines. The three packhorses are cropping grass. He sits on a cut log and looks down the valley. The mountains to his right are still white above the deep green of the treeline. The topmost peaks will remain white all summer. The first of the wild flowers are starting to appear in the ungrazed grass on the far side of the river. The pinks and yellows are the ones that always shock him the most, colours he has not seen since the previous year and still does not quite believe. The river is in spate. Come summer you will be able to walk across by hopping from boulder to boulder, but right now it is a rage of melt-water. Sometimes, early in the morning, he sees chunks of ice tumbling downstream. Directly in front of him the little plateau drops away to a sea of bright spring grass which runs unbroken to the horizon. A lammergeyer turns. He unclasps the lid of the iron pot sitting beside the log and takes out some hard mare's cheese and a length of dried goat sausage.

He does not wear the pointed hat but he has adopted the weasel-fur cloak, the felt leggings, the long boots. His hair is cut short but he has a thick beard. His face is sunburnt and webbed with fine lines. He has lost two fingers on his right hand to frostbite. Under his jerkin his upper arms, chest and shoulder blades are covered in tattoos, a rolling cartoon of hunting scenes – lions killing rams, an elk brought down by two dogs, a vulture pouncing on a small fantastical monster. The seamstress Azhana did it during a long ceremony whose meaning was opaque, the obscure details doubly obscured by the pain and the hemp he smoked to dull it. Lampblack, urine and a bone needle, the most exquisite handiwork. He is half barbarian now.

He has been travelling and trading for fourteen years. The ocean betrayed him so he turned inland. He took two slaves, eleven horses, rolls of embroidered cloth, dried fruit, double-lined leather bags stuffed with cinnamon, nutmeg, star anise ... One slave was killed and five horses were stolen along with most of his saleable goods in a short, brutal encounter on the shores of the Black Sea. The second slave slipped away into the back streets of Trapezus. He thought briefly of returning to Tyre but did not want to fail at simple trade, an activity by means of which numberless unremarkable men paid their way in the world. So he used the coins stitched into the underside of his saddle to invest in more produce and kept riding north-east.

It was easier alone. He could move more swiftly, drawing less attention to himself. He was reliant only on his own devices when he entered a new town or met new travellers on the road. He spoke three languages. He could be whoever he needed to be at every fresh encounter. He has travelled to the Greek-speaking colonies of Odessus and Apollonia in the west. He has travelled to Samarkand and ridden east through the Hindu Kush and over the Taklamakan Desert to Tun Huang. He has journeyed south into the deserts where the Persian empire thins to nothing and north by boat into the great frozen forest where there is no summer. He is exhausted. He has deliberately chosen a life in which he is seldom allowed to rest and must be always on his guard and it has worn him down so that he feels and looks like a much older man. These days he sticks to a route he knows well, moving back and forth once every year between Paphlagonia on the southern shores of the Black Sea in the winter then eastwards to the foothills of the Altai mountains during the summer, staying and trading with the same families and villages every year.

He has bought felt hats and silk stockings. He has sold tiger skins and earrings. He has bought dried amber, carnelian, peppercorns and gold toothpicks. He has sold ointments and powders for tumours, impotence, migraines, diarrhoea. He has bought tiny models of men and women carved from deer antlers which can be given the name of one's enemy and thrown into a fire to bring them bad luck. He has tried it himself, giving the tiny man his own name before burning it, with no discernible ill-effect, unless the continuance of his present life were already damnation enough. He has traded star charts from Chang-yeh and mathematical treatises from Athens. In lonely drunkenness he has paid to lie with women but seldom finished the act, their face overlaid suddenly with the remembered face of Chloë or, worse, the invented face of Marina.

He has seen holes drilled into men's skulls to release malign spirits. He has seen a chieftain's dead wife eviscerated and stuffed with hay and chamomile and parsley to keep her body fresh until the ground thawed enough to permit her burial in a holy place. He has seen raiders sweep into a camp at night, hurl lit torches onto tents, rope men to horses and ride in circles over rocky ground for an hour until one can no longer tell whether the meat they are dragging is human or animal. Having misjudged one journey in seven different ways he slept in a cavern dug from a snow bank and, after lighting a small fire, found it not unpleasant, though he came out the next morning to find that two of his four horses were dead. He has seen men who, whilst riding at speed, can fire two arrows simultaneously from one bow and kill a pair of running deer. He has smoked opium and felt an easeful bliss surpassing any he has ever felt and would have smoked it repeatedly were it not for the demons that visited him in the hours following.

He hears, every so often, of a city ruled by two sisters. Some assume that the story is a fabrication. How could women rule a city? Others assume that it is a dire portent of some greater collapse. He hears of their cruelty and of their magnanimity, and gives little credence to either rumour. More significantly he hears of no threats to their reign from inside the kingdom or to their borders from outside. He hears sometimes about their brother, Pericles of Tyre, the would-be king who lost his mind and became a beggar or possibly a disciple of the Buddha, or who died of a snake bite or who lives off fish and meltwater in the great northern forest. Sometimes the story is told as a tragedy and sometimes it is told as a comedy and sometimes it is told as a cautionary tale. He listens long enough so as not to arouse suspicion then leaves the fireside to take a turn in the dark.

For the first few years he is haunted daily by thoughts of the daughter he abandoned, berating himself constantly for his dereliction, his cowardice, trying to palliate the hurt by reminding himself that he would have made a desperately poor father. Occasionally he convinces himself that his actions were altruistic, a self-sacrifice that allowed her to live a better life, but those moments are rare. In the last two or three years, however, he has found himself thinking about her less and less. He no longer feels in control of his life. It is merely the string of events which happen to this body. He can no more blame himself for what he has done than he can blame a dog for killing a rabbit or an old horse for failing to climb a slope of scree.

But today everything will change.

Evening is coming on, that long moment when the light in the valley is both dim and luminous, the colours glowing before they disappear. He finishes his sausage and cheese and has removed his left boot to cut his toenails with the little knife he carries in a tin scabbard on his belt. He can hear drumming from beyond the wagons and the insect buzz of a khomus being played. His horses are settling at last. There is no wind. This is when he sees it, a dark object in the sheer white froth of the churning water.

It is one of the girls from the village, he is certain of it. She will have been playing with friends upstream and lost her footing. He gets to his feet and starts to run, trying to keep pace with the tumbling body. He can see her arms raised. She is alive. 'Hoy!' he shouts, though she will not be able to hear anything above the roar of water. 'Hoy!' He is wearing only one boot. The current is carrying her too fast. He stubs his toes on a stone hidden by the grass. Only later will he find that two of them are broken so that for several weeks he will be able to ride but not to walk. She snags on a rock and her descent is momentarily paused. Now is his chance. If he leaves it any longer she will be carried over the falls and he will be forced to take a longer route to descend the rocky escarpment to the plain below. By the time he rejoins the river, if she has not cracked her head open on a rock, she will have been swept beyond anyone's help. He thinks of Marina. This girl is someone's daughter. He runs into the shallows at the river's edge. The water is spectacularly cold. The stones under his feet are slippery and though the water is only up to his knees the current is muscular and relentless. The girl's parents turned away for a single moment and lost her. He turned away from his own daughter for fourteen years. She could be dead. He has managed to keep this thought at bay for all that time. He moves deeper into the angry water. The girl is nearly level with him. He has only moments to reach out and grab her. The river sweeps his legs from beneath him. He is underwater, thrashing in the dark and the cold for a foothold. The drowning girl is his daughter. He is convinced of this. He must save her. If he can save her then he can undo those years of wrong.

225

Something solid thumps him across the shoulders. He twists and grabs hold. A dead larch trunk has been wedged against the rocks by the force of the current. He grabs it and hauls himself upwards. His jerkin snags on the snapped-off stump of a broken branch. He is still underwater. He rips his jerkin free. He is desperately short of breath. He breaks the surface and looks left, expecting to see the river empty and Marina gone, but the larch must extend halfway across the river because she has been trapped in the same way. 'Hoy!' If only she can hold on long enough, if only he can get to her. Reach, grip and haul. Reach, grip and haul. The water yanks and twists at his lower body. He grabs her forearm. There is no time for niceties. He needs to get them both back to the bank before the temperature of the water does the job the current could not do. This will hurt her. He will apologise later. He must drag her along the trunk, yanking her free of the snapped-off branch-stumps in the way he was forced to yank his jerkin free. A third of the way. Half. He can feel rocks under his feet. He has a double purchase now. Ten strides left. He counts them. He must pause to take a breath and gather his strength between each stride and the next. Three. Two.

He grabs a shank of reed and hauls himself onto the bank, dragging Marina behind him. When her feet are out of the water and he knows that she is safe he loses consciousness and falls face first into the grass. He is a bird, seeing the world from high up. It is night and the endless forest below him is split from horizon to horizon by a ragged line of fire which is doggedly consuming the world. He can hear the echoing shouts of Dorkas, his old nurse, telling him to come and eat with his sisters. He opens his eyes. He is lying on his back looking up into a sky of dark blue velvet, his clothes are sodden and he is shaking. Figures stand over him. Twenty-five years in a moment. His daughter was drowning and he pulled her out of the river. He rolls over and reaches out to stroke her hair. She stares back at him blankly. Something is wrong. She is not moving. 'Marina?' Her eye sockets are empty. One of her arms is missing. His daughter has been replaced by the corpse of a deer, broken, half-rotted. 'Marina?'

He is lifted up, arms over the shoulders of two big men. A group of children lift the deer, swing it once, twice, then launch it back into the river. He wants to cry out, to tell them that it is not really a deer, but he does not have the energy. His daughter sails into the dark. A splash then she is swept away.

He is carried back towards the camp. Snowy peaks float halfway up the sky. Silhouettes of wagons. Tents are lit up by the light of the fires which burn inside. Everyone is watching. He doesn't understand the language. Then he does understand the language. The foreigner has lost his mind. They strip his clothes. 'Bring him inside.' It is Berlan, from whom he buys the horses. He is placed on a low stool facing a fire of turf and bones. Smoke rises into the high cone of the tent. A pelt is laid around his shoulder. It is the skin of his dead daughter. Berlan's wife, Madya, hands him an earthenware cup of hot milk. It is not the skin of his daughter. He must hang onto these dependable, earthbound people. He looks at the zigzag weave of the carpet under his feet, the flame-light reflected by the tiny squares of silver stitched to the breast of Madya's smock, her young son and daughter who watch, half terrified, half fascinated, from the shadows. He knows now what he has been looking for, and the only mystery is why it has taken him so many thousands of miles to understand something which would have been obvious even to a fool on that rainy quay at Tarsus.

'Drink,' says Madya.

He drinks and shivers. In the centre of the fire the hot bones crack and spit. He has one final journey to make.

THE HUNT

She never says the word 'murder', even in the confessional of her own mind. This is not an act she is planning, it does not come from her. Something unpleasant is happening in the world to which she is forced to respond. Like bad weather it is wholly beyond her control. Above all, she does not look ahead, she never asks herself where all of this is heading. No decisions are made. The whole thing runs slowly but ineluctably downhill like a river. She does not hate the child, no one can hate a child, but the child is irritating, the child grates. She neither stokes this irritation nor shares it with other people. Instead she lets it fester like the rot that burns in packed silage. She begins to understand something that has not been clear before. The way the child acts, the things the child does, these are not accidents. The child is no more intelligent than her daughter, no more beautiful, no more winning, but she is driven by an overpowering need to make her daughter look and feel inferior. In other circumstances there would be ways of resolving the situation, but the child has seduced everyone with her supposed charm. If she tries to separate the two girls she will be hated, however much she is acting in her daughter's best interests.

She is careful not to put herself in the mind of the child. She cannot risk seeing things from the child's point of view. Best not to think of the child as a child at all.

She pictures an accident in which the child dies. Everyone does this kind of thing. The imagination wanders where it will. There is neither intention nor guilt in doing this. We picture ourselves flying, we hear animals talking in voices we recognise, we bring the dead briefly back to life. The gates of horn and the gates of ivory. But the relief she feels when she pictures this accident is blissful. And maybe what she pictures is not in truth an accident. Maybe what she pictures only looks like an accident, a terrible accident.

She begins to flirt with ideas she would have found abhorrent only months ago. She still finds them abhorrent but she imagines a conversation in which she justifies these actions, a hypothetical scene set at some time in the future, in a law court for example. She is contrite. She weeps a little, because when she thinks of what happened to the girl whom she is finally allowed to think of as 'that poor child', she does indeed feel sad. She defends herself, she is articulate, she is persuasive. Her audience are moved unexpectedly by her description of the situation in which she found herself and by the terrible quandary she consequently faced. She had, if truth be told, the courage to solve the problem when others would have crumpled. She is absolved, she is forgiven.

It occurs to her that someone else could carry out this work on her behalf. *Work* is a good word. She will use it from now on. This person could take the child elsewhere and do the work out of sight. People would know only that the child had disappeared. It would be sad, but it would be a mystery no one could solve. This is how she, too, would think of it. The child had simply disappeared. People who were fond of the child could hope that she was alive somewhere, or that she died swiftly and with no pain.

This feels like a good compromise, a generous pulling back from the very worst scenarios she has entertained. The person who carries out this work will, of course, have to be someone exceptional, someone for whom this kind of thing is ordinary and easy – a soldier, perhaps, or a butcher – someone utterly loyal, someone who would do her bidding without question or regret. She could cement that loyalty with a payment. Indeed, she could spread that payment over time, a retainer for the remainder of their life, dependent upon their silence. Such a person would be poor. She is wealthy. The cost would be negligible. The neatness of this plan pleases her, and that pleasure is enough for the moment. There is no need to rush.

At this precise moment, however, she is standing at a window outside the library looking down into the second court where the tutor Mesomedes is sitting in front of the two girls. He draws a circle on a large slate with a metal stylus. 'Pythagoras believed the earth to be round because a circle was, for him and his disciples, the most perfect shape.' Phoebe scratches her nose. There is a skirl of white cloud in the shape of a seahorse suspended above the tutor's shoulder. A rug is being beaten in a courtyard nearby. 'But Aristotle was the first thinker to offer up logical reasons for this. Firstly that during an eclipse the earth casts a circular shadow on the moon, secondly that when ships sail over the horizon they vanish hull first, and thirdly that different constellations are seen from different positions on the earth at the same time during the year.' Mesomedes is a dry little man with a trim white beard who rubs his hands together when thinking, as if ideas were a feast spread before him. His spine curves a little to the right and his breath is not good. 'But it was Eratosthenes who was clever enough to measure the size of this great sphere upon which we live.' He scratches two dots on the slate circle. He labels one Alexandria and the other Syene. The cloud vanishes behind his head. 'He had heard that in Syene on the summer solstice the sun shone directly down a steep well illuminating the water at the bottom and creating no shadow. This was not the case in Alexandria ...'

The girls are fourteen years old. Phoebe has still not shaken off the plumpness that will fall away in the next two years, but she is athletic in the way that her mother was once athletic before she reached the age where being athletic was declared unseemly. Her hair is the taut globe of black frizz her father possessed before the plague aged him two decades in a year. She is funny and self-effacing and does uncannily accurate impersonations of almost everyone at court which might be considered cruel if done by someone older.

Marina is the taller of the two, a fawn of a girl, still unused to her long limbs. Fawnlike in temperament, too, jittery, laughing in a way that seems more nervous than amused, seldom holding anyone's eye and relaxing only when she is in the sole company of her adoptive sister. She has smooth brown skin and hair the colour of mahogany, though what everyone remembers is her eyes, almost black in some lights, so that her beauty always carries with it some hint of the otherworldly.

'The angle of the shadow in Alexandria was one fiftieth part of a circle. Now, Eratosthenes knew that the distance between the two cities was five thousand stadia ...'

They have grown up as twins, spending every day together with the exception of a single fortnight during which Phoebe suffered one of the lesser poxes which left her face a little pitted, a fact which would not trouble her except for the silences which settle on a room when Marina's looks are accidentally praised by strangers who do not understand the unspoken family rule.

Like many real twins they have created a world which only the two of them can enter, a world with its own mythology, its own stories, its own language. Phoebe's mother spent her youth in Baghdad speaking

Aramaic. In deference to her husband she never uses the language except in moments of anger and when she needs to speak confidentially to the slaves who came with her from her home city. The girls, in consequence, know a handful of words and have built on this rickety foundation a fictional language spoken on the fictional island of Panchaia where there are cyclopes and centaurs and wolves and birds big enough to carry off adult goats. The girls have magical powers by means of which they converse with these creatures. There are tunnels underground and so many interconnecting chambers that they have explored only a fraction. Every chamber contains something magical, extraordinary or terrifying – a flame which does not burn and can be carried around in one's hand to illuminate the lightless tunnels ahead, an entire chamber carpeted with dead crows, a mechanical woman made of brass, a subterranean forest which appears to extend for ever and in which they become utterly lost until they are rescued by the brass woman.

They are intelligent girls, both of them, and if Marina is a little quicker, a little sharper, a little more capable of those intuitive leaps ahead of rational thought, then the difference is small and of little consequence. They are too close for enmity. Phoebe is proud of her friend's achievements and Marina sometimes withholds answers to ensure that praise is more evenly distributed.

Only their origins separate them. Phoebe knows that she must count herself lucky. If she is not always in agreement with her mother and father, they are alive and they care for her. Yet everything that has happened in her life has happened in this city, most of it within these walls. She quietly yearns for the sadness that marks her friend out as special, deeper, more serious. She cannot imagine herself as the centre of a story. Marina is a story in herself.

Now, for example, the lesson over and Mesomedes dispatched, they sit on the fluted rim of the pool at the centre of the peristyle with a small bowl each, feeding fine shreds of raw chicken to the fat, orange carp in the fountain, the little O's of their hungry mouths breaking the surface to drag the treats down. Water falls from the tipped conches of the stone sea nymphs, peacocks scream faintly from the walled garden and suddenly Marina is elsewhere, one hand on her knee, the bowl tilting in the other, eyes blank, her spirit gone to the place where her mother is still alive and her father has not abandoned her. That is Phoebe's guess at least, though Marina always brushes the questions aside, after which it seems unkind to pry further. Then Phoebe's foolish envy is swept away by a vision of the reality – that bloody cabin, the dirty hands of some ham-fisted sea-doctor fighting to haul the slippery body out before it is sealed inside a corpse, the coffin sinking into the freezing dark. Would she accept any of this in return for the thrill of being special, deeper, more serious?

In truth, though Marina is sometimes melancholy, she rarely thinks about her parents. They are characters from a romance. Her mother died giving birth, her father saved the city then lost his mind and became a scattering of tall tales and dubious reports. How could such things be connected to this dull round of sleeping and bathing and eating and dressing and learning? Phoebe, Dionyza and Cleon are the only real family she has ever known. Lychorida told her the stories, but Lychorida told stories about many things, all of which seemed equally make-believe. Besides, Lychorida has been dead of a tumour these four years and she has taken with her the last, tenuous link between Marina's life in Tarsus and that exotic supposed prehistory.

In any case, she is not prone to regret about the past or anxiety about the future. She has her father's resourcefulness and her mother's

236

confidence, and something else which neither of them possessed. It is this, perhaps, which is the main legacy of her calamitous entry into the world. She understands other people, she watches, she analyses. She knows, without ever being quite aware of this, that she does not belong here, that she does not belong anywhere, that she can take nothing for granted, that she must always keep a weather eye out for those crises when people look to their own.

Only one thing genuinely troubles her. Dionyza does not like her. It has become obvious only over the past few years. It is not overt. Indeed, Dionyza is always polite and always careful to treat the girls as equals. But Marina turns sometimes and catches her stepmother looking at her with an unexpected hardness in her eyes which vanishes in a moment. She tries broaching the subject with Phoebe. They are on the verge of becoming young women and Phoebe's own relationship with her mother is sometimes prickly and difficult, so Marina assumes that she will empathise. On the contrary, Phoebe is unexpectedly defensive. Are they beginning to grow apart? Or has Marina simply broken the universal rule that one can disparage one's own parents without limit but woe betide anyone else who joins in? Either way, Marina realises that she must deal with this problem alone.

Then, quite suddenly, it is no longer a problem. As Marina and Phoebe's sixteenth birthdays approach Dionyza softens. The politeness seems real again, the equal treatment both natural and unforced. There is a kinder edge to her voice and no hard looks. Marina feels more at ease in her adoptive mother's presence than she has done for a very long time. Perhaps Phoebe has intervened on her behalf. Perhaps the previous ill-feeling was a consequence of some complex adult problem which has been invisibly resolved.

A complex adult problem has indeed been solved. Dionyza has found a man who will kill her adopted daughter. She can now relax in the company of this cuckoo who has galled her for so long. She can afford to be sympathetic, to listen, to care, knowing that she will not have to do so for much longer. Indeed, it is diplomatically wise to act in such a way so that no hint of suspicion should cling to her.

Lucius is a member of the palace guard. She has never taken much notice of him, or indeed any of the palace guard, before. But she steps quietly into the Court of Five Hares one day and sees a house martin lying at the far end of the cloisters with an injured wing. Lucius appears only moments later and without pausing, places his foot on top of the bird and slowly crushes it, twisting his sandal once left and once right when the sole is flush with the floor. It is as if the Fates had arranged the little drama entirely for her benefit. Lucius removes his foot to examine what he has done then kicks the damp, feathery mess into the little rainwater channel which runs between the feet of the columns. Dionyza has a hard heart when such a thing is called for but even she is chilled by his actions. She has found her man. She will give him his orders and arrange the payment, then she will be relieved for ever of a pain from which she has suffered for too long.

Lucius might be cruel but he is not stupid. He demands half the payment up front and half as soon as the girl is dead. The queen will become nervous soon enough and arrange for another man to kill him in turn. It is what he would do himself if he were in her position. So he needs to be long gone before she takes that decision. The job itself is simple and pigs are the key. A sty of five or six will churn through a human body in no time – bones, teeth, hair, the lot. He will pay his idiot brother to spend a few days by the coast. He will take her clothes, boots and travelling cloak to give the impression that she has run away. He will drive her into the hills bound and gagged, stove her head in with a rock, hoist her into the pen and burn the rope along with the rest of her belongings. Once he's got the remainder of the money he will board a ship for Thebes or Alexandria and start a new life.

He walks the route between the sleeping quarters and the loading bay for six consecutive nights to make sure he can do it unseen. He times the gaps between patrols, he oils hinges. On the seventh night there is dense, propitious cloud. He douses the sconces in the corridor. The girls don't sleep with slaves in their chambers, thankfully. He snuffs the oil lamp beside the bed and gets the gag on hard before telling Marina that she will remain alive if and only if she stays quiet. He blindfolds her so that she will not remember his face if he is forced to bail halfway. She is surprisingly strong for such a skinny girl but he gets her hands and feet tied soon enough. He wraps her in the square of stiff canvas folded inside his travelling bag and ropes her like a carpet so that she is easier to carry. He goes through the big chest at the foot of the bed and fills the empty bag with clothes a young girl might take if she were planning a night-time journey. Using other clothes he makes a rudimentary body shape under the blankets. He closes the trunk and hoists her onto his shoulders.

No one sees them on their winding path through the palace complex apart from an eagle owl who watches from a bay tree, as they pass through the deep shadows that border the Hexagonal Garden, head rotating slowly, big eyes locked. Is this where the message begins its journey? Or does the non-human world simply know these things, information beyond the end of the spectrum passing from creature to creature, the way decisions flash through a flock of starlings?

High in the hills is an oak grove which conceals a spring. Behind the spring stands a cave of tufa and pumice. There is no moonlight, but the flesh of arms and legs, of necks and faces, glows with its own light. The sweet rot of earth and the musk of sleeping bodies, water trickling into water. Twenty young women stir from sleep and stand and stretch. Some walk away to relieve themselves, others bend to fill cupped hands with water. They don tunics and hunting boots. They knot their hair and loop the leather straps of full quivers over their shoulders. They pick up bows and javelins. In the shadows between the trees stand twenty red deer, white-spotted hides, barrel chests and taut, sinewy legs, twitchy as tripwires. Consorts, familiars. At the head of the pool the twenty-first woman rises. She is taller by a head than all of them, long muscular arms, long muscular legs, the virgin herself, daughter of Jupiter and Latona, sister of Apollo, the hunting goddess, goddess of trees and animals, goddess of deer and oaks and high places. She leads the women out of the grove and onto the open hills, grainy and mono-chrome in this almost-nothing light. The long grass is full of animals, the air alive with wings. Boar and fox, lynx and leopard. Kestrels and crows, long-eared bats. She begins to walk and the wild world follows in her wake.

Is this what gives Marina strength, the knowledge of what's out there, messages coming back the other way? Or are these things manifestations of her own strength? She has grown up as a woman. She has been taught to flatter, to please, to depend, to give way, to make herself small and quiet. She has been told to be soft so that men will always have a means by which they can hurt and control her, that ring through the nose which men call femininity. But she has silently refused to accept these lessons.

She is roped inside a tube of rough material that smells of tar and damp. Breathing is difficult. The gag in her mouth smells of sweat and tastes of rank fish. Tight cord digs into her wrists and ankles, cutting off the blood, less painful when cobbles give way to earth under the wheel rims but more painful as minutes become an hour and an hour becomes two. She does not struggle, she makes no noise. She must conserve her energy until the moment when it can be most profitably spent. She will be angry, she will be ugly. She will get through this and she will be revenged upon those who have done it to her.

They are nearing the farm when it happens. The horses sense it first, becoming skittish and unwilling. There is a wolf upwind perhaps, or a thunderstorm in the offing. Lucius whips the reins and pushes them on as the road rises and turns deeper into the hills. Only a league or so left. The darkness is almost impenetrable, but that is all to the good. Then he begins to sense it himself. Nothing obviously wrong, no other lights on the lonely road. He is not superstitious, he is sceptical about the divine, seldom feels strong emotion and never without good cause. But he is inexplicably afraid, his body preparing itself for some kind of attack though he has no idea what form this attack might take. He turns round repeatedly to scan the dark out of which they have climbed but sees nothing and hears nothing. He covers the lantern. He is sweating, his hands shake, his stomach rolls and twists like a restless dog. He wants to turn back. He cannot turn back. What if he pulled over here, carried her into the dark and dug a grave? He has no spade, and meat buried less than waist deep is always found by hungry animals. Would that matter? What if he simply strangled her and ditched the cart and rode on? He would have two horses. He would have half the money. He is finding it hard to think rationally.

Suddenly there is light. Winds high up rake the cloud away from a full moon and a hard blue radiance falls on the earth. He should be relieved. He no longer needs the lantern, he can see where he is going, he can see anyone who might be approaching. But the vastness of the landscape makes him hanker for the little tent of light inside which he was previously travelling. The horses are still spooked. He lashes them on.

The road turns sharply at a blind bend, a house-sized slab of rock to the right, thorny scrub sliding so steeply to the left that he hears but cannot see water tumbling over rocks at its base. There is something over his head. He looks up and sees bats beyond number, like ash-flakes from a brazier but thicker and faster and more numerous, some dodging around him so closely that he can feel the tiny rushes of air displaced by their frail, veined wings.

The horses rear and whinny, trying to wrench themselves from their traces, but it is not the bats of which they are frightened. There is a single deer blocking the road, only ten paces away, staring, implacable. On any other night he would assume that the deer is sick or blind, but this deer is not sick. He knows this for certain but cannot say why.

The spooked horses become still. The deer has calmed them somehow. The deer is not a deer. Or not only a deer. He could jump down from the cart and run but he would not get far. He understands that too. He does not want to die. He has never had this thought before. More deer come out of the dark. Fifteen? Twenty? Equally indifferent, equally unafraid. Then, behind the deer, he sees the women. If he had been asked what would frighten him most at night in the hills he would have said a hungry bear, or a band of armed men perhaps. But this scares him more than anything he could imagine. Tunics, javelins. The world turned upside down, the weak given power. The revenge they could justify if they had the means at their disposal. A life would not be long enough to repay the debt.

In the middle of the band there is a woman taller by a head than all the rest. He has known her all his life, he is certain of this, but he has no idea who she is. He wants her to pull an arrow from the quiver and fire it deep into his chest so that he goes swiftly.

This does not happen.

The deer scatter, bouncing with unearthly grace up the rock face, down the little ravine and round the cart. Then the women are running and whooping and holding their bows and javelins aloft and there are lynx and wolves and boar running beside them and the horses are released from their trance and rear up again, but more violently this time so that the right wheel of the cart is lifted from the ground and several spokes in the opposite wheel snap under the extra weight. The wheel collapses altogether, the left-hand side of the cart sinks suddenly and the whole contraption rolls towards the edge of the narrow roadway. The horses try to right themselves, hooves scrabbling desperately on the gritty earth, but they no longer have sufficient purchase and the lead horse is hoisted onto the flank of its partner. Lucius grabs the seat beneath him but he cannot stop himself sliding sideways and tumbling into the dark. As he falls he is flipped onto his back and sees the cart begin to tumble after him together with the princess in her roll of canvas. Then the fallen horses themselves are flipped onto their backs and hauled off the roadway by the falling cart, vehicle and animals tethered together.

He lands flat on his back in shallow water. He has one long moment to realise that he is not dead, then the cart and the horses land. The iron rim of a wheel smashes his left ankle and pins it to the ground. A horse lands beside him, the river bed under him shaking with the impact. The horse's big moonlit head lies beside his own, lips pulled back, broken, yellow teeth, nostrils wide, terrified black eyes, hot breath. A hoof kicks him hard in the hip, then kicks him again. His trapped ankle prevents him moving away. The horse cannot get to its feet. It kicks him a third time. The other horse is dead, one of the shafts through its neck. The remaining wheel revolves slowly in silhouette. The women and their animal companions are picking their way down the bank.

Saved by three layers of canvas and the thick undergrowth that slowed her descent, Marina lies on a bank of rough grass a little way downstream. There were three loops of rope holding the canvas fast. The top one was yanked off during her descent. Her blindfold, too, has gone, at the cost of a bloody scrape down the side of her head.

What happens next is not clear. No, that's not right. What's next is the clearest memory of the whole night, but it makes no sense. A woman is crouching beside Marina – tunic and boots, spear and bow. The woman slices through the remaining two ropes around the canvas and unrolls her. She is holding a small knife. She cuts the gag from Marina's mouth then turns her onto her side and frees her hands and feet. It is hard to make anything out in this low light and Marina has seen her own reflection only in rudimentary mirrors and on the surface of still water, but the woman looks like her. Exactly like her. She holds Marina's face with both hands and looks into her eyes. Marina is giddy with the strangeness of the encounter. The woman lays Marina's head gently back on the grass then stands. Marina hears the growl and yap of animals and the voices of other women. Her otherworldly twin turns and walks away.

There is a river, there is a steep chine, there are hills. Bats scribble back and forth over the moon which burns overhead. Is this real, or is this the mind losing its footing as it crosses the border between life and death? She was taken from her bed in the middle of the night. She was driven out of the city and into the hills. She rolls over, lifts herself onto all fours and looks back upstream. The woman has gone. All the women have gone. If there really were other women. She feels very much alive, rope-burns around her wrists and ankles, a stabbing pain in the side of her head. Further upstream the cart in which she was travelling lies snapped and folded on the stream bed. Beside it lies a horse which must surely be dead. But she can see movement on the far side of the wreckage and hear the noises of someone or something in pain. It is surely safest to walk away, but she can see a fat leather satchel lying beside the cart. The night is bitter and she needs everything useful she can lay her hands on.

She picks her way between the slippery rocks. She can hear two separate noises now. A man is whimpering and the second horse is making a desperate noise for which she has no words. Carefully she steps round the cart to see what is happening. The horse is still alive, just, though it will not be alive for long. Three wolves are tearing into its abdomen, the ripped-out organs glittering with reflected moonlight. The man lies beside the horse, his leg trapped under a smashed wheel. His face is familiar. Someone from the palace. Every time the man breathes out he makes a sad, wheezing noise as if he has run a very long way.

He turns to look at Marina. It is no surprise to him that she is alive. Nothing is a surprise any more. He feels no pain, not yet, despite the injury he has sustained. He cannot beg for help. It is not in his nature. He is, in any case, beyond help of any kind. Nevertheless he wants to prove that he has agency even at this final moment. He says, 'The queen ordered this. She wanted you dead.'

Somewhere deep down Marina knew it already. The revelation holds no significance. That was her old life. A wolf pauses and looks at her, mouth rimmed with bloody fur. The horse is no longer moving. The wolf returns to its meal, as if to say, *A scrawny thing like you is of no interest to us.* She kneels beside the leather bag and unbuckles the strap.

Her would-be abductor has filled it with her clothes, as if he were taking her on a holiday. There is bread, too, and sausage. She puts on the sandals and the travelling cloak and throws the bag over her shoulder.

The man says, 'I was going to feed you to the pigs on my brother's farm. I was going to smash your skull with a rock and feed you to the pigs.'

She steps around him and starts to follow the river up the stony little valley. She does not know where she is going, only that she will be travelling for a long time.

❧

The nurse arrives later the same day, briefed so completely that she could have been doing the job for a month. Her name is Deborah. She doesn't give her surname. She comes from Cardiff and wears a navy-blue uniform with a white trim and chocolate-brown, mannish shoes. She carries a suitcase containing medical equipment and a smaller bag containing a flask of coffee and a Tupperware box of sandwiches so that her interaction with the family can be kept to a minimum.

She bathes Angelica and rubs cream gently into her sores and rashes. Angelica allows Dottie's scrambled egg to be placed into her mouth but will not chew so that Deborah must lean her over and get her to spit the food back into a bowl. When Deborah pours only the smallest amount of milk into her mouth she chokes and coughs. A bed is made up in the adjacent room. Deborah wakes at two-hourly intervals during the night to check on her charge.

Dr Kellaway returns early the following morning and fits a nasogastric tube. Philippe cannot bear to watch. Angelica struggles but does not attempt to remove it once it is in place. A bag of liquid food is connected to the other end of the tube and hung on a stand beside the bed. It is Germolene pink and plump as a stomach. The doctor says that he cannot promise anything but hopes that she will now stabilise at the very least. He will return the following day.

A second nurse arrives mid-morning to relieve Deborah, a third in the evening. The three women will take it in turns to watch over Angelica just as three nurses were paid to watch over her at the beginning of her life. Deborah, Joyce and Gillian. These may not be their real names. They are unfailingly polite but do not encourage personal questions. They are all delivered to the house in a dark green VW Polo by one of two taciturn, besuited men who look Turkish and must surely be brothers. Not once do they leave the car.

The doctor returns the following day as promised, and the day after that. He seems cautiously confident. Angelica is bathed regularly. The bag is replaced once every twelve hours. The house enters a state that mirrors Angelica's motionless drift. Even Hervé who is normally impervious to the emotions of those around him feels as if he is moving underwater.

It takes the best part of a week for Dottie to realise that Nikki has abandoned them. She decides that she must do something herself. She calls the surgery where she herself is registered in Winchester meaning to ask for help, but Hervé appears in the kitchen as she is talking. She pretends that she is ringing Skates about a faulty tumble dryer. Hervé scares her. She does not ring again.

Philippe glides slowly through the house and gardens like the resident ghost, only partially present, unable to settle, unable to read, unable to watch television or listen to the radio, unable to sleep.

And Angelica herself?

She no longer hears the voices around her. And if the owners of those voices could hear her thoughts, would they understand them? She cruises at depth, many fathoms below the world, ticking over in a state which is neither sleep nor wakefulness.

August turns to September. September turns to October. Unnaturally warm nights mean more sugar in the leaves and new colours sweeping over the hill. The drier, wind-exposed trees turn first. Orange and brown, russet, auburn, bronze. Arcturus is gone and Pegasus is rising. There are leafless branches now, bare ruined choirs. Only robin, chaffinch, blackbirds and blue tits are left, the occasional buzzard circling. The temperature drops. Bitter winds, early frosts and the Pleiades visible on cloudless nights.

Only one story ties her to the world.

Tashkent, Zadracarta, Ecbatana, Nineveh …

❧

Two and a half thousand leagues and four months of riding. He has sold five horses and two camels en route, keeping only one horse for his own use and another as insurance. Sold them at poor prices, too, wanting only a swift sale and sufficient supplies for the next leg of the journey. With the exception of a bout of fever just after crossing the Oxus, he has not spent two nights in the same place. He has felt, always, at the back of his mind, the low rumble of fear, wondering if he has left it too late to prevent something terrible happening to his daughter. If he rises early and eats and drinks in the saddle he can outride the anxiety for half a day or more, but it always catches him by the evening. As the year turns he is grateful for the lengthening days so that he can travel further and sleep more deeply afterwards.

He has little money left. He is exhausted. He cannot imagine his life beyond reunion with his daughter, or rejection by her. He knows that Cleon and Dionyza remain in power. Such facts are part of the bedrock upon which all trade is done, but news about adopted daughters has little commercial value and about Marina he has heard nothing.

When he arrives in Tarsus he will send a message to Cleon and Dionyza saying that he has news from the lost prince. He will prove his credentials by handing over a little bag of sunflower seeds and macadamia nuts and say, 'These are for the king's three parrots,' though the parrots are probably long dead by now. From that point on events are beyond his control. What if Marina sees his mutilated hand and is revolted? What if Cleon and Dionyza decide that he no longer has the right to claim paternity? What power does he have to gainsay them?

He spends his penultimate night in a post-station just north of the Cilician Gates. Traders, messengers and civil servants. He removes his travelling clothes and gives them to one of the house slaves as a gift. He bathes, cuts his hair and shaves off his beard. He oils his body and changes into the clothes he purchased in Nicomedia – a tan linen chiton, a cloak in cream wool with a patterned red border, new fawn-skin boots. He feels effete, metropolitan.

He has gifts for Marina in a travelling bag – a tiny box of black walnut with a marquetry dolphin on the lid which seems, at first, to be a solid block of wood unless one tilts and shakes it in the right way so as to release the hidden bolts; a bullfinch carved in such exquisite detail and painted in such vivid colours that every time he unwraps it he thinks, all over again, that it is a real sleeping bird; and a painting in ink on a paper scroll of a black-and-white bear climbing a gnarled tree in the snow from Yang Kuan which is now a little kinked but which struck him at the time, and still strikes him, as a perfect gift for a girl. He hopes that these things are not so shoddy as to seem insulting to someone who can doubtless have anything she wants. Perhaps modest is good. He does not want her to think that he is trying to buy the forgiveness for which he must beg and which, in truth, he does not deserve. He long ago forfeited any rights he had as a father. If she rejects him it will be neither wrong nor cruel, but his life will no longer have meaning or purpose. He puts these thoughts to the back of his mind as he has put so many similar thoughts to the back of his mind over the previous sixteen years.

He sleeps fitfully and rises early. As he is saddling the roan and loading the skewbald he sees a young man being dragged from the building by two Tarsian soldiers. Murder? Fraud? The settling of scores? The soldiers are rougher than they need be and the young man is weeping. He is drunk perhaps, or feeble-minded. He is bound, laid unceremoniously across the back of a pony and led away.

Pericles fights the urge to turn and ride back the way he came. The easy call of a perpetual journey where he can leave names and obligations behind at every border. A magpie paddles and sips in the shallow end of the water trough. Already the road shimmers in the heat. He tightens the buckle of the roan and puts his foot into the stirrup.

He enters Tarsus as he has entered every city on his travels, trusting no one and gathering information before offering any. He has seen men stabbed to death for using the wrong dialect. He has returned to cities after a single year to find the entire ruling class butchered. He stables his horses at an unassuming tavern on the western side of the Bridge of the Virgin, watches his belongings deposited in the locked cellar and attaches the numbered brass tag to his belt. The box of black walnut, the bullfinch and the painted scroll he keeps in the leather bag slung across his chest. There is a dagger beside the brass tag should anyone plan to take it from him.

He stands on the bridge itself. The crowds flow back and forth at his back. The tide flows out beneath his feet. Shelduck and goldeneye paddle in the eddies at the river's edge where rushes and garbage comb the current into curls. He feels unsteady on his feet. Sections of palace roof are visible through the highest arches of the amphitheatre. The family quarters, or near enough, with their high ceilings and windows full of ocean. His daughter is in there somewhere. *Poor bird, why art thou singing in the shadows at this late hour?* He wants opium, he wants trees. He wants a hot fire, the steamy breath of horses and the music of bridles.

He must keep himself moving if he is to do this. He steps away from the balustrade and lets the crowd carry him towards the centre of the city. He enters the warren of the old market which clings to the side of the palace wall like mussels on a rock. He should feel at home here but it is too crowded, too loud. Tunics of peach-coloured silk, striped linen shalvars in gold and sky blue, simlahs, keffiyehs. A fashion for preposterous hats seems to have taken hold since he was last in this part of the world, none of them possessing any obvious function apart from drawing attention to the wearer. The alleys are rammed. The sound of a psaltery, the sound of a flute. Several trained monkeys are ferrying cash to upper windows. Cardamom, turmeric, aniseed. Sappho and Herodotus on papyrus. Two old men are deep in a game of Go. There are squirrels, tailed, skinned, gutted and smoked into big leathery stars. There are great curtains of hung sausage. There are spotted furs and striped hides. A poorly played bagpipe sounds like a dying elk. There is bolt upon bolt of silk at such stupid prices he regrets not having loaded up a third horse. Little gods in ivory soapstone, antler and oak.

A woman reads entrails. Caged falcons, caged doves, caged parrots, a caged eagle. Two leopard cubs are being sold by a man who seems unaware of what they will become. Suspended from a hook an entire tuna is being hacked into oval steaks from the tail up. Stalls sell salep and sweet spiced milk and black tea from Hastinaptur. Gossip and haggling in Greek, Latin, Hebrew, Phoenician, Persian, Aramaic. He smells myrrh and sandalwood and sweat and woodsmoke and burnt sugar. He runs his fingers over fabrics, tastes dabs of paprika and sumac, asks for prices reflexively, shakes his head and walks away. He buys a cheap tart containing a stringy meat which is almost certainly not the promised pigeon.

'Titus ...!' It takes him a few moments to realise that it is he who is being addressed and a few more moments to connect the deep voice with the tiny man, no taller than his waist at most, who sits on a barrel so that he can bargain eye to eye with potential customers for the dyes whose garish, powdery cones sit in the mouths of little sacks ranged on the trestle table beside him.

Pericles can remember using the name but not the location in which he used it. The man laughs gently, perhaps understanding the quandary in which Pericles finds himself. 'It matters little, my friend.' He puts his hand against the flat of his chest and Pericles mirrors the gesture. 'May the gods keep you well,' they say almost simultaneously.

'What news?' asks Pericles. 'I arrived this morning.'

'Three donkey trains in yesterday,' says the man. 'Salt, spices, dried meats. Some slaves taken in Melitene. Strong, healthy, very ill-tempered.'

The man's wife appears from a dark arch behind him. He remembers the two of them now. Talub and Amira. She cannot speak, as a result of some terrible event to which Talub made only a passing reference. He met them at a trading post in the Caucasus mountains. Cow bells and driving rain. Not even a village, closed during the winter. Talub is lame in one leg as well as short. Pericles was profoundly touched by the way they looked after one another, each performing the tasks the other couldn't, with an effortless synchrony which required neither request nor thanks. Amira smiles. Hand to chest. Does she recognise him? He smiles back.

'... but the horse-market is empty,' says Talub.

'And up there?' Pericles gestures towards the palace whose outer wall blocks the sunlight at the alley's end. 'There were two daughters, one by blood and one adopted.'

'I would set your sights a little lower, my friend.' Talub laughs, then he pauses, seeing something serious in the face of this not-quite-stranger. 'You have not heard.'

'Heard what?' His heart thumps.

Talub nods towards the arched alcove in front of which their stall is pitched. Amira is listening intently to a talkative Ethiopian merchant. Without a glance in the direction of her husband she reaches out, he takes her hand and she helps him down from the barrel. Pericles feels the faintest prickle of a tear at the corner of his eye.

'Follow me,' says Talub.

They step into the dark. Brick barrel roof, hessian sacks and locked boxes. A white duck sleeps in a bell-shaped bamboo cage. Talub ascends another barrel via a makeshift staircase of two trunks. 'You will like this.'

'Like what?'

'The troubles of our supposed betters.'

Pericles feels nauseous.

'Only one daughter remains.' Talub rubs his hands together and spreads his fingers as if warming them in front of a fire.

'Which …?' He cannot speak.

'The daughter by blood. The other vanished in the night.' Talub makes an explosive gesture with his hands. *Boom. Gone.* Then he hotches forward on the barrel and looks theatrically first to one side then the other, though it is clearly not possible for a third person to be hiding in this overfilled nook. 'The official story is that she ran away. Two weeks ago.'

None of this is real. He and Talub, they are puppets in a little theatre. The sacks, the abacus, the white duck, they are all made of painted wood.

'Unofficially …?' Talub is enjoying this. 'A palace guard disappeared the same night. A wrecked cart was found in the hills. At the bottom of a ravine. Skeletons of two horses and human remains, all picked clean. Gold brooch as big as an apple in the pocket of a travelling cloak.'

Pericles steadies himself. 'She may have escaped.'

Talub laughs. 'In the hills? Alone? At night? Two weeks? Most of them would die if they didn't have a pillow.'

It was Dionyza's doing. Pericles knows instantly. A memory of the first time he saw her, on the quay which lies only a league away from this market. Eyes that refused to look away. Her husband knelt but she did not.

'They say – and this is obviously a piece of scurrilous gossip which I reject wholly – that the queen …'

Pericles holds up his hand to stop Talub talking. He needs to get out of here before he hurts someone, before the world bursts into flame. He is in the alleyway again. A blind woman is doing conjuring tricks, coloured pebbles appearing and disappearing in her dancing hands. He turns a corner. A boy has stolen a loaf. The baker curses but does not give chase. The boy is a rabbit vanishing into brambles. He turns another corner. A donkey lifts its tail and sprays wet shit all over the white toga of a man at the adjacent stall. The crowd applaud. Pericles leaves the market through the triple arch of the eastern gate and stumbles down the zigzag cobbles to the agora.

Hot sun sings on the white stone. Fourteen cypresses chop up a sheer blue sky. A group of workmen are constructing a monument of some kind, two freshly cut marble blocks sitting on log rollers. A small pyramidal crane squats on the half-completed pediment. A chisel rings out. *Ting ... ting ...*

Was she killed and then driven into the hills or was she still alive when the cart fell? What if the wolves found her lying in the dark unable to defend herself? He left his daughter in the care of strangers. He falls to his knees and throws up into a gutter. Was Cleon party to the plan? There is nothing he can do now. They will not let him into the palace, not if they have any sense.

His wife died in childbirth because he refused to take the advice of her parents. Their daughter died because he did not have the strength to look after her himself. A kingdom was lifted from his hands in the way that a precious object is carefully lifted from the hands of a clumsy child. He has thrown away everything of value in his life.

He wipes the last of the vomit from his mouth with the back of his hand. A little boy is staring at him. A nurse pulls the child away. He gets slowly to his feet. He must go somewhere. There is nowhere to go. He no longer has the energy for high passes and nights under canvas and hard bargaining in a fifth language. His feet follow the slope of the tilted city down to the harbour.

A train of yoked slaves carrying water buckets trudge blankly uphill in the heat. An elderly African man plays a sad tune on a gourd-harp at the roadside. If only he could lie down and slip from the world like an old dog. He wants desperately to know how Marina died. He wants desperately not to know. He wants to know what else was done to her by his palace guard. He wants to know none of these things.

Marina. Simply to say the name is to take a brand from the forge fire and press it to his chest. *Marina.* He never knew what his daughter looked like. Did she know who her father was? What did Cleon and Dionyza tell her? Is it possible that she died without being aware of his existence? This has never occurred to him before. So many things have never occurred to him before.

He pictures the tangled mess of horses, cart, rider and cargo being cantilevered into the dark. The terrified whinnies, everything clattering and thundering onto the river bed. A hoof comes down hard on the face of a girl.

He leans against a wall and bends over to bring the blood back to his head. The darkness swings close but stops short of sucking him in. For the smallest fraction of a second the veil grows thin. He sees, on the far side, images from lives he has not lived – a slab of liquid light swaying in the dark, a bird's-eye view of islands peppering a sun-skimmed estuary, a woman's voice, saying, *For at the first glance of the glory of God in the east he worships in his way ...*

He sits in the harbour, back against a wall, sweating in the relentless heat. In front of him a boat is being unloaded – sardine, hake, mullet, a speckled ray the size of a large carpet. A row of octopuses are carried ashore skewered on a pole. When the whole catch is landed the boat is rowed out to its mooring and a second takes its place at the quay. A third waits at anchor. To his left new boats are under construction, hulls rest on stilts like wooden spiders as men nail and mitre the superstructures into place. An older, upturned boat is being stripped and re-tarred. A fin breaks the water in the harbour's mouth.

He does nothing. It is a skill he has learnt in the mountains, to be a horse, a stone. Hours pass. The sun arcs slowly down into the west and the air begins to cool. Darkness thickens under the trees. The shadow thrown by the steep hill above the eastern side of the harbour swings slowly across the water, swallowing the boats one by one. Gulls high up catch the red of the dying sun while flying against the deep blue. They are some of the most beautiful things he has ever seen. Venus rises. His stomach is empty. He has drunk nothing all day. His head thumps. He can think of no reason to remain alive. His simple presence in the world is an offence.

The sun is gone. Stevedores and fishermen are leaving with it, sailors and shipbuilders, tax collectors, guards. Perseus rises. An idea begins to form. He will return to the ocean. He will join Chloë. It makes no sense, and yet it makes more sense than any other thought he has had for a very long time.

For several hours there are only drunks and prostitutes in the harbour. A woman sings loudly to herself. She must surely be insane. Two men have a loud argument in a language he does not recognise. They stagger away and the harbour is empty. Just a fat moon and its less substantial twin swaying tipsily beyond the breakwater.

He no longer believes in the gods. He has heard too many contradictory stories on his travels. Better, surely, that everyone is deluded than that revelation has been so parsimoniously handed out. If he has a religion it is that of grass and rivers, of mountains and of skies that continue beyond the ends even of our longest journeys. He will sink among the hammerheads and the lobsters, be eaten, be taken back.

He will do it when the moonshadow thrown by the battered statue of the goddess Galene touches the limestone mounting block. He has decided on the boat, a tiny thing, clinker-built, two stowed oars, moored not too far out. He will swim across this water for a second time. For the last time. This is the place where Marlenus drowned. Another death for which he is responsible. He will not have to bear the pain of remembering these things for much longer.

The shadow touches the mounting block. He gets to his feet. His knees are stiff. He has not moved for seven, eight hours. There is a tight, hard throb at the back of his head. He walks across the cobbles to the quay. He takes his boots off. He keeps the leather bag over his shoulder. He will give Marina the gifts when he sees her, when they are all reunited. He has made his decision. He has momentum. He walks down the stone steps. Freezing shackles of water are snapped around his ankles. Further down. Waist deep. Marlenus again. Kallios. The swung lamp in the dark. If only one of those thrown spears had thumped home through the bloody barrel of his own chest. Further in, the shackles rising, becoming a belt, a vest. He lets the water take his weight, pushes out, paddling like a dog while hanging onto the bag, hoping that no one hears the splashing and intervenes. He unloops a slick of greasy weed from round his neck. How low it seems down here at the water's surface, everything above him – moon, city, hulls. He swims on. A flotilla of dozing cormorants grumpily squawk and flap. He rests briefly halfway, holding an anchor chain, regaining his breath. He is getting rapidly colder. He swims on. Water in his mouth. Tar and sewage. The scroll is inside a metal tube. He hopes it is waterproof.

It is difficult getting into the boat. He is not as strong as he once was and the day has sapped his energy. He throws the bag in first, puts his foot on the rudder and hauls himself up over the transom. The boat is small, he is heavy and the prow is hoisted so high out of the water he fears that the whole vessel might flip end to end and land on top of him. Four attempts and he is in. There is no space to lie down in the boat so he sits, head in hands, on the single bench, getting his breath back, letting the water run from his clothes, waiting for the pain in his head to ebb enough to let him row.

Voices on the quay. Surely, he cannot be seen from this distance. He unknots the rope which tethers the boat to the nearest buoy. Carefully he lays the oars into their rudimentary notches. Wet wood squeaks quietly against wet wood. He reaches forward, dips the oars into the black water, feels for a decent purchase then pulls. Lifts, reaches, dips, pulls. He moves along the broadening channel between the moored boats. The soft slap of sisal on pine as they rock at anchor. A figure appears in silhouette as he passes one of the bigger fishing vessels. Do people spend the night out here? He keeps rowing. The figure says nothing, does nothing. Perhaps it is a ghost summoned by his own imagination. The silhouette is swallowed by the greater silhouette of hills.

He is exhausted. *Reach, dip, pull.* Saying the words to himself, the way one might encourage a child. The distance expanding as he moves into it. *Reach, dip, pull.* If he can get just outside the harbour's mouth there will be a current flowing south, not much but enough to carry him without any effort of his own. He needs to rest. He pulls the oars in. He sits and breathes. The hull rocks, the first intimation of those bigger waves out there. He looks over his shoulder at a little arc of uninterrupted horizon. But the boat is starting to drift sideways and he does not want to end up on the rocks. He extends the oars again. *Reach, dip, pull.* He counts each cycle. One hundred, one hundred and fifty. He is in the little narrows now. He looks over his shoulder again at the growing emptiness. Another fifty strokes, a hundred. He pulls the oars in, sits, watches, waits. He can see the crisp, ragged outline of coast moving faintly, the harbour mouth slowly closing. He is out. He raises the left-hand oar from its notch, lifts it above his head and pitches it as far as he can. The oar splashes, the boat rocks and settles. He throws the other oar in the opposite direction. The boat rocks and settles again. His clothes are sodden. He is no longer exerting himself and he is very cold indeed. He sees Chloë in the shadow of a scarlet awning. *Men accuse women of being fickle* ... The small of her naked back striped in shutter-light. Little stone boys urinating. A magical bronze horse. *Fair glass of light, I loved you, and could still.* A Chinese artist paints a cave, steps into it and vanishes ...

He shrinks his mind again. Horse-stillness, stone-stillness. Time passes. He slips briefly into a kind of sleep but the shivering and the pain in his head will not release him. He must do it now. If he leaves it any longer he will die in the boat and he and Chloë will never be reunited. He will get to his feet and simply step overboard. He will not be able to get back into the boat. There will be a brief struggle as the body clings to life, then it will all be over. He tries to stand. He cannot stand. He is too cold, too weak. It does not matter. He does not need to stand. He needs only to get to his knees and roll himself over the side of the boat. He does not have the courage. He does not want to die. He is terrified. He is a small boy. He is lost and he is desperately lonely. He begins to weep.

She has just watched a horse being eaten alive. The wolves will be eating the man by now. The hatred in his eyes. He planned to kill her. His crime and his punishment should cancel out. Instead they combine to form some terrible new thing.

She continues in the same direction they had been driving. Behind her is the woman who gave the man his orders. Strange that it should not be a surprise. Did Phoebe know? That discomfort when Marina ventured to question her mother. Did Cleon know? Dionyza will want reassurance that the job has been done. So how long does Marina have before the hunt begins? A day? Two days? If she is found she will not be allowed to live. She knows too much. She wraps the travelling cloak a little tighter. The night is vast. Hill beyond hill beyond hill, each fainter than the other as they step back into the dark. It is like leaning over a high parapet, the same queasy tingle in the soles of her feet, the same fear that she might be seduced into letting go of the earth and tumble into the void. She has never properly looked at the moon before, never felt this close to it. The poets are wrong. It is neither blue nor silver. It is the white of iron in the heart of a fire. The Milky Way is so bright that it seems in places more like a single substance than individual stars. Those individual stars, she can see for the first time, are different colours. The gold of Capella, the red of Aldebaran, the blue of Elnath.

By the river there was a woman who looked like her – tunic, spear, bow. She cut the rope from Marina's hands and feet. The image is as clear and nonsensical as the dream images one retains upon waking. But unlike those images this one does not fade. The woman's hands are on the side of her face. What if, in extremity, the voice you used to encourage and sustain yourself was made flesh and walked in the world of its own accord? She heard other women, too. Are they all out there now, some-where in the dark?

She lost her best friend, her second self, yet she feels bigger, stronger, more complete. Is this a truth revealed or the mind's temporary self-protection?

The slip and crumble of pebbles under her sandals, the cold biting her uncovered toes. Every now and then she is convinced that she is being watched by a creature crouched in one of the shadows beside the road. Perhaps the imagination creates phantoms to keep the body primed. She has spent every night of her life under a roof. She is outside the palace, but she is outside something more nebulous which constrained her more than walls. Even the fear is good. Cold water sluicing a dirty floor.

She takes the sausage from the bag, rips off the end with her teeth and puts the remainder back. It is the cheapest, most ordinary food she has ever eaten and the most satisfying.

The road rises and twists. Step by step she is leaving behind everything she once thought of as the world.

Dawn comes. She is tired. She thinks at first that something is burning behind the hills. The grass? Not a forest, surely. The prospect is terrifying. Then she understands. She watches for a long time. She has never seen the whole arc of a sunrise, never seen a black sky brighten to full radiance. She lets it fill her. No painting has come close to this. In the growing light she can now make out the road ahead, the pale, dirty ribbon swallowed by the ripples in the land, reappearing, disappearing. Short, sun-parched grass, the occasional thorny shrub, the wrinkles of tiny streams finding their way downhill. There are two small buildings in the distance. Byres? Barns?

There will be men on the road soon. She is a young woman alone. There are few places to hide and she has surely used up the greater part of her allotted good fortune. Or perhaps there will be no one on the road. She is unsure which is worse. She dips her cupped hands in one of the streams. The water tastes ... wrong. She drinks only a small amount for fear that it might make her ill. She drinks instead from the precious bottle in her bag. It is some kind of cordial. Apple? Pear? A couple of sips, just enough to keep her going. She must find somewhere to sleep so that she can stay awake and walk during the night. When she briefly locked eyes with the wolf something passed between them, more acknowledgement than agreement. *This is how things are.* Things might be different if she is asleep when they next meet.

The sun is fully risen and the day is rapidly heating up. She watches a honey buzzard turn on stiff wings until it lets go of the air and drops like a stone in a black bag, slowing at the very last moment, talons open. It is invisible for a couple of seconds then it grabs two wingfuls of the air and hoists itself aloft, a rat struggling in its grip. There is a vehicle of some kind heading towards her, the dark shape wobbling in the hot air. She leaves the road and heads towards a kink in the dry ground where one of the half-sunken streams dodges a big rock, jogging through the sharp, short grass with high steps to protect her toes from thorns. If she sits in the shallow water with her back against the stone and draws her legs in she is fairly sure that she will not be seen from the road. She cups a hand and drinks some of the water. Either it tastes better or she is thirstier now.

A scorpion emerges from a little forest of dry stalks, so close to her leg that she could touch it if she reached out. Ever since she was small scorpions have been a reason for running out of a room and calling for a slave. The creature crouches, motionless, only the faintest tremor in its curled tail. Is it looking at her? Do scorpions have eyes? She scoops up another palmful of water and throws it. The creature scuttles back to the shade and safety of the grass. She can smell lavender and hear the soft rasp of crickets.

Finally, axle-squeak and wheel-rims crunching on the uneven road, the surly snort of a donkey, conversation in a language she does not recognise. A dog yaps. The cart shuffles and clatters past. Gingerly she twists and looks round the edge of the rock. The cart is carrying five fat sacks of grain or rice or dried beans. The old woman rides, the old man walks. The dog stops and turns and looks directly at Marina. She slips back behind the rock, heart thumping. Then the old man whistles loudly and when she next looks out the dog has returned to its allotted place and the whole ensemble is starting its slow descent into the next rolling dip of the road.

She evades two more parties before the sun reaches its zenith – a pair of soldiers and four Persian traders with a train of wretched slaves shackled to a wagon. Some of them are children. She drinks the rest of the cordial and refills the bottle from a stream. She eats the rest of the sausage. She is thin, she does not need much, but she has never walked this distance in one day and she is very hungry indeed. She picks five brown fruits from an ugly little shrub, eats one now and saves the others for when she knows what effect the first has on her. The rind is thick, the flesh leathery and bitter. They are, by some margin, the nastiest thing she has ever eaten. There is a perverse satisfaction in this. Her stomach hurts a little but she keeps the fruit down. After an hour or so she eats another.

There is a cluster of tiny buildings up ahead – a rudimentary house, a low barn, a stone pen. She should walk on. Every person who sees her becomes a clue for her pursuers. But her thinking is becoming less clear; it seems to her that people in their own homes must surely be less dangerous than the random strangers one meets on the road, and

as her energy ebbs she finds herself relying on the presumption of deference which previously underpinned her entire life.

She walks up the gritty track from the main road. The smell is
appalling, a stronger version of the stench which lingers in parts of the
palace in those first hot weeks of late spring before the household
decamps to the summer villa while the privies and the sump are cleared.
As she gets closer she hears the grunt and squeal of pigs. It is only when
she is leaning on the wall, reassured by the grubby jostle of the busy
piglets, that she starts to wonder. Was this where he was bringing her?
She has been very foolish. If he was bringing her here then he was very
probably in league with whoever is behind that wall right now. She
needs to leave quickly and without being seen.

Unless . . . Scroll backwards. The shutters were closed when she walked
up the gritty track, she is sure of this. She gingerly circles the building,
ready to break and run at the faintest noise. The door is bolted from
the outside. Her heart slows. She breathes out.

A tiny black oval flutters above the horizon. Travellers. She needs to
get inside. There will be shade, she can sleep. She presses her face to
the crack between frame and door to double-check. It takes a few
moments for her eye to become accustomed to the dark of the interior.
A rudimentary stool on a dirt floor, a stoppered amphora, dust turning
in slices of white sunlight. A face looms suddenly – eyes, teeth, spittle.
There is a loud bang and the door smacks her hard in the forehead. She
falls backwards. The door is hammered from the inside, bolt and hinges
clanking.

A dog. It's a dog. Breathing hard she gets to her feet. Her left hand
is bleeding where it broke her fall. She shakes the bigger lumps from
the wound. She can clean it later. She walks to the door despite her fear
of dogs. The conviction that she and the dog are on the same side, that

they can talk to one another. Either a night in the open air has brought her closer to the natural world or she is losing her grip on reason.

She puts the palm of her uninjured hand on the hot flank of the door. 'I'm a friend.' The dog stops barking, listens, smells, then barks again, just once, more quietly this time. She twists and shoots the stiff bolt. The door swings open of its own accord. The dog is huge, a Kangal mastiff bitch, the type shepherds use to keep wolves away, its back higher than Marina's waist. Marina holds out her bloody hand. The act feels both reckless and right. The dog licks the wound. Marina flinches. The dog tilts her head just a little as if thinking something over, then returns to the far side of the room where she curls herself into a great torus of fur and muscle on the dirt. Marina shuts the door, locking it with the rusted bolt which mirrors the one on the outside.

Dust catches in her throat. The muffled noise of pigs rootling and jostling beyond the wall. The smell of dog urine mixes with the smell of the pigs to make a concoction of peculiar pungency. Four skinned rabbits hang from the roof, veiny, pink and dry as leather. There is a larger joint of meat lying in front of the dog, the bone mostly stripped now. There is a knife thrust into the central upright and a low tub of rank water. She kneels and gathers some in her cupped hands. The liquid is cloudy and contains shreds of matter which might or might not be moving. The taste is not quite as bad as the smell in the room.

She looks through the crack between the shutters. When the travellers breast the nearest rise she sees a small camel train, five heavily laden beasts, the first bearing a merchant extravagantly outfitted in rainbow silks. A pointed hood makes him simultaneously sinister and toy-like. He is flanked by a pair of heavily armed guards on small horses. She waits till they have disappeared then takes the knife from the wooden upright and lies down on the dirt floor with her rolled-up cloak as a pillow.

She slides swiftly into a profound sleep in which she runs with a band of women across rolling grassland, over hard, packed sand, through fine columns of leaf-light between trees. They turn into deer and she becomes a deer running with them. Their speed is thrilling, the earth spun to a blur by their hooves. Then they become a thousand arrows falling from a clear sky, into bark, into grass, into fur, into flesh. They are women and deer and arrows and this is no contradiction. Then they are the wolves tearing into the flesh of the dying horse and tearing out the slippery liver and kidneys of the man who kidnapped her, and this is both terrifying and absolutely right, the way lightning is terrifying and absolutely right. They snap away the white ribs with their powerful jaws and yank out the lungs and she knows without question that this is precisely how he died.

When she wakes she is a different person. She has been blooded. She is an animal now. She was always an animal. She understands this for the first time. They kept it hidden from her. They were afraid of what she could do.

The dog is standing by the door. She opens it and lets her out. The sun has just gone down, the black line of the western hills sharp against the last of a pink evening. There is something sweet in the air, part lavender, part lemon, though anything would smell sweet after the stink in which she was sleeping. The dog squats and empties its bowels. Marina takes two of the skinned animals from the roof. She throws one to the dog, wipes the knife against her linen chiton then cuts herself a slice. It does not taste like food as such but it answers a need.

She drinks again from the tub and puts the remaining brace of skinned animals in her bag along with the knife. The dog is waiting outside. It will travel with her. She bolts the door of the shed leaving it as she found it. Rags of cloud tonight, obscuring the moon, the darkness thicker than before but the white stones of the roadway soak up and radiate back what little light there is. The air is cool and the walking is easier as a result. Some final strand holding her back has been severed, and there is something drawing her on, though she has no idea what that something is. At a junction she chooses the road that promises higher ground. The dog follows. At a second junction she makes a similar choice, hoping for more covering as the vegetation thickens with altitude. She empties the bottle and refills it with clearer water at a stream.

The dog stops and tilts her big head to listen, nostrils flaring. Suddenly she bounds into the dark. A brief panic. Has someone been lying in wait for them? Marina hears scuffling and a squeal too high to be human. The dog returns with a baby boar limp in her jaws. She sits at the roadside to eat the animal. Marina takes off her bag and sits nearby to eat her own food. They walk on together.

The dog leaves her just before dawn. She knows it is going to happen a couple of minutes before it does. They both come to a halt, dog and woman beside one another. Marina cannot put it into words but something important is passing between them. The dog turns slowly and walks back the way she came. She feels a sadness made bearable by the knowledge that this is how things should be. She waits until dog and darkness are indistinguishable then continues to walk.

The road has been rising steadily for hours, dry rolling grassland giving way to sparse woods. The temperature drops and the darkness thickens, the moon increasingly obscured by trunks and foliage. Perhaps it is the growing cold, perhaps it is the difficulty of seeing anyone who might be approaching but Marina begins to feel a presence which is not wholly benign. She wishes the dog were still with her. She sees no buildings of any kind in which she might sleep covertly during the coming day, so she must keep walking until the dawn light penetrates the canopy so that she can more easily find a hiding place out of sight of the road.

It comes eventually, the weak, peach-pink sun, revealing the true extent of the forest through which she has been walking, trunks on either side of her receding to something which feels as deep and distant as the dark between the stars. But as the sun warms and rises, her surroundings become more human and less otherworldly. She sees, up the wooded slope to the right of the road, a low ruin of some kind, little more than an outline of stones, so long abandoned that any path which might once have connected it to the main thoroughfare has long been taken back.

She picks her way through the brambly thickets which grow between the old trunks to investigate her potential hiding place. Barbs scratch her bare legs and sandalled feet. She uses the leather bag to push them away and hold them back. Half submerged in vegetation and no more than knee high at most the ruin was once a single-roomed building, a store for woodcutter's equipment perhaps, or a place to sleep when logging in the hills.

She takes out the knife and cuts away at the brambles in one corner of the ghost room, holding down branches with her sandal, slicing the stems at the base and throwing them away. Something scurries off. Springy branches whip back and hit her thighs and chest and face. Her hands are soon bloody. Eventually she has cleared an area of bare earth upon which she can sleep. The shape is unnervingly like that of a coffin. She lays a loose bank of cut foliage along the wall between her and the road. She is proud of her handiwork and finally tired enough to sleep.

The air during the day is warm but wind and birdsong and noises which might or might not be animals nearby mean that her sleep is shallow and she wakes mid-afternoon only half rested. She lies looking up at the changing pattern of light and leaves, glancing periodically at the consistently empty road, wondering whether to start walking while it is still light and reminding herself repeatedly that the risk is unnecessary. And this is when the soldiers find her.

She hears the rhythmic *whack ... whack ... whack ...* first, then the dull echo of men shouting to one another. Worse, when she lifts her head over the protective rim of the stonework and looks through the tangled leaves and stalks the soldiers are already visible – one on horseback on the road, six more in a straight line on either side, doggedly thrashing the undergrowth away with short-bladed swords – which means that she, too, will be visible if she runs. She has a cloak but her legs are bare from the knees down and she is wearing sandals. She will be running through thorn bushes and climbing over fallen trunks. They are grown men wearing hessian trousers and metal greaves.

She grips the knife and lies back down, gently hauling some of the hacked-back foliage over her so that she is at least partly covered. She is a cornered animal, every part of her being focused on remaining motionless until she has to fight. When the soldier bends she will stab him in the neck. It does not matter that he is one of seven. It would not matter if he were one of fifty. She will not admit their superiority.

Tramp and crunch and whacks and yells from man to man. One is bored, another tells him to stop complaining, a third says he's stopping to take a piss. Her muscles are bowstrings pulled to breaking point. There is a tune the nurse sang to them when she was very young. *My heart sings like a sparrow among the alder trees.* The up-and-down of the tune, the way it mimicked birdsong. Right now she can remember only the first line. She sings it over and over in the quiet of her mind.

The faintest dimming of the light. A figure is blocking the sun to her left. *Whack ... whack ...* The sword stops. She can see his silhouette against the bright roof of the forest. He takes a couple of steps towards her. She does not look directly at him. She does not move her eyes. She needs him to crouch, to check her breathing, check her pulse. The tip of his sword gently hoists a tangle of shrubs aside. He knows now what he's found.

Something is not right. He is not crouching, he is not calling out. They now look directly at one another. He is nineteen at most, a fuzz of not-quite-beard, dark skin left pitted by pimples, muscular arms. The look on his face, is it cruelty or fear? Hers would be the first life he has taken. She knows it. But this is not what happens. She will tell herself afterwards that there is an obvious explanation. He does not want to kill a girl or be the reason she is killed. If he moves on and the girl keeps her mouth shut then he can pretend that he saw nothing. But while it is happening, Marina knows that the truth is very different. She is talking to him without using words, in the same way that she talked to the dog, in the same way that the dog talked to her. She cannot say precisely how, but the young man *is* the dog. She conjures a shower of imaginary arrows falling towards him out of a stone-grey sky, heads like razors, stems flexing and humming like harp strings. He takes a silent decision. He will say nothing and carry on walking. The arrows become rain, the rain becomes mist, the mist becomes empty air.

He shouts, 'Nothing here,' and he is gone, the *whack ... whack ...* of his sword growing slowly quieter with the diminishing shouts of the other men. Slowly the forest becomes silent again, only the low susurrus of wind and the trill and chirp of birdsong.

271

She gets to her feet and picks up her bag. She must walk away from the road now. So, using the knife she fashions a stout staff from a broken branch to clear a path in front of her just as the soldiers used their swords. The going is hard and slow. After a couple of hours she comes to a small ravine where a stream has cut a deep groove through the forest. Night is coming down. She is not tired but she cannot walk at night. Too great a risk of turning in a circle and heading straight back to the road without the sun to keep her on track. She sits on the edge of the ravine. The noise of the tumbling water is comforting and above her she can see a strip of star-studded black sky which generates a little light. She eats the last of her dried meat, hurls the bones into the water and washes both herself and the knife so as not to attract nocturnal animals in search of an easy meal. She climbs up the far side of the ravine, and perhaps she is tired after all, or perhaps she simply feels safe enough to admit how tired she is. Using the staff she clears the undergrowth and digs out a girl-shaped hollow.

She slips in and out of sleep. She hears scuffles and snorts, the crackle of twigs under hooves. She smells musk and dung. Perhaps she is imagining these things. Perhaps there is little distinction. She wakes feeling more rested than she expected. She rubs earth into every part of her chiton so that she does not give herself away with a distant flash of white cloth.

Keeping the sun to her left she tries to maintain her altitude so that she neither ascends into a colder, cloudier climate nor descends to a road. After several hours of walking she finds herself following deer and boar paths, narrow channels worn into the vegetation by the regular passage of animals. She finds blackberries, eats several handfuls and puts more in her bag. She sees two bear cubs and wants to stay and watch them but cannot see the mother and knows that coming between her and the cubs could be fatal.

She walks for a number of days. She does not remember what this number is. Only later will she look back and realise that one of these days was her sixteenth birthday. She sleeps in dug-out earthen hollows of her own making. Several thorn cuts on her legs become infected, the skin tight and pink and puffy around the original cut. She finds a dead hare but it is too far gone to be food. She finds hazelnuts. She is getting colder at night. The fire she might have been able to build out on the dry grassland is now impossible in this damper atmosphere. She startles a bird which explodes from the undergrowth in front of her. She walks over and finds a nest buried deep in thorns containing three little eggs which she eats raw. She was skinny to start with. She is gaunt now. Previously some nameless entity was walking beside her, holding her hand, keeping her safe. She knows this because it has abandoned her and she can feel the anxious chill of its absence.

She starts to grieve for the loss of Phoebe. How has this not happened before? Her best, her only friend. Sometimes she has to kneel down and cover her head with her arms, as if her sadness were driving hail or a flock of angry birds pecking at her. She wonders for the first time what Phoebe felt when Marina disappeared. What does Phoebe know? What has she been told? Under all these questions lies a troubling truth, that if they were to meet again Marina would be disgusted by Phoebe – her need for comfort and luxury, her desire to be liked, her affected weakness.

Every so often she senses a brightness in the trees to her left where the forest slopes away. She worries at first that something is wrong with her eyes or, worse, her mind. The brightness becomes slashes of vertical light between the trunks. She is near the coast. Is it possible that she has somehow walked in a great circle and found herself approaching

Tarsus again? She clambers onto a large rock to gain a better view and through the trees she sees a little dumb-bell-shaped island half a league offshore which she does not recognise. She should be relieved but this confirmation of the distance she has put between herself and what she once called home unnerves her. She is never going back. There is nowhere to go back to.

She picks her way gradually downhill through the trees. She is so profoundly tired. This stopped being an adventure a long way back. She has very little energy left. She comes to a road. Mud ruts and hoof-holes made in wetter weather have been hardened by the sun. A magpie sits on a stone league marker too moss-mottled to read clearly. She no longer cares about the soldiers. In her mind she has travelled a thousand miles since leaving the city. It seems impossible that she should meet anyone connected to Tarsus. She is not going to hide any longer. If she sees a passing vehicle of any kind she will beg a lift. She needs walls, a roof, human company. She needs a story, too, a way of generating sympathy without arousing suspicion. She cannot think of a story.

She walks along the road for an hour, two hours, three. There are no vehicles, no travellers. The road runs parallel to the coast, descending slowly. Night falls. She tries to sleep wedged under a fallen tree trunk a little way back from the road, but she is too cold and her hunger is a persistent ache and she is scared that if she falls asleep she might not wake up. She returns to the road and carries on walking very slowly so as not to twist her ankle in the ruts.

She finds the place mid-morning. There is a junction up ahead, five tracks coming together in a clearing. The building hoves into view only when she turns the final bend. She assumes that it must be some kind of agricultural building at first, given its location, but as she walks round to the front she sees a pediment resting on four columns.

She walks up the steps into the portico. There is a fresco on the rear wall. In the centre of the fresco stands the goddess Diana, bow in one hand, javelin in the other, quiver across her shoulders. The large, badly painted dog at her side bears a disturbing resemblance to the dog that briefly shared Marina's journey. A band of women stand around the goddess. Tunics, boots, spears, bows. Marina feels dizzy. Is she really here? She reaches out and touches the wall with her fingertips to reassure herself of its solidity. There are wild animals – deer, wolves, boars, something which might conceivably be either a badger or a piebald horse were the artist's perspective competent enough to give any sense of size.

There is a doorway in the wall. On the far side of the doorway a small painted Diana is crowning a small painted king. Marina is becoming increasingly confused. It seems to her that the doorway leads not into the back room behind the wall but into the world of the painting itself and that if she steps through she will find herself in a kinder, less cruel, more fantastical world. She hesitates. It is a journey of two or three steps but she is unsure whether it is one which can be made in reverse. She steps through.

If it is another world on the far side it is remarkably like the one she has just left. There is no charmed forest, there are no birds of prey, no tiny kings, only a small, unwindowed room, whitewashed and belted by a thin band of rust-red Solomon knots. A stone bench runs along the back wall. Her knees weaken. She unshoulders her bag and swings it onto one end of the bench to act as a pillow. She sits heavily, falls sideways and closes her eyes and this time she does enter another world.

There is light rain. There are trees of a deeper, lusher green than she has ever seen. A single crow struts and bounces through wet grass. There is a building of pale stone with high, arched windows and a square tower at one end from which a large, tiled spike thrusts into the sky. A tiny metal cross decorates its apex. Big bells are being struck, four or five different tones tumbling repeatedly over one another like the song of great metal birds. Five men stand between the building and the trees. They are dressed in black clothes of a kind she has never seen before. Four of the men are lowering a long black box into a slot cut crisply into the ground. A fat mound of moist earth sits to one side. The fifth man wears robes and reads from a book. All five seem oblivious to the rain which soaks their clothing and wets their hair and covers the pages of the little book with dark spots.

Marina is in the box. She is convinced of it. This is a ceremony to mark her own death. These men are going to bury her in the ground and throw earth on top of her. And it is not her death which makes this so desperately sad, it is the smallness of the gathering, the absence of any family, any friends, the way this obscure event is happening in a faraway place, in a language she cannot understand.

Then the truth dawns on her. She is not dead. She is alive and she is trapped inside the box. And these men know it. They are making sure that she dies a long, slow death and that the only evidence of their crime will be permanently hidden from the world – bloody, broken fingernails, scratches on the underside of the lid. '*I became dumb, and opened not my mouth,*' says the man in the robe, '*for it was thy doing. Take thy plague away from me: I am even consumed by means of thy heavy hand.*' The coffin bumps against the bottom of the hole. The ropes are let go and one of the men swings a spade into the pile of earth.

She cries out and hammers on the lid of the coffin and wakes in a small room of simple plaster walls. Through the open doorway she can see stone columns and, beyond them, trees. The smell of bark-rot and the sound of birds. A woman is sitting beside her. She has blonde hair and blue, blue eyes. There is a tiny scar on her cheek. She says, 'You're safe now.'

They find him early in the afternoon. They are carrying bags and ropes to the little crabbing pools. The man is lying in a wooden rowing boat which has been washed into a narrow channel and has now jammed sideways. The possibility that he is dead is thrilling. Some of them have seen dead bodies but they belonged to relatives and therefore had to be treated with decorum. They have all heard about corpses bloated by days at sea which burst when you push a spike into their bellies. Perhaps they can make this one burst. If the man is alive, on the other hand, it gets more complicated, and more thrilling, possibly. They scramble down the rocky slope. The sun has dried seaweed into vivid lime-green tufts. Sandals snag on barnacles and skid on popping bladderwrack. There are four sails out at sea.

The man is lying face down over the bench in the centre of the boat as if praying or vomiting. There seems to be no question that he is dead. The skin on the backs of his legs is blistered with sunburn. They know every boat in the harbour and every boat in neighbouring harbours. The man is from somewhere else, a stray dog, the sea's gift. They can do with him as they please and face no consequences.

They want to look into the eyes of death but there is some squeamishness about who is going to touch him first and turn him over. They challenge one another, call one another cowards. A boy who has wandered away returns with a small rock and breaks the impasse by throwing it at the man's head. The impact is as loud as the slap of a hand against the flank of a horse. The force of it twists the man's head to one side. He groans and rolls over so that he is sitting. He is alive. Several of them yelp in surprise. The man squints at them. He says nothing. He has a beard. His head wound is already bleeding copiously. He raises his right hand. Two fingers are missing, the little finger and its neighbour, stumps like melted candles where they have been cut off below the first joint.

They are going to do something to him, that much is obvious. Some of them are excited, some of them are scared, but the scared ones are equally scared of breaking ranks. One of the taller boys jumps into the boat. He means to kick or punch the man. But the man looks at him directly and doesn't flinch. Some deep chord resonates in the boy's chest. Deference? Self-protection? The man is his father's age, he is lean and muscular; he was strong once, perhaps he was strong only days ago. The boy wishes someone else had jumped into the boat but he is committed and must now prove himself. He grabs the collar of the man's soiled linen tunic and yanks it hard so that it rips away from his chest. It is the wrong gesture, clumsy, insufficiently violent, clear evidence of his failure of nerve. But no one is thinking about the gesture because it has revealed the tattoos which cover the man's chest – wings, claws, interwoven branches. Between his nipples two dogs are killing an elk. One has its jaws around a hind leg, another has its teeth fixed into the animal's neck. There is a general intake of breath. They knew that he was a stranger but they did not realise he came from this far away. Does this make the situation more dangerous? Or are they now more justified in treating him like a trapped animal?

The torn tunic has revealed something else too, a knife hanging from the man's belt in a leather sheath decorated with shiny foil spirals. The boy reaches down, grabs the handle and slips it out. A rod of whetstone with a brass end hangs beside the sheath. It has been used often. Sunlight flares on the blade's edge. The boy likes the knife. It is more sophisticated than a fist, he can do greater damage with less effort and he does not have to touch the man with his hands.

Now. Before he thinks too hard. He slashes the man's face. A louder intake of breath. Briefly, between ear and lip, a thin red line appears, like a single strand of dyed wool. Then the sides of the wound peel apart and there is yet more blood.

He stands back to admire his handiwork. He whoops. The noise is affected, an attempt to demonstrate how much he enjoyed doing this, how easily it came to him. But the whoop stirs something animal and ancient and the second whoop is genuinely ecstatic. He must cut the man again. He thinks about slashing through the centre of the tattoo. Then he stops. Could he cut the tattoo off? It excites him and scares him in equal measure. It would be an extraordinary object to take away.

But he is distracted. A younger boy with red hair has seen a leather bag under the seat. He drags it out of the boat and empties the contents onto the rocks, relieved that he has found himself a role which might just excuse him from joining in with whatever the others are planning to do to the man himself. There are two flatbreads inside, an empty, unstoppered bottle and four smaller bags. He rips open the smallest of these. Seeds and nuts bounce on the rocks and roll into a weedy pool of clear water. A second boy unknots the cord from a longer bag. It is a piece of exquisite craftsmanship, chevrons of thin leather in three colours stitched invisibly together. Everyone watches. It is too light for coins, that much is obvious. It is a map, perhaps, a map of the wild land from which this wild man has come. A tube of tarnished metal is pulled from the open bag and the stiff top is unscrewed. He unrolls a sheet of parchment. It is not a map, it is a painting of a black-and-white bear climbing a tree. There is writing down the side of the scroll in a script none of them recognise. The others are volubly disappointed but the boy with red hair thinks it is a beautiful image. He dares not say this. The second boy tears the picture in half. This is a transgression on a level with cutting the man's face. Parchment is valuable and documents of all kinds are sacrosanct. The boy with red hair is close to tears. He wanted very much to take the picture home. The man in the boat groans. Someone tells him to be quiet or they will cut him again. A third boy grabs the next bag. This too is exquisitely made. The boy in the boat hands him the bloody knife so that he can cut through the leather without wasting time unknotting the ties around the neck. The interior of the bag is furred, better to protect an object which puzzles all of them, a little cube of dark, polished wood no larger than an apple with a marquetry dolphin on the top. The boy turns it over in his hands. There is the faintest line around its circumference. It must be some kind of box but he is unable to open it. Several other boys grab it and take turns. None have any luck. Some are convinced that it will contain nothing of any value. Others don't want it to be thrown away in case there is some small but precious object inside.

Meanwhile a boy has opened the fourth bag and found a tiny bird inside – pink chest, grey wings, blue-black tail. He turns it over in his hands and everyone can see that it is solid. Wood? Bone? There is a general sullen murmur. Only one thing remains before violence is done. A boy retrieves the rock thrown at the stranger's head, puts the little wooden box on the ground and begins bashing it. The box cracks open at the fifth blow. It is empty.

As one, they turn to the man in the boat. The oldest boy asks him why he brought them these stupid objects. They wanted something better. They wanted something more expensive, more exciting. Did he not realise that? How could he be so stupid? How could he be so disrespectful?

The boy with red hair, who loved the picture of the bear, puts on as gruff a voice as he can and quietly asks the boy holding the bird if he can have it. It is as beautiful as the picture of the bear, if not more so. The boy holding the bird looks at him, smelling weakness and need. He turns and hurls the bird as far as he can into the sea. The boy with red hair nods and bites his lip and tries not to cry.

The oldest boy grabs the man's hair and demands an answer. Why has he insulted them with gifts for some old lady? The man groans. The boy tells him to speak clearly, but the man is way past speaking. His mouth is rimed with a dry white crust. His left eye is covered with sticky blood. The gaping wound on his cheek is still bleeding. The boy takes the knife. Speak, he says, or they will make him speak.

There is a yell from above and behind them. They spin round. It is one of their fathers looking down from the path. 'What in the name of the gods are you doing?' They crash back into the everyday world. They are children again. They cannot claim that they found the stranger in this state. The wounds are fresh and if the man lives he will condemn them all. If he dies they are murderers. So they run. The stronger swimmers climb down the rocks and dive. The more nimble scatter and choose their own routes up rocks they know better than any of the adults in the town. Only the boy with red hair does not run. It is never any use running. He learnt this a long time ago. He has never done anything bad. He has only ever watched bad things being done. But he will always be caught and he will always be punished.

The man walks over and looks into the boat. 'Who is this?'

'I don't know.' The boy bends down. The two halves of the bear picture have fallen into one of the shallow pools. He shakes off the excess water and unrolls them.

'What have you done to him?'

The ink is soluble, and the salt water has already gone to work. There is no bear. There is no tree. There is only the faintest hint of branches and the ghost of a creature thinning and sliding away like mist.

❧

Emilia eats a breakfast of olives and barley bread soaked in wine sitting on the terrace at the rear of the villa, watching the fox cubs who live under the collapsed wall at the edge of the sloping garden play-fighting until the mother chivvies them back into the den. Emilia goes into the house. She has been asked to resolve a dispute about the ownership of a large house belonging to the town's oldest and recently deceased resident. There are four long-lost supposed relatives and three not-wholly-convincing wills. So she spends the next hour writing a detailed missive to a notary in Latakia where the old man grew up. While she is doing this three men arrive to patch the reservoir which was storing a winter of rain until an otherwise ineffectual earthquake sent a hairline crack from end to end the previous week. She then splits forty or so of the logs from an old felled pine which have been sitting beside the villa for a week. Drusilla is horrified but Emilia finds herself increasingly unable to sit and read in the evening unless she has done some physical work during the day.

After her midday meal she walks to the temple. The journey is more spiritual than anything which happens in the temple itself if truth be told, moving from the mundane into something larger, disinterested, un-human. The way she shrinks as she follows the small paths uphill, the effort of it settling the mind.

It is late spring. Strawberry trees, laurel, broom. Two wild goats bleat and bounce away into the undergrowth. A bald ibis looks down from a nook in a rock face safe in the knowledge that Emilia is not a climbing animal. The rasp of cicadas gives way to forest hum as she rises. Deeper shade, more moisture in the air. There is no one at the temple. She is relieved and quietly embarrassed by her mean-spiritedness, though people do have a habit of appearing at the end of a quiet hour just when she has decided to head back home. As she walks up the steps a house martin weaves between the columns and sockets home into a nest in the far corner. She glances into the little back room. There is a girl lying on the bench. Strange. She was certain the room was empty. No premonition of human presence whatsoever. Dirty chiton, dirty hair, dirty face, skinny as a pole. Emilia's heart sinks. Either the girl has lost her mind or she has been rejected by her family. Neither situation is easily resolved. The girl is breathing at least, and not obviously pregnant.

She sits on the bench. The girl smells like a farmyard animal. Fourteen, fifteen? She is deep in some dream of fighting, arms and legs twitching and struggling. Under the dirt the girl has smooth brown skin and hair the colour of mahogany. Well fed before she stopped eating, or so it seems. White teeth. A comfortable childhood and a good family. She must have walked a long way or Emilia would doubtless have heard about her disappearance. Both ankles are raw and swollen and covered in thorn-scratches. There is a leech on her neck. A week in the woods? Two weeks? Tougher than she looks, then. Emilia lifts the hem of the chiton, licks her thumb and rubs the material. She is no expert but there seem to be threads of fine gold wire woven into the green patterned border.

'No!' says the girl. 'No!' She opens her eyes, panting hard. Those eyes are almost black. Emilia feels a tremor of something otherworldy. She turns briefly to look out through the door and check that they are alone. She turns back to the girl. 'You're safe now.' She moves a lick of greasy hair from the girl's face. Drink, food and a wash are badly needed but the girl doesn't look as if she's in a state for walking, even downhill. Emilia puts the girl's head on her thigh and opens the leather bag she was using for a pillow. A knife, some withered berries, a single hazelnut. 'What's your name?'

The girl mumbles. Emilia leans closer.

'Marina.'

The sea not the forest. That shiver again. There is something she doesn't like about this situation, some guardian deity telling her to tread carefully. 'Let's get you to your feet.'

The girl is even lighter than she looks. She staggers and collapses and staggers. Her arm over Emilia's shoulder, they follow the path into the trees. Several woodpeckers are drilling into tree trunks for insects. It sounds like men building a wooden house. Emilia and the girl round two bends and pass the rock which local children call the Tortoise. The journey will take two hours at this speed and Emilia very much does not want the girl to die before they get there, so she lowers her onto a bank of grass at the roadside. It is near enough to the temple, she hopes, for the principle of sanctuary to keep her safe. She will run. If she is in luck the men will not yet have finished mending the reservoir. She has not gone a hundred paces, however, when she sees Hesperos the forester walking towards her. She would, in most circumstances, politely decline his help because he is very keen indeed that Emilia marry him and treats her refusals as flirtatious procrastination. She keeps the request formal, a thing one does, not a thing she needs doing.

They jog back up the hill. He is a big man and, for a few moments, the way he lifts the girl like a father holding a baby genuinely touches her, but they must move swiftly and he is mostly interested in talking and the poor girl is soon bumping around like a sack of barley. With his usual clumsy enthusiasm he extemporises on the theme of selfish young people making work for others, becoming more sympathetic only when he realises that Emilia is genuinely worried about this girl.

The path twists and drops. They cross the little stream using the stepping stones and leave the forest. The ocean looms into view, then a slice of the town beyond the crest of the hill. She can see the villa itself sitting on the ridge where the land falls away to the river. A deer runs across the hillside, stops on the path and stands looking at them. Wrong place, wrong time of day. She rarely sees them after dawn or before dusk and she never sees them stop for so long in such an exposed location. There is something wrong with it, perhaps.

'Idiot creature,' says Hesperos, fondly, and it bolts.

He carries the girl into the villa and puts her down on the long green couch in the reception room. Drusilla bites back the urge to keep anything dirty off the furniture and shoos Hesperos out with flapping hands as if he were a chicken which had wandered in from the yard. Emilia steps out to thank him. 'And don't tell anyone.' She gently touches his arm. It may be nothing, but there are good and bad reasons for girls to run away and gossip cannot be called back.

'I saw nothing.' He bows theatrically, takes two steps backwards, rotates grandly and walks away wearing a broad smile.

Drusilla and Emilia give the girl a cup of water and some lentil soup. Drusilla says she'll bathe her and put her in clean clothes. Emilia insists that she help. It is the latest chapter in a long, ongoing tussle but Emilia will not back down this time. Something peculiar is happening here and she needs to remain involved. Time is repeating or rhyming, the girl arriving in the way that she herself arrived, out of nowhere, nameless, half conscious. She finds herself imagining a future in which she dies and the girl becomes the priestess and takes in another young woman in distress and the girl dies and that young woman becomes the priestess ... It is a preposterous fantasy. She found the girl less than two hours ago. Emilia knows nothing about her.

They sit her in the tub and wipe her down with warm water and a cloth each. The girl neither resists nor helps. Her ribs stick out, her hip bones stick out. Flat breasts, deep hollows above her collar bones. When they touch the swellings on her legs she flinches. Emilia has never taken care of someone in this intimate way before, not even Kerimon. She has held the hand of two old women and a small boy as they passed away, but even the boy's death did not move her in the way that this does. Is the girl casting some malign spell against which she should protect herself? Drusilla uses a brush to get the dirt out from under the girl's finger- and toe-nails, doing so a little more roughly than is strictly necessary. She is protective of Emilia and perpetually critical of her mistress's altruism. She wants the girl to know that she is here on sufferance. Or is there some jealousy, too? Is that possible?

They sit the girl on a low stool, dry her and oil her skin. They scrape away the excess, wrap her in two woollen blankets and sit her back on the couch. While Emilia builds a fire Drusilla fetches sagebrush from the garden, makes a poultice of leaves and flowers, and bandages it to the girl's swollen legs. Outside, the men who were mending the reservoir are boisterously reloading their donkey cart.

'Why do you think she ran away?' asks Drusilla.

'Only one of us knows the answer to that.' Emilia looks into the girl's black eyes. 'Perhaps we should wait for her to tell us. If she wants

286

to tell us.' Because Emilia has never told her own story to anyone, has she? Except Kerimon and only when she knew that he would take it to the grave. 'You go. I'll sit with her.'

'Be careful,' says Drusilla.

The girl sleeps hugging the blankets tight around her, head on the raised end of the couch. Emilia lights the fire and, when the flames take hold, sits beside the girl. What if Drusilla is right? What if they are all in danger? Girls have secrets. She has heard too many over the past few years. And there are plenty of men who consider their good name more valuable than a girl's life. But what is the answer? Armed guards? Depending on yet more men seems to her like part of the problem. Better to rely on their own invisibility. A memory of that deer standing on the path then sprinting away. The sisterhood of idiot creatures, the wisdom that comes with knowing you could be prey.

The girl's hair is dry now. It is, in its own way, as extraordinary as her eyes. Like the mane of a groomed chestnut horse, the way the deep colour shifts as she runs her hand across it. So much light soaked up, so much light given back. Now that her starved bones are hidden under the blanket Emilia can see how beautiful the girl's face is, even with those magnetic black eyes closed. She says, 'Where are you from?' Talking to herself, mostly.

The girl whispers, as if sharing a secret with someone in a dream. 'Tarsus.'

The city Pericles saved. The flames in the fireplace flatten and stand again the way they do when someone walks past in a great cloak. Is this a spirit girl? For reassurance Emilia lays her fingers on the inside of the girl's wrist and feels the faintest drumbeat of human blood.

They put the girl in Kerimon's old chamber, the servant girl Hamda sleeping on a thin mattress in the corner in case the girl wakes and panics. Emilia goes to bed late but she is anxious and finds it hard to drift off. She needs to know that the girl is safe, so she gets out of bed and walks through the orange-scented dark of the colonnade, lifts the heavy pine latch and steps into Kerimon's room. Hamda looks like a stone monument, flat on her back, legs straight, fingers laced across her breast. Two mice scoot from the empty plate on the bedside table and are swallowed by a crack in the plaster. Emilia tiptoes across the room. The girl is curled like a podded bean, knees up, elbows in, head down. Her long hair is spread out behind her as if she is flying through some night sky of her own creation.

This is the reason for Emilia's discomfort, isn't it? The way her heart reaches out, a hunger she has managed to ignore for years, the sudden incompleteness of her life, the fear not that someone is looking for this girl intent on doing her harm, but that someone else loves her and has lost her and will come to take her home. She is embarrassed by her own neediness. Marina says something in her sleep and turns over. Fearful of scaring the girl, Emilia retraces her steps and slips from the room.

The following morning the girl sits in front of a plate of oysters, boiled eggs and bread at the kitchen table. She is rocking gently back and forth and cradling her head. She nods when asked if she is in pain. Drusilla gives her a small cup of willow-bark-and-fennel tea. The girl swallows half, stops midway, gags, empties the cup and shivers. Emilia has drunk the stuff before at Drusilla's bidding and it is only marginally less unpleasant than having a headache.

'Thank you,' says the girl. 'Thank you for everything.'

Just six words, but it is immediately obvious to Emilia and Drusilla that the girl has been well educated in a wealthy family. 'I'm glad I found you when I did,' says Emilia.

The girl eats one of the eggs, possibly just to counteract the taste of Drusilla's concoction.

'Now, young lady,' says Drusilla. 'You need to tell us where you've come from and what you're up to.'

'You don't have to tell us anything,' says Emilia.

Drusilla gives her a stern look. How can Emilia explain that there are things she doesn't want to hear? It is hard enough explaining it to herself.

'Where are we?' asks the girl.

Drusilla tells her. The girl does not recognise the name.

'It's a long way from Tarsus,' says Emilia, hoping that this fact will make the girl feel safe but the girl looks panicked. 'You said the name in your sleep. Just the name. No more than that.' The girl nods slowly. 'I'm assuming a long way from Tarsus is good,' says Emilia.

'Please, please don't tell anyone that I'm here.'

'Why?' asks Drusilla.

Emilia rebukes her gently. 'That's enough.' She turns back to Marina. 'We won't tell anyone.'

'You are worried about your own safety,' says the girl. 'I understand that.' Her self-possession takes them by surprise. 'You seem like kind people but sometimes people are not what they seem, and sometimes being kind isn't enough. I am the only person I can trust.' She pauses to gather herself. She has not talked for two weeks. 'I am in great danger through no fault of my own. I am very grateful for what you have done for me ...'

'We have done very little for you.'

'... and I wish I could pay you back but I have nothing.' She is holding back tears and angry with herself that she must do this.

'You do not need to pay us back,' says Emilia.

'I need to keep travelling, to a place where no one knows who I am and no one knows the people who are looking for me. So I need money. I need to work. I can read and write. In Latin and Hebrew, too. I understand mathematics, astronomy. I can play ...' She pulls up. Has she revealed more than is safe? 'I could teach. I could copy. I would be diligent and dependable. I could clean,' she says, trying to make herself sound less exceptional. 'I could cook.' She has never cleaned or cooked in her life.

'You're still a child,' says Drusilla, though it is abundantly clear that she is old beyond both her years and her slight frame.

'Eat,' says Emilia. 'Drink.' The girl is clearly not someone whose mind can be changed easily. 'You need to be well before you can do anything.'

Marina eats an oyster and drinks a large beaker of water. Emilia says that she has work to do but that the girl can disturb her whenever she wants. She then retires to her study. The willow bark and the fennel slowly convert Marina's pain to a thin fog and some dizziness. Drusilla watches Marina and wants her to know that she is being watched. It is a new experience for Marina to occupy a position below a slave, but reassuring to understand exactly what this woman thinks of her. The other woman, the priestess ... there are things she is not saying and things not said are dangerous. Marina finishes eating and walks around the villa. She sits in the library leafing through some of the books. A Tanak, a Septuagint, Archimedes on polyhedra and sphere-making, Aristotle, Callisthenes ... There is an orrery on the central table over which Mesomedes would have swooned. The Sun is a central golden globe and when Marina turns the little handle the Earth and the other five wanderers spin round it.

At the rear of the villa a garden covers the flank of the hill which slopes down to the river. The gardens amongst which she grew up were extraordinary on account of their extent, their lushness, their sophistication and the work which went into their upkeep. This garden is less tidy and has fewer ornaments but there are plants here which seem to have come from the pages of a book of traveller's fables – plants with spiny jaws that eat spiders and flies, plants like brightly coloured pebbles which are soft to the touch and are presumably some kind of cactus. The bigger cacti look like geometry lessons viciously armed – spheres, triangles, ovals. The trunk of one tree is shaped like a vast, upright aubergine. A small bush is laden with bright orange bananas.

She sits on a vine-shaded bench. There is a kitten nearby, mewling, wanting attention. She shoos the creature away. She doesn't want to escape from a murderer then die of lockjaw or rabies.

She likes it here. The garden, the house, the kindness, the simple fact that it is warm and clean. She wishes she could stay. The woman would let her, Marina can see it in her eyes. But she can see a weakness too. And warmth and kindness are no replacement for being somewhere else when bad things happen. She has checked the map. Tarsus is four days' hard ride away. It is entirely possible that the soldiers have swung through here already, that there are people in the town who have been given her description and the promise of a reward. She cannot stay. It is too dangerous. Leaving by sea means paying money and trusting people and being trapped on a boat. Best to carry on walking, but better equipped this time. The woman will help. The woman is desperate to help. Warmer clothes, food, a weapon, a map. How many days will it take for her to regain her strength so that she can restart her journey? Two? Three?

She hears a faint clang of cowbells on the wind and looks over to the far side of the valley where a herd of pale cattle are passing through a narrow gate then spreading out across the dry grass of the hillside like blown seeds. Drusilla steps onto the terrace to check on the unwanted guest. She wipes her wet hands on her apron, nods dourly then retreats into the kitchen.

The future is terrifying. Marina must find a world in which everyone is a stranger then invent a life from nothing. She is a teenage girl. She has read enough to know what happens to teenage girls who are not protected by stronger, older men. But this is life. She sees that now. Every one of those cows will have its throat cut. The falcon will tear the pigeon apart. Chained women will be dragged from captured cities. *Sed omnes una manet nox.* Golden bowls and leather-bound books are palliatives and distractions. The lucky ones are those who die young and swiftly and in ignorance.

She is so profoundly tired. She gets up and walks back inside via the kitchen so that Drusilla doesn't need to track her down. She asks if she can take one of the leavened poppy-seed rolls, goes back to the chamber and falls asleep on the bed, hand still clutched around the small, uneaten fist of bread.

She dreams tangled, heady, sunless dreams. She is tied up in the back of the cart and the cart is falling down a well in Alexandria. She is drowning in a sea of brambles. The Kangal mastiff bitch has Drusilla's face, then her stepmother's face, then Phoebe's face. The dog says, 'I am even consumed by means of thy heavy hand,' and the stars are pieces of chalk being dragged screeching across the slate of the sky. She sleeps through the afternoon and into the night, waking only once to relieve herself, the empty villa as disturbing as any of the morphing phantasms of her sleep. She stumbles back to bed and is reclaimed by the relentless seasick churn of images.

She comes round early the following morning feeling wretched and wrung out. She steps over the sleeping Hamda, lifts the latch and heads to the garden. Emilia is already sitting in the shade of the figs which twist around the narrow beams of the veranda. Marina wants to turn and head back inside but she cannot antagonise the woman on whom she must depend for the next leg of her journey. Emilia puts her book down and wishes her a good morning. Marina sits.

'Help yourself.'

There are dried apricots and emmer porridge and mullet on the table. Marina eats two of the apricots to make the silence less uncomfortable. The first mouthful makes her realise how hungry she is. She spoons porridge into one of the smaller bowls. The world starts to seem a little more real, her dreams a little less. Emilia returns to her book. Night has cleaned and cooled the valley making the air chill and transparent. Marina can smell thyme and coconut. Nothing moves. The only noises are the sound of Emilia turning the papyrus pages and the dry ratchet of a complaining bird. The promise of a hot day ahead. They sit in silence for a long time.

'I need to leave,' says Marina at last. 'Tomorrow, the day after …
The longer I stay the more likely they are to find me.'

Emilia does not answer. It is like a bird landing on your arm in the garden. You can only stand still and hope in vain that time does the same.

'If you help me I promise that if I ever have the means then I will repay you fivefold.'

Why does Emilia want so badly for her to stay? The girl is not warm, the girl is not easy. She is grateful, but no more so than propriety dictates. She asks no questions, she tells no stories. 'I will help you because you are a young woman and you are on your own and you are in danger. If you want to repay me then you can help someone else who is in need whenever you are able.' Is it possible that the girl has done something bad? Is it possible that if Emilia knew the whole story she might not feel so sympathetic?

'I can do that.' The girl nods. 'I will do that.'

The only thing they have in common, thinks Emilia, is their refusal to tell anyone about themselves. And it is precisely this realisation that opens a door. 'I have a secret, too.' Why is she doing this? Does she think that handing over her most precious possession will persuade the girl to stay? 'No one here knows who I really am. Not Drusilla. Not Hamda.' This is not wise. She knows nothing about this girl. She must stop herself.

The girl herself looks wary, which is no surprise. She has enough to deal with already. Why would she wish to be burdened with the story of a middle-aged woman's life? A single white cloud sits on the far hill like a snow-white tree. Everything hangs in the balance. So many things could happen now, so many things which cannot be undone. Mother and daughter, complete strangers to one another. What if Emilia tells her story? What if Marina learns that her mother knew of her existence but never came to find her? What if Emilia discovers that her husband abandoned their daughter? Can those kinds of wound ever be healed? What if Marina continues her journey and they never discover any of these things?

What if they both keep their secrets and Marina stays the night and then another night and begins to trust this woman and decides to take a chance and create her new life right here? What if the two women get to know one another day by day, with no expectations, no looking back? What if they grasp that rarest of opportunities to consign the past to oblivion and begin life all over again? What if they become friends?

None of these things happen.

There is a banging from inside the villa. Marina jumps.

'Someone is at the door,' says Emilia. She touches the girl's hand. 'It always sounds like that. Drusilla will answer it. There is no need to worry.' The girl does not look convinced. 'Drusilla does not like you very much, but she dislikes strangers asking questions even more.'

The door is banged again, then banged for a third time. Emilia gets to her feet. 'Stay here. Don't move.'

Marina feels sick and twitchy. What can she do if it is the soldiers? Time spent gathering food and clothing is time wasted. There is a knife on the table. She grabs it. The blade is short but sharp. She jogs down the sloping path of limestone flags between the biggest cacti, then veers off right towards the collapsed wall and the compost heap. She turns round. She can see no one. She squats and squeezes herself into the gap between the tumbled stones and the great wedge of hot, rank clippings. She grips the knife. She waits.

Inside the villa Emilia slides back the little hatch and sees two men standing in the shade of the portico. They are too slovenly for soldiers. She is fairly sure that she recognises the lanky one with the great mane of hair. She closes the hatch, pulls back the bolt and swings open the heavy, squeaking door.

'Come,' says the lanky man. She recognises the lisp. A fisherman. His son has epilepsy. He ushers her outside. 'Come quickly.'

She sees now that a cart is parked in the lane, the ragged horse trying to pick the little succulents from the gaps in the stone wall.

'What is it?' She walks beside the man with the lisp. His sweat smells like warm fish.

'Perimos found him in a boat.' He nods towards his companion. 'Badly beaten.'

The man is lying on his back on the flat bed of the little cart, his ankles and feet hanging over the end. There is a long open wound across one side of his face. His dirty, sunburnt skin and black beard are clotted with dried blood. His right hand which flops between the spokes of the wheel is missing two fingers. But these are not the most striking thing about him. Whatever garment he was wearing to cover the top half of his body has been ripped away to reveal a torso covered in tattoos – dogs attacking a deer, lions, a ram, a large bird of prey ... She has never seen anything like it before. He must be a Scythian, or one of the other horse traders from north of the Caspian and Aral Seas. She steps a little closer. She can see his ribcage moving. Her heart sinks a little. She is tired of this. The men begin lifting the stranger from the cart. The assumption is that she will look after him. The assumption is always that she will solve any difficult problem. But she is tired of these assumptions, she is tired of being the first port of call, she is tired of other people. The girl will be sitting on the terrace, terrified no doubt. Emilia must get back to her.

The tattooed man is half on, half off the cart. There is nothing she can do for him which they cannot do – clean the wound, give him water, give him food, let him rest. She does not like the idea of a barbarian being in the villa. Drusilla will like it even less. They are four women living alone. Do these men not understand? Do they really think that the ability to read and write makes a woman safe?

The man is heavy. Perimos and his companion lower him to the ground so they can rest their arms.

If she lets them carry him into the villa then the girl will leave. She has no doubt whatsoever about that. What if, just this once, she uses money to solve the problem? She can pay the man to find a room for the stranger, a nurse for a few days, food and drink, clean clothes. The final outcome will be the same. Drusilla will be happier. She might even persuade the girl to stay. The stranger himself will almost certainly feel more at home in a workman's house.

The man with the lisp takes a deep, confessional breath. 'The children found him.' He pauses. 'The boys. They found him washed ashore in a boat near the crab pools, and they did this to him.' He pauses again. This is difficult. 'My son was one of the boys who did this to him.' He looks at the ground. 'If I hadn't found them in time ...'

The tattooed man lying on the ground rolls his head towards Emilia. He opens his left eye. The right is so swollen and bloodied that it refuses to open. He looks at her. He is in pain. The children of the town tried to kill him. Tattoos or not he has a soul. And he is damaged, like the girl, like herself. She can see that now. They are all missing something. She cannot turn him away.

'Bring him inside,' she says.

THE STORM

It begins mid-Channel, two big winds meeting to force a monumental updraught. Five hundred thousand tons of water vapour hoisted aloft, condensing as they rise to build a cumulus three miles high, the mountain of it sliding over the surface of the sea. The day's light is dying slowly, tankers and trawlers hardening to crisp black silhouettes on the tide, studded with lights of holly green and cherry red. At forty thousand feet, the summit of the storm cloud spreads sideways to make a grey anvil in the heavens. *Cumulonimbus incus.* Only the upper reaches are lit by the remaining sunlight as it arcs away around the earth. Crossing Portland Bill and Weymouth the vast structure heads inland. Miles up, water gathers into drops which turn to ice as they descend, leaving the cloudbase as marbles of hail which clatter against windows and drum on the roofs of cars and smash through the leaves of alder, oak and beech in the New Forest.

The lightning starts inside the summit of the cloud, the heart of the anvil momentarily luminous. Then below the base of the cloud, channels of ionised air dodge and branch downwards until the earth senses them and sends up its own streamers of ionised air and the sky is ripped by great cracks of plasma. Two million miles per hour, fifty thousand degrees centigrade. The sonic boom spreads in a fading ring of crack and rumble. The tang of ozone mixes with the smell of sodden earth in the wet night air.

It is directly above the house now. Logically it should strike one of the innumerable tall trees in the garden or in the surrounding woods, but lightning is rebellious and there is steel rebar in the refurbished parapet which borders the roof and those channels of ionised air connect the north-east corner of the roof to the tonnage of charged vapour overhead and the blinding fire rides its way down the side of the house, splitting concrete from concrete.

Philippe is woken by a loud bang. Was it real or did he imagine the noise? He sits up in bed. Nothing seems out of place at first. The faint blue outline of the armchair, a thin stripe of light between the curtains. Rain drums on the glass. A nightmare. He lies down but he is restless and uneasy and cannot drift off. Something is wrong. He sits up again. Burning. He can smell burning.

He runs to the door and opens it. The landing is an oven. There are curls of smoke in the air and a dancing glow from the ground floor. He shields his face and looks into the stairwell. He can see flames. It is no longer possible to go downstairs. The heat is unbearable, even at this distance. If the nurse does not rescue her then Angelica will die. A sick panic overwhelms him. How will he live with himself if he did nothing to save his daughter? But in the middle of his horror he sees an opportunity to escape a terrible quandary. If Angelica dies then she will take her story to the grave. She can no longer destroy them both. One of them, at least, will survive and be able to fashion a kind of life. She is unconscious. She will feel nothing, know nothing. It will be a blessing.

He coughs violently. The air is filled with soot and black flakes. His head swims. And only now does he realise that he must act fast if he himself is going to survive. He turns and climbs to the half-landing, unlocks the door and steps out onto the flat roof, shutting the door firmly behind him. He will be rescued. He has always been rescued. He walks to the front of the building and looks down. He can see no one. Then a rising curtain of smoke and heat-rippled air forces him to back away from the edge. He crosses to the other side of the roof and looks down the valley where the road winds up from Braishfield. He can hear no siren. He can see no blue lights. The roof is growing warm under his feet and he can smell the heady stink of the bitumen as it starts to soften. He is three storeys up. Below him is a four-metre band of concrete before the lawn begins. If someone is coming they will not get here in time. He must jump if he is to stand some small chance of surviving. He cannot bring himself to jump.

Downstairs, Angelica lies at the centre of the web of tubes and wires that keep her connected to the world. Cannulas, monitor, drip stand, oxygen tank. The pillows are banked behind her so that her head remains elevated. She is wearing a sky-blue blouse smart enough for a champagne reception. A mohair rug lies across her lap and legs, rainbow spots on a grass-green background.

No one will see this room again. No one will see the two Edward Ardizzone sketches of children playing on a beach. No one will see André, Angelica's toy rabbit, now worn a little thin in places, sitting slumped against the CD player. No one will see the charm bracelet which once belonged to Angelica's mother. No one will see the porcelain bowl on the base of which a porpoise is pictured, mid-leap, above a jumble of intricate waves.

The air is hot and foul but for now the bedroom door is holding back the furnace which rages in the stairwell. Grey smoke pours from the gap at the foot of the door, then flows upwards and pools on the ceiling. The centre of the door blackens and blisters and bows inwards. Emaciated and bone-white, Angelica dreams of porridge and apricots, of yew trees and pale stone, of fox cubs tumbling over one another in the corner of a garden.

Philippe jumps. He clears the concrete and hits the grass, but the impact shatters both his legs. Using the very last of his energy he crawls away from the inferno into the relative cool of the trees at the edge of the lawn, but the breaks are open and over the next fifteen minutes he will bleed out among the pine needles and the dead branches. The fire brigade will assume that his body has been incinerated completely somewhere in the house and his corpse will not be found for another three days when Hervé is showing the insurance agent round the devastated property.

Back in Angelica's bedroom the smoke on the ceiling is getting steadily thicker and lower. The windows are now coated with the soot and the only light comes from the monitor above the bed. The air reeks of burnt wood and melted plastic. Angelica no longer has any reason to remain alive. Her life is a burden she wants to put aside. But the animal body will not give in so easily. With her right hand she tears the cannula from her arm, grips the stainless-steel rail which runs along the edge of the mattress and hauls herself upright as if she could simply get to her feet and walk away. But such a thing is not possible. Such a thing has not been possible for months. Her fingers loosen, her grip fails and she collapses back onto the pillow. The green sawtooth line running across the monitor's screen goes flat. A red light flashes but the whining alarm is inaudible over the growing roar. On the far side of the room the door is punched from its frame like a playing card and flames pour in from the landing.

A woman is standing beside the bed. Tunic, boots, quiver. She seems familiar but Angelica cannot remember when or where they last met. The woman reaches out. 'Come. Take my hand.'

AUTHOR'S NOTE

The story of Appolinus / Apollonius had been around for at least eight hundred years before Gower retold it. The oldest surviving version was written by Venantius Fortunatus, a bishop and poet at the Merovingian court in the late sixth century, though that seems to have been adapted from an earlier Greek source which is now lost. After Fortunatus there were many other retellings, most of them in Latin, but an increasing number in vernacular European languages. The prose version in Anglo-Saxon has a good claim to be the first English novel.

An Antiocha Þare ceastre wæs sum cyningc Antiochus gehaten ...

From Gower onwards the story remained popular. Wilkins and Shakespeare weren't resurrecting a lost tale when they collaborated on the play *Pericles, Prince of Tyre*, they were ringing changes on a well-known theme. Indeed, one of the texts they almost certainly consulted was Lawrence Twine's prose version of the story, *The Pattern of Painful Adventures*, first published in 1576 then republished in 1607 round about the time of the first performance of *Pericles* at the Globe. Wilkins's own novelisation of the play, *The Painful Adventures of Pericles*, was published in 1608.

Over a thousand years the names of characters change and plot details alter but the template remains the same, and the daughter of the King of Antioch is rarely more than a device to set Pericles / Appolinus / Apollonius on the journey where he will have his real adventures.

There is, however, one version of the story which is different, so different that it counts perhaps as a hybrid of the Pericles / Appolinus / Apollonius story and some other lost antecedent. It is a Breton lai written in Middle English from the early fourteenth century. The eponymous *Emaré* is the daughter of Emperor Artyus and Dame Erayne. When Dame Erayne dies Artyus falls in love with his daughter. Desperate to marry her he appeals to the Pope who sanctions the union. Emaré refuses to comply, and when she argues violently with her father he orders her to be put to sea alone in a small boat in the hope that she will die somewhere out of sight. He rapidly regrets his decision but the emissaries he sends to seek his daughter come back empty-handed. Emaré meanwhile washes up in Wales, starved and emaciated. The king's steward, Sir Kadore, takes pity on this *glysteryng … lady of the see* and gives her a room in his castle. She marries the King of Wales and they have a son. Emaré's mother-in-law is murderously jealous, however, and Emaré is put to sea alone in a small boat for a second time. Eventually she lands in Rome where she is joyfully reunited with her husband and son. There is no suitor in this story; the father is the instigating device and it is the princess who travels around the Mediterranean having adventures.

Emaré is a weaver. As a girl her nurse teaches her *golde and sylke for to sewe*. Later, she herself teaches the women of Sir Kadore's household how to *sewe and marke all maner of sylkyn werke*.

Weaving also features in a strange little subplot at the beginning of the story in which the King of Sicily brings Emaré's father Artyus a tapestry studded with topaz and rubies, toad-stones and agate. Artyus is amazed and wonders if it is some otherworldly object. The King of

Sicily explains that it was made over seven years by the daughter of the Emir of heathendom. In one corner it shows the story of the lovers Ydoyne and Amadas, in the second the lovers Tristram and Isolde, in the third the lovers Floris and Blancheflour. The daughter of the Emir was in love with the Babylonian Sultan's son and hoped that he would fall in love with her after seeing this beautiful piece of work. So in the fourth corner she has pictured the two of them together. She is weaving her future.

SOURCES

The works of Venantius Fortunatus, edited and translated by Michael Roberts, are published in the Dumbarton Oaks Medieval Library series by Harvard University Press (2017).

The Anglo-Saxon prose version of the Appolonius story, dating from the mid-eleventh century, can be found in *Old and Middle English c.890–c.1450: an Anthology*, ed. Elaine Treharne, third edition (Oxford: Blackwell, 2010).

Confessio Amantis by John Gower, begun around 1386 and completed in 1390, and *Emaré*, dating from the late fourteenth century, can be read online in the Middle English Text Series, part of the Robbins Library Digital Projects Series provided by the University of Rochester.

The Miseries of Enforced Marriage by George Wilkins, first performed in 1607, can be read on a number of different websites.

The Pattern of Painful Adventures by Lawrence Twine, entered into the Stationers' Register in 1576, and a modernised version of *The Painful Adventures of Pericles Prince of Tyre* by George Wilkins, first performed in 1606 and published in 1608, can be read online in the Shakespeare Internet Editions, also part of the Robbins Library Digital Projects Series.

Pericles by William Shakespeare and George Wilkins was first performed in 1608. I recommend the Arden Shakespeare edition, edited and with an introduction by Suzanne Gossett (Bloomsbury, 2004).

The following also provided information and inspiration:

London: the Biography by Peter Ackroyd (Chatto & Windus, 2000)

Thames: Sacred River by Peter Ackroyd (Chatto & Windus, 2007)

Shakespeare: Staging the World by Jonathan Bate and Dora Thornton (British Museum Press, 2012)

Shakespeare's Restless World by Neil MacGregor (British Museum / Allen Lane, 2012)

The Lost Books of the Odyssey by Zachary Mason (Jonathan Cape, 2010)

The Time-Traveller's Guide to Elizabethan England by Ian Mortimer (Vintage, 2012)

A Stain in the Blood: The Remarkable Voyage of Sir Kenelm Digby by Joe Moshenska (William Heinemann, 2016)

The Lodger: Shakespeare's Life on Silver Street by Charles Nicholl (Allen Lane, 2007) – not just a fascinating book in and of itself but also the best source of information on Wilkins.

1599: A Year in the Life of William Shakespeare by James Shapiro (Faber & Faber, 2005)

1606: William Shakespeare and the Year of Lear by James Shapiro (Faber & Faber, 2015)

Scythians: Warriors of Ancient Siberia by St John Simpson (British Museum / Thames & Hudson, 2017)

A Sea Grammar by John Smith (1627)

Swimmer Among the Stars by Kanishk Tharoor (Aleph Book Company, 2016)

Wikipedia is one of the wonders of the modern world which is all too easy to take for granted. I use it all the time.

I can't write anything without a detailed visual image of the location where it is set and, ideally, an aerial map. *Google Maps* and *Google Street View* often provide both.

My preferred Internet map source for anywhere in the UK, however, is *Bing Maps* which gives unlimited access to the Ordnance Survey maps (Landranger *and* Explorer), one of my favourite publications of any kind.

The *Agas Map of Early Modern London* is invaluable for anyone who wants to take a walk through Elizabethan or Jacobean London. No copies of the original woodblock print from 1561 are known to have survived but a slightly different version was printed in 1633. This has now been digitised and put online in an annotated, searchable and zoomable form by the University of Victoria in Canada. It is a beautiful thing.

Jordskott is a Swedish TV series first broadcast by STV in 2015 starring Moa Gammel and Göran Ragnerstam. It is the model for *Skogen / The Forest*. Only when I rewatched it in the late stages of editing the novel did I realise how many motifs I had borrowed.

ACKNOWLEDGEMENTS

The novel exists in a world where times, locations, languages and cultures are laid one over the other with a cavalier disregard for historical and geographical fact, as does Shakespeare and Wilkins's play. But there are mistakes and there are mistakes. I want to thank the following people both for helping me to weed out the unwanted kind and for helping me shape the book as a whole: Carole Bourne-Taylor, Adam Brown, Clare Brown, Apostolos Doxiades, Oskar Moshenska, Liv Robinson, Duncan Rourke, Emma Smith and Bill Tollitt.

A huge thank you to David Cass (artwork) and Suzanne Dean (design) for a wonderful cover.

My editors, Clara Farmer at Chatto and Bill Thomas at Doubleday, are wise, thorough and excellent company.

I owe my agent Clare Alexander more than I can say.

Like everything else I've written for the last twenty-five years this novel would not have existed without the help of Sos Eltis, my wife, best friend and sternest editor.

Mark Haddon is a writer and artist. His bestselling novel, *The Curious Incident of the Dog in the Night-Time*, was published simultaneously by Jonathan Cape and David Fickling in 2003. It won seventeen literary prizes, including the Whitbread Award. In 2012, a stage adaptation by Simon Stephens was produced by the National Theatre and went on to win seven Olivier Awards in 2013 and the 2015 Tony Award for Best Play. In 2005, his poetry collection, *The Talking Horse and the Sad Girl and the Village Under the Sea*, was published by Picador, and his play, *Polar Bears*, was produced by the Donmar Warehouse in 2010. His most recent novel, *The Red House*, was published by Jonathan Cape in 2012. *The Pier Falls*, a collection of short stories, was also published by Cape in 2016. To commemorate the centenary of the Hogarth Press he wrote and illustrated a short story that appeared alongside Virginia Woolf's first story for the press in *Two Stories* (Hogarth, 2017).

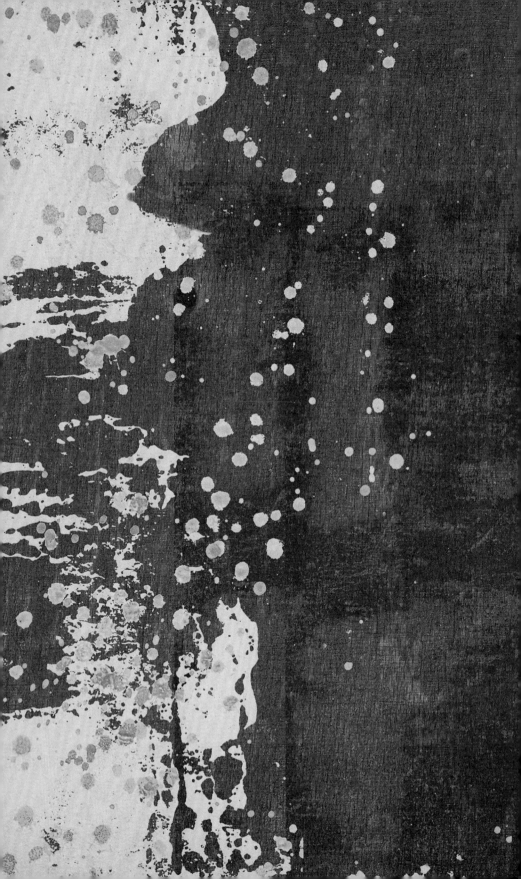